The Daft

The Dark Days

The
Daft Days

NEIL MUNRO

with an Introduction by
Ronnie Renton

Cover picture: *Under the Apple Tree* by Bessie MacNicol
Courtesy Glasgow Museums: Art Gallery & Museum, Kelvingrove

British Library Cataloguing in Publication Data
A catalogue record of this book is available from the British Library

ISBN 1 899863 77 X

First published 1907
This edition published by House of Lochar 2002

The publisher acknowledges support from the Scottish Arts Council
towards publication of this volume

Scottish
Arts Council

Typeset by XL Publishing Services, Tiverton
Printed in Great Britain
by SRP Ltd, Exeter
for House of Lochar
Isle of Colonsay, Argyll PA61 7YR

Introduction

Neil Munro (1863–1930)

Neil Munro, novelist and journalist, was born in Crombie's Land, Inveraray, Argyll on 3 June 1863. His mother, Ann Munro, was a kitchen maid, probably in Inveraray Castle. His father has been rumoured to be of the House of Argyll but there is no evidence for this. Soon after his birth Neil's mother took him to live in his grandmother's house in McVicar's Land and it was in this Gaelic-speaking household that he spent most of his childhood.

He received his formal education at Inveraray Parish School which he supplemented with his voracious appetite for books. About 1877 he became a clerk to William Douglas, a local lawyer, but found the work tedious. Like so many other young Highlanders, however, he found no other satisfactory employment locally and so on 1 June 1881 he emigrated to Glasgow where he soon began work as a reporter. After a number of posts with different newspapers he joined the *Glasgow Evening News* with which he was to remain happily for almost the rest of his life.

He made his first significant mark on the literary scene in 1896 with *The Lost Pibroch and Other Sheiling Stories,* an innovative collection of short stories which seeks to counteract the sentimentality of "Celtic Twilight" writing and to portray the Highlander accurately and in a language which captures Gaelic idiom. In 1897 he reduced his journalistic work considerably to concentrate on literature and in 1898 *John Splendid* was published, a well-judged historical novel of the seventeenth century dealing with the Montrose-Campbell conflict which culminated in the battle of Inverlochy (1645). In 1899 the partly autobiographical *Gilian the Dreamer* appeared, a study of a young boy whose undisciplined sensitivity impedes his ability act effectively. This was followed by three more novels, *Doom Castle* (1901), *The Shoes of Fortune* (1901) and *Children of Tempest* (1903), all loosely connected with the aftermath of the Jacobite Rising of 1745.

Munro published many humorous sketches in his unsigned column "The Looker-On" which appeared every Monday in the *Glasgow Evening News* and, when they later appeared in book form, he adopted for them the *nom de plume* Hugh Foulis. They included stories about the waiter and beadle Erchie MacPherson and the big hearted commercial traveller Jimmy Swan, but the most celebrated were to be his highly entertaining sketches about the crew of the puffer the *Vital Spark* and their eccentric Captain Para Handy. The first of these appeared in 1905 and Munro continued to produce them for most of his working life.

After the novel *Children of Tempest* (1903) Munro turned to the contemporary scene with *The Daft Days* (1907) and *Fancy Farm* (1910). In the meantime in 1908 he was honoured with an LL.D. from the University of Glasgow and in 1909 he was made a Freeman of Inveraray.

In 1914 he returned to the historical novel written in "the Highland manner" and published what many consider to be his finest work *The New Road*. On one level it is a Highland thriller – the hero Aeneas MacMaster's quest for information about his Jacobite father's mysterious death. At a deeper level, however, like Walter Scott's *Waverley* (1814) it examines the condition of the Highlands and the forces which shape individual destinies. It shows the hero's gradual disillusionment with the romantic glamour of the chiefs as he begins to recognise their vices. Eventually Aeneas comes to understand that only by trade and commerce will the Highlands be "civilised" and the instrument to achieve this will be the New Road Wade is building between Stirling and Inverness. The road becomes a symbol of a more prosperous Gaeldom, but at the same time it will contribute significantly to the permanent destruction of the old Gaelic way of life.

The outbreak of the First World War saw Neil Munro's return to full time journalism. In 1915 his son Hugh was killed in France, near Aveluy. This trauma coupled with enormous pressure of work – he became editor of the *Evening News* in 1918 – seemed to prevent further large scale literary production. He did, however, publish the collection of witty and sophisticated short stories *Jaunty Jock and Other Stories* (1918), and, of course, he continued with his humorous sketches.

In 1927 Munro's health began to fail and he reluctantly retired from the *Evening News* where he was loved and respected. In October 1930 he received a second LL.D., this time from the University of Edinburgh. Two months later he died at his home, "Cromalt" in Helensburgh. In 1935 a monument was erected to his memory in Glen Aray. At the dedication ceremony the writer R. B. Cunninghame Graham praised him as "the apostolic successor of Sir Walter Scott".

Munro's literary reputation declined after 1925 when he was accused by Hugh MacDiarmid of writing escapist literature that did not deal with the great national and Highland issues of the day. Modern scholarship, however, shows Munro's critique of Highland – and national – life to be much more acute than MacDiarmid had perceived. His literary reputation is being restored to its proper place.

The Daft Days

The Daft Days is a celebration of the beautiful little town of Inveraray itself. Although it is never named as such it is clearly Munro's hometown that he so vividly etches for us – and in all seasons of the year. The eighteenth-century tenements or "lands", the church and other landmarks are pictured for us in sharp detail. The visitor to the town walking up Main Street will see to this day a door with "a brass man's hand for a knocker". Behind this door is the house which Neil Munro rented and lived in with his family during his children's summer holidays. It is also the house in which he locates the Dyces, the principal family of this novel. But *The Daft Days* is much more than the evocation of a contemporary Argyllshire town and a pleasant story of the day-to-day happenings to a benign country lawyer Dan Dyce, his sisters Bell and Ailie, their lovelorn maid Kate from Colonsay and their highly intelligent little American niece.

Neil Munro has recently been identified as the author of an amusing, if somewhat satirical poem written in 1894 called *"The New Woman in Art"* which criticises the new style of the painters Margaret and Frances Macdonald, especially their treatment of the female form:

> *If you're asked for explanations,*
> *Talk vaguely of design;*
> *Or adopt a few evasions*
> *About temperament in line.*
> *But if nothing save confession*
> *Of your real intent will do,*
> *Say the hags are your impression*
> *Of the Women who are new.*

Similar humorous criticism of *art nouveau* women can be found in some of his sketches in *Erchie, My Droll Friend* (1904). In *The Daft Days* (1907), however, Munro adopts a completely different approach to women and the arts. Although the novel is lighthearted in tone, it is a subtle and serious examination, through the development of the character of the little American girl Bud, of the way women with creative gifts in the Scotland of his day are restricted by the social and religious attitudes and educational system of their country.

Bud has been orphaned and at the age of ten has come to stay with her Scottish relatives. She is highly intelligent, extrovert, articulate and has obvious acting talent. There are, however, major influences on her life in her new home in the shape of her two Aunts. Her Aunt Bell, who loves her dearly, is very Scottish and very Calvinist. She symbolises the prevailing attitude to theatre and the arts and "considers acting is almost as bad as lying, and talks about the theatre as Satan's abode". She does all in her power to stop Bud developing in this direction. Her Aunt

Ailie, on the other hand, for whom we feel much sympathy, is much more encouraging to her niece. She herself had abilities and aspirations like Bud's but societal attitudes denied their fulfilment. Like the hero in Munro's earlier novel *Gilian the Dreamer* she was circumscribed by a society that could not deal with her gifts. She sees herself in Bud:

> I thought a girl called Alison I used to know long ago was long since dead and done with, and here she's to the fore yet, daft as ever, and her name is Lennox [Bud] Dyce.

She is determined that Bud's aspirations are not to be hampered and gives permission for her to take part in Shakespeare's *King John*.

Bud proceeds in a very healthy way to a glittering career as an actress. Significantly she had ten years of American upbringing before she came to Scotland which did much to nurture her independent spirit. Being educated at home she avoided the spiritually repressive nature of Scottish primary education which Munro satirises in the stultifying philosophy of the two unimaginative spinster teachers, the Misses Duff, who consider that children who express themselves should receive punishment. Above all she had the encouragement, education and inspiration of her enlightened Aunt Ailie who ensured that the opportunities which had been denied her would not be denied her niece.

Most interesting is the ending of the story in the Imperial Theatre in London where Bud, now grown up, is playing Desdemona in *Othello*. Aunt Bell finally persuaded to come to see her niece perform, gets so caught up in the action that despite her Calvinist reservations, she forgets "it was nothing but a sinful play" and begins to feel sorry for Othello. After the rapturous applause the family go round to the dressing room where significantly Bud throws herself, not into Ailie's, but into Aunt Bell's arms – a symbolic act of reconciliation between Presbyterian Scotland and the world of the arts. Modern Scotland has accepted the theatre and the female actress!

The Daft Days, a best seller in its own day, paves the way for Munro's further treatment of the New Woman in *Fancy Farm* (1910) and points to female-affirming novels of the Scottish Renaissance like Catherine Carswell's *Open the Door!* (1920), Nan Shepherd's *The Quarry Wood* (1928) and Willa Muir's *Imagined Corners* (1931).

CHAPTER I

THE town's bell rang through the dark of the winter morning with queer little jolts and pauses, as if Wanton Wully Oliver, the ringer, had been jovial the night before. A blithe New-Year-time bell; a droll, daft, scatter-brained bell; it gave no horrid alarums, no solemn reminders that commonly toll from steeples and make good-fellows melancholy to think upon things undone, the brevity of days and years, the parting of good company, but a cheery ditty – "boom, boom, ding-a-dong boom, boom ding, hic, ding-dong," infecting whoever heard it with a kind of foolish gaiety. The burgh town turned on its pillows, drew up its feet from the bed-bottles, last night hot, now turned to chilly stone, rubbed its eyes, and knew by that bell it was the daftest of the daft days come. It cast a merry spell on the community; it tickled them even in their cosy beds. "Wanton Wully's on the ran-dan!" said the folk, and rose quickly, and ran to pull aside screens and blinds to look out in the dark on window-ledges cushioned deep in snow. The children hugged themselves under the blankets, and told each other in whispers it was not a porridge morning, no, nor Sunday, but a breakfast of shortbread, ham and eggs; and behold! a beautiful loud drum, careless as 'twere a réveille of hot wild youths, began to beat in a distant lane. Behind the house of Dyce the lawyer, a cock that must have been young and hearty crew like to burst; and at the stables of the post-office the man who housed his horses after bringing the morning mail through night and storm from a distant railway station sang a song: –

> "A damsel possessed of great beauty
> Stood near by her own father's gate;
> The gallant hussars were on duty
> To view them this maiden did wait.
> Their horses were capering and prancing,
> Their accoutrements shone like a star;
> From the plains they were quickly advancing, –
> She espied her own gallant hussar."

"Mercy on us! six o'clock!" cried Miss Dyce, with a startled jump from her dreams to the floor of her bedroom. "Six o'clock on the New Year's morning, and I'll warrant that randy Kate is sound asleep yet," she said, and quickly clad herself and went to the head of the stair and cried, "Kate, Kate! are ye up yet, Kate? Are ye hearing me, Kate MacNeill?"

1

From the cavern dark of the lower storey there came back no answer.

She stood with a curious twirly wooden candlestick in her hand in the midst of a house that was dead dumb and desperate dark, and smelled deliciously of things to eat. Even herself, who had been at the making of most of them the day before, and had, by God's grace, still much of a child's appetite, could not but sniff with a childish satisfaction at this air of a celestial grocery – of plum-puddings and currant-buns, apples and oranges, cordials and spices, toffee and the angelic treacly sweet we call Black Man – her face lit rosily by the candle lowe, a woman small and soft and sappy, with the most wanton reddish hair, and a briskness of body that showed no sign as yet of her accomplished years. What they were I will never tell you; but this I'll say, that even if they had been eighty she was the kind to cheerily dance quadrille. The daft bell, so plainly in the jovial mood of Wanton Wully Oliver, infected her: she smiled to herself in a way she had when remembering droll things or just for simple jollity, and whoever saw Bell Dyce smile to herself had never the least doubt after that she was a darling. Over the tenements of the town the song of the bell went rollicking, and in its hiccupping pauses went wonderfully another sound far, far removed in spirit and suggestion – the clang of wild geese calling: the "honk, honk" of the ganders and the challenge of their ladies come down adrift in the snow from the bitter north.

But there was no answer from the maid in the kitchen. She had rolled less deliberately than was usual from her blankets to the summons of the six o'clock bell, and already, with the kitchen window open, her bounteous form surged over the two sashes that were always so conveniently low and handy for a gossip with any friendly passer-by on the pavement. She drank the air of the clean chill morning dark, a heady thing like old Tom Watson's autumn ale, full of the sentiment of the daft days. She tilted an ear to catch the tune of the mail-boy's song that now was echoing mellow from the cobwebbed gloom of the stable stalls, and making a snowball from the drift of the window-ledge she threw it, womanwise, aimlessly into the street with a pretence at combat. The chill of the snow stung sweet in the hot palm of her, for she was young and strong.

"Kate, you wretch!" cried a voice behind her. She drew in her head, to find her mistress in the kitchen with the candlestick in her hand.

"Oh, m'em," cried the maid, no way abashed, banging up the window and hurriedly crushing her more ample parts under the final

2

hooks and eyes of her morning wrapper, "oh, m'em, what a start you gave me! I'm all in a p-p-palpitation. I was just takin' one mouthful of air and thinkin' to myself yonder in the Gaelic that it was time for me to be comin' in and risin' right."

"A Happy New Year to you, Kate MacNeill," said the mistress, taking her hand.

"Just that, just that! and the same to you yourself, Miss Dyce. I'm feeling fine; I'm that glad with everything," said the maid, in some confusion at this unusual relation with her mistress. She shook the proffered hand rapidly from side to side as if it were an egg-switch.

"And see and get the fires on quick now, like a good lass. It would never do to be starting the New Year late – it would be unlucky. I was crying to you yonder from the stair-head, and wondering if you were ill, that you did not answer me so quickly as you do for ordinar'."

"Ill, Miss Dyce!" cried the maid, astounded. "Do you think I'm daft to be ill on a New Year's day?"

"After yon – after yon shortbread you ate yesterday I would not have wondered much if you were," said Miss Dyce, shaking her head solemnly. "I'm not complaining, but, dear me! it was an awful lump; and I thought it would be a bonny-like thing too if our first-foot had to be the doctor."

"Doctor! I declare to goodness I never had need of a doctor to me since Dr Macphee in Colonsay put me in order with oil and things after I had the measles," exclaimed the maid, as if mankind were like wag-at-the-wa' clocks and could be guaranteed to go right for years if you blew through them with a pair of bellows, or touched their works with an oily feather.

"Never mind about the measles just now, Kate," said Miss Dyce, with a meaning look at the blackout fire.

"Neither I was mindin' them, m'em – I don't care a spittle for them; it's so long ago I would not know them if I saw them; I was just –"

"But get your fire on. You know we have a lot to do today to get everything nice and ready for my nephew who comes from America with the four o'clock coach."

"America!" cried the maid, dropping a saucepan lid on the floor in her astonishment. "My stars! Did I not think it was from Chickagoo?"

"And Chicago is in America, Kate," said her mistress.

"Is it? is it? Mercy on me, how was Kate to know? I only got part of my education – up to the place where you carry one and add ten.

3

America! Dear me, just fancy! The very place that I'm so keen to go to. If I had the money, and was in America –"

It was a familiar theme; Kate had not got fully started on it when her mistress fled from the kitchen and set briskly about her morning affairs.

And gradually the household of Dyce the lawyer awoke wholly to a day of unaccustomed stillness and sound, for the deep snow piled in the street and hushed the traffic of wheel, and hoof, and shoe, but otherwise the morning was cheerful with New Year's day noise. For the bell-ringing of Wanton Wully was scarcely done, died down in a kind of brazen chuckle, and the "honk, honk" of the wild geese sped seaward over gardens and back lanes, strange wild music of the north, far-fetched and undomestic – when the fife band shrilly tootled through the town to the tune of "Hey, Johnny Cope, are ye waukin' yet?" Ah, they were the proud, proud men, their heads dizzy with glory and last night's wine, their tread on air. John Taggart drummed – a mighty drummer, drunk or sober, who so loved his instrument he sometimes went to bed with it still fastened to his neck, and banged today like Banagher, who banged furiously, never minding the tune much, but happy if so be that he made noise enough. And the fifers were not long gone down the town, all with the wrong step but Johnny Vicar, as his mother thought, when the snow was trampled under the feet of playing children, and women ran out of their houses, and crossed the street, some of them, I declare, to kiss each other, for 'tis a fashion lately come, and most genteel grown wonderfully common in Scotland. Right down the middle of the town, with two small flags in his hat and holly in the lapel of his coat, went old Divine the hawker, with a great barrow of pure gold, crying "Fine Venetian oranges! wha'll buy sweet Venetian oranges, Nane o' your foreign trash. Oranges! Oranges! – rale New Year oranges, three a penny; bloods, a bawbee each!"

The shops opened just for an hour for fear anybody might want anything, and many there were, you may be sure, who did, for they had eaten and drunken everything provided the night before – which we call Hogmanay – and now there were currant-loaves and sweety biscuits to buy; shortcake, sugar and lemons, ginger cordial for the boys and girls and United Presbyterians, boiled ham for country cousins who might come unexpected, and P. & A. MacGlashan's threepenny mutton-pies (twopence if you brought the ashet back), ordinarily only to be had on fair-days and on Saturdays, and far renowned for value.

Miss Minto's Millinery and Manteau Emporium was discovered

at daylight to have magically outlined its doors and windows during the night with garlands and festoons of spruce and holly, whereon the white rose bloomed in snow; and Miss Minto herself, in a splendid crimson cloak down to the heels, and cheeks like cherries, was standing with mittens and her five finger-rings on, in the middle door, saying in beautiful gentle English "A Happy New Year" to every one who passed – even to George Jordon, the common cowherd, who was always a little funny in his intellects, and, because his trousers were bell-mouthed and hid his feet, could never remember whether he was going to his work or coming from it, unless he consulted the Schoolmaster. "The same to you, m'em, excuse my hands," said poor George, just touching the tips of her fingers. Then, because he had been stopped and slewed a little from his course, he just went back the way he had come.

Too late got up the red-faced sun, too late to laugh at Wanton Wully's jovial bell, too late for Taggart's mighty drumming, but a jolly winter sun – 'twas all that was wanted among the chimneys to make the day complete.

First of all to rise in Dyce's house, after the mistress and the maid, was the master, Daniel Dyce himself.

And now I will tell you all about Daniel Dyce; it is that behind his back he was known as Cheery Dan.

"Your bath is ready, Dan," his sister had cried, and he rose and went with chittering teeth to it, looked at it a moment, and put a hand in the water. It was as cold as ice, because that water, drinking which men never age, comes from high mountain bens.

"That for ye today!" said he to the bath, snapping his fingers. "I'll see ye far enough first!" And contented himself with a slighter wash than usual, and shaving. As he shaved he hummed all the time, as was his habit, an ancient air of his boyhood; today it was

"Star of Peace, to wanderers weary,"

with not much tone but a great conviction – a tall, lean, clean-shaven man of over fifty, with a fine long nose, a ruddy cheek, keen grey eyes, and plenty of room in his clothes, the pockets of him so large and open it was no wonder so many people tried, as it were, to put their hands into them. And when he was dressed he did a droll thing, for from one of his pockets he took what hereabouts we call a pea-sling, that to the rest of the world is a catapult, and having shut one eye, and aimed with the weapon, and snapped the rubber several times with amazing gravity, he went upstairs into an attic and laid it

5

on a table at the window with a pencilled note, in which he wrote –

NEW YEAR'S DAY PRESENT
FOR A GOOD BOY
FROM
AN UNCLE WHO DOES NOT LIKE CATS

He looked round the little room that seemed very bright and cheerful, for its window gazed over the garden to the east and to the valley where was seen the King's highway. "Wonderful! wonderful!" he said to himself. "They have made an extraordinary job of it. Very nice indeed, but just a shade ladylike. A stirring boy would prefer fewer fal-lals."

There was little indeed to suggest the occupation of a stirring boy in that attic, with its draped dressing-table in lilac print, its looking-glass flounced in muslin and pink lover's-knots, its bower-like bed canopied and curtained with green lawn, its shy scent of potpourri and lavender. A framed text in crimson wools, the work of Bell Dyce when she was in Miss Mushet's seminary, hung over the mantelpiece enjoining all beholders to

WATCH AND PRAY.

Mr Dyce put both hands into his trousers pockets, bent a little, and heaved in a sort of chirruping laughter. "Man's whole duty, according to Bell Dyce," he said, "'Watch and Pray'; but they do not need to have the lesson before them continually yonder in Chicago, I'll warrant. Yon's the place for watching, by all accounts, however it may be about the prayer. 'Watch and Pray' – h'm! It should be Watch or Pray – it clearly cannot be both at once with the world the way it is; you might as well expect a man to eat pease-meal and whistle strathspeys at the same time."

He was humming "Star of Peace" – for the tune he started the morning with usually lasted him all day – and standing in the middle of the floor contemplating with amusement the ladylike adornment of the room prepared for his Chicago nephew, when a light step fell on the attic stairs, and a woman's voice cried, "Dan! Dan Dyce! Coo-ee!"

He did not answer.

She cried again after coming up a step or two more, but still he did not answer. He slid behind one of the bed-curtains.

CHAPTER II

ALISON DYCE came lightly up the rest of the stair, whistling blithely, in spite of her sister Bell's old notion that whistling women and crowing hens are never canny. She swept into the room. People in the town – which has a forest of wood and deer behind it – used to say she had the tread and carriage of a young wild roe, and I can well assure you she was the girl to walk with on a winter day! She had in her hand a book of poems called 'The Golden Treasury' and a spray of the herb called Honesty, that thrives in poor men's gardens. Having laid them down on the table without noticing her brother's extraordinary Present for a Good Boy, she turned about and fondled things. She smoothed the bed-clothes as if they covered a child, she patted the chair-backs with an air of benediction, she took cushions to her breast like one that cuddled them, and when she touched the mantelpiece ornaments they could not help it but must start to chime. It was always a joy to see Alison Dyce redding-up, as we say; though in housewifery, like sewing, knitting, and cooking, she was only a poor second to her sister Bell. She tried, from duty, to like these occupations, but, oh dear! the task was beyond her: whatever she had learned from her schooling in Edinburgh and Brussels, it was not the darning of hose and the covering of rhubarb-tarts.

Her gift, said Bell, was management.

Tripping round the little attic, she came back by-and-by to the table at the window to take one last wee glimpse inside 'The Golden Treasury', that was her own delight and her notion of happy half-hours for the ideal boy, and her eye fell for the first time on the pea-sling and the note beside it.

She read, and laughed, and upon my word, if laughter like Ailie Dyce's could be bought in perforated rolls, there would be no demand for Chopin and Schumann on the pianolas. It was a laugh that even her brother could not resist: a paroxysm of coughing burst from behind the curtains, and he came out beside her chuckling.

"I reckoned without my host," said he, gasping.

"I was sure you were upstairs," said Alison. "You silly man! Upon my word! Where's your dignity, Mr Dyce?"

Dan Dyce stood for a second a little bit abashed, rubbing his chin and blinking his eyes as if their fun was a thing to be kept from brimming over. "I'm a great wag!" said he. "If it's dignity you're after, just look at my velvet coat!" and so saying he caught the ends of his coat skirts with his fingers, held them out at arm's-length, and turned round as he might do at a fit-on in his tailor's, laughing till his host came on again. "Dignity, quo' she, just look at my velvet coat!"

"Dan, Dan! will you never be wise?" said Ailie Dyce, a humorsome demoiselle herself, if you believe me.

"Not if I keep my health," said he. "You have made a bonny-like show of the old garret, between the two of you. It's as smart as a lass at her first ball."

"I think it's very nice; at least it might be worse," interrupted Alison defensively, glancing round with satisfaction and an eye to the hang of the frame round "Watch and Pray." Bell's wool-work never agreed with her notions, but as she knew that her tarts never agreed with Bell, she kept, on that point, aye discreetly dumb.

"Poor little Chicago!" said her brother. "I'm vexed for the wee fellow. Print chintz, or chint prints, or whatever it is; sampler texts, and scent, and poetry books – what in the world is the boy to break?"

"Oh, you have seen to that department, Dan!" said Ailie, taking the pea-sling again in her hand. "'A New Year's Day Present for a Good Boy from an Uncle who does not like Cats.' I declare that *is* a delightful way of making the child feel quite at home at once."

"Tuts! 'Tis just a diversion. I know it'll cheer him wonderfully to find at the start that if there's no young folk in the house there's some of the eternal Prank. I suppose there are cats in Chicago. He cannot expect us to provide him with pigs, which are the usual domestic pets there, I believe. You let my pea-sling alone, Ailie; you'll find it will please him more than all the poetry and pink bows. I was once a boy myself, and I know."

"You were never anything else," said Alison. "And never will be anything else. It is a pity to let the child see at the very start what an irresponsible person his uncle is; and besides, it's cruel to throw stones at cats."

"Not at all, not at all!" said her brother briskly, with his head quizzically to the side a little, in a way he had when debating in the Court. "I have been throwing stones for twenty years at those cats of Rodger's that live in our garden and I never hit one yet. They're all about six inches too short for genuine sport. If cats were Dachshund dogs, and I wasn't so fond of dogs, I would be deadly. But my ado with cats is just one of the manly old British sports, like trout-fishing and curling. You take your fun out in anticipation, and the only difference is you never need to carry a flask. Still, I'm not without hope that my nephew from Chicago may have a better aim than I have."

"You are an old – an old goose, Dan Dyce, and a Happy New Year to you!" said his sister, putting her arms suddenly round his neck and kissing him.

"Tuts! the coming of that child's ta'en your head," said the brother, reddening, for sisters never kiss their own brothers in our part – it's so sentimental, it's so like the penny stories. "A Good New Year to you, Ailie," and "Tuts!" he said again, looking quite upset, till Ailie laughed and put her arm through his and drew him downstairs to the breakfast to which she had come to summon him.

The Chicago child's bedroom, left to itself, chilly a bit like Highland weather, but honest and clean, looked more like a bower than ever: the morning sun, peeping over garden trees and the chimneys of the lanes, gazed particularly on the table where the peasling and the poetry book lay together.

And now the town was thronged like a fair-day, with such stirring things happening every moment in the street that the servant, Kate, had a constant head out at the window, "putting by the time," as she explained to the passing inquirer, "till the Mustress would be ready for the breakfast." That was Kate – she had come from an island where they make the most of everything that may be news, even if it's only brandy-sauce to pudding at the minister's; and Miss Dyce could not start cutting a new bodice or sewing a button on her brother's trousers but the maid billowed out upon the window-sash to tell the tidings to the first of her sex that passed.

Over the trodden snow she saw the people from the country crowd in their Sunday clothes, looking pretty early in the day for gaiety, all with scent on their handkerchiefs (which is the odour of festive days for a hundred miles round burgh towns); and town people, less splendid in attire, as folks that know the difference between a holiday and a Sabbath, and leave their religious hard hats at home on a New Year's day; children, too, replete with bun already, and all succulent with the juice of Divine's oranges. She heard the bell begin to peal again, for Wully Oliver – fie on Wully Oliver! – had been met by some boys who told him the six o'clock bell was not yet rung, and sent him back to perform an office he had done with hours before. He went to his bell dubiously, something in the dizzy abyss he called his mind that half convinced him he had rung it already.

"Let me pause and consider," he said once or twice when being urged to the rope, scratching the hair behind his ears with both hands, his gesture of reflection. "Was there no' a bairn – an auld-fashioned bairn – helped to ca' the bell already, and wanted to gie

9

me money for the chance? It runs in my mind there was a bairn, and that she had us aye boil-boiling away at eggs; but maybe I'm wrong, for I'll admit I had a dram or two and lost the place. I don't believe in dram-dram-dramming, but I aye say if you take a dram, take it in the morning and you get the good of it all day. It's a tip I learned in the Crimea." But at last they convinced him the bairn was just imagination, and Wanton Wully Oliver spat on his hands and grasped the rope, and so it happened that the morning bell on the New Year's day on which my story opens was twice rung.

The Dyce handmaid heard it pealing as she hung over the window-sash with her cap agee on her head. She heard from every quarter – from lanes, closes, tavern rooms, high attics, and backyards – fifes playing; it was as if she leaned over a magic grove of great big birds, each singing its own song – "Come to the Bower," or "Monymusk," or "The Girl I left Behind Me," noble airs wherein the captain of the band looked for a certain perfection from his musicians before they marched out again at midday. "For," said he often in rehearsals, "anything will do in the way of a tune in the dark, my sunny boys, but it must be the tiptop of skill, and no discordancy, when the eyes of the world are on us. One turn more at 'Monymusk,' sunny boys, and then we'll have a skelp at yon tune of my own composure."

Besides the sound of the bell and the universal practice of the fifes there were loud vocalists at the Cross, and such laughter in the street that Kate was in an ecstasy. Once, uplifted beyond all private decorum, she kilted her gown and gave a step of a reel in her kitchen solitude.

"Isn't it cheery, the noise!" she exclaimed delightedly to the letter-carrier who came to the window with the morning's letters. "Oh, I am feeling beautiful! It is – it is – it is just like being inside a pair of bagpipes."

He was a man who roared, the postman, being used to bawling up long common-stairs in the tenements for the people to come down to the foot themselves for their letters – a man with one roguish eye for the maiden and another at random. Passing in the letters one by one, he said in tones that on a quieter day might be heard half up the street, "Nothing for you, yourself, personally, Kate, but maybe there'll be one to-morrow. Three big blue anes and seven wee anes for the man o' business himsel', twa for Miss Dyce (she's the wonderfu' correspondent!), and ane for Miss Alison wi' the smell o' scented perfume on't – that'll be frae the Miss Birds o' Edinburgh. And I near forgot – here's a post-caird for Miss Dyce: hearken to this –

"'Child arrived Liverpool yesterday; left this morning for Scotland. Quite safe to go alone, charge of conductor. Pip, pip! Molyneux.'"

"Whatna child is it, Kate?"

"'Pip, pip!' What in the world's 'Pip, pip'? The child is brother William's child, to be sure," said Kate, who always referred to the Dyce relations as if they were her own. "You have heard of brother William?"

"Him that was married on the play-actress and never wrote home?" shouted the letter-carrier. "He went away before my time. Go on; quick, for I'm in a desperate hurry this mornin'."

"Well, he died abroad in Chickagoo. God have mercy on him dying so far away from home, and him without a word of Gaelic in his head! and a friend o' his father's bringing the boy home to his aunties."

"Where in the world's Chickagoo?" bellowed the postman.

"In America, of course – where else would it be but in America?" said Kate contemptuously. "Where is your education not to know that Chickagoo is in America, where the servant-maids have a pound a-week of wages, and learn the piano, and can get married when they like quite easy?"

"Bless me! do you say so?" cried the postman in amazement, and not without a pang of jealousy.

"Yes, I say so!" said Kate in the snappish style she often showed to the letter-carrier. "And the child is coming this very day with the coach-and-twice from Maryfield railway station – oh them trains! them trains! with their accidents; my heart is in my mouth to think of a child in them. Will you not come round to the back and get the Mustress's New Year dram? She is going to give a New Year dram to every man that calls on business this day. But I will not let you in, for it is in my mind that you would not be a lucky first-foot."

"Much obleeged," said the postman, "but ye needna be feared. I'm not allowed to go dramming at my duty. It's offeecial, and I canna help it. If it was not offeecial, there's few letter-carriers that wouldna need to hae iron hoops on their heids to keep their brains from burstin' on the day efter New Year."

Kate heard a voice behind her, and pulled her head in hurriedly with a gasp, and a cry of "Mercy, the start I got!" while the postman fled on his rounds. Miss Dyce stood behind, in the kitchen, indignant.

"You are a perfect heartbreak, Kate," said the mistress. "I have

11

rung for breakfast twice, and you never heard me, with your clattering out there to the letter-carrier. It's a pity you cannot marry the glee party, as Mr Dyce calls him, and be done with it."

"Me marry him!" cried the maid indignantly "I think I see myself marryin' a man like yon, and his eyes not neighbours."

"That's a trifle in a husband if his heart is good: the letter-carrier's eyes may – may skew a little, but it's not to be wondered at, considering the look-out he has to keep on all sides of him to keep out of reach of every trollop in the town who wants to marry him."

And leaving Kate speechless at this accusation the mistress of the house took the letters from her hands and went to the breakfast-table with them.

She had read the contents of the post-card before she reached the parlour; its news dismayed her.

"Just imagine!" she cried. "Here's that bairn on his way from Liverpool his lee-lone, and not a body with him!"

"What! what!" cried Mr Dyce, whose eyes had been shut to say the grace. "Isn't that actor-fellow, Molyneux, coming with him, as he promised?"

Miss Dyce sunk in a chair and burst into tears, crushing the post-card in her hand.

"What does he say?" demanded her brother.

"He says – he says – oh dear me! – he says 'Pip, pip!'" quoth the weeping sister.

CHAPTER III

"I MISDOUBTED Mr Molyneux from the very first," said Ailie, turning as white as a clout. "From all his post-cards he was plainly too casual. Stop it, Bell, my dear – have sense; the child's in a Christian land, and in care of somebody who is probably more dependable than this delightful Molyneux."

Mr Dyce took out an old, thick, silver verge. "Nine o'clock," he said, with a glance at its creamy countenance. "Molyneux's consignment is making his first acquaintance with Scottish scenery, and finding himself, I hope, amused at the Edinburgh accent. He'll arrive at Maryfield – poor wee smout! – at three; if I drive over at twelve I'll be in time to meet him. Tuts, Bell, give over; he's a ten-year-old and a Dyce at that – there's not the slightest fear of him."

"Ten years old, and in a foreign country – if you can call Scotland a foreign country," cried Miss Dyce, still sobbing with anger and grief. "Oh, the cat-witted scamp, that Molyneux – if I had him here!"

The dining-room door opened and let in a yawning dog of most plebeian aspect, longest lie-abed of the household, the clamour of the street, and the sound of sizzling bacon, followed by Kate's majestic form at a stately glide, because she had on her new stiff lilac print that was worn for breakfast only on Sundays and holidays. "You would think I was never coming," she said genially, and smiled widely as she put the tray on the sideboard. This that I show you, I fear, is a beggarly household, absurdly free from ceremony. Mr Dyce looked at his sister Ailie and smiled; Ailie looked at her sister Bell and smiled. Bell took a hairpin or two out of their places and seemed to stab herself with them viciously in the nape of the neck, and smiled not at all nor said anything, for she was furious with Molyneux, whom she could see in her mind's eye – an ugly, tippling, frowsy-looking person with badly polished boots, an impression that would have greatly amused Mrs Molyneux, who, not without reason, counted her Jim the handsomest man and the best dressed in the profession in all Chicago.

"I'm long of coming, like Royal Charlie," Kate proceeded, as she passed the ashets on to Miss Dyce; "but, oh me! New Year's day here is no' like New Year's day in the bonny isle of Colonsay."

Mr Dyce said grace and abstractedly helped himself alternately from both ends of a new roll of powdered butter. "Dan, dear, don't take the butter from both ends – it spoils the look," said Bell. "Tuts!" said he. "What's the odds? There'll be no ends at all when we're done with it. I'm utterly regardless of the symmetrical and the beautiful this morning. I'm savage to think of that man Molyneux. If I was not a man of peace I would be wanting to wring Mr Molyneux's neck," and he twisted his morning roll in halves with ferocious hands.

"Dan!" said Ailie, shocked. "I never heard you say anything so bloodthirsty in all my life before. I would never have thought it of you."

"Maybe not," he said. "There's many things about me you never suspected. You women are always under delusions about the men – about the men – well, dash it! about the men you like. I know myself so well that there is no sin, short of one or two not so accounted, that I cannot think myself capable of. I believe I might be forced into robbing a kirk if I had no money and was as hungry as I was this morning before that post-card came to ruin a remarkably fine New-Year's-day appetite, or even into murdering a man like Molyneux who failed in the simplest duties no man should neglect."

"I hope and trust," said Bell, still nervous, "that he is a wiselike boy with a proper upbringing, who will not be frightened at travelling and make no mistakes about the train. If he was a Scotch laddie, with the fear of God in him, I would not be a bit put about for him, for he would be sure to be asking, asking, and if he felt frightened he would just start and eat something, like a Christian. But this poor child has no advantages. Just American!"

Ailie sat back in her chair, with her teacup in her hand, and laughed, and Kate laughed quietly – though it beat her to see where the fun was; and the dog laughed likewise – at least it wagged its tail and twisted its body and made such extraordinary sounds in its throat that you could say it was laughing.

"Tuts! you are the droll woman, Bell," said Mr Dyce, blinking at her. "You have the daftest ideas of some things. For a woman who spent so long a time in Miss Mushet's seminary and reads so much at the newspapers, I wonder at you."

"Of course his father was Scotch, that's one mercy," added Bell, not a bit annoyed at the reception of her pious opinions.

"That is always something to be going on with," said Mr Dyce mockingly. "I hope he'll make the most of that great start in life and fortune. It's as good as money in his pocket."

Bell put up a tiny hand and pushed a stray curl (for she had a rebel chevelure) behind her ear, and smiled in spite of her anxiety about the coming nephew. "You may laugh if you like, Dan," she said emphatically, perking with her head across the table at him; "but I'm *proud*, I'm PROUD, I'm PROUD I'm Scotch." ("Not apologising for it myself," said her brother softly.) "And you know what these Americans are! Useless bodies, who make their men brush their own boots, and have to pay wages that's a sin to housemaids, and eat pie even-on."

"Dear me! is that true, or did you see it in a newspaper?" said her brother. "I begin to be alarmed myself at the possibilities of this small gentleman now on his way to the north, in the complete confidence of Mr Molyneux, who must think him very clever. It's a land of infant prodigies he comes from; even at the age of ten he may have more of the stars and stripes in him than we can eradicate by a diet of porridge and a curriculum of Shorter Catechism and Jane Porter's 'Scottish Chiefs'. Faith, I was fond of Jane myself when I read her

14

first: she was nice and bloody. A big soft hat with a bash in it, perhaps; a rhetorical delivery at the nose, 'I guess and calculate' every now and then; a habit of chewing tobacco" ("We'll need a cuspidor," said Ailie *sotto voce.*) "and a revolver in his wee hippocket. Oh, the darling! I can see him quite plainly."

"Mercy on us!" cried the maid Kate, and fled the room all in a tremor at the idea of the revolver.

"You may say what you like, but I cannot get over his being an American," said Bell solemnly. "The dollar's everything in America, and they're so independent!"

"Terrible! terrible!" said her brother ironically, breaking into another egg fiercely with his knife, as if he were decapitating the President of the United States.

Ailie laughed again. "Dear, dear Bell!" she said, "it sounds quite Scotch. A devotion to the dollar is a good sound basis for a Scotch character. Remember there are about a hundred bawbees in a dollar: just think of the dollar in bawbees, and you'll not be surprised that the Americans prize it so much."

"Renegade!" said Bell, shaking a spoon at her.

"Provincial!" retorted Ailie, shaking a fork at Bell.

"'Star of Peace, to wanderers weary,
Bright the beams that shine on me,'

– children, be quiet," half-sung, half-said their brother. "Bell, you are a blether; Ailie, you are a cosmopolitan, a thing accursed. That's what Edinburgh and Brussels and your too brisk head have done for you. Just bring yourself to our poor parochial point of view, and tell me, both of you, what you propose to do with this young gentleman from Chicago when you get him."

"Change his stockings and give him a good tea," said Bell promptly, as if she had been planning it for weeks. "He'll be starving of hunger and damp with snow."

"There's something more than dry hose and high tea to the making of a man," said her brother. "You can't keep that up for a dozen years."

"Oh, you mean education!" said Bell resignedly. "That's not in my department at all."

Ailie expressed her views with calm, soft deliberation, as if she, too, had been thinking of nothing else for weeks, which was partly the case. "I suppose," she said, "he'll go to the Grammar School, and get a good grounding on the classic side, and then to the

University. I will just love to help him so long as he's at the Grammar
School. That's what I should have been, Dan, if you had let me – a
teacher. I hope he's a bright boy, for I simply cannot stand what Bell
calls – calls –"

"Diffies," suggested Bell.

"Diffies; yes, I can *not* stand diffies. Being half a Dyce I can hardly
think he will be a diffy. If he's the least like his father, he may be a
little wild at first but at least he'll be good company, which makes
up for a lot, and good-hearted, quick in perception, fearless, and –"

"And awful funny," suggested Bell, beaming with old, fond, glad
recollections of the brother dead beside his actor wife in far Chicago.

"Fearless, and good fun," continued Ailie. "Oh, dear Will! what
a merry soul he was. Well, the child cannot be a fool if he's like his
father. American independence, though he has it in – in – in clods,
won't do him any harm at all. I love Americans – do you hear that,
Bell Dyce? – because they beat that stupid old King George, and
have been brave in the forest and wise on the prairie, and feared no
face of king, and laughed at dynasties. I love them because they gave
me Emerson, and Whitman, and Thoreau, and because one of them
married my brother William, and was the mother of his child."

Dan Dyce nodded; he never quizzed his sister Ailie when it was
her heart that spoke and her eyes were sparkling.

"The first thing you should learn him," said Miss Dyce, "is 'God
save the Queen'. It's a splendid song altogether; I'm glad I'm of a
kingdom every time I hear it at a meeting, for it's all that's left of the
olden notions the Dyces died young or lost their money for. You'll
learn him that, Ailie, or I'll be very vexed with you. I'll put flesh on
his bones with my cooking if you put the gentleman in him."

It was Bell's idea that a gentleman talked a very fine English
accent like Ailie, and carried himself stately like Ailie, and had wise
and witty talk for rich or poor like Ailie.

"I'm not so sure about the university," she went on. "Such stirks
come out of it sometimes; look at poor Maclean, the minister! They
tell me he could speak Hebrew if he got anybody to speak it back
slow to him, but just imagine the way he puts on his clothes! And his
wife manages him not so bad in broad Scotch. I think we could do
nothing better than make the boy a lawyer; it's a trade looked up to,
and there's money in it, though I never could see the need of law
myself if folk would only be agreeable. He could go into Dan's office
whenever he is old enough."

"A lawyer!" cried her brother. "You have first of all to see that he's
not an ass."

16

"And what odds would that make to a lawyer?" said Bell quickly, snapping her eyes at the brother she honestly thought the wisest man in Scotland.

"Bell," said he, "as I said before, you're a haivering body – nothing else, though I'll grant you bake no' a bad scone. And as for you, Ailie, you're beginning, like most women, at the wrong end. The first thing to do with your nephew is to teach him to be happy, for it's a habit that has to be acquired early, like the liking for pease-brose."

"You began gey early yourself," said Bell. "Mother used to say that she was aye kittling your feet till you laughed when you were a baby. I sometimes think that she did not stop it soon enough."

"If I had to educate myself again, and had not a living to make, I would leave out a good many things the old dominie thought needful. What was yon awful thing again? – mensuration. To sleep well and eat anything, fear the face of nobody in bashfulness, to like dancing, and be able to sing a good bass or tenor – that's no bad beginning in the art of life. There's a fellow Brodie yonder in the kirk choir who seems to me happier than a king when he's getting in a fine boom-boom of bass to the tune Devizes; he puts me all out at my devotions on a Lord's day with envy of his accomplishment."

"What! envy too!" said Alison. "Murder, theft, and envy – what a brother!"

"Yes, envy too, the commonest and ugliest of our sins," said Mr Dyce. "I never met man or woman who lacked it, though many never know they have it. I hope the great thing is to be ashamed to feel it, for that's all that I can boast of myself. When I was a boy at the school there was another boy, a great friend of my own, was chosen to compete for a prize I was thought incapable of taking, so that I was not on the list. I envied him to hatred – almost; and saying my bits of prayers at night I prayed that he might win. I felt ashamed of my envy, and set the better Daniel Dyce to wrestle with the Daniel Dyce who was not quite so big. It was a sair fight, I can assure you. I found the words of my prayer and my wishes considerably at variance –"

"Like me and 'Thy will be done' when we got the word of brother William," said Bell.

"But my friend – dash him! – got the prize. I supppose God took a kind of vizzy down that night and saw the better Dan Dyce was doing his desperate best against the other devil's-Dan, who mumbled the prayer on the chance He would never notice. There was no other way of accounting for it, for that confounded boy got the prize, and he was not half so clever as myself, and that was Alick Maitland. Say nothing about envy, Ailie; I fear we all have some of it until we are perhaps well up in years, and understand that between the things we envy and the luck we have there is not much to choose. If I got all I wanted, myself, the world would have to be much enlarged. It does not matter a docken leaf. Well, as I was saying when my learned friend interrupted me, I would have this young fellow healthy and happy and interested in everything. There are men I see who would mope and weary in the middle of a country fair – God help them! I want to stick pins in them sometimes and make them jump. They take as little interest in life as if they were undertakers."

"Hoots! nobody could weary in this place at any rate," said Bell briskly. "Look at the life and gaiety that's in it. Talk about London! I can hardly get my sleep at night quite often with the traffic. And such things are always happening in it – births and marriages, engagements and tea-parties, new patterns at Miss Minto's, two coaches in the day, and sometimes somebody doing something silly that will keep you laughing half the week."

"But it's not quite so lively as Chicago," said Mr Dyce. "There has not been a man shot in this neighbourhood since the tinker kind of killed his wife (as the fiscal says) with the pistol. You'll have heard of him? When the man was being brought on the scaffold for it, and the minister asked if he had anything to say before he suffered the extreme penalty of the law, 'All I have got to say,' he answered, starting to greet, 'is that this'll be an awful lesson to me.'"

"That's one of your old ones," said Bell: but even an old one was welcome in Dyce's house on New Year's day, and the three of them laughed at the story as if it had newly come from London in Ailie's precious 'Punch'. The dog fell into a convulsion of merriment, as if inward chuckles tormented him – as queer a dog as ever was, neither Scotch terrier nor Skye, Dandy Dinmont nor Dachshund, but just dog – dark wire-haired behind, short ruddy -haired in front, a stump tail, a face so fringed you could only see its eyes when the wind blew. Mr Dyce put down his hand and scratched it behind the ear. "Don't laugh, Footles," he said. "I would not laugh if I were you, Footles – it's just an old one. Many a time you've heard it before, sly rogue. One would think you wanted to borrow money." If you could hear Dan Dyce speak to his dog, you would know at once he was a bachelor: only bachelors and bairnless men know dogs.

"I hope and trust he'll have decent clothes to wear, and none of their American rubbish," broke in Bell, back to her nephew again. "It's all nonsense about the bashed hat; but you can never tell what way an American play-actor will dress a bairn: there's sure to be something daft-like about him – a starry waistcoat or a pair of spats – and we must make him respectable like other boys in the place."

"I would say Norfolk suits, the same as the banker's boys," suggested Ailie. "I think the banker's boys always look so smart and neat."

"Anything with plenty of pockets in it," said Mr Dyce. "At the age of ten a boy would prefer his clothes to be all pockets. By George! an entire suit of pockets, with a new penny in every pocket for luck, would be a great treat," – and he chuckled at the idea, making a mental note of it for a future occasion.

"Stuff and nonsense!" cried Bell emphatically, for here she was in her own department. "The boy is going to be a Scotch boy. I'll have the kilt on him, or nothing."

"The kilt!" said Mr Dyce.

"The kilt!" cried Ailie.

Rat-tat-tat-tat-tat-tat!

It was a loud knocking at the front door. They stopped the talk to listen, and they heard the maid go along the lobby from the kitchen. When she opened the door, there came in the cheerful discord of the street, the sound of a pounding drum, the fifes still busy, the orange-hawker's cry, but over all they heard her put her usual interrogation to visitors, no matter what their state or elegance.

"Well, what is't?" she asked, and though they could not see her, they knew she would have the door just a trifle open, with her shoulder against it, as if she was there to repel some chieftain of a wild invading clan. Then they heard her cry, "Mercy on me!" and her footsteps hurrying to the parlour door. She threw it open, and stood with some one behind her.

"What do you think? Here's brother William's wean!" she exclaimed in a gasp.

"My God! Where is he?" cried Bell, the first to find her tongue. "He's no' hurt, is he?"

"*It's no' a him at all – it's a her!*" shrieked Kate, throwing up her arms in consternation, and stepping aside she gave admission to a little girl.

CHAPTER IV

THE orphan child of William and Mary Dyce, dead, the pair of them, in the far-off city of Chicago, stepped quite serenely into an astounded company. There were three Dyces in a row in front of her, and the droll dog Footles at her feet, and behind her, Kate, the servant, wringing her apron as if it had newly come from the washing-boyne, her bosom heaving. Ten eyes (if you could count the dog's, hidden by his tousy fringe) stared at the child a moment, and any ordinary child would have been much put out; but this was no common child, or else she felt at once the fond kind air of home. I will give you her picture in a sentence or two. She was black-haired, dark and quick in the eye, not quite pale but olive in complexion, with a chin she held well up, and a countenance neither shy nor bold, but self-possessed. Fur on her neck and hood (Jim Molyneux's last gift), and a muff that held her arms up to the elbows, gave her an aspect of picture-book cosiness that put the maid in mind at once of the butcher's Christmas calendar.

It was the dog that first got over the astonishment: he made a dive at her with little friendly growls, and rolled on his back at her feet, to paddle with his four paws in the air, which was his way of showing he was in the key for fun.

With a cry of glee she threw the muff on the floor and plumped beside him, put her arms about his body and buried her face in his fringe. His tail went waving, joyous, like a banner. "Doggie, doggie, you love me," said she in an accent that was anything but American. "Let us pause and consider – you will not leave this house till I boil you an egg."

"God bless me, what child's this?" cried Bell coming to herself with a start, and, pouncing on her, she lifted her to her feet. Ailie sank on her hands and knees and stared in the visitor's face. "The kilt, indeed!" said Mr Dyce to himself. "This must be a warlock wean, for if it has not got the voice and sentiment of Wanton Wully Oliver I'm losing my wits."

"Tell me this, quick, are you Lennox Dyce?" said Bell all trembling, devouring the little one with her eyes.

"Well, I just guess I am," replied the child calmly, with the dog licking her chin. "Say, are you Auntie Bell?" and this time there was no doubt about the American accent. Up went her mouth to them to be kissed, composedly: they lost no time, but fell upon her, Ailie half in tears because at once she saw below the childish hood so

20

much of brother William.

"Lennox, dear, you should not speak like that; who in all the world taught you to speak like that?" said Bell, unwrapping her.

"Why, I thought that was all right here," said the stranger. "That's the way the bell-man speaks."

"Bless me! Do you know the bell-man?" cried Miss Dyce.

"I rang his old bell for him this morning – didn't you hear me?" was the surprising answer. "He's a nice man; he liked me. I'd like him too if he wasn't so tired. He was too tired to speak sense; all he would say was, 'I've lost the place; let us pause and consider,' and 'Try another egg.' I said I would give him a quarter if he'd let me ring his bell, and he said he'd let me do it for nothing and my breakfast besides. 'You'll not leave this house till I boil an egg for you' – that's what he said, and the poor man was so tired and his legs were dre'ffle poorly!" Again her voice was the voice of Wully Oliver; the sentiment, as the Dyces knew, was the slogan of his convivial hospitality.

"The kilt, indeed!" said Mr Dyce, feeling extraordinarily foolish, and, walking past them, he went upstairs and hurriedly put the peasling in his pocket.

When he came down, Young America was indifferently pecking at her second breakfast with Footles on her knee, an aunt on either side of her, and the maid Kate with a tray in her hand for excuse, open-mouthed, half in at the door.

"Well, as I was saying, Jim – that's my dear Mr Molyneux, you know – got busy with a lot of the boys once he landed off that old ship, and so he said, 'Bud, this is the – the – justly cel'brated Great Britain; I know by the boys; they're so lonely when they're by themselves; I was 'prehensive we might have missed it in the dark, but it's all right.' And next day he bought me this muff and things and put me on the cars – say, what funny cars you have! – and said 'Goodbye, Bud; just go right up to Maryfield, and change there. If you're lost anywhere on the island just holler out good and loud, and I'll hear!' He pretended he wasn't caring, but he was pretty blinky 'bout the eyes, and I saw he wasn't anyway gay, so I never let on the way I felt myself."

She suggested the tone and manner of the absent Molyneux in a fashion to put him in the flesh before them. Kate almost laughed loud out at the oddity of it; Ailie and her brother were astounded at the cleverness of the mimicry; Bell clenched her hands, and said for the second time that day, "Oh! that Molyneux, if I had him!"

"He's a nice man, Jim. I can't tell you how I love him – and he

21

gave me heaps of candy at the depot," proceeded the unabashed new-comer. "'Change at Edinburgh,' he said; 'you'll maybe have time to run into the Castle and see the Duke; give him my love, but not my address. When you get to Maryfield hop out slick and ask for your uncle Dyce.' And then he said, did Jim, 'I hope he ain't a loaded Dyce, seein' he's Scotch, and it's the festive season.'"

"The adorable Jim!" said Ailie. "We might have known."

"I got on all right," proceeded the child, "but I didn't see the Duke of Edinburgh; there wasn't time, and uncle wasn't at Maryfield, but a man put me on his mail carriage and drove me right here. He said I was a caution. My! it was cold. Say, is it always weather like this here?"

"Sometimes it's like this, and sometimes it's just ordinary Scotch weather," said Mr Dyce, twinkling at her through his spectacles.

"I was dre'ffle sleepy in the mail, and the driver wrapped me up, and when I came into this town in the dark he said, 'Walk right down there and rap at the first door you see with a brass man's hand for a knocker; that's Mr Dyce's house.' I came down, and there wasn't any brass man, but I saw the knocker. I couldn't reach up to it, so when I saw a man going into the church with a lantern in his hand, I went up to him and pulled his coat. I knew he'd be all right going into a church. He told me he was going to ring the bell, and I said I'd give him a quarter – oh, I said that before. When the bell was finished he took me to his house for luck – that was what he said – and he and his wife got right up and boiled eggs. They said I was a caution, too, and they went on boiling eggs, and I couldn't eat more than two and a white though I tried *and* tried. I think I slept a good while in their house; I was so fatigued, and they were all right; they loved me, I could see that. And I liked them some myself, though they must be mighty poor, for they haven't any children. Then the bell-man took me to this house, and rapped at the door, and went away pretty quick for him before anybody came to it, because he said he was plain-soled – what's plain-soled anyhow? – and wasn't a lucky first-foot on a New Year's morning."

"It beats all, that's what it does!" cried Bell "My poor wee whitterick! Were ye no' frightened on the sea?"

"Whitterick, whitterick," repeated the child to herself, and Ailie, noticing, was glad that this was certainly not a diffy. Diffies never interest themselves in new words; diffies never go inside themselves with a new fact as a dog goes under a table with a bone.

"Were you not frightened when you were on the sea?" repeated Bell.

22

"No," said the child promptly. "Jim was there all right, you see, and he knew all about it. He said, 'Trust in Providence, and if it's very stormy, trust in Providence *and* the Scotch captain.'"

"I declare! the creature must have some kind of sense in him, too," said Bell, a little mollified by this compliment to Scotch sea-captains. And all the Dyces fed their eyes upon this wonderful wean that had fallen among them. 'Twas happy in that hour with them; as if in a miracle they had been remitted to their own young years; their dwelling was at long last furnished! She had got into the good graces of Footles as if she had known him all her life.

"Say, uncle, this is a funny dog," was her next remark. "Did God make him?"

"Well – yes, I suppose God did," said Mr Dyce, taken a bit aback.

"Well, isn't He the darnedst! This dog beats Mrs Molyneux's Dodo, and Dodo was a looloo. What sort of a dog is he? Scotch terrier?"

"Mostly not," said her uncle, chuckling. "It's really an improvement on the Scotch terrier. There's later patents in him, you might say. He's a sort of mosaic; indeed, when I think of it you might describe him as a pure mosaic dog."

"A Mosaic dog!" exclaimed Lennox. "Then he must have come from scriptural parts. Perhaps I'll get playing with him Sundays. Not playing loud out, you know, but just being happy. I love being happy, don't you?"

"It's my only weakness," said Mr Dyce emphatically, blinking through his glasses. "The other business men in the town don't approve of me for it; they call it frivolity. But it comes so easily to me I never charge it in the bills, though a sense of humour should certainly be worth 12s. 6d. a smile in the Table of Fees. It would save many a costly plea."

"Didn't you play on Sunday in Chicago?" asked Ailie.

"Not out loud. Poppa said he was bound to have me Scotch in one thing at least, even if it took a strap. That was after mother died. He'd just read to me Sundays, and we went to church till we had pins and needles. We had the Reverend Ebenezer Paul Frazer, M.A., Presbyterian Church on the Front. He just preached *and* preached till we had pins and needles all over."

"My poor Lennox!" exclaimed Ailie, with feeling.

"Oh, I'm all right!" said young America blithely "I'm not kicking."

Dan Dyce, with his head to the side, took off his spectacles and rubbed them clean with his handkerchief; put them on again, looked at his niece through them, and then at Ailie, with some emotion struggling in his countenance. Ailie for a moment suppressed some inward convulsion, and turned her gaze embarrassed from him to Bell, and Bell catching the eyes of both of them could contain her joy no longer. They laughed till the tears came, and none more heartily than brother William's child. She had so sweet a laugh that there and then the Dyces thought it the loveliest sound they had ever heard in their house. Her aunts would have devoured her with caresses. Her uncle stood over her and beamed, rubbing his hands, expectant every moment of another manifestation of the oddest kind of child mind he had ever encountered. And Kate swept out and in between the parlour and the kitchen on trivial excuses, generally with something to eat for the child who had eaten so much in the house of Wanton Wully Oliver that she was indifferent to the rarest delicacies of Bell's celestial grocery.

"You're just – just a wee witch!" said Bell, fondling the child's hair. "Do you know, that man Molyneux –"

"Jim," suggested Lennox.

"I would Jim him if I had him! That man Molyneux in all his scrimping little letters never said whether you were a boy or a girl, and we thought a Lennox was bound to be a boy, and all this time we have been expecting a boy."

"I declare!" said the little one, with the most amusing drawl, a memory of Molyneux. "Why, I always was a girl, far back as I can remember. Nobody never gave me the chance to be a boy. I s'pose I hadn't the clothes for the part, and they just pushed me along anyhow in frocks. Would you'd rather I was a boy?"

"Not a bit! We have one in the house already, and he's a fair heart-break," said her aunt, with a look towards Mr Dyce. "We had just made up our minds to dress you in the kilt when your rap came to the door. At least, I had made up my mind; the others are so thrawn! And bless me! lassie, where's your luggage? You surely did not come all the way from Chicago with no more than what you have on your back?"

"You'll be tickled to death to see my trunks!" said Lennox. "I've heaps and heaps of clothes and six dolls. They're all coming with the coach. They wanted me to wait for the coach too, but the mail man who called me a caution said he was bound to have a passenger for luck on New Year's day, and I was in a hurry to get home anyway."

"Home!" When she said that, the two aunts swept on her like a billow and bore her, dog and all, upstairs to her room. She was almost blind for want of sleep. They hovered over her quick-fingered, airy as bees, stripping her for bed. She knelt a moment and in one breath said –

"God-bless-father-and-mother-and-Jim-and-Mrs-Molyneux-and-my-aunts-in-Scotland-and-Uncle-Dan-and-everybody-good-night."

And was asleep in the sunlight of the room as soon as her head fell on the pillow.

"She prayed for her father and mother," whispered Bell, with Footles in her arms, as they stood beside the bed. "It's not – it's not quite Presbyterian to pray for the dead; it's very American, indeed you might call it papist."

Ailie's face reddened, but she said nothing.

"And do you know this?" said Bell shamefacedly, "I do it myself; upon my word, I do it myself. I'm often praying for father and mother and William."

"So am I," confessed Alison, plainly relieved. "I'm afraid I'm a poor Presbyterian, for I never knew there was anything wrong in doing so."

Below, in the parlour, Mr Dyce stood looking into the white garden, a contented man, humming –

"Star of Peace, to wanderers weary"

CHAPTER V

SHE was a lucky lassie, this of ours, to have come home to her father's Scotland on that New Year's day, for there is no denying that it is not always gay in Scotland, contrary land, that, whether we be deep down in the waist of the world and afar from her, or lying on her breast, chains us to her with links of iron and gold – stern tasks and happy days remembered, ancient stories, austerity and freedom, cold weather on moor and glen, warm hearths and burning hearts. She might have seen this burgh first in its solemnity, on one of the winter days when it shivers and weeps among its old memorials, and the wild geese cry more constant over the house-tops, and the sodden gardens, lanes, wynds, and wells, the clanging spirits of old citizens dead and gone, haunting the place of their follies and their good times, their ridiculous ideals, their mistaken ambitions, their broken plans. Ah, wild geese! wild geese! old ghosts that cry tonight above my dwelling, I feel – I feel and know! She

25

might have come, the child, to days of fast, and sombre dark drugget garments, dissonant harsh competing kettle bells, or spoiled harvests, poor fishings, hungry hours. It was good for her, and it is the making of my story, that she came not then, but with the pure white cheerful snow, to ring the burgh bell in her childish escapade, and usher in with merriment the New Year, and begin her new life happily in the old world.

She woke at noon among the scented curtains, in linen sea-breeze bleached, under the camceil roof that all children love, for it makes a garret like the ancestral cave, and in rainy weather they can hear the pattering feet of foes above them. She heard the sound of John Taggart's drum, and the fling of "Happy we've been a' thegether," and turning, found upon her pillow a sleeping doll that woke whenever she raised it up, and stared at her in wonderment.

"Oh! – Oh! – Oh! you roly-poly blonde!" cried the child in ecstasy, hugging it to her bosom and covering it with kisses. "I'm as glad as anything. Do you see the lovely little room? I'll tell you right here what your name is: it's Alison; no, it's Bell; no, it's Alibel for your two just lovely, lovely aunties."

Up she rose, sleep banished, with a sense of cheerfulness and expectation, nimbly dressed herself, and slid down the banisters to tumble plump at the feet of her Auntie Bell in the lobby.

"Mercy on us! You'll break your neck; are you hurt?" cried Aunt Bell. "I'm not kicking," said the child, and the dog waved furiously a gladsome tail. A log fire blazed and crackled and hissed in the parlour, and Mr Dyce tapped time with his fingers on a chair-back to an internal hymn

"My! ain't I the naughty girl to be snoozling away like a gopher in a hole all day? Your clock's stopped, Uncle Dan."

Mr Dyce looked very guilty, and coughed, rubbing his chin. "You're a noticing creature," said he. "I declare it *has* stopped. Well, well!" and his sister Bell plainly enjoyed some amusing secret.

"Your uncle is always a little daft, my dear," she said.

"I would rather be daft than dismal," he retorted, cleaning his glasses.

"It's a singular thing that the clocks in our lobby and parlour always stop on the New Year's day, Lennox.

"Bud; please, say Bud," pleaded the little one. "Nobody ever calls me Lennox 'cept when I'm doing something wrong and almost going to get a whipping.".

"Very well, Bud, then. This clock gets something wrong with it every New Year's day, for your uncle, that man there, wants the folk

26

who call never to know the time so that they'll bide the longer."

"Tuts!" said Uncle Dan, who had thought this was his own particular recipe for joviality, and that they had never discovered it.

"You have come to a hospitable town, Bud," said Ailie. "There are convivial old gentlemen on the other side of the street who have got up a petition to the magistrates to shut up the inn and the public-house in the afternoon. They say it is in the interests of temperance, but it's really to compel their convivial friends to visit themselves."

"I signed it myself," confessed Mr Dyce, "and I'm only half convivial. I'm not bragging; I might have been more convivial if it didn't so easily give me a sore head. What's more cheerful than a crowd in the house and the clash going? A fine fire, a good light, and turn about at a story! The happiest time I ever had in my life was when I broke my leg; so many folk called, it was like a month of New Year's days. I was born with a craving for company. Mother used to have a superstition that if a knife or spoon dropped on the floor from the table it betokened a visitor, and I used to drop them by the dozen. But, dear me! there's a wean with a doll, and where in the world did she get it?"

Bud, with the doll under one arm and the dog tucked under the other, laughed up in his face with shy perception.

"Oh, you funny man!" she exclaimed. "I guess you know all right who put Alibel on my pillow. Why! I could have told you were a doll man: I noticed you turning over the pennies in your pants' pocket, same as poppa used when he saw any nice clean little girl like me and he was the dolliest man in all Chicago. Why, there was treasury days when he just rained dolls."

"That was William, sure enough," said Mr Dyce. "There's no need for showing us *your* strawberry mark. It was certainly William. If it had only been dolls!"

"Her name's Alibel, for her two aunties," said the child.

"Tuts!" said Mr Dyce. "If I had thought you meant to honour them that way I would have made her twins. But you see I did not know; it was a delicate transaction as it was. I could not tell very well whether a doll or a – a – or a fountain pen would be the most appropriate present for a ten-year-old niece from Chicago, and I risked the doll. I hope it fits."

"Like a halo. It's just sweet!" said the ecstatic maiden, and rescued one of its limbs from the gorge of Footles.

It got about the town that to Dyces' house had come a wonderful American child who talked language like a minister: the news was partly the news of the mail-driver and Wully Oliver, but mostly the news of Kate, who, from the moment Lennox had been taken from her presence and put to bed, had dwelt upon the window-sashes, letting no one pass that side of the street without her confidence.

"You never heard the like! No' the size of a shillin's worth of ha'pennies, and she came all the way by her lee-lone in the coach from Chickagoo – that's in America. There's to be throng times in this house now, I'm tellin' you, with brother William's wean."

As the forenoon advanced Kate's intelligence grew more surprising: to the new-comer were ascribed a score of characteristics such as had never been seen in the town before. For one thing (would Kate assure them), she could imitate Wully Oliver till you almost saw whiskers on her and could smell the dram. She was thought to be a boy to start with, but that was only their ignorance in Chickagoo, for the girl was really a lassie, and had kists of lassie's clothes coming with the coach.

The Dyces' foreigner was such a grand sensation that it marred the splendour of the afternoon band parade, though John Taggart was unusually glorious, walking on the very backs of his heels, his nose in the heavens, and his drumsticks soaring and circling over his head in a way to make the spectators giddy. Instead of following the band till its *répertoire* was suddenly done at five minutes to twelve at the door of Maggie White, the wine and spirit merchant, there were many that hung about the street in the hope of seeing the American. They thought they would know her at once by the colour of her skin, which some said would be yellow, and others maintained would be brown. A few less patient and more privileged boldly visited the house of Dyce to make their New Year compliments and see the wonder for themselves.

The American had her eye on them.

She had her eye on the Sheriff's lady, who was so determinedly affable, so pleased with everything the family of Dyce might say, do, or possess, and only five times ventured to indicate there were others, by a mention of "the dear Lady Anne – so nice, so simple, so unaffected, so amiable."

On Miss Minto of the crimson cloak, who kept her deaf ear to the sisters and her good one to their brother, and laughed heartily at all his little jokes even before they were half made, or looked at him with large, soft, melting eyes and her lips apart, which her glass had told her was an aspect ravishing. The sisters smiled at each other when she had gone and looked comically at Dan, but he, poor man, saw nothing but just that Mary Minto was a good deal fatter than she used to be.

28

On the doctor's two sisters, late come from a farm in the country, marvellously at ease so long as the conversation abode in gossip about the neighbours, but in a silent terror when it rose from persons to ideas, as it once had done when Lady Anne had asked them what they thought of didactic poetry and one of them said it was a thing she was very fond of, and then fell in a swound.

On the banker man, the teller, who was in hopeless love with Ailie, as was plain from the way he devoted himself to Bell.

On Mr Dyce's old retired partner, Mr Cleland, who smelt of cloves and did not care for tea.

On P. & A. MacGlashan, who had come in specially to see if the stranger knew his brother Albert, who he said, was "In a Somewhere-ville in Manitoba."

On the Provost and his lady, who were very old, and petted each other when they thought themselves unobserved.

On the soft, kind, simple, content and happy ladies lately married.

On the others who would like to be.

Yes, Bud had her eye on them all. They never guessed how much they entertained her as they genteelly sipped their tea, or wine, or ginger cordial – the women of them – or coughed a little too artificially over the New Year glass – the men.

"Wee Pawkie, that's what she is – just Wee Pawkie!" said the Provost when he got out, and so far it summed up everything.

The ladies could not tear away home fast enough to see if they had not a remnant of cloth that could be made into such a lovely dress as that of Dyce's niece for one of their own children. "Mark my words!" they said, "that child will be ruined between them. She's her father's image, and he went and married a poor play-actress, and stayed a dozen years away from Scotland, and never wrote home a line."

So many people came to the house, plainly for no reason but to see the new-comer, that Ailie at last made up her mind to satisfy all by taking her out for a walk. The strange thing was that in the street the populace displayed indifference or blindness. Bud might have seen no more sign of interest in her than the hurried glance of a passer-by; no step slowed to show that the most was being made of the opportunity. There had been some women at their windows when she came out of the house sturdily walking by Aunt Ailie's side, with her hands in her muff, and her keen black eyes peeping from under the fur of her hood; but these women drew in their heads immediately. Ailie, who knew her native town, was conscious that from behind the curtains the scrutiny was keen. She smiled to herself

29

as she walked demurely down the street.

"Do you feel anything, Bud?" she asked.

Bud naturally failed to comprehend.

"You ought to feel something at your back; I'm ticklish all down the back because of a hundred eyes."

"I know," said the astounding child. "They think we don't notice, but I guess God sees them," and yet she had apparently never glanced at the windows herself, nor looked round to discover passers-by staring over their shoulders at her aunt and her.

For a moment Ailie felt afraid. She dearly loved a quick perception, but it was a gift, she felt, a niece might have too young.

"How in the world did you know that, Bud?" she asked.

"I just guessed they'd be doing it," said Bud, "'cause it's what I would do if I saw a little girl from Scotland walking down the lake front in Chicago. Is it dre'ffle rude, Aunt Ailie?"

"So they say, so they say," said her aunt, looking straight forward, with her shoulders back and her eyes level, flushing at the temples. "But I'm afraid we can't help it. It's undignified – to be seen doing it. I can see you're a real Dyce, Bud. The other people who are not Dyces lose a great deal of fun. Do you know, child, I think you and I are going to be great friends – you and I and Aunt Bell and Uncle Dan."

"And the Mosaic dog," added Bud with warmth. "I love that old dog so much that I could – I could eat him. He's the becomingest dog! Why, here he is!" And it was indeed Footles who hurled himself at them, a rapturous mass of unkempt hair and convulsive barkings, having escaped from the imprisonment of Kate's kitchen by climbing over her shoulders and out across the window-sash.

CHAPTER VI

"I HEARD all about you and Auntie Bell and Uncle Dan from pop – from father," said Bud, as they walked back to the house. She had learned already from example how sweeter sounded "father" than the term she had used in America. "He was mighty apt to sit up nights talking about you all. But I don't quite place Kate: he never mentioned Kate."

"Oh, she's a new addition," explained Ailie. "Kate is the maid, you know: she came to us long after your father left home, but she's been with us five years now, and that's long enough to make her one of the family."

"My! Five years! She ain't – she isn't much of a quitter, is she? I guess you must have tacked her down," said Bud. "You don't get helps in Chicago to linger round the dear old spot like that; they get all hot running from base to base, same as if it was a game of ball. But she's a pretty – pretty broad girl, isn't she? She couldn't run very fast; that'll be the way she stays."

Ailie smiled. "Ah! So that's Chicago too, is it? You must have been in the parlour a good many times at five-o'clock tea to have grasped the situation at your age. I suppose your Chicago ladies lower the temperature of their tea weeping into it the woes they have about their domestics? It's another Anglo-Saxon link."

"Mrs Jim said sensible girls that would stay long enough to cool down after the last dash were getting that scarce you had to go out after them with a gun. You didn't really, you know; that was just Mrs Jim's way of putting it."

"I understand," said Alison, unable to hide her amusement. "You seem to have picked up that way of putting it yourself."

"Am I speaking slang?" asked the child, glancing up quickly and reddening. "Father pro – prosisted I wasn't to speak slang nor chew gum; he said it was things no real lady would do in the old country and that I was to be a well-off English undefied. You must be dre'ffle shocked, Auntie Ailie?"

"Oh no," said Ailie cheerfully; "I never was shocked in all my life, though they say I'm a shocker myself. I'm only surprised a little at the possibilities of the English language. I've hardly heard you use a word of slang yet, and still you scarcely speak a sentence in which there's not some novelty. It's like Kate's first attempt at sheep's-head broth: we were familiar with all the ingredients except the horns, and we knew them elsewhere."

"*That's* all right, then," said Bud, relieved. "But Mrs Jim had funny ways of putting things, and I s'pose I picked them up. I can't help it – I pick up so fast. Why, I had scarletina twice! and I picked up her way of zaggerating: often I zaggerate dre'ffle, and say I wrote all the works of Shakespeare, when I really didn't, you know. Mrs Jim didn't mean that she had to go out hunting for helps with a gun; all she meant was that they were getting harder and harder to get, and mighty hard to keep when you got them."

"I know," said Alison. "It's an old British story; you'll hear it often from our visitors, if you're spared. But we're lucky with our Kate;

we seem to give her complete satisfaction, or, at all events, she puts up with us. When she feels she can't put up with us any longer, she hurls herself on the morning newspaper to look at the advertisements for ladies'-maids and housekeepers with £50 a-year, and makes up her mind to apply at once, but can never find a pen that suits her before we make her laugh. The servant in the house of Dyce who laughs is lost. You'll like Kate, Bud. We like her; and I notice that if you like anybody they generally like you back."

"I'm so glad," said Bud with enthusiasm. "If there's one thing under the canopy I am, I'm a liker."

They had reached the door of the house without seeing the slightest sign that the burgh was interested in them, but they were no sooner in than a hundred tongues were discussing the appearance of the little American. Ailie took off Bud's cloak and hood, and pushed her into the kitchen, with a whisper to her that she was to make Kate's acquaintance, and be sure and praise her scones, then left her and flew upstairs, with a pleasant sense of personal good-luck. It was so sweet to know that brother William's child was anything but a diffy.

Bud stood for a moment in the kitchen, bashful, for it must not be supposed she lacked a childish shyness. Kate, toasting bread at the fire, turned round and felt a little blate herself, but smiled at her, such a fine expansive smile, it was bound to put the child at ease. "Come away in, my dear, and take a bite," said the maid. It is so they greet you – simple folk! – in the isle of Colonsay.

The night was coming on, once more with snowy feathers. Wanton Wully lit the town. He went from lamp to lamp with a ladder, children in his train chanting

"Leerie, leerie, light the lamps,
Long legs and crooked shanks!"

and he expostulating with "I know you fine, the whole of you; at least I know the boys. Stop you till I see your mothers!" Miss Minto's shop was open, and shamefaced lads went dubiously in to buy ladies' white gloves, for with gloves they tryst their partners here at New Year balls, and tonight was Samson's fiddle giggling at the inn. The long tenement lands, as flat and high as cliffs, and built for all eternity, at first dark grey in the dusk, began to glow in every window, and down the stairs and from the closes flowed exceeding cheerful sounds. Green fires of wood and coal sent up a cloud above these dwellings, tea-kettles jigged and sang. A thousand things were happening in the street, but for once the maid of Colonsay restrained her interest in the window. "Tell me this, what did you say your name was?" she asked.

"I'm Miss Lennox Brenton Dyce," said Bud primly, "but the Miss don't amount to much till I'm old enough to get my hair up."

"You must be tired coming so far. All the way from that Chickagoo!"

"Chicago," suggested Bud politely.

"Just that! Chickagoo or Chicago, it depends on the way you spell it," said Kate readily. "I was brought up to call it Chickagoo. What a length to come on New Year's day! Were you not frightened? Try one of them brown biscuits. And how are they all keeping in America?"

She asked the question with such tender solicitude that Bud saw no humour in it, and answered gravely –

"Pretty spry, thank you. Have you been there?"

"Me!" cried Kate, with her bosom heaving at the very thought. Then her Highland vanity came to her rescue. "No," she said, "I have not been exactly what you might call altogether there, but I had a cousin that started for Australia, and got the length of Paisley. It'll be a big place America? Put butter on it."

"The United States of America are bounded on the east by the Atlantic Ocean, on the west by the Pacific, on the south by Mexico and the Gulf, and on the north by an imaginary line called Canada. The State of New York alone is as large as England," said Bud glibly, repeating a familiar lesson.

"What a size!" cried Kate. "Take another of them brown biscuits. Scotland's not slack neither for size; there's Glasgow and Oban, and Colonsay and Stornoway. There'll not be hills in America?"

"There's no hills, just mountains," said Bud. "The chief mountain ranges are the Rocky Mountains and the Alleghanies. They're about the biggest mountains in the world."

"Talking about big things, look at the big pennyworth of milk we get here," said Kate, producing a can: it was almost the last ditch of her national pride.

The child looked gravely into the can, and then glanced shrewdly at the maid.

"It isn't a pennyworth," said she sharply, "it's twopence worth."

"My stars! how did you know that?" said Kate, much taken aback.

"'Cause you're bragging. Think I don't know when anybody's bragging?" said Bud. "And when a body brags about a place or anything, they zaggerate, and just about double things."

"You're not canny," said Kate, thrusting the milk-can back hastily on the kitchen dresser. "Don't spare the butter on your biscuit. They tell me there's plenty of money in America. I would not wonder, eh?"

"Why, everybody's got money to throw at the birds there," said Bud, with some of the accent as well as the favourite phrase of Jim Molyneux.

"They have little to do; forbye, it's cruelty. Mind you, there's plenty of money here too; your uncle has a desperate lot of it. He was wanting to go away to America and bring you home whenever he heard – whenever he heard. Will you not try another of them biscuits? It will do you no harm."

"I know," said Bud gravely, "whenever he heard about my father being dead."

"I think we're sometimes very stupid, us from Colonsay," said the maid regretfully. "I should have kept my mouth shut about your father. Take *two* biscuits, my dear; or maybe you would rather have short-cake. Yes, he was for going there and then – even if it cost a pound, I daresay – but changed his mind when he heard yon man Molyneux was bringing you."

Footles, snug in the child's lap, shared the biscuits and barked for more.

> "I love little Footles,
> His coat is so warm,
> And if I don't tease him
> He'll do me no harm."

said Bud, burying her head in his mane.

"Good Lord! did you make that yourself, or just keep mind of it?" asked the astounded Kate.

"I made it just right here," said Bud coolly. "Didn't you know I could make poetry? Why, you poor perishing soul, I'm just a regular wee – wee whitterick at poetry! It goes sloshing round in my head, and it's simply pie for me to make it. Here's another –

> 'Lives of great men oft remind us
> We can make our lives sublime,
> And, departing, leave behind us
> Footprints on the sands of time.'

I just dash them off. I guess I'll have to get up bright and early to-morrow and touch that one up some. Mostly you can't make them

34

good the first try, and then you're bound to go all over them from the beginning and put the good in here and there. That's art, Jim says. He knew an artist who'd finish a picture with everything quite plain about it, and then say, 'Now for the Art!' and fuzz it all with a hard brush."

"My stars! what things you know!" exclaimed the maid. "You're clever – tremendous clever! What's your age?"

"I was born mighty well near ten years ago," said Bud, as if she were a centenarian.

Now it is not wise to tell a child like Lennox Dyce that she is clever, though a maid from Colonsay could scarcely be expected to know that. Till Bud had landed on the British shore she had no reason to think herself anything out of the ordinary. Jim Molyneux and his wife, with no children of their own, and no knowledge of children except the elderly kind that play in theatres, had treated her like a person little younger than themselves, and saw no marvel in her quickness, that is common enough with Young America. But Bud, from Maryfield to her uncle's door, had been a "caution" to the plainly admiring mail-driver; a kind of fairy princess to Wanton Wully Oliver and his wife; the surprise of her aunts had been only half concealed, and here was the maid in an undisguised enchantment! The vanity of ten-year-old was stimulated; for the first time in her life she felt decidedly superior.

"It was very brave of me to come all this way in a ship at ten years old," she proceeded.

"I once came to Oban along with a steamer myself," said Kate, "but och, that's nothing, for I knew a lot of the drovers. Just fancy you coming from America! Were you not lonely?"

"I was dre'ffle lonely," said Bud, who, in fact, had never known a moment's dulness across the whole Atlantic. "There was I leaving my native land, perhaps never to set eyes on its shores evermore, and coming to a far country I didn't know the least thing about. I was leaving all my dear young friends, and the beautiful Mrs Molyneux, and her faithful dog Dodo, and –" here she squeezed a tear from her eyes, and stopped to think of circumstances even more touching.

"My poor wee hen!" cried Kate, distressed. "Don't you greet, and I'll buy you something."

"And I didn't know what sort of uncle and aunties they might be here – whether they'd be cruel and wicked or not, or whether they'd keep me or not. Little girls most always have cruel uncles and aunties – you can see that in the books."

"You were awful stupid about that bit of it," said the maid

emphatically. "I'm sure anybody could have told you about Mr Dyce and his sisters."

"And then it was so stormy," proceeded Bud quickly, in search of more moving considerations. "I made a poem about that too – I just dashed it off; the first verse goes –

'The breaking waves dashed high
   On a stern and rock-bound coast –

but I forget the rest, 'cept that

'– they come to wither there
   Away from their childhood's land.'

The waves were mountains high, and whirled over the deck, and –"

"My goodness, you would get all wet!" said Kate, putting her hand on Bud's shoulder to feel if she were dry yet. Honest tears were in her own eyes at the thought of such distressing affairs.

"The ship at last struck on a rock," proceeded Bud, "so the captain lashed me –"

"I would lash him, the villain!" cried the indignant maid.

"I don't mean that; he tied me – that's lash in books – to the mast, and then – and then – well, then we waited calmly for the end," said Bud, at the last of her resources for ocean tragedy.

Kate's tears were streaming down her cheeks at this conjured vision of youth in dire distress. "Oh dear! oh dear! my poor wee hen!" she sobbed. "I'm so sorry for you."

"Bud! coo-ie! coo-ie!" came the voice of Aunt Ailie along the lobby, but Bud was so entranced with the effect of her imaginings that she paid no heed, and Kate's head was wrapped in her apron.

"Don't cry, Kate; I wouldn't cry if I was you," said the child at last, soothingly. "Maybe it's not true."

"I'll greet if I like," insisted the maid. "Fancy you in that awful shipwreck! It's enough to scare anybody from going anywhere. Oh dear! oh dear!" and she wept more copiously than ever.

"Don't cry," said Bud again. "It's silly to drizzle like that. Why, great Queen of Sheba! I was only joshing you: it was as calm on that ship as a milk sociable."

Kate drew down the apron from her face and stared at her. Her meaning was only half plain, but it was a relief to know that things had not been quite so bad as she first depicted them. "A body's the better of a bit greet, whiles," she said philosophically, drying her eyes.

"That's what I say," agreed Bud. "That's why I told you all that. Do you know, child, I think you and I are going to be great friends." She said this with the very tone and manner of Alison, whose words they were to herself, and turned round hastily and embarrassed at a laugh behind her to find her Aunt had heard herself thus early imitated.

CHAPTER VII

IF Molyneux, the actor, was to blame for sending this child of ten on her journey into Scotland without convoy, how much worse was his offence that he sent no hint of her character to the house of Dyce? She was like the carpet-bag George Jordon found at the inn door one day without a name on it, and saying "There's nothing like thrift in a family," took home immediately, to lament over for a week because he had not the key to open it. There should have been a key to Lennox Brenton Dyce, but Molyneux, a man of post-cards and curt and cryptic epistles generally, never thought of that, so that it took some days for the folk she came among to pick the lock. There was fun in the process, it cannot be denied, but that was because the Dyces were the Dyces; had they been many another folk she might have been a mystery for years, and in the long-run spoiled completely. Her mother had been a thousand women in her time – heroines good and evil, fairies, princesses, paupers, maidens, mothers, shy and bold, plain or beautiful, young or old, as the play of the week demanded – a play-actress, in a word. And now she was dead and buried, the bright white lights on her no more, the music and the cheering done. But not all dead and buried, for some of her was in her child.

Bud was born a mimic. I tell you this at once, because so many inconsistencies will be found in her I should otherwise look foolish to present her portrait for a piece of veritable life. Not a mimic of voice and manner only, but a mimic of people's minds, so that for long – until the climax came that was to change her when she found herself – she was the echo and reflection of the last person she spoke with. She borrowed minds and gestures as later she borrowed Grandma Buntain's pelerine and bonnet. She could be all men and all women except the plainly dull or wicked – but only on each

37

occasion for a little while; by-and-by she was herself again.

And so it was that for a day or two she played with the phrase and accent of Wanton Wully Oliver, or startled her aunts with an unconscious rendering of Kate's Highland accent, her "My stars!" and "Mercy me's?" and "My wee hens!"

The daft days (as we call New Year time) passed – the days of careless merriment, that were but the start of Bud's daft days, that last with all of us for years if we are lucky. The town was settling down; the schools were opening on Han'sel Monday, and Bud was going – not to the Grammar School after all, but to the Pigeons' Seminary. Have patience, and by-and-by I will tell about the Pigeons.

Bell had been appalled to find the child, at the age of ten, apparently incredibly neglected in her education.

"Of course you would be at some sort of school yonder in America?" she had said at an early opportunity, not hoping for much, but ready to learn of some hedgerow academy in spite of all the papers said of Yales and Harvards and the like.

"No, I never was at school; I was just going when father died," said Bud, sitting on a sofa, wrapt in a cloak of Ailie's, feeling extremely tall and beautiful and old.

"What! Do you sit there and tell me they did not send you to school?" cried her aunt, so stunned that the child delighted in her power to startle and amaze. "That's America for you! Ten years old, and not the length of your alphabets – it's what one might expect from a heathen land of niggers, and lynchers, and presidents. I was the best sewer and speller in Miss Mushet's long before I was ten. My lassie, let me tell you you have come to a country where you'll get your education! We would make you take it at its best if we had to live on meal. Look at your Auntie Ailie – French and German, and a hand like copperplate; it's a treat to see her at the old scrutoire, no way put about, composing. Just goes at it like lightning! I do declare if your Uncle Dan was done, Ailie could carry on the business, all except the aliments and sequestrations. It beats all! Ten years old and not to know the A B C!"

"Oh, but I do," said Bud quickly. "I learned the alphabet off the play-bills – the big G's first, because there's so many Greats and Grands and Gorgeouses in them. And then Mrs Molyneux used to let me try to read Jim's press notices. She read them first every morning sitting up in bed at breakfast, and said, 'My! wasn't he a great man!' and then she'd cry a little, 'cause he never got justice from the managers, for they were all mean and jealous of him. Then she'd spray herself with the Peau d'espagne and eat a cracker. And the best papers there was in the land said the part of the butler in the second act was well filled by Mister Jim Molyneux; or among others in a fine cast were J. Molyneux, Ralph Devereux, and O.G. Tarpoll."

"I don't know what you're talking about, my poor wee whitterick; but it's all haivers," said Miss Bell. "Can you spell?"

"If the words are not too big, or silly ones where it's 'ei' or 'ie,' and you have to guess," said Bud.

"Spell cat."

Bud stared at her incredulously.

"Spell cat," repeated her aunt.

"K-a-t-t," said Bud (oh, naughty Bud!).

"Mercy!" cried Bell with horrified hands in the air. "Off you pack tomorrow to the Seminary. I wouldn't wonder if you did not know a single word of the Shorter Catechism. Perhaps they have not such a thing in that awful heathen land you came from?"

Bud could honestly say she had never heard of the Shorter Catechism.

"My poor neglected bairn," said her aunt piteously, "you're sitting there in the dark with no conviction of sin, and nothing bothering you, and you might be dead tomorrow! Mind this, that 'Man's chief end is to glorify God, and to enjoy Him for ever.' Say that."

"'Man's chief end is to glorify God, and to enjoy Him for ever'" repeated Bud obediently, rolling her r's and looking solemn like her aunt.

"Did you ever hear of Robert Bruce, him that watched the spiders?"

Here, too, the naughty Bud protested ignorance.

"He was the saviour of his country," said Bell. "Mind that!"

"Why, Auntie, I thought it was George Washington," said Bud, surprised. "I guess if you're looking for a little wee stupid, it's me."

"We're talking about Scotland," said Miss Bell severely. "He saved Scotland. It was well worth while! Can you do your sums?"

"I can *not*," said Bud emphatically. "I hate them."

Miss Bell said not a word more; she was too distressed at such confessed benightedness; but she went out of the parlour to search for Ailie. Bud forgot she was beautiful and tall and old in Ailie's cloak; she was repeating to herself Man's Chief End with rolling r's, and firmly fixing in her memory the fact that Robert Bruce, not George Washington, was the saviour of his country and watched spiders.

Ailie was out, and so her sister found no ear for her bewailings over the child's neglected education till Mr Dyce came in humming the tune of the day – "Sweet Afton" – to change his hat for one more becoming to a sitting of the Sheriff Court. He was searching for his good one in what he was used to call "the piety press," for there was hung his Sunday clothes, when Bell distressfully informed him that the child could not so much as spell cat.

"Nonsense! I don't believe it," said he. "That would be very unlike our William."

"It's true – I tried her myself!" said Bell. "She was never at a school: isn't it just deplorable?"

"H'm!" said Mr Dyce, "it depends on the way you look at it, Bell."

"She does not know a word of her Catechism, nor the name of Robert Bruce, and says she hates counting."

"Hates counting!" repeated Mr Dyce, wonderfully cheering up, "that's hopeful; it reminds me of myself. Forbye, it's gey like brother William. His way of counting was '£1, 10s. in my pocket; £2 that I'm owing some one, and 10s. I get tomorrow – that's £5 I have; what will I buy you now?' The worst of arithmetic is that it leaves nothing to the imagination. Two and two's four and you're done with it; there's no scope for either fun or fancy as there might be if the two and two went courting in the dark and swapped their partners by an accident."

"I wish you would go in and speak to her," said Bell, distressed still, "and tell her what a lot she has to learn."

"What, me!" cried Uncle Dan, "excuse my grammar," and he laughed. "It's an imprudent kind of mission for a man with all his knowledge in little patches. I have a lot to learn, myself, Bell; it takes me all my time to keep the folk I meet from finding out the fact."

But he went in humming, Bell behind him, and found the child still practising Man's Chief End, so engrossed in the exercise she never heard him enter. He crept behind her and put his hands over her eyes.

"Guess who," said he, in a shrill falsetto.

"It's Robert Bruce," said Bud, without moving.

"No – cold – cold! – guess again," said her uncle, growling like Giant Blunderbore.

"I'll mention no names," said she, "but it's mighty like Uncle Dan."

He stood in front of her and put on a serious face. "What's this I am hearing, Miss Lennox," said he, "about a little girl who doesn't know a lot of things nice little girls ought to know?"

40

"Man's chief end is to glorify God, and to enjoy Him for ever," repeated Bud reflectively. "I've got that all right, but what does it mean?"

"What does it mean?" said Mr Dyce, a bit taken aback. "You tell her, Bell; what does it mean? I must not be late for the court."

"You're far cleverer than I am," said Bell. "Tell her yourself."

"It means," said Daniel Dyce the lawyer, seating himself on the sofa beside his niece, "that man in himself is a gey poor soul, no' worth a pin, though he's apt to think the world was made for his personal satisfaction. At the best he's but an instrument – a harp of a thousand strings God bends to hear in His leisure. He made that harp – the heart and mind of man – when He was in a happy hour. Strings hale and strings broken, strings slack or tight, there are all kinds of them; the best we can do's to be taut and trembling for the gladness of God Who loves fine music, and set the stars themselves to singing from the very day He put them birling in the void. To glorify's to wonder and adore, and who keeps the wondering humble heart, the adoring eye, is to God pleasing exceedingly. Sing, lassie, sing, sing, sing, inside ye, even if ye are as timmer as a cask. God knows I have not much of a voice myself, but I'm full of nobler airs than ever crossed my rusty thrapple. To be grateful always, and glad things are no worse, is a good song to start the morning."

"Ah, but sin, Dan, sin!" said Bell, sighing, for she always feared her own light-heartedness. "We may be too joco."

"Say ye so?" he cried, turning to his sister with a flame upon his visage. "By the heavens above us, no! Sin might have been eternal; each abominable thought might have kept in our minds, constant day and night from the moment that it bred there; the theft we did might keep everlastingly our hand in our neighbour's kist as in a trap; the knife we thrust with might have kept us thrusting for ever and for ever. But no – God's good! sleep comes, and the clean morning, and the morning is Christ and every moment of time is a new opportunity to amend. It is not sin that is eternal, it is righteousness and peace. Joco! We cannot be too joco, having our inheritance."

He stopped suddenly, warned by a glance of his sister's, and turned to look in his niece's face to find bewilderment there. The mood that was not often published by Dan Dyce left him in a dash, and he laughed and put his arms round her.

"I hope you're a lot wiser for my sermon, Bud," said he; "I can see you have pins and needles worse than under the Reverend Mr Frazer on the Front. What's the American for haivers – for foolish speeches?"

"Hot air," said Bud promptly.

41

"Good!" said Dan Dyce, rubbing his hands together. "What I'm saying may seem just hot air to you, but it's meant. You do not know the Shorter Catechism; never mind; there's a lot of it I'm afraid I do not know myself; but the whole of it is in that first answer to Man's Chief End. Reading and writing, and all the rest of it, are of less importance, but I'll not deny they're gey and handy. You're no Dyce if you don't master them easily enough."

He kissed her and got gaily up and turned to go. "Now," said he, "for the law, seeing we're done with the gospels. I'm a conveyancing lawyer – though you'll not know what that means – so mind me in your prayers."

Bell went out into the lobby after him, leaving Bud in a curious frame of mind, for Man's Chief End, and Bruce's spider, and the word "joco," all tumbled about in her, demanding mastery.

"Little help I got from you, Dan!" said Bell to her brother. "You never even tried her with a multiplication table."

"What's seven times nine?" he asked her, with his fingers on the handle of the outer door, his eyes mockingly mischievous.

She flushed and laughed, and pushed him on the shoulder. "Go away with you!" said she. "Fine you ken I could never mind seven times!"

"No Dyce ever could," said he, "excepting Ailie. Get her to put the little creature through her tests. If she's not able to spell cat at ten, she'll be an astounding woman by the time she's twenty."

The end of it was that Aunt Ailie, whenever she came in, upon Bell's report, went over the street to Rodger's shop and made a purchase. As she hurried back with it, bare-headed, in a cool drizzle of rain that jewelled her wonderful hair, she felt like a child herself again. The banker-man saw her from his lodging as she flew across the street with sparkling eyes and eager lips, the roses on her cheeks, and was sure, foolish man! that she had been for a new novel or maybe a cosmetique, since in Rodger's shop they sell books and balms and ointments. She made the quiet street magnificent for a second – a poor wee second, and then, for him, the sun went down. The tap of the knocker on the door she closed behind her struck him on the heart. You may guess, good women, if you like, that at the end of the book the banker-man is to marry Ailie, but you'll be wrong; she was not thinking of the man at all at all – she had more to do; she was hurrying to open the gate of gold to her little niece.

"I've brought you something wonderful," said she to the child, "better than dolls, better than my cloak, better than everything; guess what it is."

42

Bud wrinkled her brows. "Ah, dear!" she sighed, "we may be too joco! And I'm to sing, sing, sing even if I'm as – timmer as a cask, and Robert Bruce is the saviour of his country." She marched across the room, trailing Ailie's cloak with her, in an absurd caricature of Bell's brisk manner. Yet not so much the actress engrossed in her performance, but what she tried to get a glimpse of what her aunt concealed.

"You need not try to see it," said Ailie, smiling, with the secret in her breast. "You must honestly guess."

"Better'n dolls and candies, oh, my!" said Bud; "I hope it's not the Shorter Catechism," she concluded, looking so grave that her aunt laughed.

"It's not the Catechism," said Ailie; "try again Oh, but you'll never guess! It's a key."

"A key?" repeated Bud, plainly cast down.

"A gold key," said her aunt.

"What for?" asked Bud.

Ailie sat herself down on the floor and drew the child upon her knees. She had a way of doing that which made her look like a lass in her teens; indeed it was most pleasing if the banker-man could just have seen it! "A gold key," she repeated, lovingly in Bud's ear. "A key to a garden – the loveliest garden, with flowers that last the whole year round. You can pluck and pluck at them and they're never a single one the less. Better than sweet peas! But that's not all, there's a big garden-party to be at it."

"My! I guess I'll put on my best glad rags," said Bud. "*And* the hat with pink." Then a fear came to her face. "Why, Aunt Ailie, you can't have a garden-party this time of the year," and she looked at the window down whose panes the rain was now streaming.

"This garden-party goes on all the time," said Ailie. "Who cares about the weather? Only very old people; not you and I. I'll introduce you to a lot of nice people – Di Vernon, and – you don't happen to know a lady called Di Vernon, do you, Bud?"

"I wouldn't know her if she was handed to me on a plate with parsley trimmings," said Bud promptly.

"– Di Vernon, then, and Effie Deans, and Little Nell, and the Marchioness; and Richard Swiveller and Tom Pinch, and the Cranford folks, and Juliet Capulet –"

"She must belong to one of the first families," said Bud. "I have a kind of idea that I have heard of her."

"And Mr Falstaff – such a naughty man, but nice too! And Rosalind."

43

"Rosalind!" cried Bud. "You mean Rosalind in 'As You Like It'?"

Ailie stared at her with astonishment. "You amazing child!" said she, "who told you about 'As You Like It'?"

"Nobody told me; I just read about her when Jim was learning the part of Charles the Wrestler he played on six 'secutive nights in the Waldorf."

"Read it!" exclaimed her aunt. "You mean he or Mrs Molyneux read it to you."

"No, I read it myself," said Bud.

> "'Now my co-mates and brothers in exile,
> Hath not old custom made this life more sweet
> Than that of painted pomp? Are not these woods
> More free from peril than the envious Court?'"

She threw Aunt Ailie's cloak over one shoulder, put forth a ridiculously little leg with an air of the playhouse, and made the gestures of Jim Molyneux.

"I thought you couldn't read," said Ailie. "You little fraud! You made Aunt Bell think you couldn't spell cat."

"Oh, Queen of Sheba! did she think I was in earnest?" cried Bud. "I was just pretending. I'm apt to be pretending pretty often; why, Kate thinks I make Works. I can read anything; I've read books that big it gave you cramp. I s'pose you were only making-believe about that garden, and you haven't any key at all, but I don't mind; I'm not kicking."

Ailie put her hand to her bosom and revealed the Twopenny she had bought to be the key to the wonderful garden of letters – the slim little grey-paper-covered primer in which she had learned her own first lessons. She held it up between her finger and thumb that Bud might read its title on the cover. Bud understood immediately and laughed, but not quite at her ease for once.

"I'm dre'ffle sorry, Aunt Ailie," she said. "It was wicked to pretend just like that, and put you to a lot of trouble. Father wouldn't have liked that."

"Oh, I'm not kicking," said Ailie, borrowing her phrase to put her at her ease again. "I'm too glad you're not so far behind as Aunt Bell imagined. So you like books? Capital! And Shakespeare no less! What do you like best, now?"

"Poetry," said Bud. "Particularly the bits I don't understand, but just about almost. I can't bear to stop and dally with too easy poetry; once I know it all plain and there's no more to it, I – I – I love to

44

amble on. I – why! I make poetry myself."

"Really?" said Ailie with twinkling eyes.

"Sort of poetry," said Bud. "Not so good as 'As You Like It' – not *nearly* so good, of course! I have loads of truly truly poetry inside me, but it sticks at the bends, and then I get bits that fit, made by somebody else, and wish I had been spry and said them first. Other times I'm the real Winifred Wallace."

"Winifred Wallace?" said Aunt Ailie inquiringly.

"Winifred Wallace," repeated Bud composedly. "I'm her. It's my – it's my poetry name. 'Bud Dyce' wouldn't be any use for the magazines; it's not dinky enough."

"Bless me, child, you don't tell me you write poetry for the magazines?" said her astonished aunt.

"No," said Bud, "but I'll be pretty liable to when I'm old enough to wear specs. That's if I don't go on the stage."

"On the stage!" exclaimed Ailie, full of wild alarm.

"Yes," said the child. "Mrs Molyneux said I was a born actress."

"I wonder, I wonder," said Aunt Ailie, staring into vacancy.

CHAPTER VIII

DANIEL DYCE had an office up the street at the windy corner facing the Cross, with two clerks in it and a boy who docketed letters and ran errands. Once upon a time there was a partner – Cleland & Dyce the firm had been – but Cleland was a shy and melancholy man whose only hours of confidence and gaiety came to him after injudicious drams. 'Twas patent to all how his habits seized him, but nobody mentioned it except in a whisper, sometimes as a kind of little accident, for in everything else he was the perfect gentleman, and here we never like to see the honest gentry down. All men liked Colin Cleland, and many would share his jovial hours who took their law business elsewhere than to Cleland & Dyce. That is the way of the world, too; most men keep their jovial-money in a different pocket from where they keep their cash. The time came when it behoved Mr Cleland to retire. Men who knew the circumstances said Dan Dyce paid rather dear for that retirement, and indeed it might be so in the stricter way of commerce, but the lawyer was a Christian who did not hang up his conscience in the "piety press" with his Sunday clothes. He gave his partner a good deal more than he asked.

"I hope you'll come in sometimes and see me whiles at night and join in a glass of toddy," said Mr Cleland.

"I'll certainly come and see you," said Dan Dyce. And then he put his arm affectionately through that of his old partner, and added, "I would – I would ca' canny wi' the toddy, Colin," coating the pill in sweet and kindly Scots. Thank God, we have two tongues in our place, and can speak the bitter truth in terms that show humility and love, and not the sense of righteousness, dictate.

"Eh! What for?" said Mr Cleland, his vanity at once in arms.

Dan Dyce looked in his alarmed and wavering eyes a moment, and thought, "What's the use? He knows himself, they always do!"

"For fear – for fear of fat," he said, with a little laugh, tapping with his finger on his quondam partner's widening waistcoat. "There are signs of a prominent profile, Colin. If you go on as you're doing it will be a dreadful expense for watch-guards."

Colin Cleland at once became the easy-osey man again, and smiled. "Fat, man! It's not fat," said he, clapping himself on the waistcoat; "it's information. Do you know, Dan, for a second, there, I thought you meant to be unkind, and it would be devilish unlike you to be unkind. I thought you meant something else. The breath of vulgar suspicion has mentioned drink."

"It's a pity that!" said Mr Dyce, "for a whole cask of cloves will not disguise the breath of suspicion."

It was five years now since Colin Cleland retired among his toddy rummers, and if this were a fancy story I would be telling you how he fell, and fell, and fell; but the truth – it's almost lamentable – is that the old rogue throve on leisure and ambrosial nights with men who were now quite ready to give the firm of Daniel Dyce their business, seeing they had Colin Cleland all to themselves and under observation. Trust estates and factorages from all quarters of the county came now to the office at the windy corner. A Christian lawyer with a sense of fun, unspotted by the world, and yet with a name for winning causes, was what the shire had long been wanting. And Daniel Dyce grew rich. "I'm making money so fast," he said one day to his sisters (it was before Bud came), "that I wonder often what poor souls are suffering for it."

Said Bell, "It's a burden that's easy put up with. We'll be able now to get a new pair of curtains for the back bedroom."

"A pair of curtains!" said her brother, with a smile to Ailie. "Ay, a score of pairs if they're needed, even if the vogue was Valenciennes.

Your notion of wealth, Bell, is Old Malabar's – 'Twopence more, and up goes the cuddy!' Woman, I'm fair rolling in wealth."

He said it with a kind of exultation that brought to her face a look of fear and disapproval. "Don't, Dan, don't," she cried, "don't brag of the world's dross; it's not like you. 'He that hasteth to be rich, shall not be innocent,' says the Proverbs. You must be needing medicine. We should have humble hearts. How many that were high have had a fall!"

"Are you frightened God will hear me and rue His bounty?" said the brother in a whisper. "I'm not bragging; I'm just telling you."

"I hope you're not hoarding it," proceeded Miss Bell. "It's not wise-like – "

"Nor Dyce-like either," said Miss Ailie.

"There's many a poor body in the town this winter that's needful."

"I daresay," said Daniel Dyce coldly. "The poor we have always with us. The thing, they tell me, is decreed by Providence."

"But Providence is not aye looking," said Bell. "If that's what you're frightened for, I'll be your almoner."

"It's their own blame, you may be sure, if they're poor. Improvidence and – and drink. I'll warrant they have their glass of ale every Saturday. What's ale? Is there any moral elevation in it? Its nutritive quality, I believe, is less than the tenth part of a penny bap."

"Oh, but the poor creatures!" sighed Miss Bell.

"Possibly," said Dan Dyce, "but every man must look after himself; and as you say, many a man well off has come down in the world. We should take no risks. I had Black the baker at me yesterday for £20 in loan to tide over some trouble with his flour merchant and pay an account to Miss Minto."

"A decent man, with a wife and seven children," said Miss Bell.

"Decent or not, he'll not be coming back borrowing from me in a hurry. I sent him off with a flea in his lug."

"We're not needing curtains," said Miss Bell hurriedly; "the pair we have are fine."

Dan finished his breakfast that day with a smile, flicked the crumbs off his waistcoat, gave one uneasy glance at Ailie, and went off to business humming "There is a Happy Land."

"Oh, dear me, I'm afraid he's growing a perfect miser," moaned Bell when she heard the door close behind him. "He did not use to be like that when he was younger and poorer. Money's like the toothache, a commanding thing."

Ailie smiled. "If you went about as much as I do, Bell," she said,

47

"you would not be misled by Dan's pretences. And as for Black the baker, I saw his wife in Miss Minto's yesterday buying boots for her children and a bonnet for herself. She called me Miss Ailie, an honour I never got from her in all my life before."

"Do you think – do you think he gave Black the money?" said Bell in a pleasant excitation.

"Of course he did. It's Dan's way to give it to some folk with a pretence of reluctance, for if he did not growl they would never be off his face! He's telling us about the lecture that accompanied it as a solace to our femininity. Women, you know, are very bad lenders, and dislike the practice in their husbands and brothers."

"None of the women I know," protested Bell. "They're just as free-handed as the men if they had it. I hope," she added anxiously, "that Dan got good security. Would it be a dear bonnet, now, that she was getting?"

Ailie laughed – a ridiculous sort of sister this; she only laughed.

Six times each lawful day Daniel Dyce went up and down the street between his house and the office at the windy corner opposite the Cross, the business day being divided by an interval of four hours to suit the mails. The town folk liked to see him passing; he gave the street an air of occupation and gaiety, as if a trip had just come in with a brass band banging at the latest air. Going or coming, he was apt to be humming a tune to himself as he went along with his hands in his outside pockets, and it was an unusual day when he did not stop to look in at a shop window or two on the way, though they never changed a feature once a-month. To the shops he honoured thus it was almost as good as a big turnover. Before him his dog went whirling and barking, a long alarm for the clerks to stop their game of Catch-the-Ten and dip their pens. There were few that passed him without some words of recognition.

He was coming down from the office on the afternoon of the Han'sel Monday that started Bud in the Pigeons' Seminary when he met the nurse, old Betty Baxter, with a basket. She put it down at her feet and bobbed a curtsey, a thing that nowadays you rarely see in Scotland.

"Tuts! woman," he said to her, lifting the basket and putting it in her hand. "Why need you bother with the like of that? You and your curtseys! They're out of date, Miss Baxter, out of date, like the decent men that deserved them long ago before my time."

"No, they're not out of date, Mr Dyce," said she; "I'll aye be minding yon about my mother; you'll be paid back some day."

"Tuts!" said he again, impatient. "You're an awful blether: how's

48

your patient, Duncan Gill?"

"As dour as the devil, sir," said the nurse. "Still hanging on."

"Poor man! poor man!" said Mr Dyce. "He'll just have to put his trust in God."

"Oh, he's no' so far through as all that," said Betty Baxter. "He can still sit up and take his drop of porridge. They're telling me you have got a wondeful niece, Mr Dyce, all the way from America. What a mercy for her! But I have not set eyes on her yet. I'm so busy that I could not stand in the close like the others, watching: what is she like?"

"Just like Jean Macrae," said Mr Dyce, preparing to move on.

"And what was Jean Macrae like?"

"Oh, just like other folk," said Mr Dyce, and passed on chuckling, to run almost into the arms of Captain Consequence.

"Have you heard the latest?" said Captain Consequence, putting his kid-gloved hand on the shoulder of the lawyer, who felt it like a lump of ice, for he did not greatly love the man, the smell of whose cigars, he said, before he knew they came from the Pilgrim Widow's, proved that he rose from the ranks.

"No, Captain Brodie," he said coldly. "Who's the rogue or the fool this time?" but the Captain was too stupid to perceive it. He stared perplexedly.

"I hear," said he, "the Doctor's in a difficulty."

"Is he, is he?" said Mr Dyce. "That's a chance for his friends to stand by him."

"Let him take it!" said Captain Consequence, puffing. "Did he not say to me once yonder, 'God knows how you're living.'"

"It must be God alone, for all the rest of us are wondering," said Mr Dyce, and left the man to put it in his pipe and smoke it.

Along the street came the two Miss Duffs, who kept the dame school, and he saw a hesitation in their manner when they realised a meeting was inevitable. If they had been folk that owed him he would not have wondered, from their manner, to see them tuck up their skirts and scurry down the lane. Twins they were – a tiny couple, scarcely young, dressed always in a douce long-lasting brown, something in their walk and colour that made them look like pigeon hens, and long ago conferred on them that name in Daniel Dyce's dwelling. They met him in front of his own door, and seemed inclined to pass in a trepidation.

He took off his hat to them and stood, full of curiosity about Lennox.

"What a lovely winter day!" said Miss Jean, with an air of supplication, as if her very life depended on his agreement.

"Isn't it *perfectly* exquisite!" said Miss Amelia, who usually picked up the bald details of her sister's conversation and passed them on embroidered with a bit of style.

"It's not bad," said Mr Dyce, blinking at them, wondering what ailed the dears today. They were looking uneasily around them for some way of escape; he could almost hear the thump of their hearts, he noted the stress of their breathing. Miss Jean's eyes fastened on the tree-tops over the banker's garden wall; he felt that in a moment she would spread out her wings and fly. "You have opened the school again," he said simply.

"We started again today," cooed Miss Jean.

"Yes, we resumed today," said Miss Amelia. "The common round, the daily task. And, oh! Mr Dyce –"

She stopped suddenly at the pressure of her sister's elbow on her own, and lowered her eyes, that had for a second shown an appalling area of white. It was plain they were going to fly. Mr Dyce felt inclined to cry "Peas, peas!" and keep them a little longer.

"You have my niece with you today?" he remarked. "What do you think of her?"

A look of terror exchanged between them escaped his observation.

"She's – she's a wonderful child," said Miss Jean, nervously twisting the strings of a handbag.

"A singularly interesting and – and unexpected creature," said Miss Amelia.

"Fairly bright, eh?" said Mr Dyce.

"Oh, bright!" repeated Miss Jean. "Bright is not the word for it – is it, Amelia?"

"I would rather say brilliant," said Amelia, coughing, and plucking a handkerchief out of her pocket to inhale its perfume and avert a threatening swound. "I hope – we both hope, Mr Dyce, she will be spared to grow up a credit to you. One never knows?"

"That's it," agreed Mr Dyce cheerfully. "Some girls grow up and become credits to their parents and guardians, others become reciters, and spoil many a jolly party with 'The Woman of Mumbles Head' or 'The Coffee was not Strong.'"

"I hope not," said Miss Jean, not quite understanding: the painful possibility seemed to be too much for Miss Amelia; she said nothing, but fixed her eyes on the distant tree-tops and gave a little flap of the wings of her Inverness cape.

"Peas, peas!" murmured Mr Dyce unconsciously, anxious to hold them longer and talk about his niece.

"I beg pardon," exclaimed Miss Jean, and the lawyer got very red. "I hope at least you'll like Bud," he said. "She's odd, but – but – but –" he paused for a word.

"– sincere," suggested Miss Jean.

"Yes, I would say sincere – or perhaps outspoken would be better," said Miss Amelia.

"So clever too," added Miss Jean.

"Preternaturally!" cooed Miss Amelia.

"Such a delightful accent," said Miss Jean.

"Like linkèd sweetness long drawn out," quoted Miss Amelia.

"But –" hesitated Miss Jean.

"Still –" more hesitatingly said her sister, and then there was a long pause.

"Oh, to the mischief!" said Mr Dyce to himself, then took off his hat again, said "Good afternoon," and turned to his door.

He was met by Ailie in the lobby; she had seen him from a window speaking to the two Miss Duffs. "What were they saying to you?" she asked with more curiosity in her manner than was customary.

"Nothing at all," said Mr Dyce. "They just stood and cooed. I'm not sure that a doo-cot is the best place to bring up an eagle in. How did Bud get on with them at school today?"

"So far as I can make out, she did not get on at all; she seems to have demoralised the school, and driven the Miss Duffs into hysterics, and she left of her own accord and came home an hour before closing-time. And – and she's not going back!"

Mr Dyce stood a moment in amazement, then rubbed his hands gleefully. "I'm glad to hear it," said he. "The poor birdies between them could not summon up courage to tell me what was wrong. I'm sorry for them; if she's not going back, we'll send them down a present."

CHAPTER IX

THAT the child should have gone to the dame school at all was due to her Auntie Bell. From the first Miss Ailie had been dubious of the seminary, but Bell was terribly domineering; in fact, was neither to hold nor bind, and the doo-cot it bode to be. A product herself of the old dame school in the spacious days of Barbara Mushet, whose pupils in white-seam sewing and Italian hand were nowadays married to the best, and notable as housewives, she deemed it still the only avenue to the character and skill that keep those queer folk, men when they're married, by their own fire-ends. As for Daniel Dyce, he was, I fear, indifferent how Bud came by her schooling, having a sort of philosophy that the gate of gifts is closed on us the day we're born, and that the important parts of the curriculum good or bad, are picked up like a Scots or Hielan' accent, someway in the home.

So Ailie had gone reluctant to the Misses Duff and told them that on the morrow the child would start in their academy. They currookity-cooed at the prospect, put past their crocheting, brought out their celebrated silver spoons, and made of the afternoon tea a banquet with the aid of a seed-cake hurriedly brought from P. & A. MacGlashan's. Their home was like a stall in a bazaar and smelt of turpentine. Ailie, who loved wide spaces, sat cramped between a laden what-not and a white-enamelled spinning-wheel, the feathers of her hat colliding with a fretwork bracket on the wall behind her chair, and thinking not unkindly of the creatures, wished that she could give them a good shaking. Oh! they were so prim, pernickety, and hopelessly in all things wrong! She was not very large herself, for stature, but in their company she felt gigantic. And oddly there rose in her, too, a sense of gladness that she was of a newer kind of women than those gentle slaves, prisoned in their primness, manacled by stupid old conceits. She was glad she was free, that her happy hours were not so wasted in futilities, that she saw farther, that she knew no social fears, that custom had not crushed her soul, and yet she someway liked and pitied them.

"You'll find her somewhat odd," she explained as she nibbled the seed-cake, with a silly little d'oyley of Miss Jean's contrivance on her knee, and the doves fluttering round her as timid of settling down as though they had actual feathers and she were a cat. "She has got a remarkably quick intelligence; she is quite unconventional – quite unlike other children in many respects, and it may be difficult at first to manage her."

"Dear me!" said Miss Jean. "What a pity she should be so odd! I suppose it's the American system; but perhaps she will improve."

"Oh, it's nothing alarming," explained Miss Ailie, recovering the d'oyley from the floor to which it had slid from her knee, and replacing it with a wicked little shake. "If she didn't speak much you would never guess from her appearance that she knew any more than

– than most of us. Her mother, I feel sure, was something of a genius – at least it never came from the Dyce side; we were all plain folk, not exactly fools, but still not odd enough to have the dogs bite us, or our neighbours cross to the other side of the street when they saw us coming. She died two years ago, and when William – when my brother died, Lennox was staying with professional friends of himself and his wife, who have been good enough to let us have her, much against their natural inclination."

"The dear!" said Miss Jean, enraptured.

"Quite a sweet romance!" cooed Miss Amelia, languishing.

"You may be sure we will do all we can for her," continued Miss Jean, pecking with unconscious fingers at the crumbs on her visitor's lap, till Ailie could scarcely keep from smiling.

"She will soon feel quite at home among us in our little school," said Miss Amelia. "No doubt she'll be shy at first –"

"Quite the contrary!" Ailie assured them, with a little mischievous inward glee, to think how likely Bud was to astonish them by other qualities than shyness. "It seems that in America children are brought up on wholly different lines from children here; you'll find a curious fearless independence in her."

The twins held up their hands in amazement, "tcht-tcht-tchting" simultaneously. "*What* a pity!" said Miss Jean, as if it were a physical affliction.

"But no doubt by carefulness and training it can be eradicated," said Miss Amelia, determined to encourage hope.

At that Miss Ailie lost her patience. She rose to go, with a start that sent the doves more widely fluttering than ever in their restless little parlour, so crowded out of all comfort by its fretful toys.

"I don't think you should trouble much about the eradication," she said, with some of her brother's manner at the bar. "Individuality is not painful to the possessor like toothache, so it's a pity to eradicate it or kill the nerve."

The words were out before she could prevent them; she bit her lips, and blushed in her vexation to have said them, but luckily the Pigeons in their agitation were not observant.

"Like all the Dyces, a little daft!" was what they said of her when she was gone, and they were very different women then, as they put on their aprons, rolled up the silver spoons in tissue-paper and put them in a stocking of Amelia's, before they started to their crochet-work again.

It was a bright, expectant, happy bairn that set out next day for the school. No more momentous could have seemed her start for

Scotland across the wide Atlantic; her aunties, looking after her going down the street alone, so confident and sturdily, rued their own arrangement, and envied the Misses Duff that were to be blessed all day with her companionship. To Bell it seemed as if the wean were walking out of their lives on that broad road that leads our bairns to other knowledge than ours, to other dwellings, to the stranger's heart. Once the child turned at the corner of the church and waved her hand; Miss Ailie took it bravely, but oh, Miss Bell! – Miss Bell! – she flew to the kitchen and stormed at Kate as she hung out at the window, an observer too.

Three-and-twenty scholars were there in the doo-cot of the Duffs – sixteen of them girls and the remainder boys, but not boys enough as yet to be in the Grammar School. Miss Jean came out and rang a tea-bell, and Bud was borne in on the tide of youth that was still all strange to her. The twins stood side by side behind a desk; noisily the children accustomed found their seats, but Bud walked up to the teachers and held out her hand.

"Good morning; I'm Lennox Dyce," she said, before they could get over their astonishment at an introduction so unusual. Her voice, calm and clear, sounded to the backmost seat and sent the children tittering.

"Silence!" cried Miss Jean, reddening, with a glance at the delinquents, as she dubiously took the proffered hand.

"Rather a nice little school," said Bud, "but a little stuffy. Wants air some, don't it? What's the name of the sweet little boy in the Fauntleroy suit. It looks as if it would be apt to be Percy."

She was standing between the twins, facing the scholars; she surveyed all with the look of his Majesty's Inspector.

"Hush-h-h," murmured Miss Amelia, Miss Jean being speechless. "You will sit here," and she nervously indicated a place in the front bench. "By-and-by, dear, we will see what you can do."

Bud took her place composedly, and rose with the rest to join in the Lord's Prayer. The others mumbled it; for her it was a treat to have to say it there for the first time in her life in public. Into the words she put interest and appeal; for the first time the doo-cot heard that supplication endowed with its appropriate dignity. And then the work of the day began. The school lay in the way of the main traffic of the little town: they could hear each passing wheel and footstep, the sweet "chink, chink" from the smithy, whence came the smell of a sheep's head singeing. Sea-gulls and rooks bickered and swore in the gutters of the street; from fields behind came in a ploughman's whistle as he drove his team, slicing green seas of fallow as a vessel cuts the green, green wave. Four-and-twenty children, four-and-twenty souls, fathers and mothers of the future race, all outwardly much alike with eyes, noses, hands, and ears in the same position, how could the poor Misses Duff know what was what in the stuff they handled? Luckily for their peace of mind, it never occurred to them that between child and child there was much odds. Some had blue pinafores and some white; some were freckled and some had warts and were wild, and these were the banker's boys. God only knew the other variations. 'Twas the duty of the twins to bring them all in mind alike to the one plain level.

It was lucky that the lessons of that day began with the Shorter Catechism, for it kept the ignorance of Lennox Dyce a little while in hiding. She heard with amazement of Effectual Calling and Justification and the reasons annexed to the fifth commandment as stammeringly and lifelessly chanted by the others; but when her turn came, and Miss Jean, to test her, asked her simply Man's Chief End, she answered boldly –

"Man's chief end is to glorify God, and to enjoy Him for ever."

"Very good! *very* good indeed!" said the twin encouragingly. She was passing on to the next pupil, when Bud burst out with her own particular reason annexed, borrowed from the rapturous explanation of her uncle.

"Man is a harp," she said as solemnly as he had said it, "a har-r-rp with a thousand strings; and we must sing, sing, sing, even if we're timmer as a cask, and be grateful always, and glad in the mornings with things."

If the whistling ploughman and his team had burst into the schoolroom it would have been no greater marvel, brought no more alarm to the breasts of the little teachers. They looked at her as if she had been a witch. The other pupils stared, with open mouths.

"What's that you say, my dear?" said Miss Amelia. "Did you learn that in America?"

"No," said Bud, "I just found it out from Uncle Dan."

"Silence!" cried Miss Jean, for now the class was tittering again. She went with her sister behind the blackboard, and nervously they communed. Bud smiled benignly on her fellows.

Just as disconcerting was her performance in geography. Had they tested her in her knowledge of the United States she might have come out triumphantly commonplace; but unfortunately they chose to ask her of Scotland, and there her latest teacher had been Kate.

"What are the chief towns in Scotland?" asked Miss Jean.

"Oban, and Glasgow, and 'Tornoway," replied Bud with a touch

55

of Highland accent; and, tired of sitting so long in one place, calmly rose and removed herself to a seat beside the Fauntleroy boy, who was greatly put about at such a preference.

"You mustn't move about like that, Lennox," explained Miss Amelia, taking her back. "It's not allowed."

"But I was all pins and needles," said Bud frankly, "and I wanted to speak to Percy."

"My dear child, his name's not Percy, and there's no speaking in school," exclaimed the distressed Miss Amelia.

"No speaking! Why, you're speaking all the time," said the child. "It ain't – isn't fair. Can't I just get speaking a wee teeny bit to that nice girl over there?"

The twins looked at each other in horror: the child was a thousand times more difficult than the worst her aunt had led them to expect. A sudden unpleasant impression that their familiar pupils seemed like wooden models beside her, came to them both. But they were alarmed to see that the wooden models were forgetting their correct deportment under the demoralising influence of the young invader.

Once more they dived behind the blackboard and communed.

There were many such instances during the day. Bud, used for all her thinking years to asking explanations of what she did not understand, never hesitated to interrogate her teachers, who seemed to her to be merely women, like her mother, and Mrs Molyneux and Auntie Ailie, only a little wilted and severe, grotesque in some degree because of their funny affected manner, and the crochet that never was out of their hands in oral exercises. She went further, she contradicted them twice, not rudely, but as one might contradict her equals.

"You talk to her," said Miss Jean behind the blackboard where they had taken refuge again. "I declare I'll take a fit if this goes on! Did you ever hear of such a creature?"

Miss Amelia almost cried. All her fixed ideas of children were shattered at a blow. Here was one who did not in the least degree fit in with the scheme of treatment in the doo-cot. But she went forward with a look of great severity.

"Of course, coming from America and all that, and never having been at school before, you don't know," she said, "but I must tell you that you are not behaving nicely – not like a nice little girl at all, Lennox. Nice little girls in school in this country listen, and never say anything unless they're asked. They are respectful to their teachers, and never ask questions, and certainly never contradict them, and –"

56

"But, please, Miss Duff, I wasn't contradicting," explained Bud very soberly, "and when respect is called for, I'm there with the goods. You said honor was spelt with a 'u', and I guess you just made a mistake, same as I might make myself, for there ain't no 'u' in honor, at least in America."

"I – I – I never made a mistake in all my life," said Miss Amelia, gasping.

"Oh, Laura!" was all that Bud replied, but in such a tone, and with eyes so widely opened, it set half of the other pupils tittering.

"What do you mean by 'Oh, Laura'?" asked Miss Jean. "Who is Laura?"

"You can search me," replied Bud composedly. "Jim often said 'Oh, Laura!' when he got a start."

"It's not a nice thing to say," said Miss Jean. "It's not at all ladylike. It's just a sort of profane language, and profane language is an 'abomination unto the Lord.'"

"But it was so like Jim," said Bud, giggling with recollection. "If it's slang I'll stop it – at least I'll try to stop it. I'm bound to be a well-off English undefied, you know; poppa – father fixed that."

The school was demoralised without a doubt, for now the twins were standing nervously before Bud and put on equal terms with her in spite of themselves, and the class was openly interested and amused – more interested and amused than it had ever been at anything that had ever happened in the doo-cot before. Miss Amelia was the first to comprehend how far she and her sister had surrendered their citadel of authority to the little foreigner's attack. "Order!" she exclaimed. "We will now take up poetry and reading."

Bud cheered up wonderfully at the thought of poetry and reading, but, alas! her delight was short-lived, for the reading-book put into her hand was but a little further on than Auntie Ailie's Twopenny. When her turn came to read "My sister Ella has a cat called Tabby. She is black, and has a pretty white breast. She has long whiskers and a bushy white tail," she read with a tone of amusement that exasperated the twins, though they could not explain to themselves why. What completed Bud's rebellion, however, was the poetry. "Meddlesome Matty" was a kind of poetry she had skipped over in Chicago, plunging straightway into the glories of the play-bills and Shakespeare, and when she had read that –

"One ugly trick has often spoiled
The sweetest and the best;

57

Matilda, though a pleasant child,
One ugly trick possessed" –

she laughed outright.

"I can't help it, Miss Duff," she said when the twins showed their distress. "It looks like poetry, sure enough, for it's got the jaggy edges, but it doesn't make any zip inside me same as poetry does. It wants biff."

"What's 'zip' and 'biff'?" asked Miss Amelia.

"It's – it's a kind of tickle in your mind," said Bud. "I'm so tired," she continued, rising in her seat, "I guess I'll head for home now." And before the twins had recovered from their dumfounderment she was in the porch putting on her cloak and hood.

"Just let her go," said Miss Jean to her sister. "If she stays any longer I shall certainly have a swoon; I feel quite weak."

And so Bud marched out quite cheerfully, and reached home an hour before she was due.

Kate met her at the door. "My stars! are you home already?" she exclaimed, with a look at the town clock. "You must be smart at your schooling when they let you out of the cemetery so soon."

"It ain't a cemetery at all," said Bud, standing unconcernedly in the lobby; "It's just a kindergarten."

Aunt Ailie bore down on her to overwhelm her in caresses. "What are you home for already, Bud?" she asked. "It's not time yet, is it?"

"No," said Bud, "but I just couldn't stay any longer. I'd as lief not go back there. The ladies don't love me. They're Sunday sort of ladies, and give me pins and needles. They smile and smile, same's it was done with a glove-stretcher, and don't love me. They said I was using profound language, and – and they don't love me. Not the way mother and Mrs Molyneux and you and Auntie Bell and Uncle Dan and Kate and Footles does. They made goo-goo-eyes at me when I said the least thing. They had all those poor kiddies up on the floor doing their little bits, and they made me read kindergarten poetry – that was the limit! So I just upped and walked."

The two aunts and Kate stood round her for a moment baffled.

"What's to be done now?" said Aunt Ailie.

"Tuts!" said Aunt Bell, "give the wean a drink of milk and some bread and butter."

And so ended Bud's only term in a dame school.

CHAPTER X

IT was a saying of Daniel Dyce's that all the world is under one's own waistcoat. We have a way of spacing fortunes in the North, when young, in which we count the waistcoat buttons from top to bottom, and say –

> "Tinker,
> Tailor,
> Soldier,
> Sailor,
> Rich man,
> Poor man,
> Prodigal, or
> Thief?"

Whichever name falls upon the last button tells what is your destiny, and after the county corps has been round our way recruiting, I see our schoolboys with all their waistcoat buttons, but three at the top, amissing. Dan Dyce had a different formula: he said "Luckiness, Leisure, Ill or Well, Good World, Bad World, Heaven or Hell?"

"Not Heaven, Dan!" said Bell. "The other place I'll admit, for whiles I'm in a furious temper over some trifle;" to which he would answer, "Woman! the Kingdom of Heaven is within you."

So, I think sometimes, all that's worth while in the world is in this little burgh, except a string quartette and a place called Florence I have long been ettling to see if ever I have the money. In this small town is every week as much of tragedy and comedy and farce as would make a complete novel full of laughter and tears, that would sell in a jiffy. I have started, myself, a score of them – all the essential inspiration got from plain folk passing my window, or from hearing a sentence dropped among women gossiping round a well. Many a winter night I come in with a fine catch of tales picked up in the by-going, as we say, and light the candles in a hurry, and make a gallant dash at "Captain Consequence. Chapter I." or "A Wild Inheritance. Part I. The Astounding Mary." Only the lavishness of the material hampers me: when I'm at "Captain Consequence" (which would be a splendid sombre story of an ill life, if I ever got beyond Chapter I. and the old scamp's fondness for his mother), my wife runs in with something warm to drink, and tells me Jonathan Campbell's goat has broken into the minister's garden, and then I'm off the key for villainy; there's a shilling book in Jonathan's goat herself.

But this time I'm determined to stick by the fortunes of the Dyce family, now that I have got myself inside their door. I hope we are friends of that household, dearer to me than the dwellings of kings (not that I have cognisance of many). I hope that no matter how often or how early we rap at the brass knocker, or how timidly, Kate will come, and in one breath say, "What is't? Come in!" We may hear, when we're in, people passing in the street, and the wild geese call – wild geese, wild geese! this time I will not follow where you tempt to where are only silence and dream – the autumn and the summer days may cry us out to garden and wood, but if I can manage it I will lock the door on the inside, and shut us snugly in with Daniel Dyce and his household, and it will be well with us then. Yes, yes, it will be well with us then.

The wild-goose cry, heard in the nights, beyond her comprehension, was all that Bud Dyce found foreign in that home. All else was natural and familiar and friendly, for all else she knew was love. But she feared at first the "honk, honk" of the lone wild things that burdened her with wonder and awe. Lying in her attic bower at night, they seemed to her like sore mistaken wanderers, wind-driven, lost; and so they are, I know. Hans Andersen and Grimm for her had given to their kind a forlorn and fearsome meaning. But Kate MacNeill had helped, to some degree, these childish apprehensions.

The Highland maid had brought from Colonsay a flesh that crept in darkness, a brain with a fantastic maggot in it; she declared to goodness, and to Bud sometimes, that she had no life of it with ghosts in her small back room. But Bud was not to let on to her aunties. Forbye, it was only for Kate they came, the ghosts; did Bud not hear them last night? Geese! No, not geese, Kate knew different, and if the thing lasted much longer she would stay no more in this town; she would stay nowhere, she would just go back to Colonsay. Not that Colonsay was better; there were often ghosts in Colonsay – in the winter-time, and then it behoved you to run like the mischief, or have a fine strong lad with you for your convoy. If there were no ghosts in America, it was because it cost too much to go there on the steamers. Harken to yon – "Honk, honk!" – did ever you hear the like of it? Who with their wits about them in weather like that would like to be a ghost? And loud above the wind that rocked the burgh in the cradle of the hills, loud above the beating rain, the creak of doors and rap of shutters in that old house, Bud and Kate together in the kitchen heard again the "Honk, honk!" of the geese. Then it was for the child that she missed the mighty certainty of Chicago, that Scotland somehow to her mind seemed an old unhappy place, in the night of which went passing Duncan, murdered in his sleep, and David Rizzio with the daggers in his breast, and Helen of Kirkconnel Lee. The nights but rarely brought any fear for her in spite of poor Kate's ghosts, since the warmth and light and love of the household filled every corner of lobby and stair, and went to bed with her. When she had said her prayer the geese might cry, the timbers of the old house crack, Bud was lapped in the love of God and man, and tranquil. But the mornings daunted her often when she wakened to the sound of the six o'clock bell. She would feel, when it ceased, as if all virtue were out of last night's love and prayer. Then all Scotland and its curious scraps of history as she had picked it up weighed on her spirit for a time; the house was dead and empty; not ghost nor goose made her eerie, but mankind's old inexplicable alarms. How deep and from what distant shores comes childhood's wild surmise! There was nothing to harm her, she knew, but the strangeness of the dawn and a craving for life made her at these times the awakener of the other dwellers in the house of Dyce.

She would get out of bed and go next door to the room of Ailie, and creep in bed beside her to kiss her for a little from her dreams. To the aunt these morning visitations were precious: she would take the bairn to her bosom and fall asleep with sighs of content, the immaculate mother. Bud herself could not sleep then for watching the revelation of her lovely auntie in the dawn – the cloud on the pillow that turned to masses of hazel hair, the cheeks and lips that seemed to redden like flowers as the day dawned, the nook of her bosom, the pulse of her brow.

Other mornings Wanton Wully's bell would send her in to Bell, who would give her the warm hollow of her own place in the blankets, while she herself got up to dress briskly for the day's affairs. "Just you lie down there, pet, and sleepy-bye," she would say, tying her goats with trim tight knots. "You will not grow up a fine, tall, strong girl like your Auntie Ailie if you do not take your sleep when you can get it. The morning is only for done old wives like me that have things to do and don't grudge doing them.

She would chatter away to Bud as she dressed, a garrulous auntie this, two things always for her text – the pride of Scotland, and the virtue of duty done. A body, she would say, was sometimes liable to weary of the same things to be done each day, the same tasks even-on, fires and food and cleansing, though the mind might dwell on great deeds desirable to be accomplished, but pleasure never came till the thing was done that was the first to hand, even if it was only darning a stocking. What was Bud going to be when she grew up? Bud guessed she wasn't going to be anything but just a lady. Ah, yes, but even ladies had to do something wise-like; there was Ailie – to go no farther – who could have managed a business though her darning was but lumpy. Even for a lady there was nothing nobler than the making of her own bed; besides, the doctors said it was remarkably efficacious for the figure.

Bud, snug in her auntie's blankets, only her nose and her bright bead eyes showing in the light of the twirly wooden candlestick, guessed Mrs Molyneux was the quickest woman to get through work ever she saw: why! she just waved it to one side and went out to shop or lunch with Jim.

A look of pity for Mrs Molyneux, the misguided, would come to Bell's face, but for those folk in America she never had a word of criticism in the presence of the child. All she could say was America was different. America was not Scotland. And Scotland was not England, though in many places they called Scotch things English.

Jim used to say, speaking of father, that a Scotsman was a kind of superior Englishman.

Bell wished to goodness she could see the man – he must have been a clever one!

Other mornings again would the child softly open her uncle's door and he would get a terrible fright, crying "Robbers! but you'll get nothing. I have my watch in my boots, and my money in my mouth."

She would creep beside him, and in these early hours began her education. She was learning Ailie's calm and curiosity and ambition; she was learning Bell's ideas of duty and the ancient glory of her adopted land; from her uncle she was learning many things, of which the least that seemed useful at the time was the Lord's Prayer in Latin. "Pater Noster qui es in coelis" – that and a few hundreds of Trayner's Latin maxims was nearly all of the classic tongue that survived with the lawyer from student days. It was just as good and effective a prayer in English, he admitted, but somehow, whiles, the language was so old it brought you into closer grips with the original. Some mornings she would hum to him coon songs heard in her former home; and if he was in trim he himself would sing some psalm to the tune of Coleshill, French, Bangor, or Torwood. His favourite was Torwood; it mourned so – mourned so! Or at other times a song like "Mary Morison".

"What are you humming away at up there the pair of you?" Bell would cry, coming to the stair-foot. "If you sing before breakfast, you'll greet before night!"

"Don't she like singing in the morning?" Bud asked, nestling beside him, and he laughed.

"It's an old freit – an old superstition," said he, "that it's unlucky to begin the day too blithely. It must have been a doctor that started it, but you would wonder at the number of good and douce Scots folk, plain bodies like ourselves, that have the notion in their mind from infancy, and never venture a cheep or chirrup before the day's well aired."

"My stars! ain't she Scotch, Auntie Bell?" said Bud. "So was father. He would sing any time; he would sing if it broke a tooth; but he was pretty Scotch other ways. Once he wore a pair of kilts to a Cale – to a Caledonian Club."

"I don't keep a kilt myself," said her uncle. "The thing's not strictly necessary unless you're English and have a Hielan' shooting."

"Auntie Bell is the genuine Scotch stuff, I guess!"

"There's no concealing the fact that she is," her uncle admitted. "She's so Scotch that I am afraid she's apt to think of God as a countryman of her own."

And there were the hours that Ailie gave with delight to Bud's more orthodox tuition. The back room that was called Dan's study, because he sometimes took a nap there after dinner, became a schoolroom. There was a Mercator's map of the world on the wall and another of Europe, that of themselves gave the place the right academy aspect. With imagination, a map, and the Golden Treasury, you might have as good as a college education, according to Ailie. They went long voyages together on Mercator; saw marvellous places; shivered at the poles or languished in torrid plains, sometimes before Kate could ring the bell for breakfast. There seemed no spot in the world that this clever auntie had not some knowledge of. How eagerly they crossed continents, how ingeniously they planned routes! For the lengths of rivers, the heights of mountains, the values of exports, and all the trivial passing facts that mar the great game of geography for many childish minds, they had small consideration; what they gathered in their travels were sounds, colours, scenes, weather, and the look of races. What adventures they had! as when, pursued by elephants and tigers, they sped in a flash from Bengal to the Isle of Venice, and saw the green slime of the sea on her steeping palaces. Yes, the world is all for the folk of imagination. "Love maps and you will never be too old or too poor to travel," was Ailie's motto She found a hero or a heroine for every spot upon Mercator, and nourished so the child in noble admirations.

You might think it would always be the same pupil and the same teacher; but no, they sometimes changed places. If Ailie taught Bud her own love for the lyrics that are the best work of men in their hours of exaltation, Bud sent Ailie back to her Shakespeare, and sweet were the days they spent in Arden or Prospero's Isle.

It was well with them then; it was well with the woman and the child, and they were happy.

CHAPTER XI

BUT the Dyces never really knew how great and serious was the charge bequeathed to them in their brother William's daughter till they saw it all one night in March in the light of a dozen penny candles.

Lennox had come from a world that's lit by electricity, and for weeks she was sustained in wonder and amusement by the paraffin lamps of Daniel Dyce's dwelling. They were, she was sure, the oldest kind of light in all the world, Aladdin-lights that gleamed of old on caverns of gems, till Kate on this particular evening came into the kitchen with the week-end groceries. It was a stormy season – the year of the big winds; moanings were at the windows, sobbings in the chimney-heads, and the street was swept by spindrift rain. Bell and Ailie and their brother sat in the parlour, silent, playing cards with a dummy hand, and Bud, with Footles in her lap, behind the winter-dykes on which clothes dried before the kitchen fire, crouched on the fender with a Shakespeare, where almost breathlessly she read the great, the glorious Macbeth.

"My stars! what a night!" said Kate. "The way them slates and chimney-cans are flying! It must be the anti-nuptial gales. I thought every minute would be my next. Oh towns! towns! Stop you till I get back to Colonsay, and I'll not leave it in a hurry, I'll assure you."

She threw a parcel on the kitchen-dresser, and turned to the light a round and rosy face that streamed with clean cooling rain, her hair in tangles on her temples and her eyes sparkling with the light of youth and adventure – for to tell the truth she had been flirting at the door a while, in spite of all the rain, with some admirer.

Bud was the sort of child whose fingers itch in the presence of unopened parcels: in a moment the string was untied from the week-end groceries.

"Candles!" she cried. "Well, that beats the band! I've seen 'em in windows. What in the world are you going to do with candles? One, two, three, four, five, six, seven, eight, nine, ten, eleven, twelve – oh Laura, ain't we grand!"

"What would we do with them but burn them?" said the maid; "we'll use them in the washing-house," and then she sank into a chair. "Mercy on me, I declare I'm dying!" she exclaimed in a different key, and Bud looked round and saw Kate's face had grown of a sudden very pale.

"Oh dear! what is the matter?" she asked, her eyes large, innocent, and anxious.

"Pains," moaned the maid. "Pains inside me and all over me, and shiverings down the spine of the back. Oh, it's a sore thing pain, especially when it's bad! But don't – don't say a word to the mustress; I'm not that old, and maybe I'll get better."

"Try pain-killer," recommended Bud. "And if I was you I'd start just here and say a prayer. Butt right in and I'll not listen."

"Pain-killer! – what in all the world's pain-killer? I never heard of it. And the only prayer I know is 'My Father which art' in Gaelic, and there's nothing in it about pains in the spine of the back. No, no! I'll just have to take a tablespoonful of something or other three times a-day, the way I did when the doctor put me right in Colonsay. Perhaps it's just a chill – but oh! I'm sorrowful, sorrowful!" and Kate, the colour coming slowly back to her, wept softly to herself, rocking in the kitchen chair. It was sometimes by those odd hysterics that she paid for her elations with the lads.

"I know what's wrong with you," said Bud briskly, in the manner of Mrs Molyneux. "It's just the croodles. Bless you, you poor perishing soul! I take the croodles myself when it's a night like this, and I'm alone. The croodles ain't the least wee bit deadly; you can put them away by hustling at your work, or banging an old piano, or reading a story, or playing that you're somebody else! Well, I declare I think I could cure you right now with these twelve candles, far better than you'd do by shooting drugs into yourself."

"I never took a single candle in all my life," said Kate, "far less twelve, and I'll die first."

"Silly!" exclaimed Bud. "You'd think to hear you speak you were a starving Eskimo. I don't want you to eat the candles. Wait a minute." She ran lightly upstairs, and was gone for ten minutes.

Kate's colour all revived; she forgot her croodles in the spirit of anticipation that the child had roused. "Oh, but she's the clever one that!" she said to herself, drying the rain and tears from her face and starting to nibble a biscuit. "She knows as much as two ministers, and still she's not a bit proud. Some day she'll do something desperate."

When Bud came back she startled the maid by her appearance, for she had clad herself, for the first time in Scotland, with a long, thin, copious dancing-gown, in which a lady of the vaudeville, a friend of Mrs Molyneux's, had taught her dancing.

"Ain't this dandy?" she said, closing the kitchen door, and there was a glow upon her countenance and a movement of her body that, to the maid's eyes, made her look a little woman. "Ain't this bully? Don't you stand there looking like a dying Welsh rabbit, but help me light them candles for the footlights. Why! I knew there was some use for these old candles first time I set eyes on them; they made me think of something I couldn't 'zactly think of – made me kind of gay, you know, just as if I was going to the theatre. They're only candles, but there's twelve lights to them all at once, and now you'll see some fun."

"What in the world are you going to do, lassie?" asked the maid.

"I'm going to be a Gorgeous Entertainment; I'm going to be the Greatest Agg-Aggregation of Historic Talent now touring the Middle West. I'm Mademoiselle Winifred Wallace of Madison Square Theatre, New York, positively appearing here for one night only. I'm the whole company, and the stage manager, and the band, and the boys that throw the bouquets. Biff! I'm checked high: all you've got to do is to sit there with your poor croodles and feel them melt away. Let's light the foot-lights."

There was a row of old brass bedroom candlesticks on the kitchen-shelf that were seldom used now in the house of Dyce, though their polish was the glory of Miss Bell's heart. The child kilted up her gown, jumped on a chair, and took them down with the help of Kate. She stuck in each a candle, and ranged them in a semicircle on the floor, then lit the candles and took her place behind them.

"Put out the lamp!" she said to Kate, in the common voice of actors' tragedy.

"Indeed and I'll do nothing of the kind," said the maid. "If your Auntie Bell comes in she'll – she'll skin me alive for letting you play such cantrips with her candles. Forbye, you're going to do something desperate, something that's not canny, and I must have the lamp behind me or I'll lose my wits."

"Woman, put out the light!" repeated Bud, with an imperious pointing finger, and, trembling, Kate turned down the lamp upon the wall and blew down the chimney in the very way Miss Dyce was always warning her against. She gasped at the sudden change the loss of the light made – at the sense of something idolatrous and bewitched in the arc of flames on her kitchen-floor, each blown inward from the draught of a rattling window.

"If it is *buidseachas* – if it is witchcraft of any kind you are on for, I'll not have it," said Kate firmly. "I never saw the like of this since the old woman in Pennyland put the curse on the Colonsay factor, and she had only seven candles. Dear, *dear* Lennox, do not do anything desperate; do not be carrying on, for you are frightening me out of my judgment. I'm – I'm maybe better now, I took a bite at a biscuit; indeed I'm quite better, it was nothing but the cold – and a lad out there that tried to kiss me."

Bud paid no heed, but plucked up the edges of her skirt in outstretched hands and glided into the last dance she had learned from the vaudeville lady, humming softly to herself an appropriate tune. The candles warmly lit her neck, her ears, her tilted nostrils, her brow was high in shadow. First she rose on tiptoe and made her feet to twitter on the flags, then swayed and swung a little body that seemed to hang in air. The white silk swept around and over her – wings with no noise of flapping feather, or swirled in sea-shell coils, that rose in a ripple from her ankles and swelled in wide circling waves above her head, revealing her in glimpses like some creature born of foam on fairy beaches, and holding the command of tempest winds. Ah, dear me! many and many a time I saw her dance just so in her daft days before the chill of wisdom and reflection came her way; she was a passion disembodied, an aspiration realised, a happy morning thought, a vapour, a perfume of flowers, for her attire had lain in lavender. She was the spirit of Spring, as I have felt it long ago in little woods, or seen it in pictures, or heard it in songs; she was an ecstasy, she was a dream.

The dog gave a growl of astonishment, then lay his length on the hearth-rug, his nose between his paws, his eyes fixed on her. "I'll not have it," said the maid piteously. "At least I'll not stand much of it, for it's not canny to be carrying-on like that in a Christian dwelling. I never did the like of that in all my life."

"*Every* move a picture," said the child, and still danced on, with the moan of the wind outside for a bass to her low-hummed melody.

Her stretching folds flew high, till she seemed miraculous tall, and to the servant's fancy might have touched the low ceiling; then she sank – and sank – and sank till her forehead touched the floor, and she was a flower fallen, the wind no more to stir its petals, the rain no more to glisten on its leaves. 'Twas as if she shrivelled and died there, and Kate gave one little cry that reached the players of cards in the parlour.

"Hush! what noise was that?" said Ailie, lifting her head.

"It would be Kate clumping across the kitchen-floor in the Gaelic language," said Mr Dyce, pushing his specs up on his brow.

"Nothing but the wind," said Bell. "What did you say was trumph?" – for that was the kind of player she was.

"It was not the wind, it was a cry; I'm sure I heard a cry. I hope there's nothing wrong with the little one," said Ailie, with a throbbing heart, and she threw her cards on the table and went out. She came back in a moment, her face betraying her excitement, her voice demanding silence.

"Of all the wonders!" said she. "Just step this way, people, to the pantry."

They rose and followed her. The pantry was all darkness. Through its partly open door that led into the kitchen they saw their child in the crescent of the candles, though she could not see them, as no more could Kate, whose chair was turned the other way. They stood in silence watching the strange performance, each with different feelings, but all with eeriness, silent people of the placid, old, half-rustic world, that lives for ever with realities, and seldom sees the passions counterfeited.

Bud had risen, her dark hair looking unnaturally black above her brow, and, her dancing done, she was facing the dog and the servant, the only audience of whose presence she was aware.

"Toots!" said the maid, relieved that all seemed over, "that's nothing in the way of dancing; you should see them dancing Gillie-Callum over-bye in Colonsay! There's a dancer so strong there that he breaks the very boards."

Bud looked at her, and yet not wholly at her – through her, with burning eyes.

"Hush!" she said, trembling. "Do you not hear something?" and at that moment, high over the town went the "honk, honk" of the wild geese.

"Devil the thing but geeses!" said the maid whose blood had curdled for a second. The rain swept like a broom along the street, the gutters bubbled, the shutters rapped, far above the dwelling went the sound of the flying geese.

"Oh, hush, woman, hush!" implored the child, her hands over her ears, her figure cowering.

"It's only the geeses. What a start you gave me!" said the maid again.

"No, no," said Bud, "Methought I heard a voice cry 'Sleep no more! Macbeth does murder sleep, the innocent sleep, Sleep that knits up the ravell'd sleeve of care, sore labour's bath, Balm of hurt minds, great nature's second course, Chief nourisher in life's feast –'"

"What do you mean?" cried Kate

"Still it cried, 'Sleep no more!' to all the house: Glamis hath murder'd sleep, and therefore Cawdor shall sleep no more; Macbeth shall sleep no more."

The child filled each phrase with a travesty of passion; she had seen the part enacted. It was not, be sure, a great performance. Some words were strangely mutilated; but it was a child, and she had more than a child's command of passion – she had feeling, she had heart.

"I cannot look at you!" exclaimed Kate. "You are not canny, but oh! you are – you are majestic! There was never the like of it in all the isles."

Bell, in the darkness of the pantry, wept silently at some sense of sin in this play-acting on a Saturday night; her brother held her arm tightly; Ailie felt a vague unrest and discontent with herself, a touch of envy and of shame.

"Please collect the bouquets," said the child, seating herself on the floor with her knees tucked high in her gown. "Are the croodles all gone?"

"It did me a lot of good yon dancing," said Kate. "Did you put yon words about Macbeth sleep no more together yourself?"

"Yes," said Bud, and then repented. "No," she added hurriedly, "that's a fib; please, God, give me a true tongue. It was made by Shakespeare – dear old Will!"

"I'm sure I never heard of the man in all my life before; but he must have been a bad one."

"Why, Kate, you are as fresh as the mountain breeze," said Bud. "He was Great! He was born at Stratford-on-Avon, a poor boy, and went to London and held horses outside the theatre door, and then wrote plays so grand that only the best can act them. He was – he was not for an age, but all the time."

She had borrowed the lesson as well as the manner of Auntie Ailie, who smiled in the dark of the pantry at this glib rendering of herself.

69

"Oh, I should love to play Rosalind," continued the child. "I should love to play *everything*. When I am big, and really Winifred Wallace, I will go all over the world and put away people's croodles same as I did yours, Kate, and they will love me; and I will make them feel real good, and sometimes cry – for that is beautiful too. I will never rest, but go on, and on, and on; and everywhere everybody will know about me – even in the tiny minstrel towns where they have no or'nary luck but just coon shows, for it's in these places croodles must be most catching. I'll go there and play for nothing, just to show them what a dear soul Rosalind was. I want to grow fast, fast! I want to be tall like my Auntie Ailie, and lovely like my dear Auntie Ailie, and clever like my sweet sweet Aunt Ailie."

"She's big enough and bonny enough, and clever enough in some things," said the maid; "but can she sew like her sister? – tell me that!"

"Sew!" exclaimed the child, with a frown. "I *hate* sewing. I guess Auntie Ailie's like me, and feels sick when she starts a hem and sees how long it is, and all to be gone over with small stitches."

"Indeed, indeed I do," whispered Ailie in the pantry, and she was trembling. She told me later how she felt – of her conviction then that for her the years of opportunity were gone, the golden years that had slipped past in the little burgh town without a chance for her to grasp their offerings. She told me of her resolution there and then that this child, at least, should have its freedom to expand.

Bud crept to the end of the crescent of her footlights and blew out the candles slowly one by one. The last she left alight a little longer, and, crouched upon the floor, she gazed with large and dreaming eyes into its flame as if she read there.

"It is over now," said Mr Dyce in a whisper to his sisters, and, with his hands on their shoulders, led them back into the parlour.

CHAPTER XII

SHE was wayward, she was passionate, she was sometimes wild. She was not what, in the Pigeons' Seminary, could be called a good child, for all her sins were frankly manifest, and she knew no fear nor naughty stratagem; her mind, to all but Kate, was open as the day, and there it was the fault of honest Kate's stupidity. But often Miss Bell must be moaning at transgressions almost harmless in themselves, yet so terribly unlike a Christian bairn, as when Bud spent an afternoon in a tent with some gipsy children, changed clothes with them the better to act a part, and stormed because she could not have them in to tea with her. Or when she asked Lady Anne, bazaar-collecting in the house of Dyce, if she ever had had a proposal. It was a mercy that Lady Anne that very week had had one, and was only too pleased to tell of it and say she had accepted.

"Then *you're* safe out of the woods," said Bud gravely. "There's our Kate, she hasn't had a proposal yet, and I guess she's on the slopey side of thirty. It must be dre'ffle to be as old – as old as a house and have no beau to love you. It must be 'scrutiating."

Lady Anne let her eyes turn for a moment on the sisters Dyce, and the child observed and reddened.

"Oh! Auntie Bell!" she said quickly. "Auntie Bell had heaps and heaps of beaux all dying to marry her, but she gave them the calm cold eye and said she had to cling to Uncle Dan. It was very noble of her, wasn't it?"

"Indeed it was!" admitted Lady Anne, very much ashamed of herself.

"And Auntie Ailie is not on the slopey side of thirty," continued Bud, determined to make all amends. "She's young enough to love dolls."

It was Bell who censured her for this dreadful behaviour. "You are a perfect torment, Lennox," she said, at the first opportunity. "A bairn like you must not be talking about beaux, and love, and proposals, and nonsense of that kind – it's fair ridiculous."

"Why, I thought love was the Great Thing!" exclaimed Bud, much astonished. "It's in all the books, there's hardly anything else, 'cept when somebody is murdered and you know that the man who did it is the only one you don't suspect. Indeed, Auntie, I thought it was the Great Thing!"

"And so it is, my dear," said Ailie. "There's very little else in all the world, except – except the children," and she folded her niece in her arms. "It *is* the Great Thing; it has made Lady Anne prettier than ever she was in her life before, it has made her brighter, humbler, gentler, kinder. God bless her, I hope she will be happy."

"But it was very wrong; it was a kind of fib for you to talk about me having lots of lads in my time," said Auntie Bell. "You do not know whether I had or not."

Bud looked at her and saw a flush on her face. "I think," said she, "the beaux must have been very stupid, then. But I guess there must

have been one, Auntie Bell, and you have forgotten all about him."
And at that Miss Bell went hurriedly from the room, with a pretence
that she heard a pot boil over, and Ailie in a low voice told her niece
all about Bell's beau, deep drowned in the Indian Ocean.

For days after that the child was tender with her elder aunt, and
made a splendid poem in blank verse upon the late Captain James
Murray, which Bell was never to see, but Ailie treasured. For days
was she angelic good. Her rages never came to fever heat. Her rebel-
lions burned themselves out in her bosom. Nobly she struggled with
Long Division and the grammar that she abominated; very meekly
she took censure for copy-books blotted and words shamefully
misspelled in Uncle Daniel's study. Some way this love that she had
thought a mere amusement like shopping in Chicago, took a new
complexion in her mind – became a dear and solemn thing, like her
uncle's Bible readings, when, on Sunday nights at worship in the
parlour, he took his audience through the desert to the Promised
Land, and the abandoned street was vocal with domestic psalm from
the Provost's open windows. She could not guess – how could she,
the child? – that love has its variety. She thought there was but the
one love in all the world – the same she felt herself for most things –
a gladness and agreement with things as they were. And yet at times
in her reading she got glimpses of love's terror and empire, as in the
stories of Othello and of Amy Robsart, and herself began to wish she
had a lover. She thought at first of Uncle Dan; but he could not be
serious, and she had never heard him sigh – in him was wanting
some remove, some mystery. What she wanted was a lover on a milk-
white steed, a prince who was "the flower o' them a',"
as in Aunt Ailie's song "Glenlogie"; and she could not imagine
Uncle Dan with his spectacles on riding any kind of steed, though
she felt it would be nice to have him with her when the real prince
was there.

Do you think it unlikely that this child should have such dreams?
Ah, then, you are not of her number, or you have forgotten. She
never forgot. Many a time she told me in after-years of how in the
attic bower, with Footles snug at her feet, she conjured up the lad
on the milk-white steed, not so much for himself alone, but that she
might act the lady-love. And in those dreams she was tall and
slender, sometimes proud, disdainful, wounding the poor wretch
with sharp words and cold glances; or she was meek and languishing,
sighing out her heart even in presence of his true-love gifts of candy
and P. & A. MacGlashan's penny tarts. She walked with him in
gardens enchanted; they sailed at nights over calm moonlit seas, and

she would be playing the lute. She did not know what the lute was like; but it was the instrument of love, and had a dulcet sound, like the alto flutes in the burgh band.

But, of course, no fairy prince came wooing Daniel Dyce's little niece, though men there were in the place – elderly and bald, with married daughters – who tried to buy her kisses for sixpences and sweets, and at last she felt vicariously the joys of love by conducting the affairs of Kate.

Kate had many wooers – that is the solace of her class. They liked her because she was genial and plump, with a flattering smile and a soft touch of the Gaelic accent that in the proper key and hour is the thing to break hearts. She twirled them all round her little finger, and Bud was soon to see this and to learn that the maid was still very far from the slopey side of thirty. But Kate, too, had her dreams – of some misty lad of the mind, with short, curled hair, clothes brass-buttoned, and a delicious smell of tar – something or other on a yacht. The name she had endowed him with was Charles. She made him up from passing visions of seamen on the quays, and of notions gleaned from her reading of penny novelettes.

One week-night Bud came on her in the kitchen dressed in her Sunday clothes and struggling with a spluttering pen.

"Are you at your lessons too?" said the child. "You naughty Kate! there's a horrid blot. No lady makes blots."

"It wasn't me, it was this devilish pen; besides, I'm not a lady," said Kate, licking the latest blot with her tongue and grimacing. "What way do you spell weather?"

"W-e-t-h-e-r," said Bud. "At least, I think that's the way! but I'd best run and ask Aunt Ailie – she's a speller from Spellerville."

"Indeed and you'll do nothing of the kind," cried the maid, alarmed and reddening. "You'll do nothing of the kind, Lennox, because – I'm writing to Charles."

"A love-letter! Oh, I've got you with the goods on you!" exclaimed Bud, enchanted. "And what are you doing with your hurrah clothes on?"

"I like to put on my Sunday clothes when I'm writing Charles," said the maid, a little put-about. "Do you think it's kind of daft?"

"It's not daft at all, it's real 'cute of you; it's what I do myself when I'm writing love-letters, for it makes me feel kind of grander. It's just the same with poetry; I simply can't make sure enough poetry unless I have on a nice frock and my hands washed."

"*You* write love-letters!" said the maid, astounded.

"Yes, you poor perishing soul!" retorted Bud. "And you needn't

73

yelp. I've written scores of loveletters without stopping to take breath. Stop! stop!" she interrupted herself, and breathed an inward little prayer. "I mean that I write them – well, kind of write them – in my mind." But this was a qualification beyond Kate's comprehension.

"Then I wish you would give me a hand with this one," said she despairingly. "All the nice words are so hard to spell, and this is such a bad pen."

"They're *all* bad pens; they're all devilish," said Bud, from long experience. "But I'd love to help you write that letter. Let me see – pooh! it's dre'ffle bad, Kate. I can't read a bit of it, almost."

"I'm sure and neither can I," said Kate, distressed.

"Then how in the world do you expect Charles to read it?" asked Bud.

"Oh, he's – he's a better scholar than me," said Kate complacently. "But you might write this one for me."

Bud washed her hands, took a chair to the kitchen table, threw back her hair from her eyes, and eagerly entered into the office of love-letter-writer. "What will I say to him?" she asked.

"My dear, dear Charles," said the maid, who at least knew so much.

"My adorable Charles," said Bud, as an improvement, and down it went with the consent of the dictator.

"I'm keeping fine, and I'm very busy," suggested Kate, upon deliberation. "The weather is capital here at present, and it is a good thing, for the farmers are busy with their hay."

Bud sat back and stared at her in amazement. "Are you sure this is for a Charles?" she asked. "You might as well call him Sissy and talk frocks. Why! you must tell him how you love him."

"Oh, I don't like," said Kate, confused. "It sounds so – so bold and impudent when you put it in the English and write it down. But please yourself; put down what you like, and I'll be dipping the pen for you."

Bud was not slow to take the opportunity. For half an hour she sat at the kitchen table and searched her soul for fitting words that would convey Kate's adoration. Once or twice the maid asked what she was writing, but all she said was "Don't worry, Kate. I'm right in the throes." There were blots and there were erasions, but something like this did the epistle look when it was done: –

"MY ADORABLE CHARLES, – I am writeing this letter to let you know how much I truly love you. Oh Charles, dear, you are the

Joy of my heart. I am thinking of you so often, often, till my Heart just aches. It is lovely wether here at present. Now I will tell you all about the Games. They took place in a park near here Friday and there was seventeen beautiful dancers. They danced to give you spassums. One of them was a Noble youth. He was a Prince in his own write, under Spells for sevn years. When he danced, lo and behold he was the admiration of all Beholders. Alas! poor youth. When I say alas I mean that it was so sad being like that full of Spells in the flower of his youth. He looked at me so sad when he was dancing, and I was so glad. It was just like money from home. Dear Charles, I will tell you all about myself. I am full of goodness most the time for God loves good people. But sometimes I am not and I have a temper like two crost sticks when I must pray to be changed. The dancing gentleman truly loves me to distruction. He kissed my hand and hastily mountain his noble steed, galoped furiously away. Ah, the coarse of true love never did run smooth. Perhaps he will fall upon the forein plain. Dearest Charles – adorable – I must now tell you that I am being educated for my proper station in life. There is Geograpy, and penmanship with the right commas, and Long Division and conjunctives which I abomiate. But my teacher, a sweet lady named Miss Alison Dyce, says they are all truly refining. Oh I am weary, weary, he cometh not. That is for you, darling Charles, my own. – Your true heart love, KATE MACNEILL."

"Is that all right?" asked Bud anxiously.

"Yes; at least it'll do fine," said the maid, with that Highland politeness that is often so bad for business. "There's not much about himself in it, but och! it'll do fine. It's as nice a letter as ever I saw: the lines are all that straight."

"But there's blots," said Bud regretfully. "There oughtn't to be blots in a real love-letter."

"Toots! just put a cross beside each of them, and write 'this is a kiss'," said Kate, who must have had some previous experience. "You forgot to ask him how's his health, as it leaves us at present."

So Bud completed the letter as instructed. "Now for the envelope," said she.

"I'll put the address on it myself," said Kate, confused. "He would be sure somebody else had been reading it if the address was not in my hand of write," – an odd excuse, whose absurdity escaped the child. So the maid put the letter in the bosom of her Sunday gown against her heart, where meanwhile dwelt the only Charles. It is, I sometimes think, where we should all deposit and retain our love-letters; for the lad and lass, as we must think of them, have no existence any more than poor Kate's Charles.

Two days passed. Often in those two days would Bud come, asking anxiously if there was any answer yet from Charles. As often the maid of Colonsay reddened, and said with resignation there was not so much as the scrape of a pen. "He'll be on the sea," she explained at last, "and not near a post-office. Stop you till he gets near a post-office, and you'll see the fine letter I'll get."

"I didn't know he was a sailor," said Bud. "Why, I calculated he was a Highland chieftain or a knight, or something like that. If I had known he was a sailor I'd have made that letter different. I'd have loaded it up to the nozzle with sloppy weather, and said, Oh, how sad I was – that's you, Kate – to lie awake nights thinking about him out on the heaving billow. Is he a captain?"

"Yes," said Kate promptly. "A full captain in the summer time. In the winter he just stays at home and helps on his mother's farm. Not a cheep to your aunties about Charles, darling Lennox," she added anxiously. "They're – they're that particular!"

"I don't think you're a true love at all," said Bud, reflecting on many interviews at the kitchen window and the back-door. "Just think of the way you make goo-goo eyes at the letter-carrier, and the butcher's man, and the ashpit gentleman. What would Charles say?"

"Toots! I'm only putting by the time with them," explained the maid. "It's only a diversion. When I marry I will marry for my own conveniency, and the man for me is Charles."

"What's the name of his ship?" asked the child.

"The *Good Intent*," said Kate, who had known a skiff of the name in Colonsay. "A beautiful ship, with two yellow lums, and flags to the masthead."

"That's fine and fancy!" said Bud. "There was a gentleman who loved me to destruction, coming over on the ship from New York, and loaded me with candy. He was not the captain, but he had gold braid everywhere, and his name was George Sibley Purser. He promised he would marry me when I made a name for myself, but I 'spect Mister J.S. Purser'll go away and forget."

"That's just the way with them all," said Kate.

"I don't care, then," said Bud. "I'm all right; I'm not kicking."

Next day the breakfast in the house of Dyce was badly served, for Kate was wild to read a letter that the post had brought, and when she opened it, you may be sure Bud was at her shoulder.

"DEAREST KATE [it said], – I love you truly and I am thinking of you most the time. Thank God we was all safed. Now I will tell you all about the Wreck. The sea was mountains high, and we had a cargo of spise and perils from Java on the left-hand side the map as you go to Australia. When the Pirite ship chased us we went down with all hands. But we constrickted a raft and sailed on and on till we had to draw lots who would drink the blood. Just right there a sailor cried 'A sail, A sail,' and sure enough it was a sail. And now I will tell you all about Naples. There is a monsterious mountain there, or cone which belches horrid flames and lavar. Once upon a time it belched all over a town by the name of Pompy and it is there till this very day. The bay of naples is the grandest in the world it is called the golden horn. Dearest Katherine, I am often on the mast at night. It is cold and shakey in that place and oh how the wind doth blow, but I ring a bell and say alls well which makes the saloon people truly glad. We had five stow-ways. One of them was a sweet fair-haired child from Liverpool, he was drove from home. But a good and beautious lady, one of the first new england families is going to adopt him and make him her only air. How beautiful and bright he stood as born to rule the storm. I weary for your letters darling Katherine. – Write soon to your true love till death,   "CHARLES."

Kate struggled through this extraordinary epistle with astonishment. "Who in the world is it from?" she asked Bud.

"Charles, stupid," said Bud, astonished that there should be any doubt about that point. "Didn't I – didn't we write him the other night? It was up to him to write back, wasn't it?"

"Of course," said Kate, very conscious of that letter still unposted, "but – but he doesn't say Charles anything, just Charles. It's a daft-like thing not to give his name; it might be anybody. There's my Charles, and there's Charles Maclean from Oronsay – what way am I to know which of them it is?"

"It'll be either or eyether," said Bud. "Do you know Charles Maclean?"

"Of course I do," said the maid. "He's following the sea, and we were well acquaint."

"Did he propose to you?" asked Bud.

"Well, he did not exactly propose," admitted Kate, "but we sometimes went a walk together to the churchyard on a Sunday, and you know yourself what that means out in Colonsay. I'll just keep the letter and think of it. It's the nicest letter I ever got, and full of information. It's Charles Maclean, I'll warrant you, but he did not use to call me Katherine – he just said Kate, and his face would be as red as anything. Fancy him going down with all hands! My heart is sore for him," and the maid there and then transferred her devotion from the misty lad of her own imagination to Charles Maclean of Oronsay.

"You'll help me to write him a letter back tonight," she said.

"Yes, indeed, I'll love to," said the child wearily. But by the time the night came on, and Wanton Wully rang his curfew bell, and the rooks came clanging home to the tall trees of the forest, she was beyond all interest in life or love.

CHAPTER XIII

WANTON WULLY only briefly rang the morning bell, and gingerly, with tight-shut lips and deep nose breathings, as if its loud alarm could so be mitigated. Once before he had done it just as delicately – when the Earl was dying, and the bell-ringer, uncertain of his skill to toll, when the time came, with the right half-minute pauses grieved the town and horrified the Castle by a rehearsal in the middle of a winter night. But no soul of mercy is in brazen bells that hang aloof from man in lofty steeples, and this one, swung ever so gently, sullenly boomed – boomed – boomed.

"Oh to the devil wi' ye!" said Wanton Wully, sweating with vexation. "Of all the senseless bells! A big, boss bluiter! I canna compel nor coax ye!" and he gave the rope one vicious tug that brought it, broken, round his ears; then went from the church into the sunny, silent, morning street, where life and the day suspended.

In faith! a senseless bell, a merciless bell, waking folk to toil and grief. Dr Brash and Ailie heavy-eyed, beside the bed in the attic bower, shivered at the sound of it, and looked with fear and yearning at the sleeping child.

Bud moved her head from side to side a little on the pillow, with a murmur from her parched lips, and there was a flicker of the eyelids – that was all. Between her and the everlasting swound, where giddily swings the world and all its living things, there seemed no more than a sheet of tissue-paper: it was as if a breath of the tender morning air would quench the wavering flame that once was joy and Lennox Dyce. The heart of Auntie Ailie rose clamouring in her bosom; her eyes stung with the brine of tears restrained, but she clenched her teeth that she might still be worthy of the doctor's confidence.

He saw it, and put out his hand and pressed her shoulder, a fat old-fashioned man, well up in years, with whiskers under his chin like a cravat, yet beautiful as a prince to Ailie, for on him all her hopes were cast. "They call me agnostic – atheist even, whiles, I hear," he had said in the midst of their vigil; "and, indeed, I'm sometimes beat to get my mind beyond the mechanism, but – h'm! – a fine child, a noble child; she was made for something – h'm! That mind and talent – h'm! – that spirit – h'm! – the base of it was surely never yon grey stuff in the convolutions." And another time the minister had come in (the folk in the street were furious to see him do it!), and timidly suggested prayer. "Prayer!" said Dr Brash, "before this child, and her quite conscious! Man, what in God's own name are we doing here, this – h'm! – dear good lady and I, but fever ourselves with sleepless, silent prayer? Do you think a proper prayer must be official? There's not a drop of stuff in a druggist's bottle but what's a solution of hope and faith and – h'm! – prayer. Con-found it, sir!"

He put out his hand and pressed her on the shoulder, and never said a word. Oh, the doctors! the doctors! Hale men and hearty, we can see their shortcomings and can smile at them, but when the night-light burns among the phials!

It was the eighth day after Kate, with a face of clay, and her sleeves rolled up, and the dough still on her elbows as she had come from the baking-board, burst upon the doctor in his surgery with the cry, "Dr Brash, Dr Brash! ye're to haste ye and come at once to the wee one!" He had gone as nearly on the wings of the wind as a fat man may in carpet-slippers, and found a distracted family round the fevered child.

"Tut, tut, lassie," said he, chucking her lightly under the chin. "What new prank is this, to be pretending illness? Or if it's not a let-on, I'll be bound it's MacGlashan's almond tablet."

"It's these cursèd crab-apples in the garden; I'm sure it's the crab-apples, doctor," said Miss Bell, looking ten years older than her usual.

"H'm! I think not," said Dr Brash more gravely, with his finger on the pulse.

"It's bound to be," said Bell, piteous at having to give up her only hope. "Didn't you eat some yesterday, pet, after I told you that you were not for your life to touch them?"

"No," said Bud, with hot and heavy breathing.

"Then why didn't ye, why didn't ye; and then it might have been the apples?" said poor Miss Bell. "You shouldn't have minded me; I'm aye so domineering."

"No, you're not," said Bud, and wanly smiling.

"Indeed I am; the thing's acknowledged, and you needn't deny it," said her auntie. "I'm desperate domineering to you."

"Well, I'm – I'm not kicking," said Bud. It was the last cheerful expression she gave utterance to for many days.

Wanton Wully was not long the only one that morning in the sunny street. Women came out, unusually early, as it seemed, to beat their basses; but the first thing that they did was to look at the front of Daniel Dyce's house with a kind of terror lest none of the blinds should be up, and Mr Dyce's old kid glove should be off the knocker. "Have you heard what way she is keeping today?" they asked the bell-man.

"Not a cheep!" said he. "I saw Kate sweepin' out her door-step, but I couldna ask her. That's the curse of my occupation; I wish to goodness they had another man for the grave-diggin'."

"You and your graves!" said the women. "Who was mentioning them?"

He stood on the syver-side and looked at the blank front of Daniel Dyce's house with a gloomy eye. "A perfect caution!" he said, "that's what she was – a perfect caution! She called me Mr Wanton and always asked me how was my legs."

"Is there anything wrong with your legs?" said one of the women.

"Whiles a weakness," said Wanton Wully, for he was no hypocrite. "Her uncle tellt me once it was a kind o' weakness that they keep on gantrys down in Maggie White's. But she does not understand – the wee one; quite the leddy! she thought it was a kind o' gout. Me! I never had the gout – I never had the money for it, more's the pity."

He went disconsolate down the street to get his brush and barrow, for he was, between the morning bell and breakfast-time, the burgh's Cleansing Department. Later – till the middle of the day – he was the Harbour-Master, wore a red-collared coat and chased the gulls from the roofs of the shipping-boxes and the boys from the slip-side where they might fall in and drown themselves; his afternoons had half a dozen distinct official cares, of which, in that wholesome air, grave-digging came seldomest. This morning, he swept assiduously and long before the house of Daniel Dyce. Workmen passing yawning to their tasks in wood and garden, field and shed, looked at the muffled knocker and put the question; their wives, making, a little later, a message to the well, stopped too, put down their water-stoups, and speculated on the state of things within. Smoke rose from more than one chimney in the Dyces' house. "It's the parlour fire," said Wanton Wully. "It means breakfast. Cheery Dan, they say, aye makes a hearty breakfast; I like to see the gift in a man mysel', though I never had it; it's a good sign o' him the night before."

Peter the post came clamping by-and-by along the street with his letters, calling loudly up the closes, less willing than usual to climb the long stairs, for he was in a hurry to reach the Dyces'. Not the window for him this morning, nor had it been so for a week, since Kate no longer hung on the sashes, having lost all interest in the outer world. He went tiptoe through the flagged close to the back-door and lightly tapped.

"What way is she this morning?" said he, in the husky whisper that was the best he could control his voice to, and in his eagerness almost mastered his roving eye.

"She's got the turn! – she's got the turn!" said the maid, transported. "Miss Dyce was down the now and told me that her temper was reduced."

"Lord help us! I never knew she had one," said the post.

"It's no temper that I mean," said Kate, "but yon thing that you measure wi' the weather-glass the doctor's aye so cross wi' that he shakes and shakes and shakes at it. But anyway she's better. I hope Miss Ailie will come down for a bite; if not, she'll starve hersel'."

"That's rare! By George, that's tip-top!" said the postman, so uplifted that he went off with the M.C. step he used at Masons' balls, and would have clean forgotten to give Kate the letters if she had not cried him back.

Wanton Wully sat on a barrow-tram waiting the postman's exit. "What way is she?" said he, and Peter's errant eye cocked to all airts of the compass. What he wanted was to keep this tit-bit to himself, to have the satisfaction of passing it along with his letters. To give it to Wanton Wully at this stage would be to throw away good fortune. It was said by Daniel Dyce that the only way to keep a dead secret in the burgh was to send Wully and his handbell round the town with it as public crier. When Wanton Wully cried, it beat you to understand a word he said after "Notice!" but unofficially he was marvellously gleg at circulating news. "What way is she?" he asked again, seeing the postman's hesitation.

"If ye'll promise to stick to the head o' the toun and let me alone in the ither end, I'll tell ye," said Peter, and it was so agreed.

But they had not long all the glory of the good tidings to themselves. Dr Brash came out of Dyce's house for the first time in two days, very sunken in the eyes and sorely needing shaving, and it could be noticed by the dullest that he had his jaunty walk and a flower in the lapel of his badly-crushed coat. Ailie put it there with trembling fingers; she could have kissed the man besides, if there had not been the chance that he might think her only another silly woman. Later Footles hurled himself in fury from the doorway, his master close behind him. At the sight of Mr Dyce the street was happy; it was the first time they had seen him for a week. In burgh towns that are small enough we have this compensation, that if we have to grieve in common over many things, a good man's personal joy exalts us all.

"She's better, Mr Dyce, I'm hearing," said P. & A. MacGlashan, wiping his hands on his apron, to prepare for a fervent clasp from one who, he ought to have known, was not of the fervent-clasping kind.

"Thank God! Thank God!" said Mr Dyce. "You would know she was pretty far through!"

"Well – we kind of jaloused. But we kent there was no danger – the thing would be ridiculous!" said P. & A. MacGlashan, and went into his shop in a hurry, much uplifted too, and picked out a big bunch of black grapes and sent his boy with them, with his compliments, to Miss Lennox Dyce, care of Daniel Dyce, Esquire, Writer.

Miss Minto so adored the man she could not show herself to him in an hour like that; for she knew that she must weep, and a face begrutten ill became her, so in she came from the door of her Emporium and watched him pass the window. She saw in him what she had never seen before – for in his clothing he was always trim and tidy, quite perjink, as hereabouts we say: she saw, with the sharp eyes of a woman who looks at the man she would like to manage, that his hat was dusty and his boots not very brightly polished. More than all the news that leaked that week from the Dyces' dwelling it realised for her the state of things there.

"Tcht! tcht! tcht!" she said to herself; "three of them yonder, and he's quite neglected!" She went into a back room, where gathered the stuff for her Great Annual Jumble Sales with ninepenny things at sevenpence ha'penny, and searched a drawer that sometimes had revealed tremendous joy to Lennox and other bairns who were privileged to see what they called "Miss Minto's back." In the drawer there was a doll called Grace, a large, robust, and indestructible wooden child that had shared Miss Minto's youth and found the

years more kindly than she, since it got no wrinkles thinking on the
cares of competition in the millinery and mantua-making trade, but
dozed its days away upon feathers and silk and velvet swatches.
Grace was dressed like a queen – if queens are attired in gorgeous
hand-stitched remnants; she had so long been part of Miss Minto's
life that the mantua-maker swithered in her first intention. But she
thought how happy Mr Dyce must be that day, and hurriedly packed
the doll in a box and went round herself with it for Lennox Dyce.

As she knocked lightly at the front door, the old kid glove came
loose in her hand – an omen! One glance up and down the street to
see that no one noticed her, and then she slipped it in her pocket,
with a guilty countenance. She was not young, at least she was not
in her 'teens, but young enough to do a thing like that for luck and
her liking of Daniel Dyce. Yet her courage failed her, and when Kate
came to the door the first thing she handed to her was the glove.

"It fell off," she said. "I hope it means that it's no longer needed.
And this is a little thing for Miss Lennox, Kate; you will give her it
with my compliments. I hear there's an improvement?"

"You wouldna *believe* it!" said Kate. "Thank God, she'll soon be
carrying-on as bad as ever!"

Mr Dyce would not have cared a rap that morning if he had come
upon his clerks at Catch-the-Ten, or even playing leapfrog on their
desks. He was humming a psalm you may guess at as he looked at
the documents heaped on his table – his calf-bound books and the
dark japanned deed-boxes round his room.

"Everything just the same, and business still going on!" he said to
his clerk. "Dear me! dear me! what a desperate world! Do you know,
I had the notion that everything was stopped. No, when I think of it
I oftener fancied all this was a dream."

"Not Menzies *v.* Kilblane at any rate," said the clerk, with his
hand on a bulky Process, for he was a cheery soul and knew the mind
of Daniel Dyce.

"I daresay not," said the lawyer. "That plea will last a while, I'm
thinking. And all about a five-pound fence! Let you and me,
Alexander, thank our stars there are no sick bairns in the house of
either Menzies or Kilblane, for then they would understand how
much their silly fence mattered, and pity be on our canty wee Table-
of-Fees!" He tossed over the papers with an impatient hand.
"Trash!" said he. "What frightful trash! I can't be bothered with
them – not today. They're no more to me than a docken leaf. And
last week they were almost everything. You'll have heard the child
has got the turn?"

"I should think I did!" said Alexander. "And no one better pleased to hear it!"

"Thank you, Alick. How's the family?"

"Fine," said the clerk.

"Let me think, now – seven, isn't it? A big responsibility."

"Not so bad as long's we have the health," said Alexander.

"Yes, yes," said Mr Dyce. "All one wants in this world is the health – and a little more money. I was just thinking –" He stopped himself, hummed a bar of melody, and twinkled through his spectacles. "You'll have read Dickens?" said he.

"I was familiar with his works when I was young," said Alexander, like a man confessing that in youth he played at bools. "They were not bad."

"Just so! Well, do you know there was an idea came to my mind just now that's too clearly the consequence of reading Dickens for a week back, so I'll hold my hand and keep my project for another early occasion when it won't be Dickens that's dictating."

He went early back that day, to relieve Ailie at her nursing, as he pretended to himself, but really for his own delight in looking at the life in eyes where yesterday was a cloud. A new, fresh, wholesome air seemed to fill the house. Bud lay on high pillows, with Miss Minto's Grace propped against her knees, and the garret was full of the odour of flowers that had come in a glorious bunch from the banker's garden. Bell had grown miraculously young again, and from between Ailie's eyebrows had disappeared the two black lines that had come there when Dr Brash had dropped in her ear the dreadful word pneumonia. But Dr Brash had beaten it! Oh, if she only knew the way to knit a winter waistcoat for him!

The child put out her hand to her uncle, and he kissed her on the palm, frightful even yet of putting a lip to her cheek, lest he should experience again the terror of the hot breath from that consuming inward fire.

"Well," said he briskly, "how's our health, your ladyship? Losh bless me! what a fine, big, sonsy baby you have gotten here; poor Alibel's nose will be out of joint, I'm thinking."

"Hasn't got any," said Bud, still weakly, in her new, thin, and unpractised voice, as she turned with a look that showed no lessening affection for the old doll, badly battered in the visage and wanting in the limbs, which lay beside her on the pillow.

"Blythmeat and breadberry," said Daniel Dyce. "In the house of Daniel Dyce! Bell and Ailie, here's an example for you!"

CHAPTER XIV

FOLLOWING on stormy weeks had come an Indian summer, when the world was blessed with Ailie's idea of Arden weather, that keeps one wood for ever green and glad with company, knows only the rumour of distant ice and rain, and makes men, reading thereof by winter fires, smell fir and feel the breeze on their naked necks and hunger for the old abandoned bed among the brackens. "It is better to hear the lark sing than the mouse squeak," was the motto of Daniel Dyce, and though the larks were absent, he would have the little one in the garden long hours of the day. She beiked there like a kitten in the sunlight till her wan cheek bloomed. The robin sang among the apples – pensive a bit for the ear of age, that knows the difference between the voice of spring and autumn – sweet enough for youth that happily does not have an ear for its gallant melancholy; the starlings blew like a dust about the sky; over the garden wall – the only one in the town that wanted broken bottles – far-oft hills raised up their heads to keek at the little lassie, who saw from this that the world was big and glorious as ever.

"My! ain't this fine and clean?" said Bud. "Feels as if Aunt Bell had been up this morning bright and early with a duster." She was enraptured with the blaze of the nasturtiums, that Bell would aye declare should be the flower of Scotland, for "Indian cress here, or Indian cress there," as she would say, "they're more like Scots than any flower I ken. The poorer the soil the better they thrive, and they come to gold where all your fancy flowers would rot for the want of nutriment. Nutriment! give them that in plenty and you'll see a bonny display of green and no' much blossom. The thing's a parable – the worst you can do with a Scotsman, if you want the best from him's to feed him ower rich. Look at Captain Consequence; never the same since he was aboard – muligatawny even-on in India; a score of servant-men, and never a hand's-turn for himself – all the blossom from that kind of Indian cress is on his nose."

"Lands sake! I *am* glad I'm not dead," said Bud, with all her body tingling as she heard the bees buzz in the nasturtium bells and watched the droll dog Footles snap at the butterflies.

"It's not a bad world, one way and the other," said Miss Bell, knitting at her side; "It would have been a hantle worse if we had had the making o't. But here we have no continuing city, and yonder – if the Lord had willed – you would have gone sweeping through the gates of the new Jerusalem."

"Sweeping!" said the child. "I can't sweep for keeps; Kate won't give me a chance to learn. But anyhow I guess this is a good enough world for a miserable sinner like me."

Mr Dyce, who had carried her, chair and all, into the garden, though she could have walked there, chuckled at this confession.

"Dan," said Bell, "think shame of yourself! You make the child light-minded."

"The last thing I would look for in women is consistency," said he, "and I daresay that's the way I like them. What is it Ailie quotes from Emerson? 'A foolish consistency is the hobgoblin of little minds,' – that kind of goblin never scared a woman in the dark yet. But surely you'll let me laugh when I think of you chiding her gladness in life today, when I mind of you last week so desperate throng among the poultices."

"I'm for none of your lawyer arguments," said Bell, trying in vain to gag herself with a knitting-pin from one of the Shetland shawls she had been turning out for years with the hope that some day she could keep one for herself. "It might have been that 'she pleased God and was beloved of Him, so that, living among sinners' – among sinners, Dan – 'she was translated. Yea, speedily was she taken away, lest that wickedness should alter her understanding, or deceit beguile her soul.'"

"I declare if I haven't forgot my peppermints!" said her brother, quizzing her, and clapping his outside pockets. "A consoling text! I have no doubt at all you could prelect upon it most acceptably, but confess that you are just as glad as me that there's the like of Dr Brash."

"I like the Doc," the child broke in, with most of this dispute beyond her; "he's a real cuddley man. Every time he rapped at my chest I wanted to cry 'Come in.' Say, isn't he slick with a poultice!"

"He was slick enough to save your life, my dear," said Uncle Dan soberly. "I'm almost jealous of him now, for Bud's more his than mine."

"Did he make me better?" asked the child.

"Under God. I'm thinking we would have been in a bonny habble wanting him."

"I don't know what a bonny habble is from Adam," said Bud, "but I bet the Doc wasn't *everything*: there was that prayer, you know."

"Eh?" exclaimed her uncle sharply.

"Oh, I heard you, Uncle Dan," said Bud, with a sly look up at him. "I wasn't sleeping really that night, and I was awful liable to have tickled you on the bald bit of your head. I never saw it before.

I could have done it easily if it wasn't that I was so tired; and my breath was so sticky that I had to keep on yanking it, just; and you were so solemn and used such dre'ffle big words. I didn't tickle you, but I thought I'd help you pray, and so I kept my eyes shut and said a bit myself. Say, I want to tell you something," – she stammered, with a shaking lip. "I felt real mean when you talked about a sinless child; of course you didn't know, but it was – it wasn't true. I know why I was taken ill: it was a punishment for telling fibs to Kate. I was mighty frightened that I'd die before I had a chance to tell you."

"Fibs!" said Mr Dyce seriously. "That's bad. And I'm loth to think it of you, for it's the only sin that does not run in the family, and the one I most abominate."

Bell stopped her knitting, quite distressed, and the child lost her new-come bloom. "I didn't mean it for fibs," she said, "and it wasn't anything I said, but a thing I did when I was being Winifred Wallace. Kate wanted me to write a letter –"

"Who to?" demanded Auntie Bell.

"It was to – it was to – oh, I daren't tell you," said Bud, distressed. "It wouldn't be fair, and maybe she'll tell you herself, if you ask her. Anyhow I wrote the letter for her, and seeing she wasn't getting any answer to it, and was just looney for one, and I was mighty keen myself, I turned Winny on, and wrote one. I went out and posted it that dre'ffle wet night you had the party, and I never let on to Kate, so she took it for a really really letter from the person we sent the other one to. I got soaked going to the post-office, and that's where I guess God began to play *His* hand. Jim said the Almighty held a royal flush every blessed time; but that's card talk, I don't know what it means, 'cept that Jim said it when the 'Span of Life' manager skipped with the boodle – lit out with the cash, I mean, and the company had to walk home from Kalamazoo on the railroad ties."

"Mercy on us! I never heard a word of it," cried Miss Bell. "This'll be a warning! People that have bairns to manage shouldn't be giving parties; it was the only night since ever you came here that we never put you to your bed. Did Kate not change your clothes when you came in wet?"

"She didn't know I was out, for that would have spoiled everything, 'cause she'd have asked me what I was doing out, and I'd have had to tell her, for I can't fib that kind of fib. When I came in all soaking, I took a teeny-weeny loan of Uncle's tartan rug, and played to Kate I was Helen Macgregor, and Kate went into spasms, and didn't notice anything till my clothes were dry. Was it very very naughty of me?"

"It was indeed! It was worse than naughty, it was silly," said her Uncle Dan, remembering all the prank had cost them.

"Oh, Lennox! my poor sinful bairn!" said her aunt, most melancholy.

"I didn't mean the least harm," protested the child, trembling on the verge of tears. "I did it all to make Kate feel kind of gay, for I hate to see a body mope – and I wanted a little fun myself," she added hastily, determined to confess all.

"I'll Kate her, the wretch!" cried Auntie Bell quite furious, gathering up her knitting.

"Why, Auntie Bell, it wasn't her fault, it was –"

But before she could say more, Miss Bell was flying to the house for an explanation, Footles barking at her heels astonished, for it was the first time he had seen her trot with a ball of wool trailing behind her. The maid had the kitchen window open to the last inch, and looked out on a street deserted but for a ring of bairns that played before the baker's door. Their voices, clear and sweet, and laden with no sense of care or apprehension, filled the afternoon with melody –

> "Water, water wall-flowers,
> Growing up so high,
> We are all maidens,
> And we must all die."

To the maid of Colonsay in an autumn mood, the rhyme conveyed some pensive sentiment that was pleasant though it almost made her cry: the air slipped to her heart, the words in some way found the Gaelic chord that shakes in sympathy with minor keys, for beautiful is all the world, our day of it so brief! Even Miss Bell was calmed by the children's song as it came from the sunny street into the low-ceiled shady kitchen. She had played that game herself, sung these words long ago, never thinking of their meaning: how pitiful it was that words and a tune should so endure, unchanging and all else alter!

"Kate, Kate, you foolish lass!" she cried, and the maid drew in with the old astonishment and remorse, as if it was her first delinquency.

"I – I was looking for the post," said she.

"Not for the first time, it seems," said her mistress. "I'm sorry to hear it was some business of yours that sent Miss Lennox to the post-office on a wet night that was the whole cause of our tribulation. At least you might have seen the wean was dried when she came back."

"I'm sure and I don't know what you're talking about, me'm," said the maid, astounded.

"You got a letter the day the bairn took ill; what was it about?"

The girl burst into tears and covered her head with her apron. "Oh, Miss Dyce, Miss Dyce!" she cried "You're that particular, and I'm ashamed to tell you. It was only just diversion."

"Indeed, and you must tell me," said her mistress, now determined. "There's some mystery here that must be cleared, as I'm a living woman. Show me that letter this instant!"

"I can't, Miss Dyce, I can't, I'm quite affronted. You don't ken who it's from."

"I ken better than yourself; it's from nobody but Lennox," said Miss Bell.

"My stars!" cried the maid, astonished. "Do you tell me that? Amn't I the stupid one? I thought it was from Charles. Oh, me'm! what will Charles Maclean of Oronsay think of me? He'll think I was demented," and turning to her servant's chest she threw it open and produced the second sham epistle.

Miss Bell went in with it to Ailie in the parlour, and they read it together. Ailie laughed till the tears came at the story it revealed. "It's more creditable to her imagination than to my teaching in grammar and spelling," was her only criticism. "The – the little rogue!"

"And is that the way you look at it?" asked Bell, disgusted. "A pack of lies from end to end. She should be punished for it; at least she should be warned that it was very wicked."

"Stuff and nonsense," said Miss Ailie. "I think she has been punished enough already, if punishment was in it. Just fancy if the Lord could make so much ado about a little thing like that! It's not a pack of lies at all, Bell; it's literature, it's romance."

"Well, romancing!" said Miss Bell. "What's romancing, if you leave out Walter Scott? I am glad she has a conviction of the sin of it herself. If she had slipped away from us on Wednesday this letter would have been upon her soul. It's vexing her now."

"If that is so, it's time her mind was relieved," said Ailie, and rising, sped to the garden with the letter in her hand. Her heart bled to see the apprehension on Bud's face, and beside her, Dan, stroking her hair and altogether bewildered.

"Bud," cried Ailie, kissing her, "do you think you could invent a lover for me who would write me letters half so interesting as this? It's a lover like that I have all the time been waiting for: the ordinary kind, by all my reading, must be very dull in their correspondence, and the lives they lead deplorably humdrum –

"'Oh, Charlie is my darling, my darling, my darling;
    Oh, Charlie is my darling, the young marineer.'

After this I'll encourage only sailors: Bud, dear, get me a nice clean sailor. But I stipulate that he must be more discriminating with his capitals, and know that the verb must agree with its nominative, and not be quite so much confused in his geography."

"You're not angry with me, Aunt?" said Bud, in a tone of great relief, with the bloom coming back. "Was it very, very wicked?"

"Pooh!" said Ailie. "If that's wicked, where's our Mr Shakespeare? Oh, child! child! you are my own heart's treasure. I thought a girl called Alison I used to know long ago was long since dead and done with, and here she's to the fore yet, daft as ever, and her name is Lennox Dyce."

"No, it wasn't Lennox wrote that letter," said Bud; "It was Winifred Wallace, and oh, my! she's a pretty tough proposition. You're quite, *quite* sure it wasn't fibbing."

"No more than Cinderella's fibbing," said her aunt, and flourished the letter in the face of Dan, who she saw was going to enter some dissent. "Behold, Dan Dyce, the artist b-r-r-rain! Calls sailor sweethearts from the vasty deep, and they come obedient to her bidding. Spise and perils, Dan, and the golden horn a trifle out of its latitude, and the darling boy that's *always* being drove from home. One thing you overlooked in the boy, Bud – the hectic flush. I'm sure Kate would have liked a touch of the hectic flush in him."

But Bud was still contrite, thinking of the servant. "She was so set upon a letter from her Charles," she explained, "and now she'll have to know that I was joshing her. Perhaps I shouldn't say joshing, Auntie Ailie – I s'pose it's slang."

"It is," said her aunt, "and most unladylike; let us call it pulling her le-let us call it – oh, the English language! I'll explain it all to Kate, and that will be the end of it."

"Kate 'd be dre'ffle rattled to talk about love to a grown-up lady," said Bud, on thinking. "I'd best go in and explain it all myself."

"Very well," said Auntie Ailie; so Bud went into the house and through the lobby to the kitchen.

"I've come to beg your pardon, Kate," said she hurriedly. "I'm sorry I – I – pulled your leg about that letter you thought was from Charles."

"Toots! Ye needn't bother about my leg or the letter either," said Kate, most cheerfully, with another letter open in her hand, and Mr Dyce's evening mail piled on the table before her; "letters are like herring now, they're comin' in in shoals. I might have kent yon one never came from Oronsay, for it hadn't the smell of peats. I have a real one now that's new come in from Charles, and it's just a beauty! He got his leg broken on the boats a month ago, and Dr Macphee's attending him. Oh, I'm that glad to think that Charles's leg is in the hands of a kent face!"

"Why! that's funny," said Bud. "And we were just going to write – oh, you mean the other Charles?"

"I mean Charles Maclean," said Kate, with some confusion. "I – I – was only lettin'-on about the other Charles; he was only a diversion."

"But you sent him a letter?" cried Bud.

"Not me!" said Kate composedly. "I kept it, and I sent it on to Charles out in Oronsay when you were poorly; it did fine! He says he's glad to hear about my education, and doesn't think much of gentlemen that dances, but that he's always glad to get the scrape of a pen from me, because – because – well, just because he loves me still the same, yours respectfully, Charles Maclean. And oh, my stars, look at what a lot of crosses!"

Bud scrutinised them with amazement. "Well *he's* a pansy!" said she.

CHAPTER XV

SUDDENLY all the town began to talk of the pride of Kate MacNeill. She took to wearing all her best on week-days; abandoned the kitchen window, and ruined an old-established trade in pay-night sweeties, that used to shower on her in threepenny packets at the start of every autumn when the days grew short. No longer blate young lads scraped with their feet uneasily in the sawdust of P. & A. MacGlashan's, swithering between the genteel attractions of Turkish Delight and the eloquence of conversation lozenges, that saved a lot of thinking, and made the blatest equal with the boldest when it came to tender badinage below the lamp at the back-door close with Dyce's maid. Talk about the repartee of salons! wit moves deliberately there compared with the swift giff-gaff that Kate and her lads were used to maintain with sentiments doubly sweet and ready-made at threepence the quarter-pound. So fast the sweeties passed, like the thrust and riposte of rapiers, that their final purpose was forgotten; they were sweeties no longer to be eaten, but scented billets-doux, laconic of course, but otherwise just as satisfactory as those that high-born maidens get only one at a time and at long intervals when their papas are out at business.

> "Are you engaged?
> "Just keep spierin'."
> " Absence makes the heart grow fonder."
> "You are a gay deceiver."
> "My heart is yours."
> "How are your poor feet?"

By the hour could Kate sustain such sparkling flirtations, or at least till a "Kiss me, dearest" turned up from the bottom of the poke, and then she slapped his face for him. It is the only answer out in Colonsay unless he's your intended.

But it stopped all at once. P. & A. was beat to understand what way his pay-night drawings fell, until he saw that all the lads were taking the other side of the street. "That's *her* off, anyway!" said he to Mrs P. & A., with a gloomy visage. "I wonder who's the lucky man? It's maybe Peter – she'll no' get mony losengers from him."

And it was not only the decline in votive offerings that showed the vital change; she was not at the Masons' ball, which shows how wrong was the thought of P. & A., for Peter was there with another lady. Very cheery, too; exceedingly cheery, ah, desperately gay, but quite beyond the comprehension of his partner, Jenny Shand, who was unable to fathom why a spirit so merry in the hall should turn to groans and bitterness when, feeling a faintish turn, she got him in behind the draft-screen on the landing of the stair to sit the "Flowers o' Edinburgh." He was fidging fain to tell her plainly what he thought of all her sex, but strove like a perfect gentleman against the inclination, and only said "Ha! ha! do you say so, noo?" and "Weemen!" with a voice that made them all out nothing more nor less than vipers. Poor Jenny Shand! bonny Jenny Shand! what a shame she should be bothered with so ill-faured a fellow! When she was picking bits of nothing off his coat lapel, as if he was her married man, and then coming to herself with a pretty start and begging pardon for her liberty, the diffy paid no heed; his mind was down the town, and he was seeing himself yesterday morning at the first

delivery getting the window of Dyce's kitchen banged in his face
when he started to talk about soap, meaning to work the topic round
to hands and gloves. He had got the length of dirty hands, and asked
the size of hers, when bang! the window went, and the Hielan' one
in among her pots and pans.

It was not any wonder, for other lads as deliberate and gawky as
himself had bothered her all the week with the same demand.
Hands! hands! you would think, said she, they were all at the door
wi' a bunch of finger-rings bound to marry her right or wrong, even
if they had to put them on her nose. Of course she knew finely what
they were after – she knew that each blate wooer wanted a partner
for the ball, and could only clench the compact with a pair of gloves;
but just at present she was not in trim for balls, and landsmen had
no interest for her since her heart was on the brine. Some of them
boldly guessed at seven-and-a-halfs without inquiry and were
dumfoundered that she would not look at them; and one had
acquired a pair of roomy white cotton ones with elastic round the
top – a kind of glove that plays a solemn part at burials, having come
upon Miss Minto when her stock of festive kids was done. They
waylaid Kate coming with her basket from the mangle – no, thanky,
she was needing no assistance; or she would find them scratching at
the window after dark; or hear them whistling, whistling, whistling
– oh, so softly! – in the close. There are women rich and nobly born
who think that they are fortunate, and yet, poor dears! they never
heard the whistling in the close. Kate's case was terrible! By day, in
her walks abroad in her new merino, not standing so much as a wink,
or paying any heed to a "Hey, Kate, what's your hurry?" she would
blast them with a flashing eye. By night, hearing their signals, she
showed them what she thought of them by putting to the shutters.
"Dir-r-rt!" was what she called them, with her nose held high and
every "r" a rattle on the lug for them – this to Bud, who could not
understand the new distaste Kate had to the other sex. "Just dirt
below my feet! I think myself far far above them."

One evening Mr Dyce came in from his office and quizzed her in
the lobby. "Kate," said he, "I'm not complaining, but I wish you
would have mercy on my back-door. There's not a night I have come
home of late but if I look up the close I find a lad or two trying to
bite his way into you through the door. Can you no' go out, like a
good lass, and talk at them in the Gaelic – it would serve them right!
If you don't, steps will have to be taken with a strong hand, as you
say yourself. What are they wanting? Bless my soul! can this – can
this be love?"

She ran to the sanctuary of the kitchen, plumped in a chair, and was swept away in a storm of laughter and tears that frightened Bud, who waited there a return of her aunts from the Women's Guild. "Why, Kate, what's the matter?" she asked.

"Your un – your un – un – uncle's blaming me for harbouring all them chaps about the door, and says it's l – l – love: oh dear! I'm black affronted."

"You needn't go into hysterics about a little thing like that," said Bud; "Uncle Dan's tickled to death to see so many beaux you have, wanting you to that ball; he said last night he had to walk between so many of them waiting for you there in front, it was like shassaying up the middle in the Haymakers."

"It's not hysterics, nor hersterics either," said the maid; "and oh, I wish I was out of here and back in the isle of Colonsay!"

Yes, Colonsay became a great place then. America, where the prospects for domestics used to be so fascinating, had lost its glamour since Bud had told her the servants there were as discontented as in Scotland, and now her native isle beat Paradise. She would talk by the hour, at a washing, of its charms, of which the greatest seemed to be the absence of public lamps and the way you heard the wind! Colonsay seemed to be a place where folk were always happy, meeting in each other's houses, dancing, singing, courting, marrying, getting money every now and then from sons or wealthy cousins in Australia. Bud wondered if they never did any work in Colonsay. Yes, yes, indeed! Kate could assure her, they worked quite often out in Colonsay – in the winter time.

But one thing greatly troubled her – she must write back at once to the only Charles, who so marvellously had come to her through Bud's unconscious offices and she knew she could never sustain the standard of hand-write, spelling, and information Bud had established in her first epistle. Her position was lamentable. It was all very well to be the haughty madam on the street, and show herself a wise-like modest gyurl, but what was that without the education? C. Maclean was a man of education – he got it on the yats among the gentry, he had travelled all the world!

Kate's new airs, that caused such speculation in the town, were – now let me tell you – all the result of a dash at education. She wanted to be able to write a letter as good as Bud in a week or two, and had engaged the child to tutor her.

Bud never found a more delicious game in all her life, and it hurried her convalescence, for to play it properly she must be Aunt Ailie, and Aunt Ailie was always so strong and well.

"Education," said Bud, who had a marvellous memory, and was now, you will notice, Ailie Dyce sitting on a high chair, with the maid on a stool before her, "education is not what a lot of sillies think it is; it isn't knowing everything. Lots try for it that way, and if they don't die young, just when they're going to win the bursary, they grow up horrid bores, that nobody asks to picnics. You can't know everything, not if you sit up cramming till the cows come home; and if you want to see a brainy person jump, ask him how his mother raised her dough. Miss Katherine MacNeill, never – NEVER – NEVER be ashamed of not knowing a thing, but always be ashamed of not wanting to know. That's Part One. Don't you think you should have an exercise-book, child, and take it down?"

"Toots! what's my head for?" said the servant.

"Uncle Dan says education is knowing what you don't know, and knowing where to find it out without the other people knowing; but he says in most places you can get the name of having it fine and good by talking loud and pushing all your goods in front of you in a big enough barrow. And Auntie Bell – she says the fear of God is the beginning of wisdom, and the rest of it is what she skipped at Barbara Mushet's Seminary. But I tell you, child (said the echo of Ailie Dyce), that education's just another name for love."

"My stars! I never knew that before," cried the servant; "I'm awful glad about Charles!"

"It isn't that kind of love," Bud hurriedly explained, "though it's good enough, for that's too easy. You're only on the trail for education when you love things so you've simply *got* to learn as much as is good for your health about them. Everything's sweet – oh, so sweet – all the different countries, and the different people, when you understand, and the woods, and the things in them, and all the animals – 'cepting maybe puddocks, though it's likely God made them too when He was kind of careless – and the stars, and the things men did, and women – 'specially those that's dead, poor dears! – and all the books, 'cepting the stupid ones Aunt Ailie simply *can't* stand, though she never lets on to the ladies who like that kind."

"My Lord! must you love them all?" asked the maid, astonished.

"Yes, you must, my Lord," said Bud. "You'll never know the least thing well in this world unless you love it. It's sometimes mighty hard, I allow. I hated the multiplication table, but now I love it – at least, I kind of love it up to seven times nine, and then it's almost horrid, but not so horrid as it was before I knew that I would never have got to this place from Chicago unless a lot of men had learned

95

the table up as far as twelve times twelve."

"I'm not particular about the multiplication table," said the maid, "but I want to be truly refined, the same as you said in yon letter to Charles. I know he'll be expecting it."

"H-m-m-m-m!" said Bud thoughtfully, "I s'pose I'll have to ask Auntie Ailie about that, for I declare to goodness I don't know where you get it, for it's not in any of the books I've seen. She says it's the One Thing in a lady, and it grows inside you someway, like – like – like your lungs, I guess. It's no use trying to stick it on outside with lessons on the piano or the mandoline, and parlour talk about poetry, and speaking mim as if you had a clothes-pin in your mouth, and couldn't say the least wee thing funny without it was a bit you'd see in 'Life and Work'. Refinement, some folk think, is not laughing right out."

"My stars!" said Kate.

"And Auntie Bell says a lot think it's not knowing any Scotch language and pretending you never took a tousy tea."

"I think," said Kate, "we'll never mind refining; it's an awful bother."

"But every lady must be refined," said Bud. "Ailie prosists in that."

"I don't care," said the maid; "I'm not particular about being very much of a lady – I'll maybe never have the jewellery for it – but I would like to be a sort of lady on the Sundays, when Charles is at home. I'm not hurryin' you, my dear, but – but when do we start the writin'?" and she yawned in a way that said little for the interest of Professor Bud's opening lecture.

Whereupon Bud explained that in a systematic course of education reading came first, and the best reading was Shakespeare, who was truly ennobling to the human mind. She brought in Auntie Ailie's Shakespeare, and sat upon the fender, and plunged Kate at once into some queer society at Elsinore. But, bless you! nothing came of it: Kate fell asleep, and woke to find the fire cold and the child entranced with Hamlet.

"Oh dear! it's a slow job getting your education," she said pitifully, "and all this time there's my dear Charles waiting for a letter!"

CHAPTER XVI

"I CANNA be bothered with that Shakespeare," Kate cried hopelessly, after many days of him; "the man's a mournin' thing! Could he not give us something cheery, with 'Come, all ye boys!' in it, the same as the trawlers sing in Colonsay? There was far more fun last week in the penny Horner."

So Bud dipped in the bottomless well of knowledge again and scooped up Palgrave's 'Golden Treasury,' and splashed her favourite lyrics at the servant's feet. Kate could not stand the 'Golden Treasury' either; the songs were nearly all so lamentable they would make a body greet. Bud assured her on the best authority that the sweetest songs were those that told of saddest thought, but Kate said that might be right enough for gentry who had no real troubles of their own, but they weren't the thing at all for working folk. What working folk required were songs with tunes to them, and choruses that you could tramp time to with your feet. History, too, was as little to her taste; it was all incredible – the country could never have kept up so many kings and queens. But she liked geography, for the map enabled her to keep an eye on Charles as he went from port to port, where letters in her name, but still the work of Lennox, would be waiting for him.

The scheme of education was maintained so long because the town had come upon its melancholy days and Bud began to feel depression, so that playing teacher was her only joy. The strangers had gone south with the swallows; the steamer no longer called each day to make the pavement noisy in the afternoon with the skliff of city feet, so different from the customary tread of tackety boots; the coachman's horn, departing, no longer sounded down the valley like a brassy challenge from the wide, wide world. Peace came to the burgh like a swoon, and all its days were pensive. Folk went about their tasks reluctant, the very smoke of the chimneys loitered lazily round the ridges where the starlings chattered, and a haze was almost ever over the hills. When it rose, sometimes, Bud, from her attic window, could see the road that wound through the distant glen. The road! – the road! – ah, that began to have a meaning and a kind of cry, and wishfully she looked at it and thought upon its other end, where the life she had left and read about was loudly humming and marvellous things were being done. Charles Maclean of Oronsay, second mate, whom she loved unto destruction, now that he was writing regularly, fairly daft himself to get such charming curious letters as he thought from Kate, had been adjusted by the doctor, and was once again on the heaving main. It would be Cardiff or Fleetwood, Hamburg, Santander, or Bilbao, whose very name is like a story, and his tarry pen, infected by the child's example, induced to emulation, always bravely sought to give some picture of the varied world through which he wandered. Of noisy ports did he communicate, crowded with ships, of streets and lofty warehouses, and places where men sang, and sometimes of the playhouse, where the villain was a bad one and the women were so braw.

"What is braw?" asked Bud.

"It's fine clothes," said Kate; "but what's fine clothes if you are not pure in heart and have a figure?" and she surveyed with satisfaction her own plump arms.

But the child guessed at a wider meaning for the word as Charles used it, and thought upon the beauteous clever women of the plays that she had seen herself in far Chicago, and since her vicarious lover would have thought them braw and plainly interesting, she longed to emulate them, at least to see them again. And, oh! to see the places that he wrote of, and hear the thundering wheels and jangling bells! And there was also Auntie Ailie's constant stimulus to thoughts and aspirations that could meet no satisfaction in this little town. Bell dwelt continually within the narrow walls of her immediate duty, content, like many, thank the Lord! doing her daily turns as best she could, dreaming of nothing nobler. Dan had ranged wider in his time, and knew the world a great deal better, and had seen so much of it was illusion, its prizes "Will-o'-the-wisp," that now his wild geese were come home. He could see the world in the looking-glass in which he shaved, and there was much to be amused at. But Ailie's geese were still flying far across the firmament, knowing no place of rest. The child had bewitched her! it was often the distant view for her now, the region unattainable; and though apparently she had long ago surrendered to her circumstances, she now would sometimes silently irk at her prisoning here, in sleeptown, where we let things slide until tomorrow, while the wild birds of her inclination flew around the habitable wakeful world. Unwittingly – no, not unwittingly always – she charged the child with curiosity unsatisfiable, and secret discontent at little things and narrow, with longings for spacious arenas and ecstatic crowded hours. To be clever, to be brave and daring, to venture and make a glorious name! – how her face would glow and all her flesh would quiver picturing lives she would have liked to live if only she had had the chance! How many women are like that! silent by the hearth, seemingly placid and content as they darn and mend and wait on the whim and call of dullards.

Bell might be content and busy with small affairs, but she had a quick, shrewd eye, and saw the child's unrest. It brought her real distress, for so had the roving spirit started in her brother William. Sometimes she softly scolded Lennox, and even had contemplated turning her into some other room from the attic that had the only window in the house from which the highroad could be seen, but Ailie told her that would be to make the road more interesting for the child. "And I don't know," she added, "that it should worry us if she does indulge herself in dreams about the great big world and its possibilities. I suppose she'll have to take the road some day."

"Take the road!" cried Bell, almost weeping. "Are you daft, Ailie Dyce? What need she take the road for? There's plenty to do here, and I'm sure she'll never be better off anywhere else. A lot of nonsense! I hope you are not putting notions in her head; we had plenty of trouble with her father."

"It would break my heart to lose her, I assure you," said Aunt Ailie softly; "but –" and she ended with a sigh.

"I'm sure you're content enough yourself?" said Bell; "and you're not by any means a diffy."

"Indeed I am content," admitted Ailie; "at least – at least I'm not complaining. But there is a discontent that's almost holy, a roving mood that's the salvation of the race. There were, you mind, the Pilgrim Fathers –"

"I wish to the Lord they had bided at home!" cried Bell. "There's never been happy homes in this Christian land since they started emigration." And at that Miss Ailie smiled and Dan began to chuckle.

"Does it not occur to you, Bell," said he, "that but for the Pilgrim Fathers there would never have been Bud?"

"I declare neither there would!" she said, smiling. "Perhaps it was as well they went, poor things! And, of course, there must be many an honest decent body in America."

"Quite a number!" said Ailie. "You would not expect this burgh to hold them all, or even Scotland: America's glad to get the overflow."

"Ah, you're trying to make me laugh, the pair of you, and forget my argument," said Bell; "but I'll not be carried away this time. I'm feared for the bairn, and that's telling you. Oh, Ailie, mind what her mother was – poor girl! poor dear girl! playacting for her living, roving from place to place, with nothing you could call a home;

99

laughing and greeting and posturing before lights for the diversion of the world –"

"We might do worse than give the world diversion," said Ailie soberly.

"Yes, yes; but with a painted face and all a vain profession – that is different, is it not? I love a jovial heart like Dan's, but to make the body just a kind of fiddle! It's only in the body we can be ourselves – it is our only home; think of furnishing it with shams, and lighting every room that should be private, and leaving up the blinds that the world may look in at a penny a-head! How often have I thought of William, weeping for a living, as he had to do sometimes, no doubt, and wondered what was left for him to do to ease his grief when Mary died. Oh, curb the child, Ailie! curb the dear wee lassie – it's you it all depends on; she worships you; the making of her's in your hands. Keep her humble. Keep her from thinking of worldly glories. Teach her to number her days, that she may apply her heart unto wisdom. Her mind's too often out of here and wandering elsewhere: it was so with William – it was once the same with you."

Indeed it was no wonder that Bud's mind should wander elsewhere, since the life about her had grown so suddenly dull. In these days Wanton Wully often let his morning sleep too long possess him, and hurrying through the deserted dawn with his breeches scarcely on, would ring the bell in a hasty fury half an hour behind the proper time. But a little lateness did not matter in a town that really never woke. Men went to work in what we call a dover – that is, half asleep; shopkeepers came blinking drowsily down and took their shutters off, and went back to breakfast, or, I fear sometimes, to bed, and when the day was aired and decency demanded that they should make some pretence at business, they stood by the hour at their shop doors looking at the sparrows, wagtails, and blue-bonnets pecking in the street, or at the gulls that quarrelled in the syver sand. Nothing doing. Two or three times a-day a cart from the country rumbled down the town, breaking the Sabbath calm; and on one memorable afternoon there came a dark Italian with an organ who must have thought that this at last was Eldorado, so great was his reward from a community sick of looking at each other. But otherwise nothing doing, not a thing! As in the dark of the fabled underland the men who are blind are kings, George Jordon, the silly man, who never had a purpose, and carried about with him an enviable eternal dream, seemed in that listless world the only wideawake, for he at least kept moving, slouching somewhere, sure there was work for him to do if only he could get at it. Bairns dawdled to the schools, dogs slept in the track where once was summer traffic; Kate, melancholy, billowed from the kitchen window, and into the street quite shamelessly sang sad old Gaelic songs which Mr Dyce would say would have been excellent if only they were put to music, and her voice was like a lullaby.

One day Bud saw great bands of countless birds depart, passing above the highroad, and standing in the withering garden heard as it were without a breath of wind the dry rattle of dead leaves fall. It frightened her. She came quickly in to the tea-table, almost at her tears.

"Oh, it's dre'ffle," she said. "It's Sunday all the time, without good clothes and the gigot of mutton for dinner. I declare I want to yell."

"Dear me!" said Miss Bell cheerfully, "I was just thinking things were unusually lively for the time of year. There's something startling every other day. Aggie Williams found her fine new kitchen-range too big for the accommodation, and she has covered it with cretonne and made it into a what-not for her parlour. Then there's the cantata – I hear the U.P. choir is going to start to practise it whenever Duncan Gill, next door to the hall, is gone: he's near his end, poor body! they're waiting on, but he says he could never die a Christian death if he had to listen to them at their operatics through the wall."

"It's not a bit like this in Chicago," said the child, and her uncle chuckled.

"I daresay not," said he. "What a pity for Chicago! Are you wearying for Chicago, lassie?"

"No," said Bud, deliberating. "It was pretty smelly, but my! I wish to goodness folk here had a little git-up-and-go to them!"

"Indeed, I daresay it's not a bit like Chicago," admitted Auntie Bell. "It pleases myself that it's just like Bonnie Scotland."

"It's not a bit like Scotland either," said Bud. "I calc'lated Scotland 'd be like a story-book all the time, chock-full of men-at-arms and Covenanters, and things father used to talk about, Sundays, when he was kind of mopish, and wanted to make me Scotch. I've searched the woods for Covenanters and can't find one; they must have taken to the tall timber, and I haven't seen any men-at-arms since I landed, 'cepting the empty ones up in the castle lobby."

"What *did* you think Scotland would be like, dear?" asked Ailie.

"Between me and Winifred Wallace, we figured it would be a

great place for chivalry and constant trouble among the crowned heads. I expected there'd be a lot of 'battles long ago,' same as in the Highland Reaper in the sweet, sweet G.T."

"What's G.T.?" asked Auntie Bell; and Bud laughed slyly, and looked at her smiling Auntie Ailie, and said: "We know, Auntie Ailie, don't we? It's GRAND! And if you want to know, Auntie Bell, it's just Mister Lovely Palgrave's 'Golden Treasury'. *That's* a book, my Lord! I expected there'd be battles every day –"

"What a bloodthirsty child!" said Miss Ailie.

"I don't mean truly truly battles," Bud hurried to explain, "but the kind that's the same as a sound of revelry off – no blood, but just a lot of bang. But I s'pose battles are gone out, like iron suits. Then I thought there'd be almost nothing but cataracts and ravines and – and – mountain-passes, and here and there a right smart Alick in short trunks and a feather in his hat, winding a hunting-horn. I used to think, when I was a little, wee, silly whitterick, that you wound a horn every Saturday night with a key, just like a clock; but I've known for years and years it's just blowing. The way father said, and from the things I read, I calc'lated all the folk in Scotland 'd hate each other like poison, and start a clan, and go out chasing all the other clans with direful slogans and bagpipes skirling wildly in the genial breeze. And the place would be crowded with lovelorn maidens – that kind with the starched millstones round their necks, like Queen Mary always wore. My, it must have been rough on dear old Mary when she fell asleep in church! But it's not a bit like that; it's only like Scotland when I'm in bed, and the wind is loud, and I hear the geese. Then I think of the trees all standing out in the dark and wet, and the hills too, the way they've done for years *and* years, and the big lonely places with nobody in them, not a light even; and I get the croodles and the creeps, for that's Scotland, full of bogies. I think Scotland's stone-dead."

"It's no more dead than you are yourself," said Miss Bell, determined ever to uphold her native land. "The cleverest people in the world come from Scotland."

"So father used to say; but Jim, he said he guessed the cleverer they were the quicker they came. I'm not a bit surprised they make a dash from home when they feel so dead and mopish and think of things and see that road."

"Road?" said Uncle Dan. "What road?"

"My road," said the child. "The one I see from my window: oh, how it rises and rises and winds and winds, and it just *shrieks* on you to come right along and try."

"Try what?" asked her uncle curiously.

"I dunno," said Bud, thinking hard; "Auntie Ailie knows, and I 'spect Auntie Bell knows too. I can't tell what it is, but I fairly tickle to take a walk along. Other times I feel I'd be mighty afraid to go, but Auntie Ailie says you should always do the things you're afraid to do, for they're most always the only things worth doing."

Mr Dyce, scratching the ear of Footles, who begged at the side of his chair, looked over the rims of his glasses and scrutinised the child.

"All roads," said he, "as you'll find a little later, come to the same dead end, and most of us, though we think we're picking our way, are all the time at the mercy of the Schoolmaster, like Geordie Jordon. The only thing that's plain in the present issue is that we're not brisk enough here for Young America. What do you think we should do to make things lively?"

"Hustle," said Bud. "Why, nobody here moves faster'n a funeral, and they ought to gallop if they want to keep up with the band."

"I'm not in a hurry myself," said her uncle, smiling. "Maybe that's because I think I'm all the band there is, myself. But if you want to introduce the Chicago system you should start with Mrs Wright's Italian warehouse down the street – the poor body's losing money trying to run her shop on philanthropic principles."

Bud thought hard a while. "Phil – phil – What's a philanthropic principle?" she asked.

"It's a principle on which you don't expect much interest except in another world," said her uncle. "The widow's what they call a Pilgrim, hereabouts; if the meek were to inherit the earth in a literal sense, she would long ago have owned the whole county."

"A truly Christian woman!" said Miss Bell.

"I'm not denying it," said Mr Dyce; "but even a Christian woman should think sometimes of the claims of her creditors, and between ourselves it takes me all my time to keep the wholesale merchants from hauling her to court."

"How do you manage it?" asked Ailie, with a twinkle in her eyes; but Dan made no reply – he coughed and cleaned his spectacles.

CHAPTER XVII

THERE was joy a few days later in the Dyce's kitchen when Peter the postman, with a snort that showed the bitterness of his feelings, passed through the window a parcel for Kate, that on the face of it had come from foreign parts. "I don't ken who it's from, and ye're no' to think I'm askin'," said he; "but the stamps alone for that thing must have cost a bonny penny."

"Did they, indeed!" said Kate, with a toss of her head. "Ye'll be glad to ken he can well afford it!" and she sniffed at the parcel, redolent of perfumes strange and strong.

"Ye needna snap the nose off me," said the postman, "I only made the remark. What – what does the fellow do?"

"He's a traveller for railway tunnels," retorted the maid of Colonsay, and shut the window with a bang, to tear open the parcel in a frenzy of expectation, and find a bottle of Genuine Riga Balsam – wonderful cure for sailors' wounds! – another of Florida Water, and a silver locket, with a note from Charles saying the poem she had sent was truly grand, and wishing her many happy returns of the day. Like many of Charles's letters now, its meaning was, in parts, beyond her, until she could learn from Bud the nature of the one to which it was an answer – for Bud was so far enraptured with the wandering sailor that she sometimes sent him letters which the servant never saw. That day the breakfast service smelt of Florida Water, for Kate had drenched herself with the perfume, and Miss Bell was sure she had washed the dishes again with scented soap, as was the habit of the girl when first she came from Colonsay, and thought that nothing but Brown Windsor would do justice to Grandma Buntain's tea-set used on Sundays. But Bud could see the signs of Shipping Intelligence, and, as soon as she could, she hastened to the kitchen, for it was Saturday, and on Saturdays there were no lessons in the Dyce Academy. Oh! how she and Kate fondled the bottles lovingly, and sniffed passionately at their contents, and took turn about of the locket! The maid had but one regret, that she had no immediate use for Riga Balsam; but Bud was more devoted than that – she gently pricked the palm of her hand with a pin and applied the Genuine. "Oh! how he must love me – us, I mean," she exclaimed, and eagerly devoured his letter.

"What did you say to him in the last?" asked Kate. "He's talking there about a poetry, and happy returns of the day."

Bud confessed she had made a poem for him from his beloved

Kate, and had reckoned on fetching a gift of candy by telling him her birthday was on Monday. "But really I'd just as lief have the balsam," said she, "it's perfectly lovely; how it nips!"

"It's not my birthday at all," said Kate. "My birthday's always on the second Sunday in September. I was born about the same time as Lady Anne – either a fortnight before or a fortnight after; I forget mysel' completely which it was, and I daresay so does she."

"No, but Monday's my birthday, right enough," said Bud, "and seeing that we're sort of loving him in company, I s'posed it would be all the same."

"So it is, I'm not complainin'," said the maid. "And now we'll have to send him something back. What would you recommend?"

They considered many gifts appropriate for a sailor – sou'-westers, Bible-markers, woollen comforters, and paper-knives, scarf-pins, gloves, and ties. Bud was sure that nothing would delight him like a book about a desert island, but Kate said no, a pipe was just the very ticket – a wooden pipe with silver mountings; the very one to suit was in the window of Mrs Wright's Italian warehouse.

"What's an Italian warehouse?" asked the child

"You have me there!" said Kate, "unless, maybe her husband was Italian before he went and died on her. 'Italian Warehouse' is the only thing that's, on her sign. She sells a thing for almost any price you like to offer, because the Bible says it's not the thing at all to argy-bargy."

"*I* know," said Bud; "It's what we call running a business on – on – on philanthropic principles. I'd love to see a body do it. I'll run out and buy the pipe from Mrs Wright, Kate."

She departed on her errand down the town, at the other side of the church; and the hours of the forenoon passed, and dinner-time was almost come, and still there was no sign of her returning. Kate would have lost her patience and gone to seek for her, but found so much to interest at the window that she quite forgot her messenger. Something out of the ordinary was happening on the other side of the church. Wanton Wully knew what it was, but of course he was not telling, for he was out as public crier, rousing the town with his hand-bell, and shouting "Notice!" with an air that promised some tremendous tidings; but beyond mysterious words like "bed-rock prices," which he mumbled from a paper in his hand, there was nothing to show this proclamation differed from the common ones regarding herring at the quay or a sale of delf down-by at John Turner's corner. "What are ye crying?" they asked him, but being a man with the belief that he had a voice as clear as a concert-singer, he would not condescend to tell them. Only when some one looked across his shoulder and read the paper for himself was it found that a sale described as "Revolutionary" was taking place at the Italian warehouse. Half the town at once went to see what the decent body was up to. Kate saw them hurrying down, and when they came back they were laughing. "What's the ploy?" she asked a passer-by.

"A sale at the Pilgrim weedow's," she was told. "She's put past her Spurgeon's Sermons and got a book about business, and she's learnin' the way to keep an Italian warehoose in Scotch."

Kate would have been down the town at once to see this marvel for herself, but her pot was on the boil, and here was the mistress coming down the stair, crying, "Lennox, Lennox!" The maid's heart sank. She had forgotten Lennox, and how could she explain her absence to a lady so particular? But for the moment she was spared the explanation, for the bark of Footles filled the street and Mr Dyce came into the lobby, laughing.

"You're very joco!" said his sister, helping him off with his coat. "What are you laughing at?"

"The drollest thing imaginable," said he. "I have just left Captain Consequence in a terrible rage about a letter that a boy has brought to him from Mrs Wright. He's one of the folk that boast of paying as they go but never make a start. It seems he's as much in debt to her as to most of the other merchants in the place, but wasn't losing any sleep about it, for she's such a softy. This letter has given him a start. He showed it to me, with the notion that it was a libel or a threat that might be actionable, but I assured him I couldn't have written one more to the point myself. It said that unless he paid at once, something would be apt to happen that would create him the utmost astonishment."

"Mercy on us! That's not very like the widow: she must be getting desperate."

"It was the wording of the thing amused me," said Mr Dyce, walking into the parlour, still chuckling – "'something will be apt to happen that will create you the utmost astonishment' – it suggests such awful possibilities. And it's going to serve its purpose too, for the Captain's off to pay her, sure it means a scandal."

Kate took the chance to rush round the kirk in search of her messenger. "This way for the big bargains!" cried some lads coming back from the Italian warehouse, or, "Hey! ye've missed a step" – which shows how funny we can be in the smallest burgh towns; but Kate said nothing, only "trash!" to herself in indignation, and tried by holding in her breath to keep from getting red.

The shop of the Pilgrim widow suffered from its signboard, that was "far too big for its job, like the sweep that stuck in my granny's chimney," as Mr Dyce said. Once the sign had been P. & A.'s, but P. & A.'s good lady tired of hearing her husband nick named the Italian, and it went back to the painter, who partly paid with it a debt to the Pilgrim widow, who long singe rued her acquisition. She felt in her soul it was a worldly vanity – that a signboard less obtrusive on the public eye would more befit herself and her two meek little windows, where fly-papers fancy goods, sweetmeats, cigarettes, country eggs, and cordial invitations to the Pilgrims Mission Bethel every Friday (*D. V.*), eight o'clock, kept each other incongruous and dusty company. A decent pious widow, but ah! so wanting any saving sense of guile. The Pilgrim Mission was the thing she really lived for, and her shop was the Cross she bore. But today it was scarcely recognisable: the windows had been swept of their stale contents, and one was filled with piles of rosy apples, the other with nuts that poured in a tempting cataract from a cask upset with an air of reckless prodigality. A large hand-lettered bill was in each window; one said –

HALLOWE'EN! ARISE AND SHINE!

and the other –

DO IT NOW!

what was to be done being left to the imagination. All forenoon there had been a steady flow of customers, who came out of the shop with more than nuts or apples, greatly amazed at the change in the Pilgrim widow, who was cracking up her goods like any common sinner. Behind the railed and curtained box in which she was supposed to keep her books and pray for the whole community, there seemed to be some secret stimulating influence, for when bad payers tried today to get a thing on credit, and she was on the point of yielding, she would dart into the box and out again as hard as steel, insisting that at every Revolutionary Sale the terms were cash. She was giving bargains, but at her own price, never at her customers, as it used to be. The Health Saline – extract of the finest fruit, Cooling, Refreshing, Invigorating, Tonic (though indeed it looked like an old friend from Rochelle with a dash of sugar and tartaric) – was down a ha'penny, to less than what it cost, according to another hand-done bill upon the counter. When they asked her how she could afford to sell the stuff below its cost, she seemed ashamed and startled, till she had a moment in behind the curtains, and then she told them it was all because of the large turn-over; she could not afford to sell the saline under cost if she did not sell it in tremendous quantities.

Did they want Ward's Matchless Polishing Paste? – alas! (after a dash behind the curtains) she was completely out of it. Of late it bad been in such great demand that she got tired of ordering it every other week wholesale. Yes, she was out of Ward's, but (again the curtained box) what about this wonderful line in calf-foot jelly, highly praised by the – by the connoisseurs? What were connoisseurs? A connoisseur (again on reference behind the curtains) was one of those wealthy men who could swallow anything.

"I'll tell ye what it is," said the tailor, "I see's at last! She's got a book in there; I've seen't before – 'The Way to Conduct a Retail Business' – and when she runs behind, it's to see what she should say to the customers. That's where she got the notions for her windows and the 'Do it Now!'"

But he was wrong – completely wrong, for when Kate came into the shop with "Have you seen Miss Lennox, Mrs Wright? I sent her here a message hours ago," Lennox herself came from the curtained box, saying, "Hello, Kate; saw you first! What can we do for you today?"

"My stars! my lady, you'll catch it!" said the maid. "They're waiting yonder on you for your dinner."

"I was just heading for home," said Bud, making for the door.

"My child! my child! my angel child!" cried the Pilgrim widow, going to kiss her, but Bud drew back.

"Not today, please; I'm miles too big for kissing today," said she, and marched solemnly out of the Italian warehouse.

"What in the world were you doing away so long?" asked Kate. "Were you carrying on at anything?"

"I was paying for Charles's pipe," said the child, returning the money she had got for its purchase. "That's the sweetest lady, Mrs Wright, but my! ain't she Baby Mine when it settles down to business? When I wanted to buy the pipe, she was so tickled she wanted me to have it for nothing, seeing I was Mr Dyce's niece. She said Uncle Dan was a man of God who saved her more than once from bankruptcy, and it was a pretty old pipe anyway, that had been in the window since the time she got changed and dropped brocaded dolmans. You'd think it made her ache to have folk come in her shop and spend money; I guess she was raised for use in a free soup-kitchen. I said I'd take the pipe for nothing if she'd throw in a little game with it. 'What game?' said she – oh, she's a nice lady! – and I said I was just dying to have a try at keeping a really really shop, and would show her Chicago way. *And you bet I did, Kate MacNeill!"*

She came in with the soup, but no question was put till her uncle asked the blessing, and then, before a spoon was lifted, Auntie Bell said, "Lassie, lassie, where in the world have you been?"

"Keeping shop for Mrs Wright," said Bud.

"Tcht! tcht! you're beyond redemption," cried her aunt. "A child like you keeping shop!"

"A bonny pair of shopkeepers, the widow and you! Which of you counted the change?" said Uncle Dan. "Tell us all about it."

"Well, I had the loveliest time," said Bud. "It would take till tea-time to tell just 'zactly what a lovely day it was, but I'll hurry up and make it a front scene. What you said, Uncle Dan, about her running a shop on phil – on philanthropic principles made me keen to see her doing it, and I went down a message for Kate, and offered to help. She 'lowed herself she wasn't the best there was in the land at keeping shop, and didn't seem to make much money at it, but said thank the Lord she had the priceless boon of health. I was the first customer she'd set eyes on all the morning, 'cept a man that wanted change for half-a-crown and hadn't the half-crown with him, but said he'd pay it when he didn't see her again, and she said she felt sure that trade was going to take a turn. I said I thought it would turn quicker if – if – if she gave it a push herself, and she said she dared say there was something in it, and hoped I was in the fold. I said I was, sure, and at that she cried out 'Hallelujah!' Every other way she was a perfectly perfect lady; she made goo-goo eyes at me, and skipped round doing anything I told her. First she cleared all the old truck out of the windows, and filled them up with nuts and apples for Hallowe'en, till they looked the way windows never looked in Scotland in all creation before, I s'pose. 'They'll think it kind of daft,' says she, scared-like, 'they're not like any other windows in the place.' 'Of course not,' I said, 'and that's the very thing to jar the eye of the passer-by.' Jim Molyneux said a shop-window was like a play-bill, it wanted a star line – a feature – a whoop. Then I tried to think of the 'cute things shopkeepers print in Chicago, but couldn't remember any 'cepting 'Pants two dollars a leg, seats free,' but the widow said she didn't sell pants. Then I thought of some natty little cards I'd seen that said 'Arise and Shine!' and 'Do it Now!' so I got her to print these words good and big, and put them in the window. She wanted to know what they meant, but I said I couldn't tell from Adam, but they would make the people wonder, and come in the shop to find out, and then it would be up

to her to sell them something and pry the money out of them before
they baulked. Oh, Auntie, how I go on!" and here Bud stopped
almost breathless and a little ashamed.

"Go on! go on!" cried Ailie.

"Well, I got behind a curtain into a little box-office, where the
widow kept a cash-book awfully doggy-eared, and a pile of printed
sermons, and heaps of tracts about doing to others as you should be
done by, and giving to the poor and lending to the Lord. She read
bits of them to me, and said she sometimes wondered if Captain
Brodie was too poor to pay for eighteen months' tobacco, but she
didn't like to press him, seeing he had been in India and fought his
country's battles. She said she felt she must write him again for her
money, but couldn't think of what to say that would be Christian
and polite and gentle, but still make him see she wanted the money
pretty bad. I said I would tell her what to say that would suit just
fine, and I dictated it –"

"I saw the letter," said Uncle Dan, twinkling through his glasses.
"It was a work of genius – go on! go on!"

"Then folk began to come in for nuts and apples, and asked what
'Arise and Shine' and 'Do it Now' meant. She said they were
messages from the angel of the Lord – meaning me, I s'pose –
though, goodness knows, I'm not much of an angel, am I, Auntie
Bell? Then the folk would fade away, looking a bit rattled, and come
back in a while and ask the price of things. She'd say she wasn't sure,
but she thought about a shilling, or maybe ninepence seeing they
had a young family, and then they'd want the stuff on credit, and
she'd yammer away to them till I got wild. When they were gone I
had a good heart-to-heart talk with her, and said phil – philanthropic
principles were a great mistake in a small Italian warehouse, and that
she ought to give the customers a chance of doing unto others as they
would be done by. She made more goo-goo eyes at me, and said I
was a caution, sure enough, and perhaps I was right, for she had
never looked at it that way before. After that she spunked up
wonderful. I got her to send Mr Wanton through the town with his
bell, saying there was everything you wanted at Mrs Wright's at bed-
rock prices; and when people came in after that and wanted to get
things for nothing, or next to it, she'd pop into the box where I lay
low, and ask me what she was to say next, and then skip out to them
as sharp as a tack and show they needn't try to toy with her. She says
she made more money today by my playing shop Chicago-way than
she'd make in a week her own way. Why, I'm talking, and talking,
and talking, and my soup's stone-cold!"

"So's mine," said Uncle Dan, with a start.

"And mine!" said Auntie Ailie, with a smile.

"And mine too, I declare!" cried Miss Bell, with a laugh they all joined in, till Footles raised his voice protesting.

CHAPTER XVIII

YES, that was one bright day in the dismal season, the day she tutored the Pilgrim widow in the newer commerce. There was a happy night to follow soon, and it is my grief that my pen cannot grasp the spirit of it, so that reading you would laugh with her and whiles be eerie. 'Tis true, there was little in the thing itself, as in most that at the age of twelve impress us for all our lives, but it met in some degree the expectations that her father's tales of Scotland had sent home with her. Hitherto all had been natural and wellnigh commonplace that she had experienced, all except the folk so queer and kind and comical in a different way from those in Chicago, the sounds she could hear as she lay in her attic bed – the wind-call, and the honk of geese, and the feeling of an island hopelessly remote from the new bright world that best she knew – remote and lost, a speck on the sea far, far from great America. The last things vaguely troubled her. For she was child enough as yet to shiver at things not touched by daylight nor seemingly made plain by the commonsense of man. She could laugh at the ghosts that curdled the blood of the maid of Colonsay; and yet at times, by an effort of the will, she could feel all Kate's terror at some manifestation no more alarming than the cheep of mice or a death-watch ticking in a corner cupboard. These were but crude and vulgar fears, self-encouraged little actress terrors. It took more than the hint of ghost or the menace of the ticking insect in the wood to wake in her the feeling of worlds unrealised, encompassing, that she could get from casual verses in her Auntie Ailie's book of Scottish ballads, or find overwhelm her of a sudden on looking from her window into the garden bare and pallid below the moon.

This night there should be moon according to the penny almanac, and Wanton Wully lit no lamps, but went home for a good sleep to himself, as his saying went, and left the burgh to such illumination as should come to it by the caprice of the clouds. It lay, the little place, for most of the night in darkness: a mirk so measureless deep, when the shops were shut, that the red-lit skylight windows at the upper end of the town seemed by some miracle to lift themselves and soar into the heavens – square, monstrous flitting stars to the vision of Bud, as she stood with Auntie Ailie at the door watching for Uncle Dan's return from his office. To bring the soaring windows back to their natural situation, she had to stand a little way inside the lobby and establish their customary place against the darkness by the lintel of the door.

From the other side of the church came a sound of dull monotonous drumming – no cheerful rhythmic beat like the drumming of John Taggart, but a mournful thumping, fitful in flaws of the bland night wind.

"What's that, Auntie?" she asked.

"The guizards," said Miss Ailie, looking down upon her in the lobby light with a smile she could not see. "Did you never hear of the guizards, Bud?"

Bud had never heard of the guizards; that was one thing, surely, her father had forgotten. She had heard of Hallowe'en, she said, when further questioned. Wasn't it the night for ducking into tubs for apples? The Pilgrim widow had told her Hallowe'en was coming, and it was for Hallowe'en she had sold so many nuts and apples; but the widow said she felt ashamed to do it, for Hallowe'en was not approved of by the Mission, being idolatrous and gay. "Is it very gay?" asked Bud anxiously.

" So I used to think it," said her aunt.

"Then I s'pose it must be wicked," said the child regretfully. "I'd have expected you'd have Hallowe'en night here in the house if it hadn't been very bad. That widow did me a lot of good, showing me what a heap of happy things are full of sin. She knew them all! I s'pose she got them in the tracts. Yes, she did me a lot of good; I – I almost wish I hadn't met that widow."

"Do you feel wicked when you're gay?" asked Miss Ailie.

"Mercy on us! not a mite!" said Bud. "I feel plumb full of goodness when I'm gay; but that's my youth and innocence. The widow says it is, and I guess what she says goes."

"Still, do you know, my dear, I'd risk a little gaiety now and then," said Auntie Ailie. "Who knows? The widow, though a worthy lady, is what in Scotland we call an auld wife, and it's generally admitted that auld wives of either sex have no monopoly of wisdom. If you're wanting pious guidance, Bud, I don't know where you'll get it better than from Auntie Bell; and she fairly dotes on Hallowe'en and the guizards. By-and-by you'll see the guizards, and – and – well, just wait and we'll find what else is to be seen. I do wish your Uncle Dan would hurry."

The street was quite deserted, but did not show its vacancy until the clouds for a moment drifted off the moon that rolled behind the steeple. Then the long grey stretch of tenements came out unreal and pale on the other side of the street, their eaves and chimneys throwing inky shadows, their red-lit windows growing of a sudden wan. Over them hung the ponderous kirk, the master shadow, and all – the white-harled walls, the orange windows, the glittering cold and empty street – seemed like the vision of a dream. Then the clouds wrapped up the moon again, and the black was the black of Erebus. But as it fell, the dull drums seemed to come nearer, and from the head of the street, the windy corner where Uncle Dan had his office, small moons came, purple and golden, fantastically carved. They ran from house to house, and grouped in galaxies, or singly fell apart, swinging and giddy orbs. For a moment Bud looked at them bewildered, then gave a happy scream.

"The lanterns! the lanterns! look at the lanterns, Auntie. Is that Hallowe'en?"

"That's part of it, at least," said her Aunt. "These are the guizards with their turnip lanterns; they're going round the houses singing; by-and-by we'll hear them."

"My! I wish to goodness I had a lantern like that. To swing a lantern like that 'd feel like being a lighthouse or the statue of Liberty at New York. I'd rather have a turnip lantern than a raft of dolls."

"Did you never have one?"

"No," said Bud sorrowfully. "You have no idea what a poor mean place Chicago is; not a thing but common electric light!" and Miss Ailie smiled gleefully to herself again like one possessed of a lovely secret. "I wish that brother of mine would come quickly," she said, and at the moment he came out of the darkness to them with a comical look of embarrassment in his face and in his hand an unlighted turnip lantern!

"Here, Bud," said he, "take this, quickly, before some silly body sees me with it and thinks it's for myself. I have the name, I know, of being daft enough already, and if it gets about the country that Daniel Dyce was going round at Hallowe'en with a turnip lantern, they would think he had lost his head in a double sense and it would be very bad for business."

"Uncle!" cried the child in ecstasy, "you're the loveliest, sweetest man in the whole wide world."

"I daresay," said he. "I have been much admired when I was younger. But in this case don't blame me. I wash my hands of the responsibility. I got my orders for that thing from your Auntie Bell."

"My! ain't it cute? Did you make it?" asked Bud, surveying the rudely carved exterior with delight, and her uncle, laughing, put on his glasses to look at it himself.

"No," said he, "though I've made a few of them in my time. All that's needed is a knife or a mussel-shell, and a dose of Gregory's Mixture in the morning."

"What's the Gregory's Mixture for?"

"In making a turnip lantern you eat the whole inside of it," said Mr Dyce. "Perhaps I might have made this one myself if it wasn't that I know I would hate to see the inside wasted, and still I have mind of the Gregory. I bought the lantern from a boy at the head of the street who was looking very gash and ill, and seemed suspiciously glad to get quit of it I'm thinking that his Gregory's nearly due."

Bud hardly listened – she was so taken up with her gift. She pounced at the handle of the kitchen door and found it snibbed within. "Kate! Kate!" she cried, "let me in to light my lantern."

Kate was to be heard moving within, and there was a curious sound of giggling, but no answer.

"Open the door, quick, quick!" cried Bud again; and this time Auntie Bell, inside, said, "Yes, open, Kate, I think we're ready."

The door of the kitchen opened, and before the eyes of the child was a spectacle the more amazing and delightful since all day they had taken pains to keep the preparations secret. A dozen children, who had been smuggled in by the back-door in the close, were seated round a tub of water with floating apples, and they were waiting her presence to begin their fun.

Oh, how happy was that hour! But not just then came the thrill of which I'm thinking. It was not the laughter and the ducking in the tub, the discoveries of rings and buttons, thimbles, and scuddy little dolls and silver pieces hidden in the mound of champed potatoes Kate had cooked; nor the supper that followed, nor the mating of nuts on the fire-ribs that gave the eerie flavour of old time and the book of ballads. She liked them all; her transport surely was completed when the guizards entered black-faced, garmented as for a masque, each thumping a sheepskin stretched on a barrel-hoop – the thing we call a dallan. She had never discovered before what a soul of gaiety was in Auntie Bell, demure so generally, practising sobriety, it might seem, as if she realised her daffing days were over and it was time for her to remember all her years. Tonight Miss Bell outdid even Ailie in her merriment, led the games in the spacious kitchen, and said such droll things, and kept the company in such a breeze that Ailie cried at last, "I think, Bell, that you're fey!"

"Indeed, and I daresay you're right," admitted Bell, sinking in a chair exhausted. "At my time of life it's daft; I have not laughed so much since I was at Barbara Mushet's seminary."

Not these things, but the half-hour after, was what made the evening memorable for the child. Nothing would satisfy her but that she should light her lantern and convoy the other children home, so Kate went with her, and the happy band went through the street, each dropping off at her own house front till the last was gone, and then Bud and the maid turned back.

But Kate had a project in her mind that had been there all night since she had burned two nuts for herself and Charles in the kitchen fire, and found them willing to flame quite snug together. That so far, was satisfactory, but she wanted more assurance of the final triumph of her love. There was, it seemed, a skilful woman up the lane who knew spells and magic, read tea-cups and the cards, and could unravel dreams. Notably was she good at Hallowe'en devices, and Bud must come and see her, for it would not take a minute.

They found their way by the light of the lantern to the spaewife's door, and to a poor confidant of fate and fortune surely, since she had not found them kinder to herself, for she dwelt in a hovel where foolish servant-girls came at night with laughter and fears to discover what the future held for them. Bud, standing on the floor in the circle of light from her own lantern, watched the woman drop the white of an egg in a glass of water. In the clot of the albumen, which formed some wavering vague figures, she peered and found, she said, the masts of ships and a crowded harbour, and that meant a sailor husband.

"Was I not sure of it!" cried Kate, triumphant; but that was not the end of the ceremony, for she was bidden to sip a little from the glass, without swallowing, and go dumb into the night till she heard the Christian name of a man, and *that* was the name of the sailor husband. Kate sipped from the glass of destiny, and passed with Bud into the darkness of the lane. It was then there came to the child the delicious wild eeriness that she was beginning now to coax to her spirit whenever she could, and feed her fancies on. The light of the lantern only wanly illumined the lane they hurried through; so plain and grey and ancient and dead looked the houses pressing on either hand with windows shuttered, that it seemed to Bud she had come by magic on a shell as empty of life as the armour in the castle hall.

115

By-and-by the servant, speechless, stopped at a corner listening. No sound of human life for a moment, but then a murmur of voices up the town, to which on an impulse she started running with Lennox at her heels, less quickly since the light of her lantern must be nursed from the wind. Bud fell behind in the race for the voice of fate; the sound of the footsteps before her died away in the distance, and her light went out, and there she stood alone for the first time in the dark of Scotland – Scotland where witches still wrought spells! A terror that was sweet to think of in the morning, whose memory she cherished all her days, seized on her, and she knew that all the ballad book was true! One cry she gave, that sounded shrilly up the street – it was the name of Charles, and Kate, hearing it, gulped and came back.

"I guessed that would fetch you," said Bud, panting. "I was so scared I had to say it, though I s'pose it means I've lost him for a husband."

"My stars! you are the clever one! said the grateful maid.

CHAPTER XIX

SPRING came, and its quickening; forest and shrub and flower felt the new sap rise; she grew in the garden then, the child – in that old Scottish garden, sheltered lownly in the neuk of the burgh walls. It must have been because the Dyces loved so much their garden, and spent so many hours there, that they were so sanely merry, nor let too often or too long the Scots forebodings quell their spirits, but got lessons of hope from the circling of the seasons, that give us beauty and decay in an unvarying alternation.

"It is the time," used Ailie to say of the spring, "when a delicious feeling steals over you of wanting to sit down and watch other people work."

"I'll need to have the lawn-mower sharpened; it may be needed at any moment by the neighbours," said her brother Dan.

They watched upspring the green spears of the daffodils, that by-and-by should bear their flags of gold.

And Wanton Wully, when he was not bell-ringing or cleaning the streets, or lounging on the quay to keep tally of ships that never came, being at ports more propinque to the highways of the world, where folks are making fortunes and losing much innocent diversion, wrought – as he would call it – in the Dyce's garden. Not a great gardener, admittedly, for to be great in versatility is of necessity to miss perfection in anything, so that the lowest wages in the markets of the world are for the handy man. But being handy is its own reward, carrying with it the soothing sense of self-sufficiency, so we need not vex ourselves for Wully. As he said himself, he "did the turn" for plain unornamental gardening, though in truth he seemed to think he did it best when sitting on his barrow trams, smoking a thoughtful pipe, and watching the glad spring hours go by at a cost of sixpence each to the lawyer who employed him.

Bud often joined him on the trams, and gravely listened to him, thinking that a man who did so many different and interesting things in a day was wise and gifted beyond ordinary. In the old and abler years he had been a soldier, and, nursing flowers nowadays, his mind would oft incongruously dwell on scenes remote and terribly different, where he had delved in foreign marl for the burial of fallen comrades.

"Tell me Inkermann again, Mr Wanton," Bud would say, "and I'll shoo off the birds from the bulb-flowers."

"I'll do that, my dearie!" he would answer, filling another pipe, and glad of an excuse to rest from the gentle toil of raking beds and chasing the birds that nipped the tips from peeping tulip leaves. "To the mischief with them birds! the garden's fair polluted wi' them! God knows what's the use o' them except for chirping, chirping – Tchoo! off wi' ye at once or I'll be after ye! – Ay, ay, Inkermann. It was a gey long day, I'm tellin' ye, from a quarter past six till half-past four; slaughter, slaughter a' the time: me wi' an awfu' hacked heel, and no' a bit o' anything in my stomach. A nesty saft day, wi' a smirr o' rain. We were as black as – as black as – as –"

"As black as the Earl o' Hell's waistcoat," Bud prompted him. "Go on! I mind the very words."

"I only said that the once, when I lost the place," said Wully, shocked at her glibness in the uptake. "And it's not a thing for the like o' you to say at all; it's only the word o' a rowdy sodger."

"Well, ain't I the limb! I'll not say it again," promised the child; "You needn't look as solemn's the Last Trump; go on, go on!"

"As black as a ton o' coal, wi' the creesh o' the cartridges and the poother; it was the Minie gun, ye ken. And the Rooshians would be just ower there between the midden and the cold frame, and we would be coming down on them – it micht be ower the sclates o' Rodger's hoose yonder. We were in the Heavy Diveesion, and I kill't my first man that I kent o' about where the yellow crocus is. Puir sowl! I had nae ill-will to the man, I'll guarantee ye that! but we were baith unloaded when we met each other, and it had to be him or me."

He paused and firmed his mouth until the lips were lost among the puckers gathered round them, a curious glint in his eyes.

"Go on!" cried Bud, sucking in her breath with a horrid expectation; "Ye gie'd him – ye gie'd him –"

"I gie'd him – I tell's ye what I gie'd him before. Will I need to say't again?"

"Yes," said Bud, "for that's your top note."

"I gie'd him – I gie'd him the – the BAGGONET!" cried the gardener, with a sudden, frightful, furious flinging of the arms, and then – oh, silly Wully Oliver! – began to weep, or at least to show a tear. For Bud had taught him to think of all that lay beyond that furious thrust of the bayonet – the bright brave life extinguished, the mother rendered childless, or the children fatherless, in some Russian home.

Bell, the thrifty woman, looking from the scullery window, and seeing time sadly wasted at twelve bawbees the hour, would drop the shawl she was making, and come out and send the child in to her lessons, but still the orra gardener did not hurry to his task, for he knew the way to keep Miss Dyce in an idle crack although she would not sit on his barrow trams.

"A wonderfu' wean that!" would be his opening. "A perfect caution! I can see a difference on her every day; she grows like a willow withy, and she's losin' yon awfu' Yankee awcent she had about her when she came at first. She can speak as bonny English noo as you or me when she puts her mind to't."

"I'm afraid it would not be very difficult for her to do that, Willy," said Miss Bell. "She could always speak in any way she wanted, and indeed the first time that we heard her she was just yoursel' on a New Year's morning, even to the hiccough. I hope you'll keep a watch on what you say to her; the bairn picks up the things she hears so fast, and she's so innocent, that it's hardly canny to let her listen much to the talk of a man that's been a soldier – not that I blame the soldiers, Willy, bless them all for Scotland, young or old!"

"Not a word out of place from me, Miss Dyce," would he cry, emphatic. "Only once I lost the place and slippit out a hell, and could have bit my tongue out for it. We heard, ye ken, a lot o' hell, out yonder roond aboot Sevastapol: it wasna Mr Meikle's Sunday-school. But ye needna fear that Wully Oliver would learn ill language to a lady like the wee one. Whatever I am that's silly when the dram is in, I hope I'm aye the perfect gentleman."

"Indeed I never doubted it," said Miss Bell. "But you know yourself we're anxious that she should be all that's gentle, nice, and clean. When you're done raking this bed – dear me! I'm keeping you from getting at it – it'll be time for you to go home for dinner. Take a bundle of rhubarb for the mistress."

"Thanky, thanky, me'm," said Wanton Wully, "but to tell the truth we're kind o' tired o' rhubarb; I'm getting it by the stone from every bit o' grun' I'm labourin' in. I wish folk were so rife wi' plooms or strawberries."

Bell smiled. "It's the herb of kindness," said she. "There's aye a reason for everything in nature, and rhubarb's meant to keep our generosity in practice."

And there she would be – the foolish woman! keeping him at the crack, the very thing he wanted, till Mr Dyce himself, maybe, seeing his silver hours mishandled, would come to send his sister in, and see that his gardener earned at least a little of his wages.

"A terrible man for the ladies, William! You must have had a taking way with you when you were in the Army," was all that the lawyer had to say. "There was some talk about doing a little to the garden, but, hoots man! don't let it spoil your smoke!"

It was then you would see Wanton Wully busy.

Where would Bud be then? At her lessons? no, no, you may be sure of it, but in with Kate of Colonsay giving the maid the bloody tale of Inkermann. It was a far finer and more moving story as it came from Bud than ever it was on the lips of Wanton Wully. From him she only got the fling of the arms that drove the bayonet home, the lips pursed up, as if they were gathered by a string, the fire of the moment, and the broad Scots tongue he spoke in. To what he gave she added fancy and the drama.

"– as black as a ton o' coal wi' the creesh o' the cartridges . . . either him or me . . . I gie'd him . . . I gie'd him . . . I shut my eyes, and said, 'O God, Thy pardon!' and gie'd him the BAGGONET!"

Kate's apron at that would fly up to cover her eyes, for she saw before her all the bloody spectacle. "I'm that glad," she would say, "that my lad's a sailor. I couldna sleep one iota at night thinkin' of their baggonets if he was a man-o'-war. And that puts me in mind, my dear, it's more than a week since we sent the chap a letter. Have you time the now to sit and write a scrape to Hamburg on the Elbow – imports iron ore?"

And Bud had time, and sit she would and write a lovely letter to

Charles Maclean of Oronsay. She told him that her heart was sore, but she must confess that she had one time plighted her troth to a Russian army officer, who died, alas! on the bloody field. His last words, as his life-blood slowly ebbed away, were –

"What *would* be the last words of a Russian officer who loved you?" asked Bud, biting her pen in her perplexity.

"Toots! anything – 'my best respects to Kate'," said the maid, who had learned by this time that the letters Charles liked the most were the ones where Bud most freely used imagination.

"I don't believe it would," said Bud. "It 'd sound far too calm for a man that's busy dying;" but she put it down all the same, feeling it was only fair that Kate should have some say in the letters written in her name.

That was the day they gave him a hint that a captain was wanted on the yacht of Lady Anne.

And still Kate's education made some progress, as you may see from what she knew of Hamburg, though she was not yet the length of writing her own love-letters. She would sit at times at night for hours quite docile, knitting in the kitchen, listening to the reading of the child. A score of books had been tried on her by Aunt Ailie's counsel (for she was in the secret of this Lower Dyce Academy), but none there was that hit the pupil's fancy half so much as her own old favourite penny novelettes till they came one happy day to 'The Pickwick Papers'. Kate grew very fond of 'The Pickwick Papers'. The fun of them being in a language quite unknown in Colonsay, was almost all beyond her. But "that poor Mr Pickwick!" she would cry at each untoward accident; "oh, the poor wee man!" and the folk were as real to her as if she had known them all in Colonsay. If Dickens could have known the curious sentiments his wandering hero roused in this Highland servant mind, he would have greatly wondered.

While Bud was tutoring Kate that spring, Miss Bell was thinking to take up the training of Bud herself in wiselike housekeeping. The child grew as fast in her mind as in her body: each day she seemed to drift farther away from the hearth and into the world from which her auntie would preserve her – into the world whose doors books widely opened, Auntie Ailie's magic key of sympathy, and the genius of herself. So Bell determined there and then to coax her into the gentle arts of domesticity that ever had had a fascination for herself. She went about it oh, so cunningly! letting Bud play at the making of beds and the dusting of the stair-rails and the parlour beltings – the curly-wurly places, as she called them, full of quirks and holes and corners that the unelect like Kate of Colonsay will always treat perfunctorily in a general wipe that only drives the dirt the farther in. Bud missed not the tiniest corner nor the deepest nook: whatever she did, she did fastidiously, much to the joy of her aunt, who was sure it was a sign she was meant by the Lord for a proper housewife. But the child soon tired of making beds and dusting, as she did of white-seam sewing; and when Bell deplored this falling off, Ailie said: "You cannot expect everybody to have the same gifts as yourself. Now that she has proved she's fit to clean a railing properly, she's not so much to blame if she loses interest in it. The child's a genius, Bell, and to a person of her temperament the thing that's easily done is apt to be contemptuous: the glory's in the triumph over difficulties, in getting on – getting on – getting on," and Ailie's face grew warm with some internal fire.

At that speech Bell was silent. She thought it just another of Ailie's haiverings; but Mr Dyce, who heard, suddenly became grave.

"Do you think it's genius or precocity?" he asked.

"They're very much the same thing," said Ailie. "If I could be the child I was; if I could just remember –" She stopped herself and smiled. "What vanity!" said she; "what conceit! If I could be the child I was, I dare say I would be pretty commonplace after all, and still have the same old draigled pinnies; but I have a notion that Lennox was never meant to make beds, dust stair-railings, or sit in a parlour listening, demure, to gossip about the village pump and Sacrament Sunday bonnets. To do these things is no discredit to the women who are meant to do them, and who do them well; but we cannot all be patient Marthas. I know, because I've honestly tried my best myself."

"When you say that, you're laughing at me, I fear," said Bell, a little blamefully.

"I wasn't thinking of you," said her sister, vexed. "And if I was, and had been laughing, I would be laughing at the very things I love; it's only the other things that make me solemn. Your way, Bell, was always clear before you – there you were the lucky woman; with genius, as we have it in the child, the way's perplexed and full of dangers."

"Is she to be let drift her own way?"

"We got her ten years too late to prevent it," said Miss Ailie firmly, and looked at her brother Dan for some assistance. He had Footles on his lap, stroking his tousy back, and he listened with twinkling eyes to the argument, humming the air of the day, that happened to be "Robin Tamson's Smiddy, O!"

121

"You're both right and you're both wrong, as Mr Cleland used to say if he was taking a dram with folk that had an argument," said the lawyer. "But I'm not so clever as Colin Cleland, for I can't ring the bell and order in the *media sententia*. This I'll say, that, to my mind, the child is lucky if she's something short of genius. If I had had a son, my prayer would always be that he should be off and on about the ordinary. It's lonely on the mountaintop, and genius generally seems to go with a poor stomach or a bad lung, and pays an awful price for every ecstasy!"

"Shakespeare!" suggested Miss Ailie.

"And Robert Burns!" cried Bell. "Except for the lass and the glass and the ran-dan – Poor misguided laddie! he was like the folk he lived among. And there was Walter Scott, the best and noblest man God ever gave to Scotland, he was never on the mountain-top except it was to bring a lot of people with him there."

Mr Dyce cleaned his glasses and chuckled. "H'm," said he, "I admit there are exceptions. But please pass me my slippers, Bell: I fall back on Colin Cleland – you're both right and you're both wrong."

Miss Bell was so put about at this that she went at once to the kitchen to start her niece on a course of cookery.

CHAPTER XX

"KATERIN!" she said, coming into the kitchen with a handful of paper cuttings, and, hearing her, the maid's face blenched.

"I declare I never broke an article the day!" she cried protestingly, well accustomed to that formal address when there had been an accident among her crockery.

"I wasn't charging you," said her mistress. "Dear me! It must be an awful thing a guilty conscience! I was thinking to give you – and maybe Lennox, if she would not mind – a lesson or two in cookery. It's a needful thing in a house with anything of a family. You know what men are!"

"Fine that!" said Kate. "They're always thinking what they'll put in their intervals, the greedy deevils! – beg your pardon, but it's not a swear in the Gaelic."

"There's only one Devil in any language, Kate," said Miss Bell. "'How art thou fallen from Heaven, O Lucifer, son of the morning!'

And I am glad to think he is oftener on our foolish tongues than in our hearts. I have always been going to give you a cookery-book –"

"A cookery-book!" cried the maid. "Many a time I saw one out in Colonsay: for the minister's wife had one they called Meg Dods, that was borrowed for every wedding. But it was never much use to us, for it started everything with 'Take a clean dish,' or 'Mince a remains of chicken,' and neither of them was very handy out in the isle of Colonsay."

Miss Bell laid out her cuttings on the dresser – a mighty pile of recipes for soups and stews, puddings and cakes, sweetmeats, and cordial wines that could be made deliciously from elder and mulberry, if hereabouts we had such fruits to make them with. She had been gathering these scraps for many years, for the household column was her favourite part of the paper after she was done with the bits that showed how Scotsmen up in London were at the head of everything, or did some doughty deed on the field of war. She hoarded her cuttings as a miser hoards his notes, but never could find the rich sultana cake that took nine eggs, when it was wanted, but only the plain one costing about one-and-six. Sometimes Ailie would, in mischief, offer to look through the packet for recipes rich and rare that had been mentioned; they were certainly there (for Bell had read them gloatingly aloud when she cut them out) but Bell would never let her do it, always saying, "Tuts! never mind; Dan likes this one better, and the other may be very nice in print but it's too rich to be wholesome, and it costs a bonny penny. You can read in the papers any day there's nothing better for the health than simple dieting." So it was that Mr Dyce had some monotony in his meals, but luckily was a man who never minded that, liking simple old friends best in his bill-of-fare as in his boots and coats and personal acquaintances. Sometimes he would quiz her about her favourite literature, pretending a gourmet's interest for her first attempt at something beyond the ordinary, but never relished any the less her unvarying famous kale and simple entremets, keeping his highest praise for her remarkable breakfasts. "I don't know whether you're improving or whether I am getting used to it," he would say, "but that's fish! if you please, Miss Bell."

"Try another scone, Dan," she would urge, to hide the confusion that his praise created. "I'm sure you're hungry."

"No, not hungry," would he reply, "but, thank Providence, I'm greedy – pass the plate."

Bell was busy at her cookery lesson, making her cuttings fill the part of the book that was still to buy, doing all she could to make

Bud see how noble was a proper crimpy paste, though her lesson was cunningly designed to look like one for Kate alone. Her sleeves were rolled up, and the flour was flying, when a rat-tat came to the door. They looked up from their entrancing occupation, and there, in front, was the castle carriage!

Miss Bell made moan. "Mercy on us! That'll be Lady Anne, and Ailie out, and I cannot go to speak to anybody, for I'm such a ticket. Run to the door, dear, and take her into the parlour, and keep her there till I am ready. Don't forget to say 'My Lady,' – No, don't say 'My Lady,' for the Dyces are of old, and as good as their neighbours, but say 'Your Ladyship'; not too often, but only now and then, to let her see you know it."

Bud went to the door and let in Lady Anne, leading her composedly to the parlour.

"Aunt Ailie's out," she said, "and Aunt Bell is *such* a ticket. But she's coming in a minute, your – your – your –" Bud paused for a second, a little put about. "I forget which it was I was to say. It was either 'Your Ladyship' or 'My Lady'. You're not my lady, really, and you're not your own, hardly, seeing you're promised to Colonel George. Please tell me which is right, Lady Anne."

"Who told you it was Colonel George, my dear?" asked Lady Anne, sitting down on the proffered chair and putting her arms around the child.

"Oh, it's just the clash of the parish," said my little Scot who once was Yankee. "And everybody's so glad."

"Are they, indeed?" said Lady Anne, blushing in her pleasure. "That is exceedingly kind of them. I always thought our own people the nicest and kindest in the world."

"That's just it!" said Bud cheerfully. "Everybody everywhere is just what one is oneself – so Aunt Ailie says; and I s'pose it's because you're – Oh! I was going to say something about you, but I'll let you guess. What lovely weather! I hope your papa is well? And Mr Jones?"

"Thank you; papa is very well indeed," said Lady Anne. "And Mr Jones –" She hung upon the name with some dubiety.

"The coachman, you know," said Bud placidly. "He's a perfectly lovely man: so fat and smiley. He smiles so much his face is all in gathers. So kind to his horses too, and waves his whip at me every time he passes. Once he gave me a ride on the dickey: it was gorgeous. Do you often get a ride on the dickey, Lady Anne?"

"Never!" said Lady Anne, with a clever little sigh. "Many a time I have wished I could get one, but they always kept me inside the carriage. I don't seem to have had much luck all my life till – till – till lately."

"Did Mr Jones never take you on his knee and tell you the story of the Welsh giants?"

"No," said Lady Anne, solemnly shaking her head.

"Then you're too big now. What a pity! Seems to me there isn't such a much in being a big L Lady after all. I thought you'd have everything of the very best. You have no idea what funny ideas we had in America about dukes and lords and ladies in the old country. Why, I expected I'd be bound to hate them when I got here, because they'd be so proud and haughty and tyrannical. But I don't hate them one little bit; they don't do anybody any harm more'n if they were knockabout artistes. I suppose the Queen herself 'd not crowd a body off the sidewalk if you met her there. She'd be just as apt to say 'What ho! little girl. Pip! pip!' and smile, for Auntie Bell is always reading in the newspapers snappy little parts about the nice things the Royal family do, just the same as if they weren't royal a bit."

"Yes, I sometimes see those touching domestic incidents," said her ladyship. "You mean such things as the Prince helping the cripple boy to find his crutch? They make me almost cry."

"I wouldn't wet a lash, if I were you,' said Bud. "That's just the Press: like as not there's nothing behind it but the agent in advance."

"Agent in advance?" said Lady Anne, perplexed.

"Yes. He's bound to boom the show somehow: so Jim Molyneux said, and he knew most things, did Jim."

"You wicked Republican!" cried her ladyship, hugging the child the closer to her.

"I'm not a Republican," protested Bud. "I'm truly Scotch, same as father was, and Auntie Bell is – that's good enough for me. I'd just *love* to be a My Lady myself, it must be so nice and – and fairy. Why! it's about the only fairy thing left anywhere, I guess. There's nothing really to it; it's not being richer nor powerfuller nor more tyrannical than anybody else, but it's – it's – it's I dunno 'zactly what it is, but it's something – it – it's romantic, that's what it is, to be a King, or a Duke, or a My Lady. The fun of it is all inside you, like poetry. I hope, My Lady Anne, you 'preciate your privileges! You must 'preciate your privileges always, Auntie Bell says, and praise the Lord without ceasing, and have a thankful heart."

"I assure you I do," replied her ladyship.

"That's right," said Bud encouragingly. "It's simply splendid to be a really Lady with a big L without having to play it to yourself. I've been one as Winifred Wallace quite often; with Auntie Ailie's fur jacket and picture-hat on I'd sit and sit, and feel so composed and grand in the rocker, and let on it was Mr Jones's carriage, and bow sweetly to Footles who'd be a poor man passing to his work, and mighty proud to have me notice him. I'd be sort of haughty, but not 'bominable haughty, 'cause Auntie Bell says there's nothing beats a humble and a contrite heart. But then you see something would happen to spoil everything; Kate would laugh, or Auntie Bell would pop in and cry 'Mercy on me, child, playacting again! Put away that jacket instantly.' Then I'd know I was only letting on to be a really Lady; but with you it's different – all the time you're It. Auntie Bell says so, and she knows everything."

"It really looks as if she did," said her ladyship, "for I've called to see her today about a sailor."

"A sailor!" Bud exclaimed, with wild surmise.

"Yes. He wants to be captain of my yacht, and he refers me to Miss Dyce, for all the world as if he were a housemaid."

"I'm *so* glad," cried Bud. "For it was I who advised him to, and I'm – I'm the referee."

"You!"

"Yes; it was Kate's letter, and she – and we – and I said there was a rumour you wanted a captain, and he should apply, saying if you wanted to know just what a clean, good, brave sailor he was you should ask Kate MacNeill or Miss Dyce, and I'm the Miss Dyce this time, and you're – why, you're really visiting me!"

Lady Anne laughed. "Really, Miss Lennox," she said, "you're a wonderful diplomatist. I must get the Earl to put you in the service. I believe there's a pretty decent salary goes to our representative in the United States."

"But don't laugh at me, Lady Anne," pleaded Bud earnestly. "I'm dre'ffle set on having Charles off the cargo boats, where he's thrown away. You don't know how Kate loves him, and she hasn't seen him – not for years and years. You know yourself what it is to be so far away from anybody you love. He'd just fit your yacht like a glove – he's so educated, having been on the yachts and with the gentry round the world. He's got everything nice about him you'd look for in a sailor – big brown eyes so beautiful there's only Gaelic words I don't know, but that sound like somebody breaking glass, to describe how sweet they are. And the whitest teeth! When he walks, he walks so straight and hits the ground so hard you'd think he owned the land."

"It seems to me," said Lady Anne, "that you couldn't be more enthusiastic about your *protégé* if you loved him yourself."

"So I do," said Bud, with the utmost frankness. "But there's really nothing between us. He's meant for Kate. She's got heaps of beaux, but he's her steady. I gave him up to her for good on Hallowe'en, and she's so happy."

Bell had thrown off her cooking-apron and cleaned her hands, and ran up the stairs to see that her hair was trim, for though she loved a Lady for the sake of Scotland's history, she someway felt in the presence of Lady Anne the awe she had as a child for Barbara Mushet. That Ailie in such company should be, on the other hand, so composed, and sometimes even comical, was a marvel she never could get over. "I never feared the face of earl or man," she would say, "but I'm scared for a titled lady."

When she came down to the parlour the visitor was rising to go.

"Oh, Miss Dyce," said she, "I'm so glad to see you, though my visit this time's really to Miss Lennox. I wished to consult her about a captain for my little yacht."

"Miss Lennox!" exclaimed Miss Bell, shaking hands, and with a look of apprehension at her amazing niece.

"Yes," said Lady Anne; "she has recommended a man who seems in all respects quite suitable, if he happens to know a little about sailing; and I'm going to write to him to come and see me."

At that, I must confess it, Lennox for once forgot her manners and darted from the parlour to tell Kate the glorious news.

"Kate, you randy!" she cried, bursting into the kitchen –

"'I sent a letter to my love and by the way I dropped it, I dropped it, I dropped it; I dree – I dree – I dropped it'" –

"I've fixed it up for Charles; he's to be the captain." The servant danced on the floor in a speechless transport, and Bud danced too.

CHAPTER XXI

Too slow, far too slow, passed the lengthening days. Kate was bedded by nine to make them shorter by an hour or two, but what she took from the foot of the day she tacked to the head of it, as Paddy in the story eked his blanket, and she was up in the mornings long before Wanton Wully rang the six-hours' bell. The elder Dyces – saving Ailie, who knew all about it, hearing it from Bud in passionate whispers as they lay together in one bed in the brightening morns of May – might think summer's coming was what made the household glad, Kate sing like the laverock, and Lennox so happy and so good, but it was the thought of Charles. "Dear me! you've surely taken a desperate fancy for Prince Charlie songs," would Miss Bell remark to Bud and the maid of Colonsay. "Is there not another ditty in the ballant?" and they would glance at each other guiltily but never let on.

"Come o'er the stream, Charlie, dear Charlie, brave Charlie,
    Come o'er the stream, Charlie, and I'll be Maclean."

– Bud composed that one in a jiffy sitting one day at the kitchen window, and of all the noble Jacobite measures Kate liked it best, "it was so clever, and so desperate like the thing!" Such a daft disease is love! To the woman whose recollection of the mariner was got from olden Sabbath walks 'tween churches in the windy isle, among the mossy tombs, and to Bud, who had never seen him, but had made for herself a portrait blent of the youth so gay and gallant Kate described, and of George Sibley Purser, and of dark ear-ringed men of the sea that in "The Tempest" cry "Heigh, my hearts! cheerily, cheerily, cheerily, my hearts! yare, yare," the prospect of his presence was a giddy joy.

And after all the rascal came without warning, to be for a day and a night within sound of Kate's minstrelsy without her knowing it, for he lodged, an ardent but uncertain man, on the other side of the garden wall, little thinking himself the cause and object of these musical mornings. Bud found him out – that clever one! who was surely come from America to set all the Old World right – she found him at the launching of the *Wave*.

Lady Anne's yacht dozed like a hedgehog under leaves through the winter months below the beeches on what we call the hard – on the bank of the river under Jocka's house, where the water's brackish, and the launching of her was always of the nature of a festival, for the Earl's men were there, John Taggart's band, with "A life on the Ocean Wave" between each passage of the jar of old Tom Watson's home-made ale – not tipsy lads but jovial, and even the children of the schools, for it happened on a Saturday.

Bud and Footles went with each other and the rest of the bairns, unknown to their people, for in adventures such as these the child delighted, and was wisely never interdicted.

The man who directed the launch was a stranger in a foreign-looking soft slouch hat – Charles plain to identify in every feature, in the big brown searching eyes that only Gaelic could do justice to, and his walk so steeve and steady, his lovely beard, his tread on the hard as if he owned the land, his voice on the deck as if he were the master of the sea. She stood apart and watched him, fascinated, and could not leave even when the work was done and the band was home-returning, charming the road round the bay with "Peggy Baxter's Quickstep." He saw her lingering, smiled on her, and beckoned on her to cross the gangway that led to the yacht from the little jetty.

"Well, wee lady," said he, with one big hand on her head and another on the dog, "is this the first of my crew at a quay-head jump? Sign on at once and I'll make a sailor of you."

"Oh, please," said she, looking up in his face, too anxious to enter into his humour, "are you our Kate's Charles?"

"Kate!" said he, reflecting, with a hand in his beard, through which his white teeth shone. "There's such a wheen of Kates here and there, and all of them fine, fine gyurls! Still-and-on, if yours is like most of her name that I'm acquaint with, I'm the very man for her; and my name, indeed, is what you might be calling Charles. In fact," – in a burst of confidence, seating himself on a water-breaker – "my Christian name is Charles – Charlie, for short among the gentry. You are not speaking, by any chance, of one called Kate MacNeill?" he added, showing some red in the tan of his countenance.

"Of course I am," said Bud reproachfully. "Oh, men! men! As if there could be any other! I hope to goodness you love her same as you said you did, and haven't been – been carrying-on with any other Kates for a diversion. I'm Lennox Dyce. Your Kate stays with me and Uncle Dan, and Auntie Bell, and Auntie Ailie, and this sweet little dog by the name of Footles. She's so jolly! My! won't she be tickled to know you've come? And – and how's the world, Captain Charles?"

"The world?" he said, aback, looking at her curiously as she seated herself beside him on a hatch.

"Yes, the world, you know – the places you were in," with a wave of the hand that seemed to mean the universe.

> "'Edinburgh, Leith,
> Portobello, Musselburgh, *and* Dalkeith?'

– No, that's Kate's favourite geography lesson, 'cause she can sing it. I mean Rotterdam, and Santander, and Bilbao – all the lovely places on the map where a letter takes four days and a twopence-ha'penny stamp, and's mighty apt to smell of rope."

"Oh, them!" said he, with the warmth of recollection, "They're not so bad – in fact, they're just A1. It's the like of there you see life and spend the money."

"Have you been in Italy?" asked Bud. "I'd love to see that old Italy – for the sake of Romeo and Juliet, you know, and my dear, dear Portia."

"*I* know," said Charles. "Allow me! Perfect beauties, all fine, fine gyurls; but I don't think very much of dagoes. I have slept in their sailors' homes, and never hear Italy mentioned but I feel I want to scratch myself."

"Dagoes!" cried Bud; "that's what Jim called them. Have you been in America?"

"Have I been in America? I should think I have," said he emphatically. "The Lakes. It's yonder you get value – two dollars a-day and everywhere respected like a perfect gentleman. Men's not mice out yonder in America."

"Then you maybe have been in Chicago?" cried Bud, her face filled with a happy expectation as she pressed the dog in her arms till its fringe mixed with her own wild curls.

"Chicago?" said the captain. "Allow me! Many a time. You'll maybe not believe it, but it was there I bought this hat."

"Oh!" cried Bud, with the tears in her eyes and speechless for a moment, "I – I – could just hug that hat. Won't you please let me – let me pat it?"

"Pat away," said Captain Charles, laughing, and took it off with the sweep of a cavalier that was in itself a compliment. "You know yon place – Chicago?" he asked, as she patted his headgear fondly and returned it to him. For a little her mind was far away from the deck of Lady Anne's yacht, her eyes on the ripple of the tide, her nostrils full, and her little bosom heaving.

"You were there?" he asked again.

"Chicago's where I lived," she said. "That was mother's place," and into his ear she poured a sudden flood of reminiscence – of her father and mother, and the travelling days and lodging-houses, and Mr and Mrs Molyneux, and the graves in the far-off cemetery. The very thought of them all made her again American in accent and in phrase. He listened, understanding, feeling the vexation of that far-sundering by the sea as only a sailor can, and clapped her on the shoulder, and looking at him she saw that in his eyes which made her love him more than ever.

"Oh my!" she said bravely, "here I'm talking away to you about myself, and I'm no more account than a rabbit under these present circumstances, Captain Charles, and all the time you're just pining to know all about your Kate."

The Captain tugged his beard and reddened again. "A fine, fine gyurl!" said he. "I hope – I hope she's pretty well."

"She's fine," said Bud, nodding her head gravely. "You bet Kate can walk now without taking hold. Why, there's never anything wrong with her 'cepting now and then the croodles, and they're not anything lingering."

"There was a kind of rumour that she was at times a trifle delicate," said Charles. "In fact, it was herself who told me, in her letters."

Bud blushed. This was one of the few details of her correspondence on which she and Kate had differed. It had been her idea that an invalidish hint at intervals produced a nice and tender solicitude in the roving sailor, and she had, at times, credited the maid with some of Mrs Molyneux's old complaints, a little modified and more romantic, though Kate herself maintained that illness, in a woman under eighty was looked upon as anything but natural or interesting in Colonsay.

"It was nothing but – but love," she said now, confronted with the consequence of her imaginative cunning. "You know what love is, Captain Charles? A powerfully weakening thing, though I don't think it would hurt anybody if they wouldn't take it so much to heart."

"I'm glad to hear it's only – only what you mention," said Charles, much relieved. "I thought it might be something inward, and that maybe she was working too hard at her education."

"Oh, she's not taking her education so bad as all that," Bud assured him. "She isn't wasting to a shadow sitting up nights with a wet towel on her head soaking in the poets and figuring sums. All she wanted was to be sort of middling smart, but nothing gaudy."

Captain Charles looked sideway keenly at the child as she sat beside him, half afraid himself of the irony he had experienced among her countrymen, but saw it was not here. Indeed it never was in Lennox Dyce, for all her days she had the sweet engaging self-unconsciousness no training can command; frankness, fearlessness, and respect for all her fellows – the gifts that will never fail to make the proper friends. She talked so composedly that he was compelled to frankness himself on a subject no money could have made him speak about to any one a week ago.

131

"Between you and me and the mast," said he, "I'm feared Kate has got far too clever for the like of me, and that's the way I have not called on her."

"Then you'd best look pretty spry," said Bud, pointing a monitory finger at him; "for there's beaux all over the place that's wearing their Sunday clothes week-days, and washing their faces night and morning, hankering to tag on to her, and she'll maybe tire of standing out in the cold for you. I wouldn't be skeered, Cap', if I was you; she's not too clever for or'nary use; she's nicer than ever she was that time you used to walk with her in Colonsay." Bud was beginning to be alarmed at the misgivings to which her own imaginings had given rise.

"If you saw her letters," said Charles gloomily. "Poetry and foreign princes. One of them great at the dancing! He kissed her hand. He would never have ventured a thing like that if she hadn't given him encouragement."

"Just diversion," said Bud consolingly. "She was only – she was only putting by the time; and she often says she'll only marry for her own conveniency, and the man for her is – well, you know, Captain Charles."

"There was a Russian army officer," proceeded the seaman, still suffering a jealous doubt.

"But he's dead. He's deader 'n canned beans. Mr Wanton gied him – gied him the BAGGONET. There wasn't really anything in it anyway. Kate didn't care for him the tiniest bit, and I guess it was a great relief."

"Then she's learning the piano," said the Captain; "that's not like a working gyurl. And she talked in one of her letters about sitting on Uncle Dan's knee."

Bud dropped the dog at her feet and burst into laughter: in that instance she had certainly badly jumbled the identities.

"It's nothing to laugh at," said the Captain, tugging his beard. "It's not at all becoming in a decent gyurl; and it's not like the Kate I knew in Colonsay."

Bud saw the time had come for a full confession.

"Captain Charles," she said, when she recovered herself, "it – it wasn't Kate said that at all; it was another girl called Winifred Wallace. You see, Kate is always so busy doing useful things – *such* soup! and – and a washing every Monday, and taking her education, and the pens were all so dev – so – so stupid, that she simply had to get some one to help her write those letters; and that's why Winifred Wallace gave a hand and messed things up a bit, I guess. Where the

letters talked solemn sense about the weather and the bad fishing
and bits about Oronsay, and where they told you to be sure and
change your stockings when you came downstairs from the mast,
out the wet, and where they said you were the very, very one she
loved, that was Kate; but when there was a lot of dinky talk about
princes and Russian army officers and slabs of poetry, that was just
Winifred Wallace putting on lugs and showing off. No, it wasn't all
showing off; it was because she kind of loved you herself. You see she
didn't have any beau of her own, Mr Charles; and – and she thought
it wouldn't be depriving Kate of anything to pretend, for Kate said
there was no depravity in it."

"Who's Winifred Wallace?" asked the surprised sailor.

"I'm all the Winifred Wallace there is," said Bud penitently. "It's
my poetry name – it's my other me. I can do a heap of things when
I'm Winifred I can't do when I'm plain Bud, or else I'd laugh at
myself enough to hurt, I'm so mad. Are you angry, Mr Charles?"

"Och! just Charles to you," said the sailor. "Never heed the
honours. I'm not angry a bit. Allow me! In fact, I'm glad to find the
prince and the piano and the poetry were all nonsense."

"I thought that poetry pretty middling myself," admitted Bud,
but in a hesitating way that made him look very guilty.

"The poetry," said he quickly, "was splendid. There was nothing
wrong with it that I could see; but I'm glad it wasn't Kate's – for she's
a fine, fine gyurl, and brought up most respectable."

"Yes," said Bud; "she's better 'n any poetry. You must feel gay
because you are going to marry her."

"I'm not so sure of her marrying me. She maybe wouldn't have
me."

"But she can't help it!" cried Bud. "She's bound to, for the witch-
lady fixed it on Hallowe'en. Only, I hope you won't marry her for
years and years. Why, Auntie Bell 'd go crazy if you took away our
Kate; for good girls ain't so easy to get nowadays as they used to be
when they had three pound ten in the half-year, and nailed their
trunks down to the floor of a new place when they got it, for fear they
might be bounced. I'd be vexed I helped do anything if you married
her for a long while. Besides, you'd be sorry yourself, for her
education is not quite done; she's only up to Compound
Multiplication and the Tudor Kings. You'd just be sick sorry."

"Would I?"

"Course you would! That's love. Before one marries it's
hunkydory – it's fairy all the time; but after that it's the same old face
at breakfast, Mr Cleland says, and simply putting up with one

another. Oh, love's a wonderful thing, Charles; it's the Great Thing, but sometimes I say 'Give me Uncle Dan!' Promise you'll not go marrying Kate right off."

The sailor roared with laughter. "Lord!" said he, "if I wait too long I'll be wanting to marry yourself, for you're a dangerous gyurl."

"But I'm never going to marry," said Bud. "I want to go right on loving everybody, and don't yearn for any particular man tagging on to me."

"I never heard so much about love in English all my life," said Charles, "though it's common enough and quite respectable in Gaelic. Do you – do you love myself?"

"Course I do!" said Bud, cuddling Footles.

"Then," said he firmly, "the sooner I sign on with Kate the better, for you're a dangerous gyurl."

So they went down the road together, planning ways of early fore-gatherings with Kate, and you may be sure Bud's way was cunningest.

CHAPTER XXII

WHEN Kate that afternoon was told her hour was come, and that tomorrow she must meet her destined mariner, she fell into a chair, threw her apron over her head, and cried and laughed horribly turn about – the victim of hysteria that was half from fear and half from a bliss too deep and unexpected.

"Mercy on me!" she exclaimed. "Now he'll find out everything, and what a stupid one I am. All my education's clean gone out of my head; I'm sure I couldn't spell an article. I canna even mind the ninth commandment, let alone the Reasons Annexed; and as for grammar, whether it's 'Give the book to Bud and me' or 'Give the book to Bud and I,' is more than I could tell you if my very life depended on it. Oh, Lennox! now we're going to catch it! Are you certain sure he said tomorrow?"

Bud gazed at her disdainfully and stamped her foot. "Stop that, Kate MacNeill!" she commanded. "You mustn't act so silly. He's as skeered of you as you can be of him. He'd have been here Friday before the morning milk if he didn't think you'd be the sort to back him into a corner and ask him questions about ancient Greece and

Rome. Seems to me love makes some folk idiotic; lands sake! I'm mighty glad it always leaves me calm as a plate of pumpkin pie."

"Is – is – he looking tremendously genteel and well-put-on?" asked the maid of Colonsay, with anxious lines on her forehead. "Is he – is he as nice as I said he was?"

"He was everything you said – except the Gaelic. I knew he couldn't be so bad as that sounded that you said about his eyes. I – I never saw a more becoming man. If I had known just how noble he looked, I'd have sent him stacks of poetry," whereat Kate moaned again, rocked herself in her chair most piteously, and swore she could never have the impudence to see him till she had her new frock from the dressmakers.

"He'll be thinking I'm refined and quite the lady," she said, "and I'm just the same plain Kate I was in Colonsay, and him a regular Captain! It was all your fault, with your fancy letters. Oh, Lennox Dyce, I think I hate you, just: lend me your hanky – mine's all wet with greeting."

"If you weren't so big and temper wasn't sinful, I'd shake you!" said Bud, producing her handkerchief. "You were just on your last legs for a sailor, and you'd never have put a hand on one if I didn't write these letters. And now, when the sweetest sailor in the land is brought to your doorstep, you don't 'preciate your privileges and have a grateful heart, but turn round and yelp at me. I tell you, Kate MacNeill, sailors are mighty scarce and sassy in a little place like this, and none too easy picked up, and 'stead of sitting there, with a smut on your nose and tide-marks on your eyebrows, mourning, you'd best arise and shine, or somebody with their wits about them'll snap him up. I'd do it myself if it wouldn't be not honourable to you."

"Oh! if I just had another week or two's geography!" said Kate dolefully.

Bud had to laugh – she could not help herself; and the more she laughed, the more tragic grew the servant's face.

"Seems to me," said Bud, "that I've got to run this loving business all along the line: you don't know the least thing about it after g-o, go. Why, Kate, I'm telling you Charles is afraid of you more than you are of him. He thought you'd be that educated you'd wear specs, and stand quite stiff talking poetry all the time, and I had to tell him every dinky bit in these letters were written by me."

"Then that's worse!" cried the servant, more distressed than ever. "For he'll think I canna write myself, and I can write like fury if you only give me a decent pen, and shut the door, and don't bother me."

"No fears!" said Bud; "I made that all right. I said you were too busy housekeeping, and I guess it's more a housekeeper than a school-ma'rm Charles needs. Anyhow, he's so much in love with you, he'd marry you if you were only half-way through the Twopenny. He's plump head over heels, and it's up to you, as a sensible girl, not to conceal that you like him some yourself."

"I'll not know what to say to him," said Kate, "and he always was so clever: half the time I couldna understand him if it wasn't for his eyes."

"Well, he'll know what to say to you, I guess, if all the signs are right. Charles is not so shy as all that – love-making is where he lives; and he made goo-goo eyes at myself without an introduction. You'd fancy, to hear you, he was a school inspector, and he's only just an or'nary lover thinking of the happy days you used to have in Colonsay. If I was you I'd not let on I was anything but what I really was; I'd be natural – yes, that's what I'd be, for being natural's the deadliest thing below the canopy to make folk love you. Don't pretend, but just be the same Kate MacNeill to him you are to me. Just you listen to him, and now and then look at him, and don't think of a darned thing – I mean, don't think of a blessed thing but how nice he is, and he'll be so pleased and so content he'll not even ask you to spell cat."

"Content!" cried Kate, with conviction. "Not him! Fine I ken him! He'll want to kiss me, as sure as God's in heaven – beg your pardon."

"I expect that's not a thing you should say to me," said Bud, blushing deeply.

"But I begged your pardon," said the maid.

"I don't mean that about God in heaven, that's right – so He is, or where would *we* be? what I meant was about the kissing. I'm old enough for love, but I'm not old enough for you to be talking to me about kissing. I guess Auntie Ailie wouldn't like to have you talk to me about a thing like that, and Auntie Bell, she'd be furious – it's too advanced."

"What time am I to see him?" asked Kate.

"In the morning. If you go out to the garden just after breakfast, and whistle, he'll look over the wall."

"The morning!" cried the maid aghast. "I couldn't face him in the morning. Who ever heard of such a thing? Now you have gone away and spoiled everything! I could hardly have all my wits about me even if it was only gloaming."

Bud sighed despairingly. "Oh, you don't understand, Kate," said she. "He wanted it to be the evening, too, but I said you weren't a miserable pair of owls, and the best time for anything is the morning. Uncle Dan says the first half-hour in the morning is worth three hours at any other time of the day, for when you've said your prayers, and had a good bath, and a clean shave, and your boots new on – no slippers nor slithery dressing-gowns, the peace of God, and – and – and the assurance of strength and righteousness descends upon you so that you – you – you can tackle wild-cats. I feel so brash and brave myself in the morning I could skip the hills like a goat. It's simply *got* to be the morning, Kate MacNeill. That's when you look your very best, if you care to take a little trouble, and don't simply just slouch through, and I'm set on having you see him first time over the garden wall. That's the only way to fix the thing up romantic, seeing we haven't any balcony. You'll go out and stand against the blossom of the cherry-tree, and hold a basket of flowers and parsley, and when he peeks over and sees you looming out in the picture, I tell you he'll be tickled to death. That's the way Shakespeare 'd fix it, and he knew."

"I don't think much of Shakespeare," said Kate. "Fancy yon Igoa!"

"Iago, you mean; well, what about him?"

"The wickedness of him; such a lot of lies!"

"Pooh!" said Bud. "He was only for the effect. Of course there never really was such a mean wicked man as that Iago – there couldn't be; but Shakespeare made him just so's you'd like the nice folk all the more by thinking what they might have been if God had let Himself go."

That night Kate was abed by eight. Vainly the town cried for her – the cheerful passage of feet on the pavement, and a tinker piper at the Cross, and she knew how bright was the street, with the late-lit windows of the shops, and how intoxicating was the atmosphere of Saturday in the dark; but having said her Lord's Prayer in Gaelic, and "Now I lay me down to sleep" in English, she covered her head with the blankets and thought of the coming day with joy and apprehension, until she fell asleep.

In the morning Miss Bell had no sooner gone up to the making of beds, that was her Sabbath care to save the servant-maid from too much sin, and Ailie to her weekly reading with the invalid Duncan Gill, than Bud flew into the kitchen to make Kate ready for her tryst. Never in this world were breakfast dishes sooner cleaned and dried than by that eager pair: no sooner were they done than Kate had her chest-lid up and had dived, head foremost, among her Sunday finery.

"What's that?" asked Bud. "You're not going to put on glad rags, are you?" For out there came a blue gown, fondled tenderly.

"Of course I am," said Kate. "It's either that or my print for it, and a print wrapper would not be the thing at all to meet – meet the Captain in; he'll be expecting me to be truly refined."

"I think he'd like the wrapper better," said Bud gravely. "The blue gown's very nice – but it's not Kate, somehow: do you know, I think it's Auntie Ailie up to the waist, and the banker's cook in the lacey bits above that, and it don't make you refined a bit. It's not what you put on that makes you refined, it's things you can't take off. You have no idea how sweet you look in that print, Kate, with your cap and apron. You look better in them than if you wore the latest yell of fashion. I'd want to marry you myself if I was a captain, and saw you dressed like that; but if you had on your Sunday gown I'd – I'd bite my lip and go home and ask advice from mother."

Kate put past the blue gown, not very willingly, but she had learned by now that in some things Bud had better judgment than herself. She washed and dried her face till it shone like a polished apple, put on Bud's choice of a cap and streamered apron, and was about to take a generous dash of Florida Water when she found her hand restrained.

"I'd have no scent," said Bud. "I like scent myself, some, and I just dote on our Florida Water, but Auntie Ailie says the scent of clean water, sun, and air, is the sweetest a body can have about one, and any other kind's as rude as Keating's Powder."

"He'll be expecting the Florida Water," said Kate, "seeing it was himself that sent it."

"It don't amount to a hill of beans," said Bud; "You can wear our locket, and that'll please him."

Kate went with a palpitating heart through the scullery, out into the garden, with a basket in her hand, a pleasing and expansive figure. Bud would have liked to watch her, but a sense of delicacy prevented, and she stood at the kitchen window looking resolutely into the street. On his way down the stairs Mr Dyce was humming the Hundredth Psalm; outside the shops were shuttered, and the harmony of the morning hymn came from the baker's open windows. A few folk passed in their Sunday clothes, at a deliberate pace, to differentiate it from the secular hurry of other days. Soon the church bell would ring for the Sabbath-school, and Bud must be ready. Remembering it, a sense of some impiety took possession of her – worldly trysts in back gardens on the Sabbath were not what Aunt Bell would much approve of. Had they met yet? How did

138

Charles look? What did Kate say?

"Mercy on me!" cried the maid, bursting in through the scullery. "Did you say I was to whistle?"

"Of course," said Bud, and then looked horrified. "Oh, Kate," said she in a whisper, "I was so keen on the vain things of this wicked world I quite forgot it was the Lord's Day; of course you can't go whistling on Sunday."

"That's what I was just thinking to myself," said the maid, not very heartily. "But I thought I would ask you. It wouldn't need to be a tune, but – but – of course it would be awful wicked – forbye Miss Dyce would be sure to hear me, and she's that particular."

"No, you can't whistle – you daren't," said Bud. "It'd be dre'ffle wicked. But how'd it do to throw a stone? Not a rock, you know, but a nice little quiet wee white Sunday pebble? You might like as not be throwing it at Rodger's cats, and that would be a work of necessity and mercy, for these cruel cats are just death on birds."

"But there's not a single cat there," explained the maid.

"Never mind," said Bud. "You can heave the pebble over the wall so that it'll be a warning to them not to come poaching in our garden; there's sure to be some on the other side just about to get on the wall, and if Charles happens to be there too, can you help that?" and Kate retired again.

There was a pause, and then a sound of laughter. For ten minutes Bud waited in an agony of curiosity, that was at last too much for her, and she ventured to look out at the scullery window – to see Charles chasing his adored one down the walk, between the bleaching-green and the gooseberries. Kate was making for the sanctuary of her kitchen, her face aflame, and all her streamers flying, but was caught before she entered.

"I told you!" said she, as she came in panting. "We hadn't said twenty words when he wanted to kiss me."

"Why! was that the reason you ran?" asked Bud, astonished.

"Ye – yes," said the maid.

"Seems to me it's not very encouraging to Charles, then."

"Yes, but – but – I wasn't running all my might,' said Kate.

CHAPTER XXIII

TA-RAN-TA-RA! Ta-ran-ta-ra!

The world is coming for Lennox Dyce, the greedy world, youth's first and worst beguiler, that promises so much, but at the best has only bubbles to give, which borrow a moment the splendour of the sun, then burst in the hands that grasp them; the world that will have only our bravest and most clever bairns, and takes them all from us one by one. I have seen them go – scores of them, boys and girls, their foreheads high, and the sun on their faces, and never one came back. Now and then returned to the burgh in the course of years a man or woman who bore a well-known name, and could recall old stories, but they were not the same, and even if they were not disillusioned, there was that in their flushed prosperity which ill made up for the bright young spirits quelled.

Ta-ran-ta-ra! Ta-ran-ta-ra!

Yes, the world is coming, sure enough – on black and yellow wheels, with a guard red-coated who bugles through the glen. It is coming behind black horses, with thundering hooves and foam-flecked harness, between bare hills, by gurgling burns and lime-washed shepherd dwellings, or in the shadow of the woods that simply stand where they are placed by God and wait. It comes in a fur-collared coat – though it is autumn weather – and in a tall silk hat, and looks amused at the harmless country it has come to render discontent.

Ta-ran-ta-ra! Ta-ran-ta-ra!

Go back, world! go back, and leave the little lass among her dreams, with hearts that love and cherish. Go back, with your false flowers and your gems of paste. Go back, world, that for every ecstasy exacts a pang!

There were three passengers on the coach – the man with the fur collar who sat on the box beside the driver, and the Misses Duff behind. I am sorry now that once I thought to make you smile at the pigeon hens, for today I'm in more Christian humour and my heart warms to them, seeing them come safely home from their flight afar from their doo-cot, since they it was who taught me first to make these symbols on the paper, and at their worst they were but a little stupid, like the most of us at times, and always with the best intent. They had been to Edinburgh; they had been gone two weeks – their first adventure in a dozen years. Miss Jean was happy, bringing back with her a new crochet pattern, a book of Views, a tooth gold-filled (she was so proud and spoke of it so often that it is not rude to mention it), and a glow of art she had got from an afternoon tea in a picture-gallery full of works in oil. Amelia's spoils were a phrase that lasted her for years – it was that Edinburgh was "redolent of Robert Louis," the boast that she had heard the great MacCaskill preach, and got a lesson in the searing of harmless woods with heated pokers. Such are the rewards of travel: I have come home myself with as little for my time and money.

But between them they had brought back something else – something to whisper about lest the man in front should hear, and two or three times to look at as it lay in an innocent roll beside the purse in Miss Amelia's reticule. It might have been a serpent in its coils, so timidly they glanced in at it, and snapped the bag shut with a kind of shudder.

"At least it's not a very large one," whispered Miss Jean, with the old excuse of the unhappy lass who did the deadly sin.

"No," said her sister, "it may, indeed, be called quite – quite diminutive. The other he showed us was so horribly large and – and vulgar, the very look of it made me almost faint. But, oh! I wish we could have dispensed with the horrid necessity. After twe – after so many years it looks like a confession of weakness. I hope there will be no unpleasant talk about it."

"But you may be sure there will, Amelia Duff," said her sister. "They'll cast up Barbara Mushet to us; she will always be the perfect teacher."

"The paragon of all the virtues."

"And it is such a gossiping place."

"Indeed it is," said Miss Amelia. "It is always redolent of – of scandal."

"I wish you had never thought of it," said Miss Jean, with a sigh and a vicious little shake of the reticule. "I am not blaming you, remember, 'Melia; if we are doing wrong the blame of it is equally between us, except perhaps a little more for me, for I *did* think the big one was better value for the money. And yet it made me grue, it looked so – so dastardly."

"Jean," said her sister solemnly, "if you had taken the big one, I would have marched out of the shop affronted. If it made you grue, it made me shudder. Even with the small one, did you notice how the man looked at us? I thought he felt ashamed to be selling such a thing: perhaps he has a family. He said they were not very often asked for. I assure you I felt very small, the way he said it."

Once more they bent their douce brown hats together over the reticule and looked timidly in on the object of their shames and fears. "Well, there it is, and it can't be helped," said Miss Jean at last, despairingly. "Let us hope and trust there will not be too frequent need for it, for, I assure you, I have neither the strength nor inclination." She snapped the bag shut again, and, glancing up, saw the man with the fur collar looking over his shoulder at them.

"Strikes me, ladies," he said, "the stage coach, as an easy mark for the highwaymen who used to permeate these parts, must have been a pretty merry proposition; they'd be apt to stub their toes on it if they came sauntering up behind. John here" – with an inclination of his head towards the driver – "tells me he's on schedule time, and I allow he's making plenty fuss clicking his palate, but I feel I want to get out and heave rocks at his cattle, so's they'd get a better gait on 'em."

Miss Jean was incapable of utterance; she was still too much afraid of a stranger, who, though gallantly helping them to the top of the coach at Maryfield, could casually address herself and Miss Amelia as "dears," thrust cigars on the guard and driver, and call them John and George at the very first encounter.

"We – we think this is fairly fast," Miss Amelia ventured, surprised at her own temerity. "It's nineteen miles in two hours, and if it's not so fast as a railway train it lets you enjoy the scenery. It is very much admired, our scenery, it's so – it's so characteristic."

"Sure!" said the stranger, "it's pretty tidy scenery as scenery goes, and scenery's my forte. But I'd have thought that John here'd have all this part of Caledonia stern and wild so much by heart he'd want to rush it and get to where the houses are; but most the time his horses go so slow they step on their own feet at every stride."

"Possibly the coach is a novelty to you," suggested Miss Amelia, made wondrous brave by two weeks' wild adventuring in Edinburgh. "I – I take you for an American."

"So did my wife, and she knew, for she belonged out mother's place," said the stranger, laughing. "You've guessed right, first time. No, the coach is no novelty to me; I've been up against a few in various places. If I'm short of patience and want more go just at present, it's because I'm full of a good joke on an old friend I'm going to meet at the end of these obsequies."

"Obsequies?" repeated Miss Amelia, with surprise, and he laughed again.

"At the end of the trip," he explained. "This particular friend is not expecting me, because I hadn't a post-card, hate a letter, and don't seem to have been within shout of a telegraph office since I left Edinburgh this morning."

"We have just come from Edinburgh ourselves," Miss Jean chimed in.

"So!" said the stranger, throwing his arm over the back of his seat to enter more comfortably into the conversation. "It's picturesque. Pretty peaceful, too. But it's liable to be a little shy of the Thespian muse. I didn't know more than Cooper's cow about Edinburgh when I got there last Sunday fortnight, but I've gone perusing around a bit since; and say, my! she's fine and old! I wasn't half a day in the city when I found out that when it came to the real legit. Queen Mary was the king-pin of the outfit in Edinburgh. Before I came to this country I couldn't just place Mary; sometimes she was Bloody, and sometimes she was Bonnie, but I suppose I must have mixed her up with some no-account English queen of the same name."

"Edinburgh," said Miss Amelia, "is redolent of Mary Queen of Scots – and Robert Louis."

"It just is!" he said. "There's a little bedroom she had in the Castle yonder, no bigger than a Chicago bathroom. Why, there's hardly room for a nightmare in it – a skittish nightmare 'd kick the transom out. There doesn't seem to be a single dramatic line in the whole play that Mary didn't have to herself. She was the entire cast, and the spot light was on her for the abduction scene, the child-widow scene, the murder, the battle, and the last tag at Fotheringay. Three husbands and a lot of flirtations that didn't come to anything; her portrait everywhere, and the newspapers tracking her up like old Sleuth from that day to this! I guess Queen Lizzie put her feet in it when she killed Mary – for Mary's the star-line in history, and Lizzie's mainly celebrated for spoiling a good Prince Albert coat on Walter Raleigh."

He spoke so fast, he used such curious words and idioms which the Misses Duff had never heard before nor read in books, that they were sure again he was a dreadful person. With a sudden thought of warnings to "Beware of Pickpockets" she had seen in Edinburgh, Miss Amelia clutched so hard at the chain of the reticule which held their purse as well as their mystery that it broke, and the bag fell over the side of the coach and, bursting open, scattered its contents on the road unobserved by the guard, whose bugle at the moment, was loudly flourishing for the special delectation of a girl at work in a neighbouring corn-field.

"Hold hard, John," said the American, and before the coach had

143

quite stopped he was down on the highway recovering the little teachers' property.

The serpent had unwound its coils; it lay revealed in all its hideousness – a teacher's tawse!

At such a sad exposure its owners could have wept. They had never dreamt a tawse could look so vulgar and forbidding as it looked when thus exposed to the eye of man on the King's highway.

"Oh, thank you so much," said Miss Jean. "It is so kind of you."

"Exceedingly kind, courteous beyond measure – we are more than obliged to you," cooed Miss Amelia, with a face like a sunset as she rolled the leather up with nervous fingers.

"Got children, ma'am?" asked the American seriously, as the coach proceeded on its way.

Miss Amelia Duff made the best joke of her life without meaning it. "Twenty-seven," said she, with an air of great gratitude, and the stranger smiled.

"School-ma'rm. Now that's good, that is; it puts me in mind of home, for I appreciate school-ma'rms so heartily that about as soon as I got out of the school myself I married one. I've never done throwing bouquets at myself about it ever since, but I'm sorry for the mites she could have been giving a good time to as well as their education if it hadn't been that she's so much mixed up with me. What made me ask about children was that – that medieval animator. I haven't seen one for years and years, not since old Deacon Springfield found me astray in his orchard one night and hiking for a short cut home. I thought they'd been abolished by the treaty of Berlin."

Miss Amelia thrust it hurriedly into the reticule. "We have never used one all our life," said she, "but now we fear we have to, and, as you see, it's quite thin – it's quite a little one."

"So it is," said the stranger solemnly. "It's thin – it's translucent, you might say; but I guess the kiddies are pretty little too, and won't be able to make any allowance for the fact that you could have had a larger size if you wanted. It may be light on the fingers and mighty heavy on the feelings."

"That's what you said," whispered Miss Amelia to her sister.

"As moral suasion, belting don't cut ice," went on the American. "It's generally only a safety-valve for a wrothy grown-up person with a temper and a child that can't hit back."

"That's what *you* said," whispered Miss Jean to Miss Amelia, and never did two people look more miserably guilty.

"What beats me," said the stranger, "is that you should have got along without it so far, and think it necessary now."

"Perhaps – perhaps we won't use it," said Miss Jean.

"Except as – as a sort of symbol," added her sister. "We would never have dreamt of it if children nowadays were not so different from what they used to be."

"I guess folk's been saying that quite a while," said the American. "Children never were like what they used to be. I reckons old Mother Nature spits on her hands and makes a fresh start with each baby, and never turns out two alike. That's why it's fun to sit and watch 'em bloom. Pretty delicate blooms, too! Don't bear much pawing; just give them a bit of shelter when the weather's cold, a prop to lean against if they're leggy and the wind's high, and see that the fertiliser is the proper brand. Whether they're going to turn out like the picture on the packet or just only weeds depends on the seedsman."

"Oh, you *don't* understand how rebellious they can be!" cried Miss Amelia with feeling. "And they haven't the old deference to their elders that they used to have – they're growing bold and independent."

"Depends on the elders, I suppose. Over here I think you folks think children come into the world just to please grown-ups and do what they're told without any thinking. In America it's looked at the other way about: the children are considerably more important than their elders, and the notion don't do any harm to either, far as I can see. As for your rebels, ma'am, I'd cherish 'em: rebellion's like a rash, it's better out than in."

Ta-ran-ta-ra! The bugle broke upon their conversation; the coach emerged from the wood and dashed down hill, and, wheeling through the arches, drew up at the inn.

The American helped the ladies to alight, took off his hat, bade them good-day, and turned to speak to his friend the driver, when a hand was placed on his sleeve, and a child with a dog at her feet looked up in his face.

"Jim! Why, Jim Molyneux!" cried Bud.

CHAPTER XXIV

For only a day or two the world (in a fur-lined collar) dwelt among us, but momentous was its advent to the household Molyneux came visiting. It was as if a high tide had swept the dwelling, Bell remarked when he was gone. You might see no outward difference; the furniture might still be as it was, and in the same position as Miss Bell had found it when her mother died, but none the less there was an unseen doleful wreckage. This unco man Molyneux changed the vital thing, the atmosphere, and the house with the brass knocker was never to be altogether just the same again. It is no discovery of mine that what may seem the smallest trifles play tremendous parts in destiny.

Even the town itself was some ways altered for a little by the whim that took the American actor to it. That he should be American and actor too foredoomed the greatness of his influence, since the combination stood for much that was mysterious, half fearful, half sublime, in our simple notions of the larger world. To have been the first alone would have endowed him with the charm of wonder and romance for most of us, who, at the very sight of the name America, even if it be only on a reaper or a can of beef, have some sense of a mightiness that the roar of London cannot rouse. But to be an actor too! earning easy bread by mimicry, and in enormous theatres, before light-headed folk that have made money – God knows how! – and prospered. Sinful a little, we allow, for there are doubts if the play-actor, having to paint his face and work late hours in gas-light, finally shall obtain salvation; sinful, and yet – and yet – so queer and clever a way of making out a living! It is no wonder if we looked on Mr Molyneux with that regard which by cities is reserved for shahs of a hundred wives, and royal vagabonds. Besides, consider how the way had been prepared for him by Bud! – a child, but a child who had shown already how wonderful must be the land that had swallowed up clever men like William Dyce and the brother of P. & A. MacGlashan. Had she not, by a single object-lesson in the Pilgrim widow's warehouse, upset the local ways of commerce, so that now, in all the shops, the people were constantly buying things of which they had no earthly need; and the Pilgrim widow herself was put to the weekly trouble of washing her windows, so wasting time that might have been devoted to the Mission? Had she not shown that titled ladies were but human after all, and would not bite you if you cracked a joke politely with them? Had she not put an end to all the gallivanting of the maid of Colonsay, and given her an education that made her fit to court a captain? And, finally, had she not, by force of sheer example, made dumb and stammering bashfulness in her fellow pupils at the Sunday-school look stupid, and by her daily walk and conversation roused in them a new spirit of inquiry and independence that pleased their parents not so badly, and only the little twin teachers of the Pigeon Seminary could mistake for the kind of rebellion that calls for the application of the tawse?

Mr Molyneux might have no idea of it, but he was a lion for those few days of sequestration in what he thought the wilds. Miss Minto dressed her windows specially for his critical eye, and on the tickets of her autumn sales gave the name of "waist" to what had hitherto been a blouse or a garibaldi; P. & A. MacGlashan made the front of his shop like a wharf with piles of empty packing-cases to indicate a prosperous foreign and colonial trade; one morning Wanton Wully rang the bell at half-past five instead of six to prove how very wide-awake we were; and the band paraded once with a new tune, "Off to Philadelphia," to show that when it came to gaiety we were not, though small, so very far behind New York.

But Jim Molyneux, going up and down the street with Lennox and the dog for cicerones, peered from under the rim of his hat, and summed all up to himself in the words, "Rube town" and "Cobwebopolis."

Bell took warmly to him from the outset, so much was in his favour. For one thing he was spick and span, though not a jackanapes, with no long hair about him as she had expected, and with an honest eye and a good complexion that, for simple country ladies, readily pass as the guarantee of a being clean within. She forgave the disreputable part in him – the actor, since William had been one, and yet had taught his child her prayers; and she was willing to overlook the American, seeing William's wife had suffered from the same misfortune. But, oh! the blow she got when she unpacked what he called his grip, and found the main thing wanting!

"Where's your Bible, Mr Molyneux?" she asked solemnly. "It's not in your portmanteau?"

Again it was in his favour that he reddened, though the excuse he had to make was feeble.

"Dear me!" she said, shaking her head, with a sad sort of smile, "and you to be so regularly travelling! If I was your wife I would take you in hand! But perhaps in America there's no need for a lamp to the feet and a light to the path."

It was after their first supper, for which the patriot Bell had made a haggis, that her brother, for Molyneux's information, said was thought to be composed of bagpipes boiled; Bud was gone to bed in the attic, and Molyneux was telling how he simply *had* to come.

"It's my first time in Scotland," said he, "and when 'The Iron Hand' lost its clutch on old Edina's fancy, and the scenery was arrested, I wasn't so sore about it as I might have been, since it gave me the opportunity of coming up here to see girly-girly. 'I'll skiddoo from the gang for a day or two,' I said to the manager, when we found ourselves side-tracked, and he said that was all right, he'd wire me when he'd fixed a settlement; so I skiddid, and worked my way here with the aid of the American language, and a little Scotch – by absorption."

"We have only one fault with your coming – that it was not sooner," said Mr Dyce.

"And I'm pretty glad I came, if it was only to see what a credit Bud is to a Scottish training. Chicago's the finest city on earth – in spots; America's what our Fourth of July orators succinctly designate God's Own, and since Joan of Arc there hasn't been any woman better or braver than Mrs Molyneux. But we weren't situated to give Bud a show like what she'd get in a settled home. We did our best, but we didn't dwell, as you might say, on Michigan Avenue, and Mrs Molyneux's a dear good girl, but she isn't demonstratively domesticated. We suspected from what Bud's father was, the healthiest place she could be was where he came from, and though we skipped some sleep, both of us, to think of losing her, now that I'm here and see her, I'm glad of it, for my wife and I are pretty much on the drift most the time in England as we were in the United States."

"Yours is an exacting calling, Mr Molyneux," said Mr Dyce. "It's very much the same in all countries, I suppose?"

"It's not so bad as stone-breaking, nor so much of a cinch as being a statesman," said Mr Molyneux cheerfully, "but a man's pretty old at it before he gives up hope of breaking out into a very large gun. I've still the idea myself that if I'm not likely to be a Booth or Henry Irving, I could make a pile at management. With a millionaire at my back for a mascot, and one strong star, I fancy I could cut a pretty wide gash through the English dramatic stage. You know our Mr Emerson said, 'Hitch your waggon to a star.' I guess if I got a good star bridled, I'd hitch a private parlour-car and a steam yacht on to her before she flicked an ear. Who wants a waggon, anyway?"

"A waggon's fairly safe to travel in," suggested Mr Dyce,

148

twinkling through his glasses.

"So's a hearse," said Mr Molyneux quickly. "Nobody that ever travelled in a hearse complained of getting his funny-bone jolted or his feelings jarred, but it's a mighty slow conveyance for live folks. That's the only thing that seems to me to be wrong with this 'cute little British Kingdom: it's pretty, and it's what the school-marm on the coach would call redolent of the dear dead days beyond recall; and it's plucky – but it keeps the brakes on most the time, and don't give its star a chance to amble. I guess it's a fine, friendly, and crowded country to be born rich in, and a pretty peaceful and lonesome country to die poor in; but take a tenpenny car-ride out from Charing Cross and you're in Lullaby Land, and the birds are building nests and carolling in your whiskers. Life's short; it only gives a man time to wear through one pair of eyes, two sets of teeth, and a reputation, and I want to live every hour of it that I'm not conspicuously dead."

They were silent in the parlour of the old house that had for generations sheltered very different ideals, and over the town went the call of the wild geese. The room, low-roofed, small-windowed, papered in dull green, curtained against the noises of the street, and furnished with the strong mahogany of Grandma Buntain, dead for sixty years, had ever to those who knew it best a soul of peace that is not sometimes found in a cathedral. They felt in it a sanctuary safe from the fret and tempest, the alarums and disillusions of the life out-bye. In the light of the shaded lamp hung over the table, it showed itself to its inmates in the way our most familiar surroundings will at certain crises – in an aspect fonder than ever it had revealed before. To Bell, resenting the spirit of this actor's gospel, it seemed as if the room cried out against the sacrilege: even Ailie, sharing in her heart, if less ecstatically, the fervour for life at its busiest this stranger showed, experienced some inharmony. To Dan it was for a moment as if he heard a man sell cuckoo clocks by auction with a tombstone for his rostrum.

"Mr Molyneux," said he, "you remind me, in what you say, of Maggie White's husband. Before he died he kept the public-house, and on winter nights when my old friend Colin Cleland and his cronies would be sitting in the back room with a good light, a roaring fire, and an argument about Effectual Calling, so lively that it stopped the effectual and profitable call for Johnny's toddy, he would come in chittering as it were with cold, and his coat-collar up on his neck, to say, 'An awfu' nicht outside! As dark as the inside o' a cow, and as cauld as charity! They're lucky that have fires to sit by.'

149

And he would impress them so much with the good fortune of their situation at the time that they would order in another round and put off their going all the longer, though the night outside, in truth, was no way out of the ordinary. I feel like that about this place I was born in, and its old fashions and its lack of hurry, when I hear you – with none of Johnny White's stratagem – tell us, not how dark and cold is the world outside, but what to me, at the age of fifty-five, at any rate is just as unattractive. You'll excuse me if, in a manner of speaking, I ring the bell for another round. Life's short, as you say, but I don't think it makes it look any the longer to run through the hours of it instead of leisurely daundering – if you happen to know what daundering is, Mr Molyneux – and now and then resting on the roadside with a friend and watching the others pass."

"At fifty-five," said Mr Molyneux agreeably, "I'll perhaps think so too, but I can only look at it from the point of view of thirty-two. We've all got to move, at first, Mr Dyce. That reminds me of a little talk I had with Bud today. That child's grown, Mr Dyce – grown a heap of ways: she's hardly a child any longer."

"Tuts! She's nothing else!" exclaimed Miss Bell, with some misgiving. "When I was her age I was still at my sampler in Barbara Mushet's."

"Anyhow she's grown. And it seems to me she's about due for a little fresh experience. I suppose you'll be thinking of sending her to one of those Edinburgh schools to have the last coat of shellac put on her education?"

"What put that in your head? Did she suggest it herself?" asked Mr Dyce quickly, with his head to one side in his cross-examination manner.

"Well, she did – but she didn't know it," said Mr Molyneux. "I guess about the very last thing that child 'd suggest to anybody would be that she wanted to separate herself from folk she loves so much as you; but, if there's one weakness about her, it is that she can't conceal what she thinks, and I'd not been twenty minutes in her society before I found out she had the go-fever pretty bad. I suspect a predisposition to that complaint and a good heart was all her father and mother left her, and lolling around and dwelling on the past isn't apt to be her foible. Two or three years in the boarding-school arena would put the cap sheaf on the making of that girl's character, and I know, for there's my wife, and she had only a year and a half. If she'd had longer I guess she'd have had more sense than marry me. Bud's got almost every mortal thing a body wants here, I suppose – love in lumps, a warm moist soil, and all the rest of it; but she wants to be hardened-off, and for hardening-off a human flower there's nothing better than a three-course college, where the social breeze is cooler than it is at home."

Miss Bell turned pale – the blow had come! Dan looked at her with a little pity, for he knew she had long been fearfully expecting it.

"Indeed!" said she, "and I do not see the need for any such thing for a long while yet. Do you, Ailie?" But Ailie had no answer, and that was enough to show what she thought.

"I know how it feels at first to think of her going away from home," continued Mr Molyneux, eager to be on with a business he had no great heart for. "Bless you, I know how my wife felt about it – she cried like the cherubim and seraphim. Said it was snatching all the sunshine out of her life, and when I said, 'Millicent Molyneux, what about hubby?' she just said 'Scat!' and threw a couple of agonised throes. Now, Edinburgh's not so very far away that you'd feel desolated if Bud went to a school there."

"An unhealthy hole, with haars and horrible east wind," said Miss Bell.

"Well, it isn't the Pacific Slope, if it comes to climate," admitted Mr Molyneux.

"No, but it's the most beautiful city in the wide world, for all that," cried Miss Bell, with such spirit that it cleared the air, and made her sister and her brother smile, for Molyneux, without his knowing it, had touched her in the very heart's core of her national pride.

"You're sure you are not mistaken, and that she would wish to go to school?" asked Mr Dyce.

"Do you doubt it yourself?" asked Molyneux slyly.

"No," said Mr Dyce, "I know it well enough, but – but I don't believe it," and he smiled at his own paradox.

"I have her own words for it."

"Then she'll go!" said the lawyer firmly, as if a load was off his mind; and, oddly, there were no objections from his sisters. "You're not to imagine, Mr Molyneux," he went on, "that we have not thought of this before. It has for months been never out of our minds, as might be seen from the fact that we never mentioned it, being loth to take a step that's going to make considerable difference here. It's not that we feared we should die of ennui in her absence, for we're all philosophers and have plenty to engage our minds as well as our activities, and though you might think us rather rusty here we get a good deal of fun with ourselves. She'll go – oh, yes, of course she'll go – Ailie went, and she's no muckle the waur o't, as we say. I spent some time in the south myself, and the only harm it seems to have done me was to make me think too much perhaps of my native north. Taste's everything, Mr Molyneux, and you may retort if you please that I'm like the other Scotsman who preferred his apples small and hard and sour. I think there's no divine instruction, is there, Bell, about apples? and judgments regarding different countries and different places in them is mostly a subjective thing, like the estimate of beauty apart from its utility –"

"Oh! there you are at your metapheesics, Dan," cried Miss Bell, "and it's for me and Ailie to make ready the bairn for Edinburgh. She hasna got a stitch that's fit to be put on."

Molyneux stared at her – the tone displayed so little opposition to the project; and seeing him so much surprised, the three of them smiled.

"That's us!" said Mr Dyce. "We're dour and difficult to decide on anything involving change, and hide from ourselves as long as we can the need for it; but once our mind's made up, it's wonderful how we hurry!"

CHAPTER XXV

BELL liked the creature, as I say; not a little because she saw in him whence came some part of Bud's jocosity, and most of the daft-like language (though kind of clever too, she must allow) in which it was expressed. It was a different kind of jocosity from Dan's, whose fun, she used to say, partook of the nature of rowan jelly, being tart and sweet in such a cunning combination that it tickled every palate and held some natural virtue of the mountain tree. The fun of Molyneux had another flavour – it put her in mind of allspice, being foreign, having heat as well as savour. But in each of these droll men was the main thing, as she would aye consider it – no distrust of the Creator's judgment good intentions and ability, and a readiness to be laughed at as well as find laughter's cause in others. She liked the man, but still-and-on was almost glad when the telegram came from Edinburgh and he went back to join his company. It was not any lack of hospitality made her feel relief, but the thought that now Bud's going was determined on, there was so much to do in a house where men would only be a bother.

Mr Molyneux found himself so much at home among them, he was loth to go, expressing his contempt for a mode of transit to the railway that took two hours to nineteen miles; but Bell, defensive even of her country's coaches, told him he was haivering – that any greater speed than that was simply tempting Providence. He praised the Lord there was no Providence to be tempted inside Sandy Hook, and that he knew Beef Kings who hurled themselves across the landscape at the rate of a mile a minute. The fact inspired no admiration in Miss Bell: she wondered at the misguided wretches scudding like that regardless of their lives, and them with so much money.

Before he left he called at the Pigeons' Seminary to say good-bye to the little teachers, and sipped tea – a British institution which he told them was as deleterious as the High Ball of his native land. High Ball – what was a High Ball? asked Miss Amelia, scenting a nice new phrase; but he could only vaguely indicate that it was something made of rye and soda. Then she understood – it was a teetotal drink men took in clubs, a kind of barley-water. The tea gratified him less than the confidence of the twins, who told him they had taken what he said about the – about the shameful article so much to heart, that they had given it for a razor-strop to one George Jordon.

"Bully for you!" cried Mr Molyneux delighted. "But I'd have liked that tawse some, myself, for my wife's mighty keen on curios. She's got a sitting-room full of Navaho things: scalpin'-knives, tomahawks, and other brutal bric-a-brac, and an early British strap would tickle her to death."

Well, he was gone: the coachman's horn had scarcely ceased to echo beyond the arches, when Miss Bell had thrown herself into the task of preparing for Bud's change in life.

What school was she to go to in Edinburgh? – Ailie knew: there was none better than the one she had gone to herself.

When did it open? – Ailie knew: in a fortnight.

What, exactly, would she need? – Ailie knew that too: she had in the escritoire a list of things made up already.

"It seems to me," said Miss Bell suspiciously, "you're desperately well informed on all that appertains to this sudden necessity. How long has it been in your mind?"

"For a twelvemonth at least," answered Ailie boldly. "How long has it been in your own?"

"H'm!" said Bell. "About as long, but I refused to harbour it; and – and now that the thing's decided on, Ailie Dyce, I hope you're not going to stand there arguing away about it all day long, when there's so much to do."

Surely there was never another house so throng, so bustling, so feverish in anxiety, as this one was for the next fortnight. The upper and the lower Dyce Academy took holiday; Kate's education stopped with a sudden gasp at a dreadful hill called Popocatepetl, and she said she did not care a button, since Captain Maclean (no longer Charles to any one except himself and Bud in the more confidential moments) said the main things needed in a sailor's wife were health, hope, and temper and a few good-laying hens. Miss Minto was engaged upon Bud's grandest garments, running out and in next door herself with inch-tapes over her shoulders and a mouthful of pins, and banging up against the lawyer in his lobby to her great distress of mind. And Bell had in the seamstress, 'Lizbeth Ann, to help her and Ailie with the rest. Mercator sulked neglected on the wall of Mr Dyce's study, which was strewn with basting-threads and snippets of selvedge and lining till it looked like a tailor's shop, and Bud and Footles played on the floor of it with that content which neither youth nor dogs can find in chambers trim and orderly. Even Kate was called in to help these hurried operations – they termed it the making of Bud's trousseau. In the garden birds were calling, calling; far sweeter in the women's ears were the snip-snip of scissors and the whir of the sewing-machine; needle arms went back and forth like fiddle-bows in an orchestra, and from webs of cloth and linen came forth garments whose variety intoxicated her who was to wear them. I'm thinking Daniel Dyce lived simply then, with rather makeshift dinners, but I'm certain, knowing him well, he did not care, since his share in the great adventure was to correspond with Edinburgh, and pave the way there for the young adventurer's invasion.

He would keek in at the door on them as he passed to his office, and Ailie would cry, "Avaunt, man! here woman reigns."

"It's a pleasant change," he would say. "I would sooner have them rain than storm."

"You're as bad as Geordie Jordon," said Miss Bell, biting thread with that zest which always makes me think her sex at some time must have lived on cotton, "you're as bad as Geordie Jordon, you cannot see a keyhole but your eye begins to water."

If it had indeed been Bud's trousseau, the town folk could not have displayed more interest. Ladies came each day to see how things progressed, and recommend a heavier lining or another row of the insertion. Even Lady Anne came one afternoon to see the trousseau, being interested, as she slyly said, in such things for private reasons of her own, and dubious about the rival claims of ivory or pure white. So she said; but she came, no doubt, to assure Miss Lennox that her captain was a great success.

"I knew he'd be!" said Bud complacently. "That man's so beautiful and good, he's fit for the Kingdom of Heaven."

"So are you – you rogue!" said Lady Anne, gathering her in her arms, without a bit of awkwardness, to the great astonishment of 'Lizbeth Ann, who thought that titled folk were not a bit like that – perhaps had not the proper sort of arms for it. Yes, "So are you – you rogue!" said Lady Anne.

"No, I'm not," said the child. "Leastways only sometimes. Most the time I'm a born limb, but then again I'm nearly always trying to be better, and that's what counts, I guess."

"And you're going away to leave us," said Lady Anne, whereon a strange thing happened, for the joyous child, who was to get her heart's desire and such lovely garments, burst into tears, and ran from the room to hide herself upstairs in the attic bower, whose windows looked to a highway that seemed hateful through her tears. Her ladyship went off distressed, but Bell, as one rejoicing, said, "I always told you, Ailie – William's heart!"

But Bud's tears were transient: she was soon back among the snippets where Ailie briskly plied the sewing-machine, and sang the kind of cheerful songs that alone will go to the time of pedalling, and so give proof that the age of mechanism is the merry age, if we have the happy ear for music. And Bud, though she tired so soon of hems, could help another way that busy convocation, for she could sit tucked up in Uncle Dan's snoozing chair and read 'Pickwick' to the women till the maid of Colonsay was in the mood to take the Bardell body by the hair of the head and shake her for her brazenness to the poor wee man. Or the child would dance as taught by the lady of the Vaudeville, or start at Ailie's bidding (Bell a little dubious) to declaim a bit of "Hamlet" or "Macbeth," till 'Lizbeth Ann saw ghosts and let her nerves get the better of her, and there was nothing for it but a cheery cup of tea all round. Indeed, I must confess, a somewhat common company! I could almost wish for the sake of my story they were more genteel, and dined at half-past seven, and talked in low hushed tones of Bach and Botticelli.

But, oh! they were happy days – at least, so far as all outward symptoms went: it might indeed have been a real trousseau, and not the garments for the wedding of a maiden and the world. How often in the later years did Winifred Wallace, reading to me her own applause in newspapers, stop to sigh and tell me how she once was really happy – happy to the inward core, feeling the dumb applause of four women in a country chamber, when the world was all before her, and her heart was young.

CHAPTER XXVI

WORKING thus, furiously, at the task of love, which, in all it does for the youth it cherishes, must ever be digging a grave for its own delight, Bell could forget, for periods, that the days of Bud's presence in their midst were numbered. Had she stopped her needle and shears a moment, and let her mind contemplate all the emptiness of a fortnight hence and the months and years thereafter, she would have broken down. Ailie, knowing it, watched her anxiously, and kept the sewing briskly going as if they wrought for a living in a factory, frightened to think of her sister's desperate state when that last button, that the Armies talk about, was in its place.

But the days sped: one afternoon there was a final sweeping up of the scraps in the temporary workroom, Bell searched her mind in vain to think of anything further wanted, and, though there were still two weeks to go, became appalled to find that the only thing of any moment to be done 'twixt now and Friday fortnight was to say Good-bye!

No, stay! There was another thing to bring a little respite – the girl's initials must be sewn upon her clothing. A trivial thing to mention, you may think, but the very thought of it gave pleasure to the sisters, till Bud herself, sent to Miss Minto's for a sample of the woven letters, came back with only one – it was a W.

"Has the stupid body not got L's and D's?" asked Bell. "There's no use here for W." And Bud showed a countenance startled and ashamed.

"Oh, Auntie!" she cried, "I asked for W's. I quite forgot my name was Lennox Dyce, for in all I'm thinking of about the school and Edinburgh, I am Winifred Wallace."

It was all that was needed to bring about her aunt's prostration! "I'm far from well," said she, and took to her bed, her first confession of weakness in all the years that Dan or Ailie could remember. What ailed her she could not tell, and they sent, without acquainting

156

her, for Dr Brash. Hearing he was coming, she protested that she could not see the man – that she was far too ill to be troubled by any doctor; but Dr Brash was not so easily to be denied.

"H'm!" said he, examining her. "Your system's badly down."

"I never knew I had one," said the lady, smiling wanly, with a touch of Dan's rowan-jelly humour. "Women had no system in my young days to go up or down: if they had, they were ashamed to mention it. Nowadays, it seems as fashionable as what Kate, since she got her education, calls the boil."

"You have been worrying," he went on, "a thing that's dreadfully injudicious. H'm! worse than drink *I* say. Worry's the death of half my patients; they never give my pills a chance," and there was a twinkle in his eyes which most of Dr Brash's patients thought was far more efficacious than his pills.

"What would I worry for?" said Miss Bell. "I'm sure I have every blessing; goodness and mercy all my life."

"Just so! just so!" said Dr Brash. "Goodness and – and, h'm – mercy sometimes take the form of a warning that it's time we kept to bed for a week, and that's what I recommend you."

"Mercy on me! Am I so far through as that?" she said, alarmed. "It's something serious – I know by the cheerful face that you put on you. Little did I think that I would drop off so soon. And just at the very time when there's so much to do!"

"Pooh!" said Dr Brash. "When you drop off, Miss Dyce, there'll be an awful dunt, I'm telling you! God bless my soul, what do you think a doctor's for but putting folk on their pins again! A week in bed – and – h'm! – a bottle. Everything's in the bottle, mind you!"

"And there's the hands of the Almighty too," said Bell, who constantly deplored the doctor was so poor a Kirk attender, and not a bit in that respect like the noble doctors in her sister's latest Scottish novels.

Dr Brash went out of the room, to find the rest of the household sorely put about in the parlour, Lennox an object of woe, and praying hard to herself with as much as she could remember of her Uncle Dan's successful supplication for herself when she had the pneumonia. To see the cheerfulness of his countenance when he came in was like the sun-burst on a leaden sea. "Miss Bell's as sound as her namesake," he assured them. "There's been something on her mind" – with a flash of the eye, at once arrested, towards Lennox – "and she has worked herself into a state of nervous collapse. I've given her the best of tonics for her kind – the dread of a week in bed – and I'll wager she'll be up by Saturday. The main thing is to keep

157

her cheerful, and I don't think that should be very difficult."

Bud there and then made up her mind that her own true love was Dr Brash, in spite of his nervous sisters and his funny waistcoats. Ailie said if cheerfulness would do the thing she was ready for laughing-gas, and the lawyer vowed he would rake the town for the very latest chronicles of its never-ending fun.

But Bud was long before him on her mission of cheerfulness to the bedroom of Auntie Bell. Did you ever see a douce Scotch lass who never in her life had harboured the idea that her native hamlet was other than the finest dwelling-place in all the world, and would be happy never to put a foot outside it? – that was to be the *rôle* today. A sober little lass, sitting in a wicker-chair whose faintest creak appeared to put her in an agony – sitting incredibly long and still, and speaking Scotch when spoken to, in the most careful undertone, with a particular kind of smile that was her idea of judicious cheerfulness for a sick-room.

"Bairn!" cried her aunt at last, "if you sit much longer like that you'll drive me crazy. What in the world's the matter with you?"

"Nothing, dear Auntie Bell," said Bud, astonished.

"You needn't tell me! What was the Doctor saying?"

"He said you were to be kept cheerful," said Bud, "and I'm doing the best I can –"

"Bless me, lass! do you think it's cheery to be sitting there with a face like a Geneva watch? I would sooner see you romping."

But no, Bud could not romp that day, and when her Uncle Dan came up he found her reading aloud from Bell's favourite Gospel according to John – her auntie's way of securing the cheerfulness required. He looked at the pair, his hands in his pockets, his shoulders bent, and all the joviality with which he had come carefully charged gave place for a little to a graver sentiment. So had Ailie sat, a child, beside her mother on her death-bed, and, reading John one day, found open some new vista in her mind that made her there and then renounce her dearest visions, and thirl herself for ever to the home and him and Bell.

"Well, Dan," said his sister, when the child was gone, "what have you brought me? Is it the usual pound of grapes?" – for she was of the kind whose most pious exercises never quench their sense of fun, and a gift of grapes in our place is a doleful hint to folks bedridden: I think they sometimes might as well bring in the stretching-board.

"A song-book would suit you better," said the lawyer. "What do you think's the matter with you? Worrying about that wean! Is this your Christian resignation?"

"I am *not* worrying, Dan," she protested. "At least, not very much, and I never was the one to make much noise about my Christianity."

"You need to be pretty noisy with it nowadays to make folk believe you mean it."

"What did Dr Brash say down the stair?" she asked. "Does he – does he think I'm going to die?"

"Lord bless me!" cried her brother, "this is not the way that women die. I never heard of you having a broken heart. You're missing all the usual preliminaries, and you haven't even practised being ill. No, no, Bell; it'll be many a day, I hope, before you're pushing up the daisies, as that vagabond Wanton Wully puts it."

Bell sighed. "You're very joco'," said she; "You're aye cheery, whatever happens."

"So long as it doesn't happen to myself – that's philosophy; at least it's Captain Consequence's. And if I'm cheery today it's by the Doctor's orders. He says you're to be kept from fretting, even if we have to hire the band."

"Then I doubt I'm far far through!" said Bell; "I'm booked for a better land," – and at that the lawyer gave a chirruping little laugh, and said, "Are you sure it's not for Brisbane?"

"What do you mean?" she asked him, marvellously interested for one who talked of dying.

"It's a new one," he exclaimed. "I had it today from her ladyship's Captain. He was once on a ship that sailed to Australia, and half-way out a passenger took very ill. 'That one's booked for heaven, anyway,' Maclean said to the purser. 'No,' said the purser, who was busy, 'he's booked for Brisbane.' 'Then he would be a D. sight better in heaven,' said Maclean; 'I have been twice in Brisbane, and I know.'"

Bell did her best to restrain a smile, but couldn't. "Oh, Dan!" said she, "you're an awful man! You think there's nothing in this world to daunten anybody."

"Not if they happen to be Dyces," said he. "high heart and a humble head – you remember father's motto? And here you're dauntened because the young one's going only one or two hundred miles away for her own advantage."

"I'm not a bit dauntened," said Miss Bell with spirit. "It's not myself I'm thinking of at all – it's her, poor thing! among strangers night and day; damp sheets, maybe, and not a wise-like thing to eat. You would never forgive yourself if she fell into a decline."

"Ailie throve pretty well on their dieting," he pointed out; "and if

159

she's going to fall into a decline, she's pretty long of starting."

"But you mind they gave her sago pudding," said Miss Bell; "and if there's one thing Lennox cannot eat, it's sago pudding. She says it is so slippy, every spoonful disappears so sudden it gives her an awful start. She says she might as well sup puddocks."

Dan smiled at the picture and forced himself to silent patience.

"And they'll maybe let her sit up to all hours," Bell proceeded. "You know the way she fastens on a book at bed-time!"

"Well, well!" said he emphatically. "If you're sure that things are to be so bad as that, we'll not let her go at all," and he slyly scanned her countenance to see, as he expected, that she was indignant at the very thought of backing out now that they had gone so far.

"You needn't start to talk nonsense," said she; "of course she's going. But oh, Dan! it's not the sheets, nor food, nor anything like that, that troubles me; it's the knowledge that she'll never be the same wee lass again."

"Tuts!" said Daniel Dyce, and cleaned some moisture from his spectacles; "You're putting all the cheerful things I was going to say to you out of my head. I'm off to business; is there anything I can do for you? No. Then, remember, you're not to stir this week outside the blankets; these are the orders of Dr Brash. I have no doubt Ailie will do very well at the house-keeping," and he left her with a gleam of mischief in his eye.

The window of the bedroom was a little open; on one of the trees a blackbird sang, and there came in the scent of apple-ringie and a tempting splendour of sun. For twenty minutes the ailing lady tried to content herself with the thought of a household managed by Alison Dyce, and then arose to see if Wully Oliver was not idling in the garden. She saw him sitting on his barrow-trams, while Ailie walked among the dahlias, and chucked her favourites of them under their chins.

"William Oliver!" cried Miss Bell indignantly, having thrown a Shetland shawl about her; "Is that all the work you can do in a day?"

He looked up at the window and slowly put his pipe in his pocket.

"Well, m'em," said he, "I daresay I could do more, but I never was much of a hand for showing off."

CHAPTER XXVII

WHEN Miss Bell rose, as she did in a day or two, bantered into a speedy convalescence by Ailie and Dan, it was to mark Bud's future holidays on the calendar, and count the months in such a cunning way that she cheated the year of a whole one, by arguing to herself that the child would be gone a fortnight before they really missed her, and as good as home again whenever she started packing to return. And Edinburgh, when one was reasonable and came to think of it, was not so very awful: the Miss Birds were there, in the next street to the school where Bud was bound for, so if anything should happen – a fire, for instance – fires were desperately common just now in the newspapers, and ordinary commonsense suggested a whole clothes-rope for the tying up of the young adventurer's boxes; or if Bud should happen to be really hungry between her usual meals – a common thing with growing bairns – the Birds were the very ones to make her welcome. It was many a year since Bell had been in Edinburgh – she had not been there since mother died – she was determined that, if she had the money and was spared till Martinmas, she should make a jaunt of it and see the shops: it was very doubtful if Miss Minto wasn't often lamentably out of date with many of her fashions.

"Oh, you vain woman!" cried Ailie to her; "will nothing but the very latest satisfy you?"

Bud was to be sure and write once every week, on any day but Saturday, for if her letters came on Sunday they would be tempted to call at the post-office for them, like Captain Consequence, instead of waiting till the Monday morning. And if she had a cold or any threatening of quinsy, she was to fly for her very life to the hoarhound mixture, put a stocking round her neck, and go to bed. Above all, was she to mind and take her porridge every morning, and to say her prayers.

"I'll take porridge to beat the band," Bud promised, "even – even if I have to shut my eyes all through."

"In a cautious moderation," recommended Uncle Dan. "I think myself oatmeal is far too rich a diet for the blood. I have it from Captain Consequence that there's nothing for breakfast like curried kidney and a chop to follow. But I hope you'll understand that, apart from the carnal appetites, the main thing is to scoop in all the prizes. I'll be dreadfully disappointed if you come back disgraced, with anything less of them than the full of a cart. That, I believe, is the

161

only proof of a liberal Scottish education. In Ailie's story-books it's all the good, industrious, and deserving pupils who get everything. Of course, if you take all the prizes somebody's sure to want – but, tuts! I would never let that consideration vex me – it's their own look-out. If you don't take prizes, either in the school or in the open competition of the world, how are folk to know they should respect you?"

"You must have been a wonderfully successful student in your day," said Ailie mischievously. "Where are all your medals?"

Dan laughed. "It's ill to say," said he, "for the clever lads who won them when I wasn't looking have been so modest ever since that they've glean dropped out of sight. I never won anything myself in all my life that called for competition – except the bottom of the class! When it came to competitions, and I could see the other fellows' faces, I was always far too tired or well disposed to them to give them a disappointment which they seemingly couldn't stand so well as myself. But then I'm not like Bud here. I hadn't a shrewd old uncle egging me on. So you must be keen on the prizes, Bud. Of course there's wisdom too, but that comes later – there's no hurry for it. Prizes, prizes – remember the prizes: the more you win, the more, I suppose, I'll admire you."

"And if I don't win any, Uncle Dan?" said Bud slyly, knowing very well the nature of his fun.

"Then, I suppose, I'll have to praise the Lord if you keep your health, and just continue loving you," said the lawyer. "I admit that if you're anyway addicted to the prizes, you'll be the first of your name that was so. In that same school in Edinburgh your Auntie Ailie's quarterly reports had always 'Conduct – Good,' and 'Mathematics – Fairly moderate'. We half expected she was coming back an awful diffy; but if she did, she made a secret of it. I forgave her the 'Fairly moderate' myself, seeing she had learned one thing – how to sing. I hope you'll learn to sing, Bud, in French, or German, or Italian – anything but Scotch. Our old Scotch songs, I'm told, are not what's called artistic."

"The sweetest in the world!" cried Auntie Bell. "I wonder to hear you haivering."

"I'm afraid you're not a judge of music," said the brother. "Scotch songs are very common – every body knows them. There's no art in them, there's only heart – a trifling kind of quality. If you happen to hear me singing 'Annie Laurie' or 'Afton Water' after you come home, Bud, be sure and check me. I want to be no discredit to you."

"No, I shan't, Uncle Dan," said the child. "I'll sing 'Mary

Morison,' and 'Ae Fond Kiss,' and 'Jock o' Hazeldean' at you till you're fairly squealing with delight. I know. Allow me! why, you're only haivering."

"Have mercy on the child, Dan," said his sister. "Never you mind him, Bud; he's only making fun of you."

"I know," said Bud; "but I'm not kicking."

Kate – ah! poor Kate – how sorry I should be for her, deserted by her friend and tutor, if she had not her own consoling Captain. Kate would be weeping silently every time the pipe was on in the scullery, and she thought how lonely her kitchen was to be when the child was gone. And she had plans to make that painful exile less heartrending: she was going to write to her sister out in Colonsay and tell her to be sure and send fresh country eggs at intervals of every now and then, or maybe oftener in the winter-time, to Lennox; for the genuine country egg was a thing it was hopeless to expect in Edinburgh, where there wasn't such a thing as sand, or grass, or heather – only causeway stones. She could assure Lennox that, as for marriage, there was not the slightest risk for years and years, since there wasn't a house in the town to let that would be big enough (and still not dear) to suit a Captain. He was quite content to be a plain intended, and hold on. And as for writing, she would take her pen in hand quite often and send the latest news to Lennox, who must please excuse haste, and these d-d-desperate pens, and having the post to catch – not that she would dream of catching the poor, wee, shauchly creature: it was just a way of speaking. Would Lennox not be dreadful home-sick, missing all the cheery things, and smothered up in books in yon place – Edinburgh?

"I expect I'll be dre'ffle home-sick," admitted Bud.

"I'm sure you will, my lassie," said the maid. "I was so home-sick myself when I came here at first that my feet got almost splay with wanting to turn back to Colonsay. But if I'm not so terribly good-looking, I'm awful brave, and soon got over it. When you are home-sick go down to the quay and look at the steamboats, or take a turn at our old friend Mr Puckwuck."

Four days – three days – two days – one day – tomorrow; that last day went so fast, it looked as if Wanton Wully had lost the place again and rang the evening bell some hours before it was due. Bud could only sit by, helpless, and marvel at the ingenuity that could be shown in packing what looked enough to stock Miss Minto's shop into a couple of boxes. She aged a twelvemonth between the handglass at the bottom and the bath-sheet on the top.

"And in this corner," said Miss Bell, on her knees, "you'll find your Bible, the hoarhound mixture, and five-and-twenty three-penny-bits for the plate on Sundays. Some of them sixpences."

"Irish ones, apparently," said Uncle Dan.

"Some of them sixpences, for the Foreign Mission days, and one shilling for the day of the Highlands and Islands."

"You're well provided for the kirk at any rate," said Uncle Dan. "I'll have to put a little money for this wicked world in the other corner," and he did.

When the coach next day set out – No, no, I cannot tell you all, for I hate to think of tears, and would hurry over partings. It went in tearful weather, rain drizzling on Bud and Auntie Ailie, who accompanied her. They looked back on the hill-top, and saw the grey slates glint under a grey sky, and following them on the miry road, poor Footles, faithful heart, who did not understand. He paddled through the mud till a blast from the bugle startled him, and he seemed to realise that this was some painful new experience. And then he stood in the track of the disappearing wheels, and lifted up his voice in lamentation.

The night came on, resuming her ancient empire – for she alone, and not the day, did first possess and finally shall possess unquestioned this space dusty with transient stars, and the light is Lord of another universe where is no night, nay, nor terror thereof. From the western clouds were the flame and gold withdrawn, and the winds sighed from the mountains, as vexed for passing days. The winds sighed from the mountains, and the mists came mustering to the glens; the sea crept out on long, bird-haunted, wailing, and piping sands, nought to be seen of it, its presence obvious only in the scent of wrack and the wash on the pebbled beaches. Behind the town the woods lay black and haunted, and through them, and far upward in the valley, dripping in the rain and clamorous with hidden burns and secret wells, went the highway to the world, vacant of aught visible, but never to be wholly vacant, since whoso passes on a highway ever after leaves some wandering spirit there. Did the child, that night, think of the highway that had carried her from home? In the hoarsely crying city did she pause a moment to remember and retrace her way to the little town that now lay faintly glowing in the light of its own internal fires?

Thus Bell wondered, standing at her window, looking into the solitary street. Every mile of separating highway rose before her – she walked them in the rain and dark; all the weary longing of the world came down on her that mirk night in September, and praying that discretion should preserve and understanding keep her wanderer, she arrived at the soul's tranquillity, and heard without misgiving the wild geese cry.

Her brother took the Books, and the three of them – master, mistress, and maid – were one in the spirit of worship, longing, and hope. Where, then, I wonder, had gone Daniel Dyce, the lawyer, the gentle ironist, on whose lips so often was kindly mockery, on whose tongue levity or its pretence –

> "Never by passion quite possess'd,
> And never quite benumbed by the world's sway"?

It was Bell's nightly duty to turn the lamp out in the lobby and bolt the outer door. She went this night reluctant to perform that office, but a thought possessed her of a child from home, somewhere in the darkness among strangers, and she had to call her brother.

"What is it?" said he.

"The door," she said, ashamed of herself, "I cannot bolt it."

He looked at her flushed face and her trembling hand, and understood. "It's only the door of a house," said he; "*that* makes no difference," and ran the bolt into its staple.

CHAPTER XXVIII

FOR all the regrets of increasing age there is one alleviation among many, that days apart from those we love pass the quicker, even as our hurrying years. Thus it is that separations are divested of more and more of their terrors the nearer we are to that final parting which wipes out all, and is but the going to a great reunion. So the first fortnight, whereof Miss Bell thought to cheat the almanac under the delusion that Bud's absence would then scarcely be appreciated, was in truth the period when she missed her most, and the girl was back for her Christmas holidays before half of her threepenny-bits for the plate were done.

It was worth a year of separation to see her come in at the door, rosy from the frosty air, with sparkling eyes and the old, sweet, rippling laugh, not – outside at least – an atom different from the girl who had gone away; and it made up to Bud herself for many

165

evenings home-sick on an Edinburgh pillow to smell again the old celestial Christmas grocery and feel the warmth of her welcome.

Myself, I like to be important – not of such consequence to the world as to have it crick its neck with having to look up at me, but now and then important only to a few old friends; and Bud, likewise, could always enjoy the upper seat, if the others of her company were never below the salt. She basked in the flattery that Kate's deportment gave to her dignity as a young lady educated at tremendous cost.

It was the daft days of her first coming over again; but this time she saw all with older eyes – and, besides, the novelty of the little Scottish town was ended. Wanton Wully's bell, pealing far beyond the burgh bounds – commanding, like the very voice of God, to every ear of that community, no matter whether it rang at morn or eve – gave her at once a crystal notion of the smallness of the place, not only in its bounds of stone and mortar, but in its interests, as compared with the city, where a thousand bells, canorous on the Sabbath, failed, it was said, to reach the ears of more than a fraction of the people. The bell, and John Taggart's band on Hogmanay, and the little shops with windows falling back already on timid appeals, and the grey high tenements pierced by narrow entries, and the douce and decent humdrum folk – she saw them with a more exacting vision, and Ailie laughed to hear them all summed up as "quaint."

"I wondered when you would reach 'quaint'," said Auntie Ailie; "It was due some time ago, but this is a house where you never hear the word. Had you remained at the Pige – at the Misses Duff's Seminary Miss Amelia would have had you sewing it on samplers, if samplers any longer were the fashion."

"Is it not a nice word 'quaint'?" asked Bud, who, in four months among critics less tolerant (and perhaps less wise) than the Dyces, had been compelled to rid herself of many transatlantic terms and phrases.

"There's nothing wrong with 'quaint,' my dear," said Miss Ailie; "It moves in the most exclusive circles: if I noticed it particularly, it is because it is the indication of a certain state of mind, and tells me where you stand in your education more clearly than your first quarterly report. I came home from school with 'quaint' myself: it not only seemed to save a lot of trouble by being a word which could be applied to anything not otherwise describable, but I cherished it because its use conferred on me a kind of inward glow of satisfaction like – like – like Aunt Bell's homemade ginger-cordial. 'Quaint,'

Bud, is the shibboleth of boarding-school culture: when you can use the word in the proper place, with a sense of superiority to the thing so designated, you are practically a young lady and the polish is taking on."

"They all say it in our school," explained Bud apologetically; "at least, all except The Macintosh – I couldn't think of her saying it somehow."

"Who's The Macintosh?" asked Ailie.

"Why! was there no Macintosh in your time?" exclaimed Bud. "I thought she went away back to the – to the Roman period. She's the funniest old lady in the land, and comes twice a-week to teach us dancing and deportment. She's taught them to mostly all the nobility and gentry of Scotland; she taught Lady Anne and all her brothers when they were in St Andrews."

"I never heard of her," said Ailie; "she must be – be – be decidedly quaint."

"She's so quaint you'd think she'd be kept in a corner cupboard with a bag of camphor at the back to scare the moths away. She's a little wee mite, not any bigger than me – than I – and they say she's seventy years old, but sometimes she doesn't look a day more than forty-five if it weren't for her cap and her two front teeth missing. She's got the loveliest fluffy silver hair – pure white, like Mrs Molyneux's Aunt Tabitha's Persian cat; cheeks like an apple, hands as young as yours, and when she walks across a room she glides like this, so you'd think she was a cutter yacht –"

Bud sailed across the parlour to represent the movement of The Macintosh with an action that made her aunties laugh, and the dog gave one short yelp of disapproval.

"That was the way that Grandma Buntain walked – it used to be considered most genteel," said Bell. "They trained girls up to do it with a back-board and a book on the top of the head; but it was out before my time; we just walked anyway in Barbara Mushet's Seminary, where the main things were tambouring and the Catechism."

"Miss Macintosh is a real lady," Bud went on. "She's got genuine old ancestors. They owned a Highland place called Kaims, and the lawyers have almost lawyered it a' awa' she says, so now she's simply got to help make a living teaching dancing and deportment. I declare I don't know what deportment is no more than the child unborn, unless it's shutting the door behind you, walking into a room as if your head and your legs were your own, keeping your shoulders back, and being polite and kind to everybody, and I thought folks 'd do all that without attending classes, unless they were looney. Miss Macintosh says they are the *sine qua non* and principal branches for a well-bred young lady in these low days of clingy frocks and socialism; but the Principal she just smiles and gives us another big block of English history. Miss Macintosh doesn't let on, but I know she simply can't stand English history, for she tells us, spells between quadrilles, that there hasn't been any history anywhere since the Union of the Parliaments, except the Rebellion of 1745. But she doesn't call it a rebellion. She calls it 'yon affair'. *She's* Scotch! I tell you, Auntie Bell, you'd love to meet her! I sit, and sit, and look at her like – like a cat. She wears spectacles, just a little clouded, only she doesn't call them spectacles; she says they are preserves, and that her eyes are as good as anybody's. They're bright enough, I tell you, for over seventy."

"Indeed I would like to see the creature!" exclaimed Miss Bell. "She must be an original! I'm sometimes just a trifle tired of the same old folk about me here – I know them all so well, and all they're like to do or say, that there's nothing new or startling to be expected from them."

"Would you like to see her?" said Bud quickly; "then – then, some day I'll tell her, and I'll bet she'll come. She dresses queer – like a lady in the 'School for Scandal,' and wears long mittens like Miss Minto, and when our music-master, Herr Laurent, is round she makes goo-goo eyes at him fit to crack her glasses. 'Oh, Hair-r-r!' she says, sitting with her mitts in her lap – 'oh, Hair-r-r! can you no' give the young ladies wise-like Scotch sangs, instead o' that dreich Concone?' And sometimes she'll hit him with a fan. He says she plays the piano to our dancing the same as it was a spinet."

"I declare it beats all!" said Miss Bell. "Does the decent old body speak Scotch?"

"Sometimes. When she's making goo-goo eyes at the Herr, or angry, or finding fault with us but doesn't want to hurt our feelings."

"I can understand that," said Miss Bell, with a patriot's fervour; "there's nothing like the Scotch for any of them; I fall to it myself when I'm sentimental. And so does your Uncle Dan."

"She says she's the last of the real Macintoshes – that all the rest you see on Edinburgh signboards are only incomers or poor de-degenerate cadets; and I guess the way she says it, being a de-degenerate cadet Macintosh must be the meanest thing under the cope and canopy. Heaps of those old ancestors of hers went out in the days of the clans, fighting for any royalty that happened along. She's got all their hair in lockets, and makes out that when they disappeared Scotland got a pretty hard knock. I said to her once the same as Aunt Ailie says to you, Aunt Bell, 'English and Scots, I s'pose we're all God's people, and it's a terribly open little island to be quarrelling in, seeing all the Continent can hear us quite plain'; but she didn't like it. She said it was easy seen I didn't understand the dear old Highland mountains, where her great-great-grandfather, Big John of the Axe, could collect five hundred fighting-men if he wagged a fiery cross at them. 'I have Big John's blood in me!' she said, quite white, and her head shaking so much her preserves nearly fell off her nose. 'I've Big John's blood in me; and when I think of things, *I hate the very name o' thae aboaminable English!*' 'Why, you've never seen them, Miss Macintosh,' I said – for I knew she'd never had a foot outside Scotland. 'No,' said she, quite sharp, 'and I don't want to; for they might be nice enough, and then I wad be bound to like them.'"

"Oh, Bell!" cried Ailie, laughing, "Miss Macintosh is surely your doppelganger."

"I don't know what a doppelganger is," said Auntie Bell; "but she's a real sensible body, and fine I would like to see her."

"Then I'll have to fix it somehow," said Bud, with emphasis. "P'raps you'll meet her when you come to Edinburgh –"

"I'm not there yet, my dear."

"– Or she might be round this way by-and-by. She'd revel in this place: she'd maybe not call it quaint, but she'd find it pretty careless about being in the – in the modern rush she talks about, and that would make her happier than a letter from home. I believe The Macintosh –"

"Miss Macintosh, my dear," said Bell reprovingly, and the girl reddened.

"I know," said she. "It's mean to talk of her same as she was a waterproof, and I often try not to, because I like her immensely; but it's so common among the girls that I forget. I believe Miss Macintosh would love this place, and could stop in it for ever."

"Couldn't you?" asked Auntie Ailie slyly.

Bud hesitated. "Well, I – I like it," said she. "I just love to lie awake nights and think about it, and I can hear the wind in the trees and the tide come in, and the bell, and the wild geese; and family worship at the Provost's on Sunday nights, and I can almost *be* here, I think so powerfully about it; but – but –"

She stopped short, for she saw a look of pain in the face of her Auntie Bell.

"But what?" said the latter sharply.

"Oh! I'm a wicked, cruel, ungrateful girl, Auntie Bell; and I ought to want to love this place so much, nobody could push me out of it. And I *do* love it; but I feel if I lived here always I'd not grow any more."

"You're big enough," said Auntie Bell. "You're as big as myself now."

"I mean inside. Am I a prig, Aunt Ailie? I'd hate to be a prig! But I'd hate as bad to tell a lie; and I feel I'd never learn half so much or do half so much here as I'd do where thousands of folk were moving along in a procession, and I was with them too. A place like this is like a kindergarten – it's good enough as far's it goes, but it doesn't teach the higher branches."

Bell gazed at her in wonder and pity and blame, shaking her head. All this was what she had anticipated.

"I know the feeling," said Aunt Ailie, "for I have shared it myself; and sometimes still it will come back to me, but in my better hours I think I'm wiser and can be content. If there is growth in you, you will grow anywhere. You were born in the noise of Chicago, Bud, and I suppose it's hard to get it out of the ears. By-and-by I hope you'll find that we are all of us most truly ourselves not in the crowd but when we are alone, and that not the smallest hamlet in the world need be intellectually narrow for any one with imagination, some books, and a cheerful constitution. Do you understand that, Bud?"

Bud thought hard for a moment and then shook her head. "It sounds as if it ought to be true," said she, "and I daresay you think just now it is true; but I simply *can't* believe it." And all of them turned at the sound of a chuckling laugh, to find that Mr Dyce had heard this frank confession.

"That's the worst of you, Bud," said he. "You will never let older folk do your thinking for you."

CHAPTER XXIX

IT is another mercy, too, that in our age we learn to make the best of what aforetime might be ill to thole, as Bell made fine new garments out of old ones faded by turning them outside in and adding frills and flounces. Bud's absence early ceased to be deplorable, since it wakened cheerful expectations not to be experienced had she stayed at home; gave rise to countless fond contrivances for her happiness in exile; and two or three times a-year to periods of bliss, when her vacations gave the house of Dyce the very flower of ecstasy. Her weekly letters of themselves were almost compensation for her absence. On the days of their arrival, Peter the post would come blithely whistling with his M.C. step to the lawyer's kitchen window before he went to the castle itself, defying all routine and the laws of the Postmaster-General, for he knew Miss Dyce would be waiting feverishly, having likely dreamt the night before of happy things that – dreams going by contraries, as we all of us know in Scotland – might portend the most dreadful tidings.

Bud's envelope was always on the top of his budget. For the sake of it alone (it sometimes seemed to Peter and those who got it) had the mail come splashing through the night – the lawyer's big blue envelopes, as it were, had got but a friendly lift through the courtesy of clerks in Edinburgh, and the men on the railway train, and the lad who drove the gig from Maryfield. What were big blue envelopes of the business world compared with the modest little square of grey with Lennox Dyce's writing on it?

"Here's the usual! Pretty thick today!" would Peter say, with a smack of satisfaction on the window-sash. Ah, those happy Saturdays! Everybody knew about them. "And how's hersel'?" the bell-ringer would ask in the by-going, not altogether because his kindly interest led to an eye less strict on his lazy moods in the garden. One Fair day, when Maggie White's was Irresistible, it rang so merrily with drovers, and he lost the place again, he stopped the lawyer on the street to ask him what Miss Lennox thought of all this argument about the Churches, seeing she was in the thick of it in Edinburgh.

"Never you mind the argument, Will," said Daniel Dyce, "you do your duty by the Auld Kirk bell; and as for the Free folk's quarrelling, amang them be't!"

"But can you tell me, Mr D-D-Dyce," said Wanton Wully, with as much assurance as if he was prepared to pay by the Table of Fees, "what's the difference between the U.F.'s and the Frees? I've looked at it from every point, and I canna see it."

"Come and ask me some day when you're sober," said the lawyer, and Wanton Wully snorted.

"If I was sober," said he, "I wouldna want to ken – I wouldna give a curse."

Yet each time Bud came home she seemed, to the mind of her Auntie Bell, a little farther off from them – a great deal older, a great

171

deal less dependent, making for womanhood in a manner that sometimes was astounding, as when sober issues touched her, set her thinking, made her talk in fiery ardours. Aunt Ailie gloried in that rapid growth; Aunt Bell lamented, and spoke of brains o'ertaxed and fevered, and studies that were dangerous. She made up her mind a score of times to go herself to Edinburgh and give a warning to the teachers; but the weeks passed, and the months, and by-and-by the years, till almost three were gone, and the Edinburgh part of Lennox's education was drawing to a close, and the warning visit was still to pay.

It was then, one Easter, came The Macintosh.

Bell and Ailie were out that afternoon for their daily walk in the woods or along the shore, when Mr Dyce returned from the Sheriff Court alert and buoyant, feeling much refreshed at the close of an encounter with a lawyer who, he used to say, was better at debating than himself, having more law books in his possession and a louder voice. Letting himself in with his pass-key, he entered the parlour, and was astonished to find a stranger, who rose at his approach and revealed a figure singular though not unpleasing. There was something ludicrous in her manner as she moved a step or two from the chair in which she had been sitting. Small, and silver-grey in the hair, with a cheek that burned – it must be with embarrassment – between a rather sallow neck and sunken temples, and wearing smoked spectacles with rims of tortoise-shell, she would have attracted attention anywhere even if her dress had been less queer. Queer it was, but in what manner Daniel Dyce was not the person to distinguish. To him there was about it nothing definitely peculiar, except that the woman wore a crinoline, a Paisley shawl of silken white, and such a bonnet as he had not seen since Grandma Buntain's time.

"Be seated, ma'am," said he; "I did not know I had the honour of a visitor," and he gave a second, keener glance, that swept the baffling figure from the flounced green poplin to the snow-white lappet of her bonnet. A lady certainly – that was in the atmosphere, however odd might be her dress. "Where in the world has this one dropped from?" he asked himself, and waited an explanation.

"Oh, Mr Dyce!" said the lady in a high, shrill voice, that plainly told she never came from south of the Border, and with a certain trepidation in her manner; "I'm feared I come at an inconvenient time to ye, and I maybe should hae bided at your office; but they tell't me ye were out at what they ca'd a Pleading Diet. I've come about my mairrage."

172

"Your marriage!" said the lawyer, scarcely hiding his surprise.

"Yes, my mairrage!" she repeated sharply, drawing the silken shawl about her shoulders, bridling. "There's naething droll, I hope and trust, in a maiden lady ca'in' on a writer for his help about her settlements!"

"Not at all – not at all, ma'am," said Daniel Dyce. "I'm honoured in your confidence." And he pushed his spectacles up on his brow that he might see her less distinctly and have the less inclination to laugh at such an eccentric figure.

She broke into a torrent of explanation. "Ye must excuse me, Mr Dyce, if I'm put-about and gey confused, for it's little I'm acquent wi' lawyers. A' my days I've heard o' naething but their quirks, for they maistly rookit my grandfaither. And I cam' wi' the coach frae Maryfield, and my heart's in a palpitation wi' sic briengin' and bangin' ower heughs and hills –" She placed a mittened hand on a much-laced stomacher, and sighed profoundly.

"Perhaps – perhaps a glass of wine –" began the lawyer, with his eye on the bell-pull, and a notion in his head that wine and a little seed-cake someway went with crinolines and the age of the Paisley shawl.

"No, no!" she cried extravagantly. "I never lip it; I'm – I'm in the Band o' Hope."

The lawyer started, and scanned her again through his glasses, with a genial chuckling crow. "So's most maiden ladies, ma'am," said he. "I'm glad to congratulate you on your hopes being realised."

"It remains to be seen," said the visitor. "Gude kens what may be the upshot. The maist deleeberate mairrage maun be aye a lottery, as my Auntie Grizel o' the Whinhill used to say; and I canna plead that mine's deleeberate, for the man just took a violent fancy the very first nicht he set his een on me, fell whummlin' at my feet, and wasna to be put aff wi' 'No' or 'Maybe'. We're a puir weak sex, Mr Dyce, and men's sae domineerin'!"

She ogled him through her clouded glasses: her arch smile showed a blemish of two front teeth amissing. He gave a nod of sympathy, and she was off again. "And to let ye ken the outs and ins o't, Mr Dyce, there's a bit o' land near Perth that's a' that's left o' a braw estate my forebears squandered in the Darien. What I want to ken is, if I winna could hinder him that's my *fiancé* frae dicin' or drinkin' 't awa' ance he got me mairried to him? I wad be sair vexed at ony such calamity, for my family hae aye been barons."

"Ance a baron aye a baron," said the lawyer, dropping into her own broad Scots.

173

"Yes, Mr Dyce, that's a' very fine; but baron or baroness, if there's sic a thing, 's no great figure wantin' a bit o' grun' to gang wi' the title; and John Cleghorn – that's my intended's name – has been a gey throughither chiel in his time by a' reports, and I doubt wi' men it's the aulder the waur."

"I hope in this case it'll be the aulder the wiser, Miss –"said the lawyer, and hung unheeded on the note of interrogation.

"I'll run nae risks if I can help it," said the lady emphatically; "and I'll no' put my trust in the Edinburgh lawyers either: they're a' tarred wi' the ae stick, or I sair misjudge them. But I'm veesitin' a cousin owerby at Maryfield, and I'm tell't there's no' a man that's mair dependable in a' the shire than yoursel', so I just cam' ower ains errand for a consultation. Oh, that unco' coach! the warld's gane wud, Mr Dyce, wi' hurry and stramash, and Scotland's never been the same since... But there! I'm awa' frae my story; if it's the Lord's will that I'm to marry Johnny Cleghorn, what comes o' Kaims? Will he be owner o't?"

"Certainly not, ma'am," said Mr Dyce, with a gravity well preserved considering his inward feelings. "Even before the Married Women's Property Act, his *jus mariti*, as we ca' it, gave him only his wife's personal and moveable estate. There is no such thing as *communio bonorum* – community of goods – between husband and wife in Scotland."

"And he canna sell Kaims on me?"

"No; it's yours and your assigns *ad perpetuam remanentiam*, being feudal right."

"I wish ye wad speak in honest English, like mysel', Mr Dyce," said the lady sharply. "I've forgotten a' my Laiten, and the very sound o't gars my heid bizz. I doubt it's the lawyer's way o' gettin' round puir helpless bodies."

"It's scarcely that," said Mr Dyce, laughing. "It's the only chance we get to air auld Mr Trayner, and it's thought to be imposin'. *Ad perpetuam remanentiam* just means to remain for ever."

"I thocht that maybe John might hae the poo'er to treat Kaims as my tocher."

"Even if he had," said Mr Dyce, "a *dot*, or *dos*, or tocher, in the honest law of Scotland, was never the price o' the husband's hand; he could only use the fruits o't. He is not entitled to dispose of it, and must restore it intact if unhappily the marriage should at any time be dissolved."

"Dissolved!" cried the lady. "Fegs! ye're in an awfu' hurry, and the ring no' bought yet. Supposin' I was deein' first?"

"In that case I presume that you would have the succession settled on your husband."

"On Johnny Cleghorn! Catch me! There's sic a thing as – as – as bairns, Mr Dyce," and the lady simpered coyly, while the lawyer rose hurriedly to fumble with some books and hide his confusion at such a wild conjecture. He was relieved by the entrance of Bell and Ailie, who stood amazed at the sight of the odd and unexpected visitor.

"My sisters," said the lawyer hastily. "Miss – Miss – I did not catch the name."

"Miss Mackintosh," said the stranger nervously, and Bell cried out immediately, "I was perfectly assured of it! Lennox has often spoken of you, and I'm so glad to see you. I did not know you were in the neighbourhood."

Ailie was delighted with so picturesque a figure. She could scarcely keep her eyes off the many flounced, expansive gown of poplin, the stomacher, the ponderous ear-rings, the great cameo brooch, the long lace mittens, the Paisley shawl, the neat poke-bonnet, and the fresh old face marred only by the spectacles, and the gap where the teeth were missing.

"I have just been consultin' Mr Dyce on my comin' mairrage," said The Macintosh; and at this intelligence from a piece of such antiquity Miss Bell's face betrayed so much astonishment that Dan and Ailie almost forgot their good manners.

"Oh! if it's business –" said Bell, and rose to go; but The Macintosh put a hand on her sleeve and stayed her.

"Ye needna fash to leave, Miss Dyce," said she. "A'thing's settled. It seems that Johnny Cleghorn canna ca' a rig o' Kaims his ain when he mairries me, and that was a' I cam' to see about. Oh, it's a mischancy thing a mairrage, Miss Dyce; maist folk gang intill't heels-ower-hurdies, but I'm in an awfu' swisher, and havena a mither to guide me."

"Keep me!" said Miss Bell, out of all patience at such maidenly apprehensions, "ye're surely auld enough to ken your ain mind. I hope the guidman's worthy."

"He's no' that ill – as men-folk gang," said The Macintosh resignedly. "He's as fat's creish, and has a craighlin' cough, the body, and he's faur frae bonny, and he hasna a bawbee o' his ain, and sirs! what a reputation! But a man's a man, Miss Dyce, and time's aye fleein'."

At such a list of disabilities in a husband the Dyces lost all sense of the proprieties and broke into laughter, in which the lady joined them, shaking in her arm-chair. Bell was the first to recover with a guilty sense that this was very bad for Daniel's business. She straightened her face and was about to make apologies, when Footles bounded in at the open door, to throw himself at the feet of The Macintosh and wave a joyous tall. But he was not content there. In spite of her resistance, he must be in her lap, and then, for the first time, Bell and Ailie noticed a familiar cadence in the stranger's laugh.

Dan rose and clapped her on the back. "Well done, Bud!" said he. "Ye had us a'; but Footles wasna to be swindled wi' an auld wife's goon," and he gently drew the spectacles from the laughing eyes of his naughty niece!

"Oh, you rogue!" cried Auntie Ailie.

"You wretch!" cried Auntie Bell. "I might have known your cantrips. Where in the world did you get these clothes?"

Bud sailed across the room like a cutter yacht and put her arms about her neck. "Didn't you know me?" she asked.

"How could I know you, dressed up like that? And your teeth – you imp! they're blackened; and your neck – you jad! it's painted; and – oh' lassie, lassie! Awa'! awa'! the deil's ower grit wi' ye!"

"Didn't *you* know me, Aunt Ailie?" asked Bud.

"Not in the least," said Ailie, taking the droll old figure in her arms. "Perhaps I might have known you if I didn't think it was tomorrow you were coming."

"It was to have been tomorrow; but the measles have broken out in school, and I came a day earlier, and calculated I'd just hop in and surprise you all. Didn't you guess, Uncle Dan?"

"Not at first," said he. "I'll admit I was fairly deceived, but when you talked about being in the Band of Hope I saw at a shot through The Macintosh. I hope you liked my Latin, Bud."

CHAPTER XXX

"YOU surely did not come in these daft-like garments all the way from Edinburgh?" asked her Auntie Bell, when the wig had been removed and Bud's youth was otherwise resumed.

"Not at all!" said Bud, sparkling with the success of her deception. "I came almost enough of a finished young lady to do you credit, but when I found there was nobody in the house except Kate,

I felt I couldn't get a better chance to introduce you to The Macintosh if I waited for a year. I told you we'd been playing charades last winter at the school, and I got Jim to send me some make-up, the wig, and this real 'cute old lady's dress. They were all in my box to give you some fun sometime, and Kate helped me hook things, though she was mighty scared to think how angry you might be, Aunt Bell; and when I was ready for you she said she'd be sure to laugh fit to burst, and then you'd see it was only me dressed up, and Footles he barked, so he looked like giving the show away, so I sent them both out into the garden and sat in a stage-fright that almost shook my ear-rings off. I tell you I felt mighty poorly sitting there wondering what on earth I was to say; but by-and-by I got to be so much The Macintosh I felt almost sure enough her to have the rheumatism, and knew I could fix up gags to keep the part going. I didn't expect Uncle Dan would be the first to come in, or I wouldn't have felt so brave about it, he's so sharp and suspicious – that's with being a lawyer, I s'pose, they're a' tarred wi' the ae stick, Miss Macintosh says; and when he talked all that solemn Latin stuff and looked like running up a bill for law advice that would ruin me, I laughed inside enough to ache. Now *amn't* I just the very wickedest girl, Uncle Dan?"

"A little less Scotch and a more plausible story would have made the character perfect," said her uncle. "Where did you get them both? Miss Macintosh was surely not the only model?"

"Well, she's not so Scotch as I made out, except when she's very sentimental, but I felt she'd have to be as Scotch as the mountain and the flood to fit these clothes; and she's never talked about marrying anybody herself, but she's making a match just now for a cousin o' hers, and tells us all about it. I was partly her, but not enough to be unkind or mean, and partly her cousin, and a little bit of the Waverley Novels – in fact, I was pure mosaic, like our dog. There wasn't enough real quaint about Miss Macintosh for ordinary to make a front scene monologue go, but she's fuller of hints than – than a dictionary, and once I started I felt I could play half a dozen Macintoshes all different, so's you'd actually think she was a surging crowd. You see there's the Jacobite Macintosh, and the 'aboaminable' English Macintosh, and the flirting Macintosh who raps Herr Laurent with her fan, and the fortune-telling Macintosh who reads palms and tea-cup leaves, and the dancing and deportment Macintosh who knows all the first families in Scotland."

Bud solemnly counted off the various Macintoshes on her finger-tips.

"We'll have every one of them when you come home next winter," said Miss Ailie. "I'd prefer it to the opera."

"I can't deny but it's diverting," said Miss Bell; "still, it's dreadfully like play-acting, and hardly the thing for a sober dwelling. Lassie, lassie, away this instant and change yourself!"

If prizes and Italian songs had really been the proof that Bud had taken on the polish, she would have disappointed Uncle Dan, but this art of hers was enough to make full amends, it gave so much diversion. Character roused and held her interest; she had a lightning eye for oddities of speech and gesture. Most of a man's philosophy is in a favourite phrase, his individuality is betrayed in the way he carries his hat along the aisle on Sunday. Bud, each time that she came home from Edinburgh, collected phrases as others do postage-stamps, and knew how every hat in town was carried. Folk void of idiosyncrasy, having the natural self restrained by watchfulness and fear, were the only ones whose company she wearied of; all others she studied with delight, storing of each some simulacrum in her memory. Had she reproduced them in a way to make them look ridiculous she would have roused the Dyces' disapproval, but lacking any sense of superiority she made no impersonation look ignoble; the portraits in her gallery, like Raeburn's, borrowed a becoming curl or two and toned down crimson noses.

But her favourite character was The Macintosh in one of the countless phases that at last were all her own invention, and far removed from the original. Each time she came home, the dancing-mistress they had never really seen became a more familiar personage to the Dyces. "I declare," cried Bell, "I'm beginning to think of you always as a droll old body." "And how's the rheumatism?" Dan would ask; it was "The Macintosh said this" or "The Macintosh said that" with Ailie; and even Kate would quote the dancing-mistress with such earnestness, that the town became familiar with the name and character without suspecting they were often merely parts assumed by young Miss Lennox.

Bud carried the joke one night to daring lengths by going as Miss Macintosh with Ailie to a dance, in a gown and pelerine of Grandma Buntain's that had made tremendous conquests eighty years before.

Our dances at the inn are not like city routs: Petronella, La Tempête, and the reel have still an honoured place in them; we think the joy of life is not meant wholly for the young and silly, and so the elderly attend them. We sip claret-cup and tea in the alcove or "adjacent," and gossip together if our dancing days are done, or sit below the flags and heather, humming "Merrily danced the quaker's

wife," with an approving eye on our bonny daughters. Custom gives
the Provost and his lady a place of honour in the alcove behind the
music: here is a petty court where the civic spirit pays its devoirs,
where the lockets are large and strong, and hair-chains much
abound, and mouths before the mellowing midnight hour are apt to
be a little mim.

Towards the alcove, Ailie – Dan discreetly moving elsewhere –
boldly led The Macintosh, whose ballooning silk brocade put even
the haughtiest of the other dames in shadow. She swam across the
floor as if her hoops and not her buckled shoon sustained her, as if
she moved on air.

"Dod! here's a character!" said Dr Brash, pulling down his
waistcoat. "Where have the Dyces gotten her?"

"The Ark is landed," said the Provost's lady. "What a peculiar
creature!"

Ailie gravely gave the necessary introductions, and soon the
notable Miss Macintosh of Kaims was the lion of the assembly. She
flirted most outrageously with the older beaux, sharing roguish
smiles and taps of the fan between them, and, compelling unaccustomed gallantries, set their wives all laughing. They drank wine with
her in the old style; she met them glass for glass in water.

"And I'll gie ye a toast now," she said, when her turn came,
"Scotland's Rights," raising her glass of water with a dramatic
gesture.

"Dod! the auld body's got an arm on her," whispered Dr Brash to
Colin Cleland, seeing revealed the pink plump flesh between the
short sleeves and the top of the mittens.

They drank the sentiment – the excuse for the glass was good
enough, though in these prosaic days a bit mysterious.

"What are they?" asked the Provost.

"What are what?" said The Macintosh.

"Scotland's Rights."

"I'll leave it to my frien' Mr Dyce to tell ye," she said quickly, for
the lawyer had now joined the group. "It'll aiblins cost ye 6s. 8d.,
but for that I daresay he can gie ye them in the Laiten. But – but I
hope we're a' friens here?" she exclaimed with a hurried glance
round her company. "I hope we have nane o' thee aboaminable
English amang us. I canna thole them! It has been a sair dooncome
for Scotland since ever she drew in wi' them." For a space she dwelt
on themes of rather antique patriotism that made her audience
smile, for in truth in this burgh town we see no difference between
Scotch and English: in our calculations there are only the lucky folk,

born, bred, and dwelling within the sound of Will Oliver's bell, and the poor souls who have to live elsewhere, all equally unfortunate, whether they be English, Irish, or Scots.

"But here I'm keepin' you gentlemen frae your dancin'," she said, interrupting herself, and consternation fell on her company, for sets were being formed for a quadrille, and her innuendo was unmistakable. She looked from one to the other of them as if enjoying their discomfiture.

"I – I – I haven't danced, myself, for years," said the Provost, which was true; and Colin Cleland, sighing deeply in his prominent profile and hiding his feet, protested quadrilles were beyond him. The younger men quickly remembered other engagements and disappeared. "Will you do me the honour?" said Dr Brash – good man! a gentle hero's heart was under that wrinkled waistcoat.

"Oh!" said The Macintosh, rising to his arm, "you'll be sure and no' to swing me aff my feet' for I'm but a frail and giddy creature."

"It would be but paying you back," said the Doctor, bowing. "Miss Macintosh has been swinging us a' aff our feet since she entered the room."

She laughed behind her clouded glasses, tapped him lightly with her fan, and swam into the opening movement of the figure. The word's abused, yet I can but say she danced divinely, with such grace, lightness of foot, and rhythm of the body that folk stared at her in admiration and incredulity: her carriage, seen from behind, came perilously near betraying her, and possibly her partner might have soon discovered who he had, even if she had not made him a confession.

"Upon my word!" said he, in a pause between the figures, "Upon my word! you dance magnificently, Miss Macintosh. I must apologise for such a stiff old partner as you've gotten."

"I micht weel dance," said she. "You ken I'm a dancin'-mistress?" Then she whispered hurriedly in her natural voice to him. "I feel real bold, Dr Brash, to be dancing with you here when I haven't come out yet, and I feel real mean to be deceiving you, who would dance with an old frump just because you're sorry for her, and I *can't* do it one minute longer. Don't you know me, really?"

"Good Lord!" said he in an undertone, aghast. "Miss Lennox!"

"Only for you," she whispered. "Please don't tell anybody else."

"You beat all," he told her. "I suppose I'm making myself ridiculous dancing away here with – h'm! – auld langsyne, but faith I have the advantage now of the others, and you mustn't let on when the thing comes out that I did not know you from the outset. I have a crow to pick with Miss Ailie about this – the rogue! But, young woman, it's an actress you are!"

"Not yet, but it's an actress I mean to be," she said, pousetting with him.

"H'm!" said he, "there seems the natural gift for it, but once on a time I made up my mind it was to be poetry."

"I've got over poetry," she said. "I found I was only one of that kind of poets who always cut it up in fourteen-line lengths and begin with 'As when'. No, it's to be the stage, Dr Brash; I guess God's fixed it."

"Whiles He is – h'm – injudicious," said the Doctor. "But what about Aunt Bell?"

"There's no buts about it, though I admit I'm worried to think of Auntie Bell. She considers acting is almost as bad as lying, and talks about the theatre as Satan's abode. If it wasn't that she was from home tonight, I daren't have been here. I wish – I wish I didn't love her so – almost – for I feel I've got to vex her pretty bad."

"Indeed you have!" said Dr Brash. "And you've spoiled my dancing, for I've a great respect for that devoted little woman."

Back in the alcove The Macintosh found more to surround her than ever, though it was the penalty of her apparent age that they were readier to joke than dance with her. Captain Consequence, wanting a wife with money, if and when his mother should be taken from him, never lost a chance to see how a pompous manner and his medals would affect strange ladies. He was so marked in his attention, and created such amusement to the company, that, pitying him, and fearful of her own deception, she proposed to tell fortunes. The ladies brought her their emptied teacups; the men solemnly laid their palms before her; she divined, for all, their past and future in a practised way that astonished her uncle and aunt, who, afraid of some awkward sally, had kept aloof at first from her levee, but now were the most interested of her audience.

Over the leaves in Miss Minto's cup she frowned through her clouded glasses. "There's lots o' money," said she, "and a braw house, and a muckle garden wi' bees and trees in's, and a wheen boys speilin' the wa's – you may be aye assured o' bien circumstances, Miss Minto."

Miss Minto, warmly conscious of the lawyer at her back, could have wished for a fortune less prosaic.

"Look again; is there no' a man to keep the laddies awa'?" suggested the Provost, pawky body!

"I declare there is!" cried The Macintosh, taking the hint. "See;

there! he's under this tree, a' huddled up in an awfu' passion."

"I can't make out his head," said the Provost's lady.

"Some men hae nane," retorted the spaewife; "but what's to hinder ye imaginin' it like me?"

"Oh! if it's imagination," said the Provost's lady, "I can hear him swearin'. And now, what's my cup?"

"I see here," said The Macintosh, "a kind o' island far at sea, and a ship sailin' frae't this way, wi' flags to the mast-heid, and a man on board."

"I hope he's well, then," said the Provost's lady, "for that's our James, and he's coming from Barbadoes: we had a letter just last week. Indeed you're a perfect wizard!" She had forgotten that her darling James's coming was the talk of the town for ten days back.

Colin Cleland, rubicund, good-natured, with his shyness gone, next proffered his palm to read. His hand lay like a plaice, inelegant and large, in hers, whose fresh young beauty might have roused suspicion in observers less carried away in the general illusion.

"Ah! sir," said she with a sigh, "ye hae had your trials!"

"Mony a ane, ma'am," said the jovial Colin. "I was ance a lawyer, for my sins."

"That's no' the kind o' trial I mean," said The Macintosh. "Here's a wheen o' auld tribulations."

"Perhaps you're richt, ma'am," he admitted. "I hae a sorry lot o' them marked doon in auld diaries, but gude-be-thanked I canna mind them unless I look them up. They werena near see mony as the rattlin' ploys I've had."

"Is there no' a wife for Mr Cleland?" said the Provost – pawky, pawky man!

"There was ance, I see, a girl, and she was the richt girl too," said The Macintosh.

"Yes, but I was the wrang man," said Colin Cleland, drawing his hand away, and nobody laughed, for all but The Macintosh knew that story and made it some excuse for foolish habits.

"I'm a bit of a warlock myself," said Dr Brash, beholding the spaewife's vexation at a *faux-pas* she only guessed herself guilty of. "I'll read your loof, Miss Macintosh, if ye let me."

They all insisted she should submit herself to the Doctor's unusual art, and taking her hand in his he drew the mitten off and pretended to scan the lines.

"Travel – h'm – a serious illness – h'm – your life, in youth, was quite adventurous, Miss Macintosh."

"Oh! I'm no' that auld yet," she corrected him. "There's mony a chance at fifty. Never mind my past, Dr Brash, what about my future?"

He glanced up a moment and saw her aunt and uncle listening in amusement, unaware as yet that he knew the secret, then scanned her palm again.

"The future – h'm! let me see. A long line of life; heart line healthy – h'm – the best of your life's before you, though I cannot say it may be the happiest part of it. Perhaps my – h'm – my skill a little fails here. You have a strong will, Miss – Miss Macintosh, and I doubt in this world you'll aye have your own way. And – h'm – an odd destiny surely 's before you – I see the line of Fame, won – h'm – in a multitude of characters; by the Lord Hairry, ma'am, you're to be – you're to be an actress!"

The company laughed at such a prophecy for one so antiquated, and the Doctor's absurdity put an end to the spaeing of fortunes, but he had effected his purpose. He had found the words that expressed the hope, half-entertained, so far, of Ailie, and the fear of her brother Dan. They learned before they left that he had not spoken without his cue, yet it was a little saddened they went home at midnight with their ward in masquerade.

CHAPTER XXI

FORTUNATELY Kate's marriage came to distract them for a while from the thought of Bud's future. The essential house had been found that was suitable for a captain, yet not too dearly rented – a piece of luck in a community where dwellings are rarely vacant, and every tenant over eighty years of age has the uneasy conscious-ness that half a dozen pairs betrothed have already decided upon a different colour of paint for his windows, and have become resigned, with a not unpleasing melancholy, to the thought that in the course of nature his time cannot be long.

The Captain – that once roving eagle-heart subdued by love for the maid of Colonsay – so persistently discouraged any yachting trips which took the *Wave* for more than a night or two from her moorings, that Lady Anne and her husband, knowing the heart themselves, recommended immediate marriage; and Miss Bell, in consequence, was scouring the countryside for Kate's successor in the kitchen, but hopeless of coming on one who could cook good kail, have a cheery face, and be a strict communicant. "I can get fine cooks that are wanting in the grace of God, and pious girls who couldn't be trusted to bake a Christian scone," she said; "It's a choice between two evils."

"Of two evils choose the third, then," said Dan to his sister, flushed and exhilarated by a search that, for elderly maiden ladies, makes up for an older hunt. "The sport's agreeing with you."

It was a great distress to Bud that the wedding should take place in the house and not in church, as seemed most fitting. She felt a private ceremony deprived her of a spectacle, with Miss Amelia Duff playing the wedding march on the harmonium, and the audience filing up the aisle in their Sunday clothes, the carriage of their hats revealing character.

"Why, you're simply going to make it look like a plain tea!" she protested. "If it was my marriage, Kate, I'd have it as solemn and grand as Harvest Sunday. A body doesn't get married to a man in brass buttons every other day, and it's a chance for style."

"We never have our weddings in the church," said Kate. "Sometimes the gentry do, but it's not considered nice; it's kind of Roman Catholic. Forbye, in a church, where would you get the fun?"

If Bud hadn't realised that fun was the main thing at Scottish weddings, she got hints of it in Kate's preparation. Croodles and hysterics took possession of the bride: she was sure she would never get through the ceremony with her life, or she would certainly do something silly that would make the whole world laugh at her and dreadfully vex the Captain. Even her wedding-dress, whose prospect had filled her dreams with gladness, but deepened her depression when it came from the manteau-makers: she wept sad stains on the front width, and the orange-blossom they rehearsed with might have been a wreath of the bitter rue. Bud wanted her to try the dress on, but the bride was aghast at such an unlucky proposition; so she tried it on herself, with sweet results, if one did not look at the gathers in the back. They practised the ceremony the night before, Kate's sister from Colonsay (who was to be her bridesmaid) playing the part of a tall, brass-buttoned bridegroom.

"Oh, Kate!" cried Bud pitifully, "you stand there like's you were a soda-water bottle and the cork lost. My goodness! brisk up a bit. If it's hard on you, just remember it isn't much of a joke for Charles. Don't you know the eyes of the public are on you?"

"That's just it," said poor Kate. "I wouldn't be frightened a bit if it wasn't for that, for I'm so brave. What do you do with your hands?"

"You just keep hold of them. Mercy! don't let them hang like that – they're yours; up till now he's got nothing to do with them. Now for the tears – where's your handkerchief? That one's yards too big, and there isn't an edge of lace to peek through, but it'll do this time. It'll all be right on the night. Now the minister's speaking, and you're looking down at the carpet and you're timid and fluttered and nervous and thinking what an epoch this is in your sinful life, and how you won't be Kate MacNeill any more but Mrs Charles Maclean, and the Lord knows if you will be happy with him

The bride blubbered and threw her apron over her head as usual: Bud was in despair.

"Well, you are a silly!" she exclaimed. "All you want is a gentle tear or two trickling down the side of your nose, enough to make your eyes blink but not enough to soak your veil or leave streaks. And there you gush like a waterspout, and damp your face so much the bridegroom'll catch his death of cold when he kisses you! Stop it, Kate MacNeill – it isn't anybody's funeral: why, weddings aren't so very fatal; lots of folk get over them – leastways in America."

"I can't help it!" protested the weeping maid. "I never could be melancholy in moderation, and the way you speak you make me think it's running a dreadful risk to marry anybody."

"Well," said Bud, "you needn't think of things so harrowing, I suppose. Just squeeze your eyes together and bite your lip, and perhaps it'll start a tear: if it don't, it'll look like as if you were bravely struggling with emotion. And then there's the proud glad smile as you back out on Charles's arm – give her your arm, Minnie – the trial's over, you know, and you've got on a lovely new plain ring, and all the other girls are envious, and Charles Maclean and you are one till death do you part. Oh, Kate, Kate! don't grin; that's not a smile, it's a – it's a railroad track. Look –" Bud assumed a smile that spoke of gladness and humility, confidence and a maiden's fears – a smile that appealed and charmed.

"I couldn't smile like that to save my life," said Kate in a despair. "I wish you had learned me that instead of the height of Popacatthekettle. Do you think he'll be angry if I don't do them things properly?"

"Who? Charles! Why, Charles'll be so mortally scared himself he wouldn't notice if you made faces at him, or were a different girl alto- gether. He'll have a dull dead booming in his ears, and wonder whether it's wedding-day or apple-custard: all of them I've seen married looked like that. It's not for Charles you should weep and smile; it's for the front of the house, you know – it's for the people looking on."

"Toots!" said Kate, relieved. "If it's only for them, I needn't bother. I thought that maybe it was something truly refined that he would be expecting. It's not – it's not the front of a house I'm marrying. Tell me this and tell me no more – is there anything special I should do to please my Charles?"

"I don't think I'd worry," said Bud on reflection. "I daresay it's better not to think of anything dramatic. If I were you I'd just keep calm as grass, and pray the Lord to give me a good contented mind and hurry up the clergyman."

But yet was the maiden full of a consciousness of imperfection, since she had seen that day the bride's-cake on view in the baker's window – an edifice of art so splendid that she felt she could never be worthy of it. "How do you think I'll look?" she asked. And Bud assured her she would look magnificently lovely.

"Oh, I wish I did," she sighed. "But I'm feared I'll not look so lovely as I think I do."

"No girl ever did," said Bud. "That's impossible; but when Charles comes to and sits up he'll think you're It: he'll think you perfect."

"Indeed I'm far from that," said Kate. "I have just my health and napery and a liking for the chap, and I wish I wasn't near so red."

Bud was able to instruct her in the right deportment for a bride, but had no experience in the management of husbands: for that Kate had to take some hints from her mistress, who was under the delusion that her brother Dan was the standard of his sex.

"They're curious creatures," Bell confided. "You must have patience, ay, and humour them. They'll trot at your heels like pussy for a cheese-pudding, but they'll not be driven. If I had a man I would never thwart him. If he was out of temper or unreasonable I would tell him he was looking ill, and that would make him feared and humble. When a man thinks he's ill, his trust must be in the Lord and in his woman-kind. That's where we have the upper hand of them! First and last, the thing's to be agreeable. You'll find he'll never put anything in its proper place, and that's a heartbreak, but it's not so bad as if he broke the dishes and blackened your eyes, the way they do in the newspapers. There's one thing that's the secret of a happy home – to live in the fear of God and within your income, faith! you can't live very well without it."

"Oh, mem! it's a desperate thing a wedding," said the maid. "I never, in all my life, had so much to think about before."

There were stricken lads in these days! The more imminent became her utter loss, the more desirable Kate became. But sentiment in country towns is an accommodating thing, and all the old suitors – the whistlers in the close and purveyors of conversation lozenges – found consolation in the fun at the wedding, and danced their griefs away on the flags of the Dyces' kitchen.

A noble wedding! All the cookery skill of Kate and her mistress was expended on it, and discretion, for the sake of the incredulous, forbids enumeration of the roasted hens. Chanticleers in the town crowed roupily and ruefully for months thereafter. The bridegroom might have stepped over the wall to the wedding chamber, or walked to it in a hundred paces up the lane: he rode instead in a carriage that made a stately and circuitous approach round John Turner's Corner, and wished the distance had been twenty times as long. "It's not that I'm feared," said he, "or that I've rued the gyurl, but – but it's kind of sudden!" – a curious estimate of a courtship that had started in the burial-ground of Colonsay so many years before!

A noble wedding! – its revelry kept the town awake till morning. From the open windows the night was filled with dancing tunes, and songs, and laughter; boys cried "Fab, fab!" in the street, and a fairy lady – really a lady all grown up, alas! – stood at a window and showered pence among them.

Long before the wedding-party ended, Bud went up to bed, but she lay for hours awake in the camceil room hearing the revelry of the kitchen. She had said good-bye to the blissful pair whose wedding was the consequence of her own daft pranks as letterwriter: she would miss the maid of Colonsay. The knowledge that 'tis an uncertain world, a place of change and partings, comes to us all sooner or later in one flash of apprehension and of grief: for the first time Bud felt the irrevocable nature of the past, and that her happy world under this roof was, someway, crumbling, and the tears came to her eyes.

A hurried footstep sounded on the stairs, a rap came to her door, and the bride came in, unbid, in the darkness, whispering Lennox's name.

Her only answer was a sob from the girl in bed.

"Miss Lennox!" said the bride distressed; "what ails you? I've come up to say good-bye: it wasn't a right good-bye at all with yon folk looking. Oh, Lennox, Lennox! *ghaol ma chridhe!* my heart is sore to be leaving you, for the two of us were so merry! Now I have a man, and a good man too; it was you that gave me him, but I have lost my loving friend." She threw herself on the bed, regardless of her finery, and the Celtic fount of her swelled over in sobs and tears.

CHAPTER XXXII

IT took two maids to fill Kate's place in the Dyces' household – one for the plain boiling of potatoes and the other for her pious atmosphere, as the lawyer argued; and a period of discomfort attended on what Bell called their breaking-in. No more kitchen nights for Lennox, now that she was a finished young lady and her friend was gone: she must sit in the parlour strumming canzonets on Grandma Buntain's Broadwood, taming her heart of fire. It was as a voice from heaven's lift there came one day a letter from London in which Mrs Molyneux invited her and one of her aunts for an Easter holiday.

"Indeed and I'll be glad to be quit for a week or two of both of you," said Bell to her niece and Ailie. "Spring-cleaning, with a couple of stupid huzzies in the kitchen – not but what they're nice and willing lassies – is like to be the sooner ended if we're left to it ourselves."

A radiant visage and lips in firm control betrayed how Lennox felt. She had never been in London – its cry went pealing through her heart. Ailie said nothing, but marvelled how blithely and blindly her sister always set foot on the facile descent that led to her inevitable doom of deprivation and regret.

"The Grand Tour!" said Uncle Dan; "It's the fitting termination to your daft days, Lennox. Up by at the Castle there's a chariot with imperials that conveyed the Earl on his, the hammercloth most lamentably faded: I often wonder if his lordship takes a sly seat in it at times when no one's looking, and climbs the Alps or clatters through Italian towns again when Jones the coachman is away at his tea. It's a thing I might do myself if I had made the Tour and still had the shandrydan."

"Won't you really need me?" Aunt Ailie asked her sister, and half hoped, half feared spring-cleaning should postpone the holiday; but Bell maintained it should be now or never, more particularly as Lennox's dress was new.

Oh, London, London! siren town! how it bewitched the girl! Its cab-horse bells were fairy; its evening, as they entered, hung with a myriad magic moons and stars. The far-stretching streets with their flaming jewel windows, the temples in the upper dusk, and the solemn squares crowding round country trees; the throngs of people, the odours of fruit-shops, the passion of flowers, the mornings silvery grey, and the multitudinous monuments rimed by years, thunder of hoofs in ways without end, and the silence of mighty parks – Bud lay awake in the nights to think of them.

Jim Molyneux had the siren by the throat: he loved her, and shook a living out of her hands. At first she had seemed to him too old, too calm, too slow and stately as compared with his own Chicago, nor did she seem to have a place for any stranger: now he had found she could be bullied – that a loud voice, a bold front, and the aid of a good tailor could compel her to disgorge respect and gold. He had become the manager of a suburban theatre, where oranges were eaten in the stalls, and the play was as often as not "The Father's Curse"; but once a day he walked past Thespian temples in the city, and, groaning at their mismanagement, planned an early future for himself with classic fronts of marble, and duchesses advertising him each night by standing in rows on the pavement awaiting their carriages. Far along Grove Lane, where he dwelt in a pea-green house with nine French-bean rows and some clumps of bulbs behind, one could distinguish his coming by the smartness of his walk and the gleam of the sunshine on his hat. He had one more secret of success – teetotalism. "Scotch and soda," he would say, "that's what ails the boys, and makes 'em sleepier than Hank M'Cabe's old tom-cat. Good boys, dear boys, they've always got the long-lost-brother grip, but they're mighty prone to dope assuagements for the all-gone feeling in the middle of the day. When they've got cobwebs in their little brilliantined belfries, I'm full of the songs of spring and merry old England's on the lee. See? I don't even need to grab; all I've got to do is to look deserving, and the stuff comes crowding in: it always does to a man who looks like ready-money, and don't lunch on cocktails and cloves."

"Jim, boyette," his wife would say, "I guess you'd better put ice or something on your bump of self-esteem;" but she proudly wore the jewels that were the rewards of his confidence and industry.

Bud and Ailie, when they thought of home in these days, thought of it as a picture only, or as a chapter in a book covered in mouldy leather, with *f*'s for *s*'s. In their prayers alone were Dan and Bell real personages; and the far-off little town was no longer a woodcut, but an actual place blown through by the scented airs of forest and sea. Bell wrote them of rains and hails and misty weather; Grove Lane gardens breathed of daffodils, and the city gleamed under a constant sun. They came back to the pea-green house each day from rare adventuring, looking, in the words of Molyneux, as if they were fresh come off the farm, and the best seats in half a dozen theatres were at their disposal. "Too much of the playhouse altogether!" Bell wrote once, remonstrating. "Have you heard that man in the City Temple yet?"

In Molyneux's own theatre there was a break in the long succession of melodrama and musical comedy. He privately rejoiced that, for two ladies of such taste as Ailie and her niece, he could display a piece of the real legitimate – "King John," – though Camberwell was not very likely to make a week of Shakespeare very profitable to his treasury. Ailie and Bud were to go on Tuesday; and Bud sat up at night to read an acting copy of "King John" till every character took flesh in her imagination, and the little iron balcony behind the pea-green house became the battlemented walls of Angiers, to whose postern came trumpeters of France.

They sat in the drawing-room, astonished at her speeches –

> "You men of Angiers, open wide your gates,
> And let young Arthur, Duke of Bretagne, in,
> Who by the hand of France this day hath made
> Much work for tears in many an English mother.

Or –

> "I am not mad: this hair I tear is mine;
> My name is Constance, I was Geffrey's wife;
> Young Arthur is my son, and he is lost!"

"Bravo, Bud!" would Molyneux cry, delighted. "Why, if I was an actor-manager, I'd pay you any salary you had the front to name. Ain't she just great, Millicent? I tell you, Miss Ailie, she puts the blinkers on Maude Adams, and sends Ellen 'way back in the standing-room only. Girly, all you've got to learn is how to move. You mustn't stand two minutes in the same place on the stage, but cross 'most every cue."

"I don't know," said Bud dubiously. "Why should folk have fidgets on a stage? They don't always have them in real life. I'd want to stand like a mountain – you know, Auntie Ailie, the old hills at home! – and look so – so – so awful, the audience would shriek if I moved, the same as if I was going to fall on them."

"Is that how you feel?" asked Jim Molyneux, curiously surveying her.

"Yes; that's how I feel," said Bud, "when I've got the zip of poetry in me. I feel I'm all made up of burning words and eyes."

"Child, you are very young!" said Mrs Molyneux.

"Yes," said Bud; "I suppose that's it. By-and-by I'll maybe get to be like other people."

Jim Molyneux struck the table with his open hand. "By George!" he cried, "I wouldn't hurry being like other people; that's what every gol-darned idiot in England's trying, and you're right on the spot just now as you stand. That's straight talk, nothing but! I allow I favour a bit of leg movement on the stage – generally it's about the only life there is on it; but a woman who can play with her head don't need to wear out much shoe-leather. Girly –" he stopped a second, then burst out with the question: "How'd you like a little part in this 'King John'?"

A flame went over the countenance of the girl, and then she grew exceedingly pale. "Oh!" she exclaimed, "Oh! Jim Molyneux, don't be so cruel."

"I mean it," he said, "and I could fix it, for they've got an Arthur in the caste who's ill and bound to break down in a day or two if she had an understudy – and if I – Think you could play a boy's part? There isn't much to learn in Arthur, but that little speech of yours in front of Angiers makes me think you could make the part loom out enough to catch the eve of the cognoscenti. You'd let her, wouldn't you, Miss Ailie? It'd be great fun. She'd learn the lines in an hour or two, and a couple of nights of looking on would put her up to all the business. Now don't kick, Miss Ailie; say, Miss Ailie, have this little treat with us!"

Ailie's heart was leaping. Here was the crisis – she knew it – what was she to do? She had long anticipated some such hour – had often wrestled with the problem whether, when it came, the world should have her Bud without a struggle for the claims of Bell and the simple cloistered life of the Scottish home. While yet the crisis was in prospect only, she could come to no conclusion. Her own wild hungers as a girl, recalled one night in the light of kitchen candles, had never ceased to plead for freedom – for freedom and the space that herself had years ago surrendered: now it was the voice of the little elder sister, and the bell of Wanton Wully ringing at evening humble people home.

"Just this once!" pleaded Mr Molyneux, understanding her scruples: Bud's face mutely pleaded.

Yes, "just this once!" – it was all very well, but Ailie knew the dangers of beginnings. It would not even be, in this case, a beginning; the beginning was years ago – before the mimicry on the first New Year's morning, before the night of the dozen candles, or the creation of The Macintosh: the child had been carried onward like a feather in a stream.

"I really don't mind much, myself," said Ailie at last; "but I fancy her Aunt Bell would scarcely like it."

"Not if she knew I was going to do it," said Lennox quickly; "but when the thing was over she'd be as pleased as Punch – at least, she'd laugh the way she did when we told her I was dressed as Grandma Buntain at the ball."

The sound of Will Oliver's curfew died low in Ailie's mind, the countenance of Bell grew dim: she heard, instead, the clear young voice of Bud among the scenery and sat with an enraptured audience. "If you are all so anxious for it, then," she said, and the deed was done!

She did not rue it when the night of Bud's performance came, and her niece as the hapless young Bretagne welcomed the Dauphin before the city gates: she gloried in the natural poignancy that marked the painful scene with Hubert come to torture, but she almost rued it when Molyneux, having escorted them in an inexplicable silence home, broke out at last in fervent praise of his discovery as soon as the girl had left them for her bed.

"I've kept clutch of myself with considerable difficulty," he said, "for I didn't want to spoil girly's sleep or swell her head, but I want to tell you, Millicent, and you, Miss Ailie, that I'VE FOUND MY STAR! Why, say! she's out of sight! She was the only actor in all that company tonight who didn't know she was in Camberwell: she was right in the middle of medieval France from start to finish, and when she was picked up dead at the end of the fourth act she was so stone-cold and stiff with thinking it she scared the company. I suspect, Miss Ailie, that you're going to lose that girl!"

CHAPTER XXXIII

IT was a wet night in November. With a chuckle of horse's hoofs on shining streets, Dan Dyce, with Bell and Ailie, drove from Molyneux's fine new home to the temple of his former dreams – the proud Imperial. They sat in silence in the darkness of the cab, and in silence drifted into the entrance-hall of the theatre to mingle with the pompous world incongruously – with loud vain-glorious men, who bore to the eye of Bell some spirit of abandonment and mockery, with women lovely by the gift of God, or with dead-white faces, wax-red lips, and stealthy sidelong eyes. One there was who, passing before them, released a great fur cloak from her shoulders with a sudden movement, and, as it slowly slipped down her marble back, threatened an utter nakedness that made Bell gasp and clutch at her sister's arm.

"Look!" said Ailie eagerly – before them was a portrait of a woman in the dress of Desdemona. The face had some suggestion that at times it might be childlike and serene, but had been caught in a moment of alarm and fire, and the full black eyes held in their orbs some frightful apprehension, the slightly parted lips expressed a soul's mute cry.

"What is it? Who is it?" asked Bell, pausing before the picture with a stound of fear.

"It is Bud," said Ailie, feeling proud and sorrowful – for why she could not tell. "There is the name: 'Winifred Wallace.'"

Bell wrung her hands in the shelter of her mantle and stood bewildered, searching for the well-known lineaments.

"Let us go up," said Dan softly, with no heed for the jostling people, for ever self-possessed, sorrowful to guess at his sister's mind.

"Yes, yes, let us go up out of this crowd," said Ailie, but the little woman hung before the portrait fascinated. Round her washed the waves of rustling garments like a surf on the shore at home; scents wafted; English voices, almost foreign in their accent, fell upon her ear all unnoticed since she faced the sudden revelation of what her brother's child, her darling, had become. Seekers of pleasure, killers of wholesome cares, froth of the idle world eddied around her chattering, laughing, glancing curious or contemptuous at her grey sweet face, her homely form, her simple Sabbath garments: all her heart cried out in supplication for the child that had too soon become a woman and wandered from the sanctuary of home.

193

"We are blocking the way here, Bell. Let us go up," again said Ailie, gently taking her arm.

"Yes," said her brother. "It's not a time for contemplation of the tombs – it's not the kirkyard, Bell. You see there are many that are anxious to get in."

"Oh, Lennox, Lennox!" she exclaimed, indifferent to the strangers round about her, "my brother's child! I wish – oh, I wish ye were at home! God grant ye grace and wisdom: 'Then shalt thou walk in thy way safely, and thy foot shall not stumble. When thou liest down, thou shalt not be afraid: yea, thou shalt lie down, and thy sleep shall be sweet.'"

They went up to the box that Molyneux had kept for them, to find his wife there nursing an enormous bouquet of flowers, all white as the driven snow. "A gorgeous house!" she told them. "Everybody that's anybody, and in the front push. Half a hundred critics, two real Count Vons, a lot of benzine brougham people who never miss a first night – there are their wives, poor dears! shining same as they were Tiffany's windows. My! ain't our Bud going to have a happy night!"

They sat and looked for a while in silence at the scene before them, so pleasing to the mind that sought, in crowds, in light and warmth and gaiety, its happiest associations; so wanting in the great eternal calm and harmony that are out of doors in country places. Serpent eyes in facets of gems on women's bosoms; heads made monstrous yet someway beautiful and tempting by the barber's art; shoulders bare and bleached, devoid of lustre; others blushing as if Eve's sudden apprehension had survived the generations. Sleek shaven faces, linen breastplates, opera-glasses, flowers, fans, a murmur of voices, and the flame over all of the enormous electrolier.

It was the first time Bell had seen a theatre. Her first thought was one of blame and pity. "'He looked on the city and wept'!" said she. "Oh, Ailie, that it were over and we were home!"

"All to see Miss Winifred Wallace!" said Mrs Molyneux. "Think of that, Miss Dyce – your darling niece, and she'll be so proud and happy!"

Bell sighed. "At least she had got her own way, and I am a foolish old country-woman who had different plans."

Dan said nothing. Ailie waited too, silent, in a feverish expectation; and from the fiddles rose a sudden melody. It seemed the only wise and sober thing in all that humming hive of gaudy insects passing, passing, passing. It gave a voice to human longings for a nobler, better world; and in it, too, were memory and tears. To the

194

people in the box it seemed to tell Bud's story – opening in calm sweet passages, closing in the roll of trumpet and the throb of drum. And then the lights went down, and the curtain rose upon the street in Venice.

The early scenes were dumb and vacant, wanting Bud's presence: there was no play for them till she came slowly into the council chamber where sat the senators, timidity and courage struggling in her port and visage.

"No, no; it is not Bud," Bell whispered. "It is not our lassie, this one is too tall and – and too deliberate. I fear she has not dared it at the last, or that she has been found unsuitable."

Ailie leaned forward, quivering, feeding her eyes. "It's no one else," said she. "Dear Bud, our Bud! Those two years' training may have made her someways different, but she has not changed her smile. Oh! I am so proud, and sure of her! Hus-s-sh!"

> "I do perceive here a divided duty:
> To you I am bound for life and education;
> My life and education both do learn me
> How to respect you; you are the lord of duty:
> I am hitherto your daughter: but here's my husband."

Desdemona's first speech broke the stillness that had fallen on the house: her face was pale, they saw the rapid heaving of her bosom, they heard a moment's tremor in her voice matured and wonderful, sweet as a silver bell. To the box where she knew her friends were sitting she let her eyes for a second wander as she spoke the opening lines that had so much of double meaning – not Desdemona, but the loving and wilful child asking forgiveness, yet tenacious of her purpose.

To Ailie came relief and happiness and pride: Dan held a watching brief for his elder sister's prejudices and his own philosophy. Bell sat in tears which Shakespeare did not influence. When next she saw the stage with unblurred eyes Desdemona was leaving with the Moor.

"My dears," said Mrs Molyneux, "as Desdemona she's the Only One! and Jim was right. It's worth a thousand times more trouble than he took with her. He said all along she'd dazzle them, and I guess her fortune's made, and it's going to be the making of this house too. I feel so proud and happy I'd kiss you right here, Mr Dyce, if it wouldn't mess up my bouquet."

"A black man!" said Bell regretfully. "I know it is only paint, of course, but – but I never met him; I do not even know his name."

It seemed as if the play had nothing in it but the words and acts of Desdemona. At each appearance she became more confident, charged the part with deeper feeling, found new meaning in the time-worn words. Even Bell began to lose her private judgment, forget that it was nothing but a sinful play, and feel some pity for Othello; but, as the knavish coils closed round her Desdemona, the strain became unbearable.

"Oh! I cannot stand it any longer," she exclaimed, when the voice of Lennox quavered in the song before her last good-night, and saying so, pushed back her seat into the shadows of the box, covering her ears with her fingers. She saw no more; she heard no more till the audience rose to its feet with thunders of applause that swelled and sunk and swelled again as if it would never end. Then she dared to look, and saw a trembling Desdemona all alone before a curtain bowing.

"What is the matter? What is the matter? Why are they crying that way on her?" she asked, dumbfounded.

"Why, don't you see they're mad!" said Mrs Molyneux.

"Oh, dear! and I thought she was doing splendidly."

"Glad mad, I mean. She has carried them off their feet, and I'll bet Jim Molyneux is standing on his hands behind that drop and waving his legs in the air. Guess I needn't waste this bouquet on a girl who looks like the morning hour in Covent Garden."

Molyneux burst into the box in a gust of wild excitement. "Come round, come round at once – she wants to see you," he exclaimed, and led them deviously behind the scenes to her dressing-room.

She stood at the door, softly crying; she looked at them – the grave old uncle; Ailie who could understand, the little Auntie Bell – it was into the arms of Bell she threw herself!

CHAPTER XXXIV

"THE talk of the whole of London! The beauteous Lady Anne herself's not in it with her!" said Will Oliver, scratching behind his ears. "Man, is it no' just desperate? But I'll warrant ye there's money in it, for it's yonder folk are willing to pay well for their diversion."

"Are you sure," said P. & A., "it's not another woman altogether? It gives the name of Wallace in the paper."

The bellman, sitting on a soap-box, slapped his thigh and said, "I'm telling ye; I had it long ago from Kate MacNeill that her name on the stage was going to be Wallace – Winifred Wallace, and there it is in print. Tra – tragedienny, tragediennys are the head ones in the trade: I've seen them in the shows – tr-r-r-emendous women!"

The Provost, who had just stepped into P. & A.'s for his Sunday sweeties, smiled tolerantly and passed his taddy-box. "Bud Dyce," said he, "is never likely to be round this way in a caravan to do the deid-drap three times every night for front-seats sixpence. I doubt we have seen the last of her, unless we have the money and the clothes for London theatres."

"It's really her, then?" said the grocer.

"You can take Wull's word for that," said the Provost, "and I have just been talking to her uncle. Her history's in the morning paper, and I'm the civic head of a town renowned for genius."

Wanton Wully went out to drift along the street in the light of the bright shop-windows before which bairns played "chaps me," making choice of treasures for their gaudiness alone, like most of us, who should know better. He met George Jordan. "Geordie," said he, "you'll have heard the latest? You should be in London: yon's the place for oddity," and George, with misty comprehension, turned about for the road to London town. Out of the inn came Colin Cleland, hurried, in his hand the business-looking packet of tattered documents that were always his excuse for being there.

"Winifred Wallace – Great Tragedienny! It's a droll thing life, according to the way you look at it. Stirring times in London, Mr Cleland! Changed her name to Wallace, having come of decent worthy people. We know, but we'll not let on."

"Not a word!" said Colin Cleland comically. "Perhaps she may get better and the thing blow by. Are you under the impression that celebrity's a thing to be ashamed of? I tell you she's a credit to us all."

"Lord bless me! do you say so?" asked Wull Oliver. "If I was a tragedienny I would be ashamed to show my face in the place again. We all expected something better from the wee one – she was such a caution! It was myself, as you might say, invented her: I gave her a start at devilment by letting her ring the New Year bell. After that she always called me Mr Wanton, and kindly inquired at me about my legs. She was always quite the leddy."

Miss Minto's shop was busy: a boy was in with a very red face demanding the remnants that by rights should have gone home with his mother's jacket, and the Misses Duff were buying chiffon.

"This is startling news about young Lennox Dyce," remarked Miss Minto. "It's caused what you might call a stir. There's not a weekly paper to be had for love or money."

"She was always most peculiar," said Miss Jean.

"Bizarre," cooed Miss Amelia – it was her latest adjective.

"I was sure there was something special about in her since the very first day I saw her," said the mantua-maker. "Yon eye, Miss Duff! And what a sweet and confident expression! I am so glad she has pleased them up in London; you never can depend on them. I am thinking of a novel blouse to mark in what I think will be a pleasing way the great occasion – the Winifred Wallace Waist I'm calling it: you remember the clever Mr Molyneux?"

"I doubt we never understood her," said Miss Jean. "But we make a feature now of elocution."

"Not that we wish to turn out great tragediennes," said Miss Amelia. "There's happiness in humbler vocations."

"I daresay there is," confessed Miss Minto. "I never thought of the stage myself; my gift was always dressmaking, and you wouldn't believe the satisfaction that's in seeing a dress of mine on a woman who can do it justice. We have all our own bit art, and that's a wonderful consolation. But I'm very glad at that girl's progress, for the sake of Mr Dyce – and, of course, his sisters. Miss Ailie is transported, in the seventh heaven, and even her sister seems quite pleased. 'You'll have a high head today,' I said to her when she was passing from the coach this afternoon."

"And what did she say to that?" inquired Miss Jean, with curiosity.

"You know Miss Dyce! She gave a smile and said, 'But a humble heart – it's the Dyces' motto.'"

The doctor put his paper down, having read the great news over several times with a singular satisfaction that surprised his sisters, who were beat to see much glory in a state of life that meant your name on every wall and the picture of your drawing-room every other week in 'Homely Notes'. Drawing on his boots, he took a turn the length of the lawyer's house.

"Faith! London has the luck of it," he said on entering. "I wish I was there myself to see this wonderful Desdemona. I hope you liked your jaunt, Miss Bell?"

"It wasn't bad," said Bell, putting out the cards. "But, mercy on me! what a silly way they have of baking bread in England – all crust outside, though I grant it's sweet enough when you break into it."

"H'm!" said Dr Brash, "I've seen Scotch folk a bit like that. She has rung the bell, I see; her name is made."

"It is, they tell me," answered Bell, "but I hope it will never change her nature."

"She had aye a genius," said Mr Dyce, cutting the pack for partners.

"She had something better," said Miss Ailie, "she had love;" and on the town broke forth the evening bell.